Mayrah planted her stick on the ground and leaned on it. The white man's eyes seemed to bore into hers. There was a large bag on the ground, and he knelt by it and began taking things out of it—an axe made of the white man's stone, a knife, and pieces of the stone. Mayrah's father and Puntaru knelt and looked at them, then began separating them between them.

A chilling thought suddenly occurred to her. Weapons made of white man's stone were enormously valuable, and her father possessed only one belonging of sufficient value to barter for them.

Herself.

She looked at her mother, trembling with shock and fright. Her mother's face was averted. Her family began moving away from the white man, carrying the weapons, and her father looked at her as he passed.

"You are this man's woman. Remain here, and be obedient to him."

Mayrah felt numb, her mouth went dry, and her knees trembled. She had been given away, like an animal, to one who was likened to devils. She leaned on her stick and burst into tears of anguish.

OUTBACK

Aaron Fletcher

LEISURE BOOKS ❧ NEW YORK CITY

A LEISURE BOOK

Published by

Dorchester Publishing Co., Inc.
41 E. 60 St.
New York City

Printed in the United States of America

OUTBACK

Part One

Wayamba Station

- 1 -

The sandy soil was dry, burning hot to the touch where the sun reached it between the towering clumps of spinifex and gnarled, sun-blasted scrub acacia. It was rippled in patterns from winds which had penetrated the foliage, and strewn with small pebbles, a mottled surface of duns and browns which faded into a featureless blur in the blinding sunlight and into deep, dark shadows in the shade. But Mayrah's eyes were fixed on the virtually invisible trail across it. She was frozen into immobility and standing on one foot, her other foot poised inches above the ground in the step which had been arrested when her keen eyes detected the minute traces left by the passage of another creature.

The tough, thick soles of her bare feet insulated them against the fiery heat of the ground, and she was unconscious of the glaring sun beaming down on her naked body except for a gentle, insistent, instinctive voice which spoke in the back of her mind, reminding her that direct sunlight during the heat of the day should be avoided when possible. Her eyes moved along the ground. The trail was that of the *ooboon*, the blue-tongued lizard, and it had been made only seconds before because tiny grains of soil were still slipping down into the shallow depression. It ended at the base of a thick clump of the silvery, spiny spinifex whose blades rose above her head all around her.

She slowly lowered her foot to the ground and took a soundless step to one side, the long, heavy stick in her right hand poised to throw, her right elbow pressing against the woven grass bag hanging from her shoulder to keep it from swinging, and her neck straight to balance the *wirree*, the small bark vessel of water she carried on top of her head. There was no trail on the other side of the spinifex. The *ooboon* was still in it. She crouched slightly and her eyes narrowed to peer more closely into the shade under the blades of the spinifex, and she began stalking.

A whisper of sound carried through the grass from the distance of a spear cast ahead of her, barely audible over the rustle of the light, hot breeze through the spinifex, and she reacted instantly. It was made by her father, almost but not quite a whistle, and it was interrupted twice by his lips closing and opening again. The warning of danger. All thoughts of the lizard left her mind, and she dropped into a low crouch, lifting the bag and stick so they wouldn't make a noise against the ground and still balancing the *wirree* and its precious mouthfuls of water on her head. Then she was completely motionless again except for her eyes darting around and her nostrils flaring and testing the air for a scent of the source of danger. A soft click came from a distance on her right. It was her mother, wanting to pinpoint the location of her children. And she was risking being punished by doing so, because the warning of danger included an implicit command for absolute silence. Mayrah clicked her tongue. Off to her left and slightly in front of her there was another click, her brother. Then there was silence again.

The man's hoot and the wooden clatter of the spears shaking in his hand were muffled by distance, but she was so tense that she almost jumped at the sound. It was a sign of peaceful intentions, the loud and demonstrative announcement of a solitary man acknowledging trespass on the hunting territory of another, and she turned her head slightly to cock her ear as her father hooted and rattled his spears in reply. The man shouted louder, identifying himself as Puntaru, a Ngala of the Arunta. The Arunta was the tribe of her family, but from the way the man formed his words he was from a long distance away. Mayrah's father identified himself, his voice fading as he moved toward the man.

Their deep voices were a barely audible murmur as they talked. The minutes slowly dragged by. The muscles in her thighs began aching and her neck became cramped from keeping the *wiree* balanced on top of her head while in the crouched position, but she remained unmoving because she hadn't been released from the command for absolute silence. Life was fraught with danger, a gauntlet of hazards and perils, and from earliest childhood her mother had drummed into her by reprimands and example that safety lay in immediate and unquestioning obedience to her father's commands. There were poisonous snakes and insects, brush fires, and flash floods at times of the *dooran*, the cold winds from the North which brought dark clouds. The slightest sound when commanded to be silent could

11

frighten away game her father was stalking, which could mean starvation when food was scarce, or it could announce their presence to enemies in the area. From the time she had been able to walk, her mother's cautions had been reinforced by swift, painful, and unfailing punishment from her father, and obedience was instinctive and unthinking. For her, there was a special danger which had developed during the recent past. Invaders from other tribes occasionally roamed abroad to find and capture young women for wives. So her mother was allowed some latitude, her brother was permitted more, and she had none.

Her father whistled, calling them forward. It wasn't an imperative command, so her mind returned to the lizard. She crept forward under the fringe of stiff, prickly spinifex blades, sliding the stick through her hand and gripping the end of it, and she poked it into the left side of the base of the clump of spinifex and stirred it. The lizard leaped out, racing toward another clump. She jerked the stick back, balanced it on the tips of her fingers, and threw it like a spear. The heavy stick flashed through the air, and the end of it struck the lizard's head and crushed it into a smear. Two fat grubs fell out of the spinifex where she had pushed the stick into it, and they squirmed around, trying to crawl back into the grass. She gathered them up and put them in her mouth as she stood up, and she munched them as she stepped forward and picked up her stick and the twitching lizard. Everything eatable was saved for the common meal when food was scarce, but it had been relatively plentiful during the past few days and it was permissible to eat the grubs. She put the lizard into the bag hanging from her shoulder, knelt by the clump of spinifex again and raked the end of her stick through the base of it, and dragged out four more grubs. She gathered them up and put them in her mouth as she got back to her feet, and walked toward her father through the clumps of spinifex and acacia, automatically taking light, virtually soundless steps and avoiding blades of grass which might rustle and pebbles which might click together.

The odor of another person carried to her nostrils on the breeze through the grass, blended with the warm, appetizing scent of a fresh kill. It was a large animal, with the tangy, musky smell characteristic of a kangaroo. The smells became stronger, mixed with the omnipresent and scarcely noticed odors of her mother, brother, and father. The spinifex and brush thinned out into a small area of claypan where water had coursed sometime during the past when it had rained heavily, gushing along and sweeping away the growth as it sought lower terrain, and leaving a smooth, hard surface as it subsided and dried up. Her mother and brother were sitting on their heels in the shade of the foliage at the edge of the small opening, and her father and the other man were kneeling together on the other side of it, talking in low voices. A small kangaroo which had been gutted, folded, and tied with blades of grass to carry on the shoulder was on the ground by the other man, and the smell of the blood and fresh flesh was almost overpowering, making her salivate. She dropped her stick, slipped the bag off her shoulder, and lifted the *wirree* from her head as she sat down by her mother. Her father glanced at her, motioned and murmured a terse command for her to give the man a drink, then looked back at the man as he said something else to him.

The man glanced at her then looked back at her father as she crossed the claypan, carrying the *wirree* in her hands, and the situation suddenly changed in her mind. Meeting with another wasn't an unusual event, but it suddenly took on a special meaning. Shortly after the last cold season there had been a corroboree and male initiation rite at which many of the tribe had gathered, and for the first time others had stopped referring to her as *ipi tuntumba*, young girl with small breasts, and had referred to her as *ipi longkara*, girl of well-formed breasts. And the four days of the gathering had been four days of terror for her, followed by an exhilarating feeling of relief when they had left for their territory without her father mentioning giving her to someone. She dreaded leaving her familiar situation and departing into the unknown, leaving her father, mother, and brother and their hunting territory to go with some stranger to another place. But the man talking to her father had said he was Ngala. She was Knurair. They were eligible for marriage. A cold hand seemed to grip her entrails, and her mouth was suddenly dry.

But at the same time and without conscious volition, her walk became slower and more deliberate, her steps more graceful and her hips swinging more than in her accustomed pace. Her instinctive response to the situation demanded that she make herself attractive and desirable, even if the result were contrary to her wishes. Instead of bending over to put the *wirree* in front of the man, as she would have her father, she slowly knelt on one knee and placed it on the ground in front of him, lifting off the large leaves that kept out dust and twigs and slowed the evaporation. She kept her eyes downcast as he picked it up and drank. He passed it to her father, who took a drink, put it back down, and flicked his fingers in a gesture of dismissal. Mayrah put the leaves back on top of it, picked it up as she rose, and turned back toward the other side of the claypan.

Her brother and mother were looking at the men intently and trying to hear their conversation, and Mayrah sat by her mother and put her *wirree* down, listening. Their voices were soft as always when in the open, when it was also necessary to listen for noises which might signal danger, but she could make out a

14

few words of what they were saying. And the conversation wasn't about her. The man's attitude toward her was different from the speculative smiles and gazes with which men had looked at her during the last corroboree. His eyes had been thoughtful rather than interested, and he had apparently dismissed her from his mind. She caught a couple more words spoken by her father, and for a moment she thought they were talking about *mamu*, devils, and she felt the mixture of apprehension and awe she always experienced when the supernatural was discussed in her presence. Then she heard the qualifying particle they were using with the noun, identifying a specific type of devil. White men.

As a child she had considered them as one of the more remote dangers which had always been present to prey upon her people, then as she had grown older and had heard more about them, she had found out that some of the older people could remember when the first stories of them had begun circulating. And the stories were plentiful. They had magical weapons which killed from afar with loud noises, harnessing the frightening power of *dooloomai*, thunder. They were always accompanied by massive, strange-looking animals, which were said to have supernatural powers. But they weren't invincible. There were stories of white men and their animals being found dead, and there were stories of successful attacks against them.

And once she had seen them. It had been a long time before and from a very long distance away, but the memory of the line of hideous creatures was still clear in her mind. Her family had fled, her mother running in front and carrying her brother because he had been small at the time. Her other brother had been alive then and running beside her, and her father had followed behind everyone else, ready to defend them if necessary. The crashing sounds the white men made traveling and the strange, acrid odor from them had announced their

15

presence over a wide area, but her family had escaped detection and eventually the noise and odor had faded into the distance. And they were less strange than she had thought from the glimpse of them, because in listening to the conversation between her father and mother, she had found that they were men much like her father riding on top of the large animals, rather than all one grotesque creature, as they had seemed to her. But most strange of all, her father had seen some of the *Daen*, their own people, among them.

There had been other stories about *Daen* who had lived among the white men, and apparently Puntaru had as well. His voice rose louder and took on a boastful note as he talked about it, and he separated one of his spears and showed the point to Mayrah's father. It was a thin, flimsy-looking point in comparison with the points on his other spears and those on her father's, and it was much darker. But Puntaru talked about its superiority, pulling the kangaroo closer and turning it over to show her father the hole in the side of the carcass as he talked about the distance of the cast. Her father looked politely doubtful. Puntaru stood up, looking around and balancing the spear in his hand, then he cast it at the base of a spindly acacia bush at one end of the clearing. The point of the spear sliced the stem of the bush in two and thumped into the soil on the other side of it. The two men walked across the claypan to the spear, and her father looked at the point again with more respect. Puntaru took his axe from under his plaited kangaroo-skin belt and showed it to Mayrah's father. They were further away and she couldn't hear what they were saying, but it was apparent that the axe was also of a superior stone he had got from the white men, because he broke a couple of rocks on the edge of the claypan with it, something no one would casually do with a flint axe, then chopped the acacia bush into several pieces with effortless blows.

It was impressive, but only mildly interesting to her. Spears, axes, knives, and similar things were for men. By tradition, she was limited to carrying the smooth, heavy, hardwood stick, six feet long and three inches in diameter. Her mother had helped her make it when she approached adult size, selecting the wood and scraping and polishing it with bits of stone, then hardening the ends by heating them in a fire. It was used for purposes ranging from exploring dark places and crevices for food or dangerous snakes and insects to protection from others, and she and her mother were always ready with their sticks to assist her father if he summoned them. Over the years it had become almost like an extension of her right arm, always in her hand when moving about and at her side and under her fingertips when at rest. She could cast it with deadly, unerring accuracy over a distance of several yards, and she could manipulate it with blinding speed and lethal force within its six foot reach. It would be several years before her brother attained the size, strength, and skill to wield a spear which would be more dangerous. She moved the tips of her fingers on the stick, yawning widely and darting a glance at her mother's bag. Several lizard tails were sticking out of it, a couple of them still twitching. She was hungry, a more or less constant state, but the sight of the lizards was less appetizing than the scent of the blood and flesh of the kangaroo.

Her father and Puntaru walked back to where they had been sitting, looking at the axe and spear and talking about them. Puntaru was acting much more congenial than was ordinary for a stranger met by chance, yet he wasn't demonstrating interest in her in the usual and accepted ways. It was something of a puzzle, but her curiosity about his behavior was mild compared to her more immediate concern with the kangaroo. There seemed to be a likelihood that Puntaru might share it. The two men began gathering up their spears and settling their axes and knives in their belts, and Puntaru picked up the kangaroo and put it on his shoulder. Her father's glance passed across her, her mother, and her brother, and he pointed to the east with his chin, indicating a nearby camping place. Mayrah slipped the woven grass rope on her bag over her right shoulder, lifted her *wirree* and balanced it on her head, and picked up her stick as she rose.

The two men disappeared into the spinifex at the end of the small clearing, walking together and talking softly to each other, followed by Mayrah's mother and brother. Mayrah walked slowly for a few minutes, listening to the men and moving a few yards to the left of their path, then when they were at a distance where she could occasionally detect them by a slight sound or a whiff of their scent, she began pacing them and hunting again, and she also began gathering up sticks and twigs along the way, accumulating a bundle of them under her arm. It was the pattern that they always used in moving through the bush in their constant search for food, her father in front to hunt larger game and watch for danger, and her mother and brother on either side. Some time before, when the other and larger brother had been alive, he had always been in the position to the left and the smaller brother had been behind her. The brothers had always received the more choice portions of food, and they had always had more latitude in behavior, but she had always been more protected because she was her father's most valuable possession.

The camping place was one of several they visited on their hunts, a shallow depression in front of a layered outcropping of red sandstone at the base of a low, sandy hill. Mayrah and her mother combined the sticks and twigs they had gathered and began making a fire under the shelter of the sandstone as Mayrah's father sent her brother up to the top of the sandstone to keep watch until darkness fell. Puntaru dropped the kangaroo to the ground by Mayrah and her mother, then walked over to where Mayrah's father was settling himself and sat down, putting his spears down and making himself comfortable. Mayrah and her mother looked at the kangaroo and exchanged a hopeful smile. Mayrah's mother took her fire-making materials out of her bag, a wad of fleecy lining gathered from dried seed pods and a couple of shards of flint, and she knocked sparks onto a pinch of the tinder and blew on it gently until it was smoldering and glowing. She put a few tiny bits of bark from a stick on the tinder and continued blowing on it. The bark burst into flame, and she put splinters of wood on the finger of flame and built it higher. The blaze leaped up, and the pieces of wood cracked and popped as she stacked them on. Mayrah pulled the kangaroo closer, untying its legs and unfolding it, and she and her mother held it between them as they passed it back and forth across the flames, singeing the hair off it.

The shadows grew long, and the sun began setting in a blaze of fiery red from the dust still hanging in the air from a dust storm of three days before. Mayrah and her mother finished singeing the hair off the kangaroo, and they dug a shallow pit by the fire, pushed the fire into it, folded the kangaroo and put it on top of the embers and blazing sticks, and piled more wood on top of it. The fire blazed higher, and the appetizing odor of the burning skin and the roasting meat filled the air. Mayrah swallowed constantly as she sat by the fire, looking into the flames. The two men sat on the other side of the depression, leaning back against the dirt wall behind them and talking quietly. Their previous conversation had been muted with the caution natural when in the open and in ε potentially dangerous situation, but they still talked softly, obviously wishing to keep their conversation between themselves. It wasn't unusual for men to be secretive, and Mayrah felt totally unconcerned. All of her attention was on the kangaroo.

Darkness fell. The fire filled the depression with a ruddy glow and made wavering, flickering fingers of light on the face of the sandstone, and the sky became a soft, velvety black dotted with the brilliantly twinkling lights of the stars. The men stirred and rose to their feet, and Mayrah's father summoned her brother with a soft whistle as they walked toward the fire. Mayrah's mother rooted the kangaroo out of the fire with her stick, and Puntaru impaled it with a spear and carried it back to where they had been sitting as it hissed, smoked, and dripped on the ground. Mayrah's brother scrambled down from the sandstone and trotted eagerly toward the men. Puntaru split the kangaroo in two down the spine with his axe, put the half without the tail and head in a nearby bush, and he and Mayrah's father and brother began eating the half with the head and tail attached.

Mayrah and her mother emptied the food out of their bags. She had five lizards, and her mother had seven lizards, two small snakes, and four fat jerboa mice. It wasn't an inconsiderable amount of food, and much less had on occasion sufficed the entire family, but Mayrah's share was less that satisfying because her mind was still on the kangaroo. She and her mother ate, and she sat on her heels and absently searched her mouth with the tip of her tongue for grains of sand and spat them out as she watched the men and her brother eating. The fire died down and it was dark for a few minutes. Then the moon rose and filled the depression with light almost as bright as twilight. The men and her brother finished, and her mother rose and went to get what was left. They had eaten the tail, the tender flesh along the backbone, both legs, and the brains and tongue, but the ribs were left and shreds of flesh and cartilage still adhered to the joints and bones. Mayrah and her mother cracked the bones for the marrow, gnawed the meat and cartilage off the bones, then divided the ribs and separated them to gnaw the stringy flesh off them.

The combination of all she had eaten amounted to an exceptionally large meal, and Mayrah felt sluggish, leaden, and breathless as she chewed the last rib bone. She tossed the bone onto the glowing embers of the fire with the other bones, took a cautiously measured mouthful of water from her *wirree*, then picked up her stick and jabbed the end of it into the holes and crevices in the sandstone behind the fire. A couple of tiny rock lizards leaped out and flashed away along the rock into the darkness, and a large scorpion jumped out of a crack, poised to do battle. She swept the scorpion into the fire with the end of her stick and curled up on her side with her back to the stone and her arms wrapped around herself, settling herself to go to sleep and watching the scorpion.

It had landed on a large bone which was uncomfortably but not lethally hot. It darted back and forth with its tail curved and its stinger poised, searching for an enemy and a path out of the heat. It slid off the bone and into the dull red coals. Its limbs began smoldering, and it lashed about in an ecstasy of agony and rage, stabbing blindly with its stinger. Its movements became more languid as the fiery heat overcame it, and it fell onto its side as it twitched and jerked in its death throes. A tiny flame licked upward and raced along it as its tail lifted again to a position of attack, and its limbs and body shriveled up and faded into the ashes. The flame died away. Mayrah's brother lay down on the other side of the fire. Her mother curled up with her head near Mayrah's feet as the two men continued talking quietly. Mayrah closed her eyes, and her breathing became slow and regular as she sank into a deep, dreamless sleep.

- 2 -

A by-product of the American Revolution was the main impetus for the settlement of Australia. The prison population in England had been kept to a manageable level by transportation of felons to the American Colonies, where men were sold into bondage for fifteen to twenty guineas and women for eight to ten, providing labor and sufficient profit to interest ship owners in the undertaking. Subsequent to the American Revolution, the rapidly growing number of felons imprisoned in England made it necessary to moor decommissioned ships in the Thames and use them as prisons. The problem rapidly became something more than a nuisance, because the hulks were dangerous breeding grounds for disease and the prisoners released from them at the end of their sentences were so depraved that the moral health of the community was threatened.

Attention was turned to Australia. The existence of the continent had been known for some time, but the reports of early explorers had been consistently disparaging, describing it as a barren and worthless land. These reports were sketchy in detail, because Australia was isolated by both distance and by prevailing winds. It had been found that conditions were unpredictable and hurricanes and severe storms could sweep down around Australia between November and March, discouraging venturing into the area. From April through October the weather became more settled, but a steady wind blew from the southeast, dead against any ship approaching the eastern coast of Australia from the open sea. And the reward of a toilsome beat to windward and landfall on the northern part of the eastern coast was the uncharted hazards of the Great Barrier Reef.

But a more optimistic note had been sounded by Sir Joseph Banks, an amateur botanist who had traveled to Australia on the *Endeavour* with the famous Captain Cook and made landfall in Botany Bay. And in 1784, James Matra, who had fought on the loyalist side in the American Revolution, made a proposal to the Secretary of State that territory in Australia be developed and used to compensate loyalists for what they had lost during the Revolution. This was supported by Banks, and Sir George Young, submitted a proposal to the Admiralty pointing out the advantages of a naval station in the South Pacific to counter Spanish and French influence in the area. The main objectives of the proposals met with a cool reception, but the plans also pointed out the advantages of Australia as a penal colony. That, combined with the eternal suspicion of French intentions, stimulated interest. In May, 1787, a

23

fleet of eleven ships left England under the command of Captain Arthur Phillip with six hundred male convicts and two hundred and fifty female convicts, en route to Australia.

The first years were difficult. Many of the convicts were accustomed to a life of crime and vice, and those who survived the voyage would do manual labor only when forced. The commander of the Royal Marines who accompanied the First Fleet would permit his men to do only work which was within their accepted routine. No overseers had accompanied the convicts, and those drawn from the ranks were largely ineffective. There were no gardeners or farmers in the colony, and the soil was far different from that of England. Most of the seed which had been brought had spoiled, and some of the sheep and cattle strayed or died from eating the unfamiliar vegetation. The fishing was undependable. For the most part, the colony lived on the rations they had brought with them—salt beef and pork, ship's biscuit, flour, rice, and dried peas. The commander communicated his problems to England, and in response *HMS Guardian* was fitted out and stocked with supplies, including livestock, medicines, seeds, farming implements, and large stores of food. The ship's complement included overseers for convicts, farmers, mechanics, and selected convicts of good character. *Guardian* was to arrive in January 1789, but she foundered on an iceberg in fog and heavy seas rounding the Cape of Good Hope. For a time the colony was on starvation rations, but finally the transport *Lady Juliana* arrived in July 1790, bringing supplies, and the Second Fleet of convicts arrived shortly thereafter. A number of free settlers arrived on *Lady Juliana*; more came on *HMS Gorgon* in September 1791, and the colony began an era of relative prosperity.

Land was cleared and methods of farming were

adapted, and the settlements of Sydney and Parramatta thrived. Convicts completed their sentences or were pardoned by the Governor and took land grants, soldiers completed their terms of service and elected to take grants instead of returning to England, and more free settlers arrived. Sheep grazing became a profitable industry, and the colony rapidly developed self-sufficiency in the production of foodstuffs. Secondary colonies thrived, and on Van Diemen's Land, limited sealing and whaling industries developed and growing herds of sheep and cattle filled cleared areas in the interior. Ships began calling at Sydney to trade and to take on foodstuffs. Crime became a problem, with some convicts fleeing to the hinterlands to become bushrangers and rob, murder, and terrorize isolated settlers and small settlements.

The Blue Mountains to the west of Sydney and Parramatta were a barrier which confined the mainland settlements to a coastal strip of about forty miles until 1813. Various attempts were made to penetrate the mountain range, but the explorers turned back because of the forbidding terrain and because they persisted in following their previous experience in crossing mountain ranges, trying to find a pass through a valley when in fact they were attempting to penetrate a tableland and all the valleys had dead ends. In 1813 a small party followed the ridges, which were covered with sharp granite and quartz stones. It took them almost three weeks to cover the fifty miles to the western edge of the tableland, but on the other side they found rivers and abundant stands of trees interspersed with broad areas of thick, lush grass. When they reported back to the Governor, he organized a road-building party to open the way into the interior, clearing brushwood, filling swamps, and making a gravel roadbed across the granite and quartz ridges. The project was quickly completed, opening the route for further exploration and for herds of sheep and cattle to be driven into the interior.

Dealing with the female convicts was always a problem, beginning with the first landing when all convicts had been put on good behavior and brought ashore without fetters, promptly resulting in an orgy. While the Governor struggled with a variety of problems and gave as much attention as he could to means of keeping the male and female convicts separated, several hundred of them devoted much of their time and energy to foiling the Governor's objective, producing a steady internal growth in the population of the colony. Marriage was encouraged, and any female convict who found someone to marry her was released to live with her spouse, a free woman except for the bonds of matrimony. At other times, any man or family with sufficient resources to maintain a woman servant was allowed to select one from the female convicts, and any couple who wished to marry were allowed to do so and were assigned to a landowner to work out their sentences. Policies varied under various Governors, becoming lenient at one time and more strict at another, and for a time all female convicts who were not otherwise disposed of were assigned to the Female Factory at Parramatta.

It was a small complex of buildings and parts of buildings, a long room over the jail used for some male convicts, with a few adjacent sheds and a small wooden house. The long room was used for spinning to occupy the women's time, and there was a small fireplace where they did their cooking. Some of the women slept in the huts and others in the long room, some on cots and others on heaps of wool which was spun in the room. The sanitary facilities were buckets at each end of the room, and it was ventilated by two windows covered with wooden bars. The wide cracks in the floor resulted in the male convicts below being drenched by the

26

infrequent occasions when the floor was washed. The long room was the scene of occasional riots, drunken brawls when the women managed to get rum, and fights between the women and the guards, which the women usually won.

The Female Factory was home for a time for Sheila Garrity, who arrived on the Second Fleet. Convicted of being a shill for a purse snatcher, she was twenty, the daughter of Patrick Garrity, who had been an immigrant from Dublin to London, and a convict who had died on the First Fleet, and she was five months pregnant when she arrived as a result of a liaison with a Royal Marine guard on the voyage. Her son was born in the Female Factory, the third child to which she had given birth and the first which survived the first weeks of life, and she named him Patrick after her father. When he was something less than a year old, Sheila had an offer of employment as a house servant for a free settler and his wife, but the offer was contingent upon her giving up her child. It was a choice between keeping the child or her sanity, and she turned the child over to the orphanage at Sydney and went to work for the settler, a man named Albert Cummings.

The orphanage was located at the corner of George and Bridge Streets and supported from port dues, fines, and confiscations. It was operated by matrons selected from among the female conficts and a couple of widows under the general jurisdiction of a clergyman appointed by the Governor, and life within it was characterized by piety, industry, and discipline. Most of the children in it were the offspring of female convicts, with a few children of free settlers who had been orphaned by the death of their parents.

Garrity's first memories were of the strict routine and the immediate, severe punishment following any interruption to the routine or infraction of rules. Those who were of walking age rose each morning, hurriedly washed and dressed and folded their blankets, then assembled for morning prayer and filed into the dining room for breakfast. After breakfast the group divided, the smaller children going to workshops to card wool for spinning, the older ones going to workshops to spin wool, and the eldest ones assisting in caring for children too small to care for themselves. At midday there was another assembly for prayers, then the noon meal. Groups of the older children attended instruction in the rudiments of reading, writing, and arithmetic for a time during the afternoon, then returned to their work. In late afternoon there was an exercise period in the large yard behind the house, with the older children supervising the play of the younger ones; then another assembly for prayers and the evening meal. After supper, some of the older children or the women read aloud from books or the Bible until it was time for bed. The routine was broken on Sunday, which was devoted to religious study and worship for everyone, and the group marched along the street and was joined at the church by the children from the girls' orphanage at Parramatta for a special service for orphans. Sheila visited Garrity over a period of several years and occasionally brought him small things, a sweetmeat or a garment discarded by or stolen from one of her employer's children. Then the visits diminished and finally stopped.

To young Patrick Garrity, the stories in the books about England had the same level of reality as the stories from the Bible. And they were based on premises and assumptions which made them meaningless in realistic terms. There were no oak or hickory trees in Australia, and to turn the other cheek was to invite another blow. He was quiet and withdrawn, industrious at his work, and meticulously obedient. But he had inherited his father's substantial build and either the temper which had kept his father a private soldier during twenty years of service or the temper which had sent his maternal grandfather to prison for murder, and a surreptitious pinch from a troublemaker would always bring a direct and highly public retaliation from him. By the time Patrick was fifteen he was the size of an average adult, and he'd had innumerable thrashings by the minister for assaulting other boys for no apparent reason, because he always remained steadfastly silent as to what had been done to provoke him. The matrons were darkly suspicious and mistrustful of him because of his size and silent nature, and he was assigned to work outside the house, chopping wood and drawing water with another large boy. The other boy was a slacker, preferring the brief pain of a thrashing to hours of labor hewing wood and carrying water, and he got Garrity thrashed as well when there was insufficient wood and water. The unfairness of the situation didn't bother Garrity, because he had found out years before that life was basically unfair. But a thrashing always injured his sense of dignity. He fought the other boy and whipped him, which got him another thrashing when the minister saw the boy's battered face, but he started doing his share of the work.

At seventeen there was a major upheaval in his life. He and five other boys were called to assemble in the yard, the usual lineup when a mechanic, sawyer, carpenter, or other tradesman was looking for an apprentice. Garrity had been periodically summoned for the lineups from the age of fifteen, but a reputation for truculence had attached itself to him and was generally known among the tradesmen in Sydney and Parramatta, and he had never been selected for even a trial period.

But this man didn't look like a tradesman. He was a couple of inches shorter than Garrity, with a powerful chest, shoulders, and arms, and a trace of white showing in the hair sticking from under his hat and in

29

his mustaches and beard. His face above his beard and mustaches was leathery from exposure to the sun and wind, and he stood with his arms folded and his feet apart, somehow giving the impression that the yard behind the orphanage was too small to contain him. His piercing, pale blue eyes moved back and forth across the line as the minister made his usual speech of introduction, saying that the man was named Williamson and he was a grazier. Then the minister invited Williamson to step closer or to question each boy, but Williamson stood unmoving and silent. His eyes moved back and forth again and locked with Garrity's, and he pointed to Garrity and nodded his head.

Garrity went upstairs to the long room lined with cots where the older boys slept, and collected his blanket, his extra pair of trousers and shirt, and a small wooden box his mother had brought him on a visit several years before, and he rolled the things up into a bundle. He had hoped to be picked as an apprentice, because it had been impressed upon him that it was a worthy objective and he had been subjected to ridicule because he hadn't been selected before. But he felt a strange sadness and a dragging reluctance to leave. He put his bundle under his arm and went down the stairs. Two of the matrons were standing in the hall whispering, and as he started down the stairs they fell silent and moved away from the staircase, looking at him with their usual wary frowns.

Williamson's bullock cart was piled high with bags and barrels of foodstuffs on the street in front of the orphanage, and he was standing by it and talking to the minister. The minister shook hands with Williamson, Williamson climbed onto the cart, and the minister shook hands with Garrity for the first and last time and told him to work hard and obey Williamson. Garrity mumbled a reply, and the minister smiled, nodded, and patted his shoulder. Williamson waved toward the rear of the cart, and Garrity put his bundle in and followed after it.

The cart rumbled along the busy street, a few people glancing at it. A couple of boys who had been apprenticed sometime before were walking along the street and pushing a small cart of barrel staves, and they looked at Garrity and exchanged a quiet, laughing comment. A couple of men waved and shouted a greeting to Williamson. The houses thinned out, and the street turned into the rough road leading west from Sydney, with brush, trees, and scattered houses on both sides. A few minutes later he was further out of the settlement than he had ever been before, and he gazed around with interest.

Williamson turned and looked at him. "You're of a good size and age not to be apprenticed, boy. Do you always do as you're told?"

"Aye, I do as I'm told."

"Do you fancy yourself a fighter?"

"No more than the next one."

"I take that as you do. We can stop here so we can have our fight and get it over with."

"I want no trouble with you, and I'll do as I'm told."

Williamson looked over his shoulder at Garrity thoughtfully, his pale blue eyes penetrating, then they were suddenly twinkling with good humor and friendliness. "We'll leave it at that, then, and I won't have to take a chance on getting whipped," he chuckled. He rooted around under his seat and took out a bottle, and he motioned Garrity to move to the front of the cart. "You can have a go at this instead of me, and I warrant it'll win the fight."

Garrity climbed across the bags and barrels to the seat, and Williamson chatted cheerfully with him and passed him the bottle of rum during the first half of the trip. It was the first liquor Garrity had ever tasted, and during the second half of the trip he lay with his head

31

over the side of the cart and vomited drunkenly.

When they arrived at the station, Williamson and a couple of other men dragged Garrity out of the cart and carried him to the shed where the stockmen slept.

The trip from the orphanage to Williamson's selection was an accurate indicator in that life on the selection was far different in every respect from what Patrick had known at the orphanage. Williamson was a former convict who had worked out his term of servitude on the lands of an officer in the South Wales Guard, and over a period of years he had increased an initial small flock into thousands of sheep. He was an uncompromising man regarding work and his sheep, but he was also generous, affable, and friendly.

The clean, neat, and orderly streets of Sydney had been left behind, and the selection was a wilderness of rolling hills covered with brush, clumps of eucalyptus trees, and grass. Williamson was married to a woman of thirty, a former convict a few years younger than he, and they had two children which Williamson had delivered himself. Their house was a hovel built of sod, stones, and sheets of bark, but the pens surrounding it were neat and in good repair, and the shearing shed was sturdy and well-built. Williamson had four other stockmen, all of them convicts paroled to him to serve out their terms, and all of them were out in the bush with flocks. He also had a half dozen aborigines around his place, as well as a couple of older white men who did odd jobs. There had been occasional aborigines roaming the streets in Sydney, but those on Williamson's selection were substantially less civilized in appearance than the ones Garrity had seen before, only partially clothed or walking about naked, and living with their families in the bush in the vicinity of Williamson's house under conditions which were poorer than Williamson's only in that their huts were smaller. They located strayed sheep, tracked and killed dingoes, and did other odd jobs in return for rations, bits of clothing, and pieces of metal to make spear points, axes, and knives. They were useful, but they also had to be watched because they would steal anything made of metal which was left lying about.

Williamson taught Garrity to fire a musket and trained him in some of the tasks around the pens, then put him with one of the stockmen for a month. The stockman was a surly, withdrawn man, bitter and caustic in everything he said to Garrity, and they almost fought several times. But Garrity restrained his temper, and he watched and learned. At the end of the month, Williamson came for him and took him back to his house. He issued Garrity a musket, rations, four dogs, and camp equipment, and helped him drive a flock of two hundred sheep into the bush. Then Williamson left him alone.

At first the feeling of responsibility was so burdensome that he couldn't sleep at night, and his days were a nightmare of stumbling wearily about and compulsively counting the sheep over and over, with a cold feeling in the pit of his stomach each time he miscounted and left out a couple. Other than what little he remembered of his mother, Williamson was the first person who had been kind to him, and he had a driving need to make a success of the job. Then he began to trust his dogs more, perceiving that they knew more about sheep than he did, and they became accustomed to him. But he still slept with his musket at his side, and a growl from one of his dogs in the night would immediately awaken him and bring him out of his shelter with his musket in hand.

The days began to fade together, but there was no monotony. The flies and mosquitoes were bothersome and the torrid heat was a constant discomfort during the day, but the isolation bothered him little. Williamson's warnings about poisonous snakes and insects became more meaningful when a scorpion stung him and he was ill for several days, and he became more watchful. He killed four dingoes, and fired off his musket a few times to frighten off aborigines who were prowling about. Two sheep were bitten by snakes and died, and another died of no apparent cause beyond the possibility that it had eaten something poisonous, but Williamson had said he expected some losses.

At the end of six weeks, Williamson came to check on him, and he was highly pleased. He left and returned a few days later with three hundred more sheep to add to Garrity's flock, and he helped Garrity move them to better graze along the banks of the Nepean River, the boundary of the selection.

– 3 –

There was a feeling of accomplishment when each day
was ended and the sheep were in the fold, and there was
a satisfying contentment he had never before known as
he sat in front of his shelter with his dogs around him
and cooked his meal and boiled his tea at night. And as
opportunities developed to exchange a few words with
men who had worked for other graziers, he gained a
more complete appreciation of how fortunate he was to
be working for Williamson. Many graziers gave their
men enormous flocks to tend and still held them
responsible for the death of any sheep. They docked the
pay of hired stockmen for sheep which died, and if their
stockmen were convicts and didn't get wages, they took
them to the nearest Justice of the Peace, another

grazier, and had them punished by whipping. Garrity was still bound to the orphanage, which would receive his wages until he was nineteen in compensation for having reared him. But Williamson had driven a hard bargain with the orphanage, and he paid Garrity two shillings and sixpence per week which was unknown to them. A close friendship was developing between the two. In addition to the food and other necessities he was required to furnish Garrity, Williamson also provided him with tobacco and an occasional bottle of rum.

Cooler weather brought a different set of problems. There were fewer flies and mosquitoes, but good graze was also more scarce and the sheep had to be moved about more frequently, necessitating dismantling and moving the fold more often. The snakes were sluggish in the cooler weather, but they were also more likely to seek the warmth of the fire or the shelter. Garrity drove his sheep to the pens for shearing, and Williamson let him off for a couple of days to go to Sydney.

The city had changed. Buildings had been put up where there had been fields, and it seemed busier and more cosmopolitan. And while Sydney seemed larger, the orphanage seemed smaller. Garrity found that he had also changed, becoming moody and morose when drunk. He was arrested for public drunkeness and fighting, and the orphanage was notified. The minister came to the jail, lectured him, and left him there and sent word to Williamson where he was. Williamson came to Sydney earlier than usual for supplies and to get Garrity out of jail, but he was amused rather than resentful about the trouble.

There was a brushfire during the winter, and he lost eighteen sheep, a dog, and all of his equipment and supplies in his headlong rush to drive the sheep to the other side of the Nepean. Then it began raining heavily, and he spent several cold and miserable nights in the open and long, dreary days worrying about what he had lost, keeping on the move all the time to hold the flock bunched because he had lost his fold in the fire. It was several days before Williamson found him, and Williamson was exuberant when he did. One entire flock had been lost in the fire, there had been losses much larger than Garrity's in all the flocks. Williamson helped him get the sheep back across the river, left what he had in the way of food with him, and returned two days later with clothing, equipment, more food, and poles to make another fold. When the frigid weather set in, Williamson brought some heavy winter clothes and Garrity made himself a long, heavy coat from several sheepskins. By spring he had outgrown both the clothes and the coat he had made.

Garrity had attained his full growth by the time he drove in his sheep to be sheared again, well over six feet tall and some fifteen stone in weight, a size which made other men regard him respectfully. Williamson laughingly warned him about drinking and fighting before he left for Sydney, and Garrity remembered it on the first day and drank very little. He spent most of the day wandering around Sydney and looking at the new buildings which had been put up since he had been there last, and he visited the orphanage briefly because he felt a compulsion to see it again. But seeing it somehow failed to satisfy the need which had generated the compulsion. Then on the second day he met a man who had been an older boy at the orphanage and had been apprenticed several years before who had become a sawyer. The cuffs the man had given him as a boy were a dim, distant memory, and the man had matured to a substantially smaller size than Garrity and was heartily friendly. He had a house on the Parramatta Road, and Garrity went with him to meet his wife and see his children. They went out into the woodlot behind the man's house, where he had a bottle of rum under a pile of lumber, and a couple of hours later the man was asleep on the ground, Garrity was mildly befuddled, and the man's wife was glaring at Garrity each time she passed the back window or door in going about her tasks. Garrity left.

Darkness fell as Garrity wandered between the public houses near the docks. In one of them he got into an argument with a free settler who resented the privileges of former convicts, and he was still sober enough to realize the potential danger in the situation and left. The man followed him through an alley, pulling at his arm and snarling at him, and Garrity's temper flared. He wheeled, striking out at the man in the darkness, and his fist caught the side of the man's head and knocked him reeling toward the building on one side of the alley. The man smacked into the heavy timbers and slumped to the ground. Garrity started to go on, then he turned back and bent over the man, checking him. He was dead.

The chilling awareness of what he had done cut through the alcohol, and he was suddenly completely sober, pondering his predicament. It would probably be adjudged murder, and the minimum punishment would be transportation to one of the secondary penal colonies. But no one else had seen. Garrity moved along the dark, odorous, refuse-choked alley and looked at the pedestrians and conveyances moving along the street in the soft glow of the lamps in front of the stores. Then he went back to the man and hoisted him to his shoulder. He worked his way through the alleys to the docks, and carried his burden to the end of a deserted wharf and dropped it into the water. The tide was going out, and he watched the blur of the man's body fading into the darkness as it moved toward the bay. Then he turned and walked back through the city and along the road in the darkness.

He told Williamson what had happened, then took

his flock back out into the bush. Williamson made a special trip into Sydney on the pretext of getting supplies, and when he returned he came out into the bush to talk to Garrity. The man had been reported missing and the authorities were searching for him, but his body hadn't been found and Garrity hadn't been associated with his disappearance. Williamson talked to Garrity again about drinking and fighting, and it wasn't in a jocular tone. But it also wasn't needed, because Garrity didn't go into Sydney again. When he drank he drank alone in the bush, and when he woke with a bad hangover from drinking too much his knuckles would usually be battered from being hammered against a tree while he was drunk.

Williamson had remained on his original lands while other graziers had moved across the Blue Mountains to the interior, and he had repeatedly sought to buy adjoining properties or claim title to abandoned properties through the Governor's office in Sydney. But he had been unsuccessful in his attempts to obtain additional property, and his flock had been expanding at the normal rate of one third each year, necessitating the slaughter of many sheep to keep from overgrazing the selection. Official policy expressed in London and Sydney forbade graziers from moving onto Crown lands west of the Blue Mountains, but no direct action had been taken against those who had done so. And the interior had been explored and sketchily mapped all along the Murrumbidgee River and north and west of the Darling River.

After pondering the situation and being frustrated in further attempts to obtain more land, Williamson began making preliminary preparations to take a flock into the interior. Garrity had broken his final ties with the orphanage and was on full wages, and Williamson offered him the opportunity of going into the interior as a stockman on shares, with Williamson providing the sheep, equipment, and supplies, and Garrity receiving two thirds of the profits for his labor. Garrity quickly accepted, but he was the only stockman to do so; other men agreed to go for wages, but they refused to risk their labor on the uncertainties of the interior. Williamson hired a manager and other stockmen to see to the sheep and land he was leaving behind, and he began buying up bullocks and carts and large amounts of supplies. He waited until the next shearing had been completed, then left with Garrity and twelve other men, five thousand sheep, twenty dogs, his family, and a long line of carts loaded with supplies.

It was a year of substantial rainfall and the graze was good, but the trek took months. All of the land on the western slopes of the Blue Mountains and as far west as the headwaters of the Lachlan River had been taken by squatters, and they trudged on, finding more fences and squatters and stopping every few days to give the sheep and bullocks a full day of grazing to maintain their condition. The terrain across the vast inland area changed, becoming more arid than the land along the Nepean, but there was usually ample graze for the stock. Many squatters and stockmen came through the brush to meet them, not having seen other people for months, and some accompanied them for short distances to point out ways around difficult terrain. There were several stretches where there was no water, and some sheep were trampled in the surging rush of the flocks to water after passing through a dry stretch. Several of the bullocks died or became crippled and had to be shot, and a couple of the carts were damaged beyond use in accidents while crossing hills. Other sheep died through eating poisonous weeds and from snakebite, and dingoes killed a few which got out of the folds at night. One of the men was snakebitten and died, and another man became ill and had to ride in a cart for almost a month before he recovered. Eight months after the trek began, they crossed the Darling River with almost four thousand sheep. The last of the squatters had been left behind, and they continued on for a few days then stopped at a creek in an area of rolling hills and relatively good grasslands to establish the station.

Williamson immediately dispatched four of the men back to Sydney with the carts and bullocks to get another load of supplies and began working with other men to build pens, houses, and sheds. Garrity and the other stockmen drew their rations and equipment, sorted out their flocks and dogs, and left to establish their grazing areas. It took a period of a few weeks for Garrity to accustom himself to the unfamiliar territory. The first and primary consideration was to locate landmarks so he wouldn't become lost, because they had spread out over an enormous distance compared to the area they had occupied on the Nepean and he was many miles from the creek where the buildings were being put up. There was a peculiar, jagged hill which could be seen for a long distance, and he established it as the western and southern boundary of his grazing area. He found other landmarks, located waterholes and convenient and safe routes to drive the sheep from one area to another, and gradually became familiar with the terrain. Rations were short for a time and there was no tea, sugar, or tobacco, but the time passed quickly for him and it seemed only a short time after the next shearing that the carts returned after taking the wool to Sydney and supplies were abundant again.

The graze was much poorer than that along the Nepean, and Patrick had to move the sheep more often and over a wider range. But he had a feeling of ownership toward the sheep which had come when he started working on shares, and the work seemed less than it had before. The sheep lambed well, and he tended them more carefully, conscious that two thirds

41

of the profits were his. The new arrangement with Williamson had been effective from the time of the first shearing after arriving, and he already had two hundred guineas in the bank in Sydney, m re money than he had ever dreamed of owning.

But for some reason the isolation weighed on him more heavily. It didn't seem logical, because he had gone for weeks without seeing another person on the Nepean, and it hadn't bothered him there. And through the years he had become accustomed to the periodic stillness and silence of the bush, when it seemed that even the insects, birds, and small animals were still and silent. But during the time he had been on the Nepean, there had been the firm knowledge in the back of his mind that Sydney was a relatively short distance away. That knowledge had been replaced by an awareness that he was separated from civilization by a distance which took months to traverse.

Something of the sort also seemed to bother the others, because three stockmen drew their wages and left with the supply carts during the first year, to be replaced with others. Garrity fought it, because the wool harvest and lambing were better than they had normally been on the Nepean and his share of profits on the next shearing brought his savings up to what was to him a staggering amount. Williamson perceived that Garrity was troubled, and he took time away from other things he had to do in order to bring Garrity's supplies, instead of sending the head stockman or a rouseabout as he did with the other stockmen. And he spent all the time he could afford with Garrity, talking to him encouragingly about the profits from the wool and the possibilities for future years.

The aborigines in the area were rarely seen, because they'd had little or no contact with white people. There were isolated instances when they tried to steal a sheep, and one of the stockmen was wounded with a spear, but Garrity had no difficulty other than having to fire his musket a few times to scare them off. Then one approached· openly late one afternoon as Garrity was putting the sheep into the fold, causing some confusion as the dogs became excited and divided their attention between the sheep and the aborigine. A few sheep were frightened at a dog's barking at the aborigine and broke away, and Garrity snarled at the dog and waved it after the sheep. The dog darted away and raced around the sheep, turning them, then nipped at their heels and drove them back. Garrity slid the poles closed after the sheep, frowning suspiciously at the aborigine as he approached.

With the sheep in the fold, the dogs turned their attention to the aborigine and advanced toward him, growling threateningly and baring their teeth. He stood with his hands held over his head in a display of peaceful intentions, and he approached closer when Garrity called·the dogs back. He was a more or less typical aborigine, thin but not bony, of indeterminate age, and a dusty chocolate color from exposure to the sun and dirt. His hair was the usual untidy, lank mass of mottled brown hacked off even with his ears, his mustaches and beard covered the lower half of his face, and there were traces of faded white and red paint on his forehead, nose, cheeks, and chest. He wore a belt made of braided strips of animal skin with a knife and an axe stuck in it, and he had apparently been around white people to a considerable extent because he was fluent in the pidgin English which passed for communication between white people and aborigines.

His name was Puntaru, he had a friendly, ingratiating manner, and he was the first human being Garrity had seen for some weeks. Garrity shared his meal with him and listened to him chatter as they ate, some of what he said almost unintelligible because he talked very rapidly and because of the aborigine tendency to substitute "p" sounds for "f" sounds. Garrity let him spend the night by the fire, and the following day Puntaru cut down a tree in a nearby grove to replace a broken pole in the fold, cut strips of bark from gum trees to make a better roof for Garrity's shelter, and spent the rest of the day following Garrity around chattering to him about the numbers of sheep and white men he had seen elsewhere.

When Garrity returned the sheep to the fold that evening, he looked around in his shelter to see if he had any scraps of metal. He had broken off part of the blade of a shovel in digging in the flinty ground to place poles for his shelter, and he found the piece of metal where he had thrown it into the corner of the shelter. Puntaru's axe handle had a steel head, of which he was inordinately proud, and Garrity used a large stone and the flat side of Puntaru's axe and showed him how to shape the piece of metal into a spearpoint. Puntaru was delighted with it, and he immediately removed the flint point from one of his spears and began replacing it with the metal point as Garrity started cooking the meal. When Puntaru had the metal point fastened firmly into the shaft of the spear, Garrity showed him how to sharpen it and the blade of his axe by scraping them on a stone. Puntaru watched closely with rapt fascination, his childish exuberance over the scrap of metal humorous in a way and yet pathetic.

Puntaru didn't like tea, but he enjoyed the damper and mutton as much as he had the night before. He ate with a hearty gusto and enormous appetite, gnawed the bone, then licked his fingers and began chattering again as Garrity smoked his pipe and sipped a pannikin of tea. "Him proper bloody good, mate," he said with a gusty belch. "Gut me maybe bust now." He sighed with contentment, tossing a couple of sticks onto the fire, then looked at Garrity thoughtfully. "Pellow like you him need wooman belong him."

44

Williamson had his wife with him and he had recently hired a new head stockman who had brought his wife, and during the past year or so there had been a stockman or two who had brought their wives. But most of the men were unmarried, and the majority of those who were had left their wives in Sydney or elsewhere, either because they didn't want to subject them to the hardships of the bush or because they had refused to come. Garrity had thought about marriage, but it had been in terms of an extremely distant and possibly unlikely objective. Many men didn't get married at all. And his first concern was to build up his bank account and get his own flock of sheep. He puffed his pipe, looking at Puntaru, and he lifted his eyebrows and shrugged indifferently.

"Pellow him need wooman belong him," Puntaru said in a firm tone, nodding his head emphatically. "Pellow him need wooman to cook, talk, and puck. No good pellow him stay belong ship and dingo allatime." He waved toward the fold, where the sheep were making quiet noises as they settled for the night. "Ship him bloody good eat, but him no allasame pellow." He nodded toward the dogs lying on the other side of the fire. "Dingo him some allasame pellow, but him no talk, no cook, no puck."

Garrity took a drink of tea from his pannikin and looked at Puntaru with a musing smile as he put his pipe back in his mouth. "Where woman you?"

"Him station me," Puntaru replied promptly. "Samesame some white pellow wooman him stay belong big station Sydney. Bimeby me go station me." He tapped his axe with a finger. "Bimeby me get two, three white pellow tamaha, then me go station me." He picked up the spear with the metal point and fingered the point. "And maybe get two, three white pellow stone for *kiru*."

Garrity nodded. Puntaru's life was far different from

that of a white man, but in this respect it was similar. Some married stockmen left their wives in Sydney or elsewhere while they worked in the bush to earn enough to get established, and Puntaru was doing the identical thing. With two or three metal axes and two or three metal spearpoints, he would undoubtedly be regarded as a wealthy man when he returned to his tribe.

"Arunta wooman him work plenty bloody hard and maybe bimeby him cook white pellow eat plenty good."

The reason why Puntaru had introduced the subject became abundantly clear; he was offering his services in locating a woman, and undoubtedly anticipated receiving an axe or two or some metal to make spearpoints for his efforts. Some white men lived with aborigine women, but the idea didn't appeal to Garrity. Aborigines were far different from white people in habits, attitudes, and way of life, and most of the aborigine women Garrity had seen had been extremely ugly. He drained his pannikin and refilled it from the billy on the fire, and he silently shook his head as he put the billy back on the coals and puffed on his pipe.

"No samesame old wooman belong station," Puntaru said. "Old wooman belong station him no bloody good for puck. Me find wooman you him no have *birrahlee*, and him look good for puck. You puck and make *birrahlee* you."

Aborigines appeared to regard children highly, and it seemed likely that Puntaru was speaking from that viewpoint in calling attention to the possibility of children, but to Garrity that would be simply another undesirable feature of the situation he had no intention of becoming involved in. He shook his head again, and Puntaru dropped the subject and began talking again about the metal spearpoint and what Garrity had shown him about sharpening it. Garrity searched around on the ground and found a stone with a smooth finish, and he took the spear and began trying to explain how to hone the edge of the blade with a finer-grained stone.

Puntaru remained through the night again and followed Garrity as he took the sheep out of the fold and drove them out to graze the next morning, then he left to hunt for a kangaroo. He returned in the middle of the afternoon without having seen any, and Garrity selected a sheep to butcher and drove it away from the flock. Puntaru was appalled by what he regarded as Garrity's waste in butchering the sheep, and he searched out the heart in the pile of entrails and munched on it as he helped Garrity carry the carcass and hang it in a tree near the shelter. Garrity skinned it and covered it with a piece of canvas to keep the flies off, then went back to the flock and began moving the sheep slowly toward the fold. Puntaru continued returning to the entrails and finding tidbits to eat during the late afternoon, but he was ready for his share of the mutton and damper Garrity cooked that night. After they ate, they sat by the fire and stretched the sheepskin on a frame of boughs to scrape it and let it dry. Puntaru didn't bring up the subject of a woman, but he mentioned several times that cooking and working with animal skins were women's work.

Garrity decided to move the fold the next day, and after the sheep were pastured in the open under the watchful eyes of the dogs, he began dismantling the fold to move it and his other things to an open, grassy hillside a couple of miles away. Puntaru helped him, and it took most of the day to move everything. Since the shelter had started deteriorating, they abandoned it and Puntaru cut sheets of bark to make another one. He worked willingly, occasionally disappearing to go back to the pile of entrails to rummage through what birds and small animals had left of it, and he mentioned several times that moving belongings and constructing a shelter were women's work.

Puntaru's reminders hadn't been necessary, because the subject had been on Garrity's mind much of the time. Most of the aborigines he had seen had been aged and with pot bellies and slack, flapping dugs from hardship and childbearing, but there had been a few younger ones who had drawn a second glance from him. And biological pressures were a problem. Beyond that, there was the troublesome and in some respects frightening side to his nature which came out when drinking, and he suspected that his solitude might be a cause of it, or at least contribute to it. And there was the solitude itself, which had become harder to bear.

There was also the work. Cooking a joint of meat took hours, and there had been many times when he had dozed off in front of the fire and lost his appetite while waiting for his evening meal to cook. A woman could have it ready for him when he brought the flock back to the fold, and he could also have something more appetizing than a piece of cold, leftover damper for his morning and noon meal. There were many things. Most of all, there would be someone sitting by him in front of the fire at night when he smoked his pipe and drank his billy of tea.

Not unexpectedly, he found Puntaru more than willing to discuss the subject again. Puntaru's tribal area was to the north and west, and he was confident that he could locate and bring back a woman who would be satisfactory. And he appeared more than anxious to proceed so he could return to his own family. For his efforts he wanted an axe, a knife, and metal to fashion two more spearpoints, and he suggested that approximately the same amounts and types of items would suffice as a purchase price to be given to the woman's father. Garrity was still doubtful, and he thought about it for another night. Puntaru brought up the subject again the following morning, talking about how useful a woman would be and the many things Garrity had to do that could be done by a woman, and he emphasized the point that Garrity would be under no obligation if he considered the woman unsatisfactory. Garrity was still undecided, perceiving all the advantages but reluctant to commit himself, and it was difficult to sort it out in his mind while Puntaru continued chattering about it. During the afternoon he agreed to it after pushing himself into a decision, and Puntaru immediately collected his belongings and left, not even waiting for the evening meal.

Puntaru had alleviated the solitude during the days he had been there, and after his departure the silence of the bush descended once more. Williamson came a couple of days after Puntaru left and brought supplies, and Garrity asked him to send out a couple of small axes, a couple of knives, and a few bits of metal. Williamson assented, displaying no curiosity about the matter, and three days later a rouseabout came from the station with the things.

Garrity's mood vacillated between dread and anticipation for a time. Puntaru had given no indication of how long he might be gone, and Garrity frequently scanned the countryside as he moved about with the dogs and flock. Then a week passed, and Garrity's attitude toward the matter became something of a mix between relief and disappointment. Another week passed, and full days began to pass without his thinking of Puntaru.

The dark, slender spearpoint which had been a matter
of only mild and passing curiosity became the focus of
attention just before noon the following day. They were
moving slowly and silently through the brush in the
hunting pattern, and there was a sudden flurry of
movement and commotion in front, followed by
exhilarated whoops and shouts from Mayrah's father
and the man Puntaru. Mayrah, her mother, and her
brother raced through the brush to them, and they were
standing over an enormous red kangaroo. And from
the excited conversation, the cast of the spear had been
from an unbelievably long distance away, so far that an
ordinary spear would have only slightly wounded the
kangaroo at most. But the point on Puntaru's spear had

driven home, piercing through the ribs in a killing blow, and the kangaroo had gone only a short distance before collapsing.

Mayrah and her mother sat on their heels at one side as the men cut the kangaroo open and began eating the heart, liver, and lungs. Mayrah's brother edged forward and touched his father's arm, reminding him of his presence, and his father glanced over his shoulder, edged to one side, and indicated the kangaroo with his chin. The two men and the boy sat on their heels by the kangaroo, rooting out handfuls and eating noisily. The sun beamed down, and the odor of the blood and intestines was appetizing in the hot, still air. Mayrah had killed a bushrat and a couple of lizards and her mother had killed several lizards, and they shared them and ate them. The remainder of the small brown kangaroo had been eaten that morning and Mayrah had eaten a couple of ribs as her share, and the cumulative amount of food she had eaten during the day had been much more than usual. But the sight and smell of food stimulated her appetite, and she watched hungrily as the two men and the boy ate.

Puntaru pushed himself to his feet, belching and groaning, and he walked a few feet away and sat down in a patch of shade. Mayrah's father rose and moved away from the kangaroo, glancing at Mayrah and her mother and indicating the kangaroo with his chin. Mayrah and her mother leaped up and darted forward. Mayrah's brother was still squatting in front of the kangaroo carcass and eating, and Mayrah shouldered him aside as she reached into the kangaroo. He made a sound of protest. She looked down at him with a warning glare, baring her teeth slightly. He moved to one side and gave her more room.

There was part of the liver and lung left, and she and her mother tore out handfuls and pushed them into their mouths. Her brother leaned forward and reached in for another bite as they sat back on their heels to chew. On the edge of her vision, Mayrah noticed that Puntaru was looking at her as he and her father talked quietly and rubbed the dry, sandy soil on their hands and forearms to get the blood off them. She was squatting awkwardly, and she curled her legs under and sat down, turning her hips gracefully to one side, and she began eating less greedily to display a more restrained satisfaction with Puntaru's kill.

They finished off the lungs and liver, and the two men took a drink of water and moved off through the brush toward another camping place. Mayrah and her mother gathered up their things and the remains of the kangaroo and followed the men. The kangaroo was heavy and awkward to handle, and Mayrah's *wirree* slipped off her head and fell to the ground as they went around a thick clump of brush, spilling the water. Her mother looked at her in reproach and irritation, but in silence. Mayrah tucked the *wirree* under her arm, and they continued carrying the kangaroo along behind the men.

The camping place was a long, narrow depression between two sandy dunes, and Mayrah's brother sat on one of the dunes on watch as the two men relaxed in the shade and dozed. Mayrah and her mother made a sweep through the surrounding brush and gathered up heavy loads of firewood, built a fire and started the kangaroo roasting, and prepared to go for water. As they started to leave the camping place, Mayrah's father pointed to the south and murmured a command to her mother, indicating a source where the water was slightly brackish but where they would be within hearing distance.

It was a gnamma-hole, located at the base of a granite outcropping in the center of a blistering-hot stretch of morraine deposited by a prehistoric river eons before. The outcropping was the surface indication of a massive stretch of subterranean granite, covered by a layer of clay and the surface layers of sandy soil and morraine. During the infrequent rains, water soaked through the sandy soil to the subsurface clay at a level too deep to be reached by the roots of the stunted growth among the morraine, and it was held in the clay by the granite under it. The water collected in a small reservoir at the base of the granite outcropping, and when the reservoir was emptied it slowly refilled by drainage from the surrounding clay.

Mayrah and her mother knelt under the drooping blades of a tall clump of spinifex at the edge of the stretch of morraine and passed her mother's *wirree* back and forth, drinking the last of the water in it and slowly examining the open area and the line of brush around it for any sign of danger. When the water was finished, they rose and silently trotted across the morraine to the jutting clump of granite. Mayrah put her *wirree* down and knelt in the shadow of the granite with her back to it, bending low. Her eyes moved restlessly back and forth, her senses keenly alert, and she gripped her stick tightly in both hands, poised to bound into headlong flight. Her mother knelt behind her and began digging in the soft, sandy soil at the base of the granite.

She uncovered a piece of bark she had buried there before, and she began using it as a shovel, scraping the soil to one side. As the hole became deeper, she lay on her stomach and scraped, then climbed down into the hole and began tossing the dirt out. She disappeared from sight, and the soil continued flying from the hole. The soil changed, turning to clay and showing traces of moisture which dried rapidly in the sweltering heat, then damp clods of clay began coming from the hole. She slowed. A few more clods, then a couple of handfuls of loose clay flew out of the hole, and she clicked her tongue. Mayrah slid toward the hole, moving cautiously to keep from caving the hole in on her mother, and she reached down into it. The edge of the rough, damp slab of bark left in place to cover the water met her hand. She lifted the bark out and put it to one side, then handed her *wirree* down to her mother, leaving her arm hanging down in the hole as she turned her head sideways and continued glancing around the open area. The side of the *wirree* nudged her fingers, and she lifted it out, dripping with cool water, and handed her mother's *wirree* down to her.

The water was so cool that the brackish taste wasn't pronounced. She knelt with her stick across her toes as she held the *wirree* in both hands, drinking deeply, waiting, then drinking again. Soft, almost inaudible sounds came from the hole as her mother drank her fill. Mayrah finished the water in her *wirree*, put it down, and waited. A moment later her mother clicked her tongue. She slid back to the edge of the hole and reached down into it. The side of her mother's *wirree* touched her fingers. She lifted it out, brimming with water, put it to one side, and handed hers down. Her mother filled it and handed it back up to her, and Mayrah put it by her mother's and handed the slab of bark back down. A moment later her mother clicked her tongue again, and Mayrah moved around to the other side of the hole and began cautiously pushing the dirt back into it, starting with the clay.

Her mother's feet made soft, drumming sounds as she stamped around in the bottom of the hole, tamping the dirt back down. She clicked her tongue again, and Mayrah pushed the dirt in more rapidly. Her mother's head came back into view, then her shoulders. She climbed out of the hole and bagan pushing the dirt in, and Mayrah moved to one side and picked up her stick. Her mother finished pushing the dirt into the hole and buried the piece of bark she used as a shovel, and she began smoothing out the tracks they had made around the base of the granite. Mayrah put the leaves on her *wirree*, balanced it on her head, and moved away from the granite, crouching a few feet away and watching. Her mother finished obliterating their tracks and picked up her *wirree*, and they silently ran back across the morraine toward the edge of the brush.

Mayrah's brother was dozing in the shade of a clump of spinifex at the side of the depression, and he didn't hear them approach. When her mother kicked his foot, he sat bolt upright with a muffled exclamation and expression of surprise, and she frowned at him warningly as she passed him. The two men were dozing in the shade, and they opened their eyes as Mayrah and her mother slid down the side of the depression. They had rooted the kangaroo out of the fire and eaten the tail, leaving the remainder of it on the ground by the firepit, and Puntaru motioned toward it in permission for them to eat what they wanted.

It was virtually an entire kangaroo, an enormous amount of food, and Mayrah waited impatiently as her mother separated a front leg from the carcass. She divided it and they began eating, and her mother built up the fire again and pushed the rest of the kangaroo back into the firepit to roast it some more as she chewed a large bite. Mayrah automatically started to object, having a wishful intention of eating all of it, an intention which was untroubled by a logical analysis of how much she was capable of eating, and her mother glanced toward the men and shook her head warningly for silence, apprehensive of attracting too much attention while eating such a choice portion.

Mayrah was uncomfortably full when they finished eating. It was the middle of the afternoon, the hottest part of the day, and she felt torpid and sluggish as she lay on the ground and waited for the shadows to reach her and cover her. Her mother had given her the largest share of the kangaroo foreleg, her usual practice when food was plentiful, and she had somewhat more energy. She slid over to Mayrah with a scrap of the kangaroo skin, and she began rubbing Mayrah's face with the flesh side of the skin. Mayrah opened her eyes and looked up at her, glanced at the men on the other side of the depression, then looked back up at her mother and spoke quietly.

"Would Puntaru have me for his woman?"

Her mother pursed her lips and looked at Puntaru thoughtfully, then she looked down at Mayrah and made a negative motion with her free hand as she began wiping the piece of skin over Mayrah's face again. Mayrah glanced at Puntaru again, then dismissed the thought from her mind and closed her eyes to go to sleep.

Her brother's squealing awakened her. It was late afternoon, and the depression was filled with shadow. Both of the men were gone, and her mother was standing at the other end of the depression and looking up at the edge of the dune with a worried expression. There was a sharp slap of the shaft of a spear smacking against flesh, another howl of pain from her brother, and a growl of anger from her father. Her father had caught him sleeping. He struck him a few more times with the shaft of his spear, then she could hear the conversation between him and Puntaru fading as they walked away. Her mother waited for a moment, then quietly called her brother down into the depression. He slid down the bank, his face twisted and tears streaming from his eyes as he moaned and whimpered with pain. Mayrah's mother snapped at him irritably, taking his arm and turning him to look at his back, then she led him toward the fire. The shaft of the spear had raised thick, angry-looking weals on his back and buttocks. Her mother took a piece of kangaroo skin and began wiping the grease on the weals. He hissed

56

and winced with pain, pulling away from her, and she snapped at him angrily and jerked his arm as she continued wiping the grease on him. Mayrah yawned and stretched, and curled up on her side and closed her eyes to go back to sleep.

Most of the following day was spent in lying around the camping place and indolently munching on a piece of the kangaroo or gnawing the bones. Mayrah and her mother went out for more firewood to keep the kangaroo hot so it wouldn't spoil, and her father and Puntaru sat together at the other end of the depression and talked quietly for a long time. During the afternoon, her father told her mother to prepare to travel, and the particle he used on the end of the verb indicated that it would be for a long distance. Mayrah and her mother went for more water, and on the way back they gathered long, tough blades of spinifex to strengthen the shoulder ropes on their bags. Mayrah was curious about where they were going, as was her mother, but her father's attitude and expression didn't invite questions. Puntaru appeared to be intensely satisfied about something.

They left at daylight the following morning in a single file, with Puntaru leading the way. Mayrah and her mother carried the remainder of the kangaroo, following her father at a steady trot, with her brother a few yards behind. By midday Mayrah was starting to get a little weary from the hard, steady pace, and her brother appeared to be exhausted. They stopped for a short time, then started out again. During the middle of the afternoon they stopped again to take a drink of water and rest for a few minutes. Everyone was streaming with sweat, and it was several minutes before her brother caught up with the rest of the group. He was staggering with fatigue, and Mayrah's father gave him a warning glare. Mayrah's mother lay limply on the ground until the men started to get up again, then she pushed herself to her feet with a grim expression and gathered up her things.

They passed near the place where the last tribal corroboree had been held shortly before nightfall, but they had taken two days in traveling to it before. They sheltered in a thick stand of tall spinifex for the night, and they didn't have a fire. Mayrah ate a piece of the kangaroo and took a drink of water, then curled up and slept soundly. It seemed only moments later that her mother awakened her. The clumps of spinifex were dark shadows in the grey light of early dawn as she ate the piece of kangaroo her mother handed her and gathered up her things.

The soreness worked out of her thighs and calves during the first hour, and her stride became long and effortless. The day wasn't as hot as the previous one, the load of kangaroo was lighter because part of it had been eaten, and the effort of trotting along was easier than the previous day, even though Puntaru and her father set a harder pace. But it wasn't easier on her mother, and she was gasping with exhaustion when they stopped at midday. Mayrah filled her *wirree* with water from her mother's and took her mother's load of kangaroo meat, and her mother managed to keep up during the afternoon. When they stopped during the middle of the afternoon, they were almost ready to leave again before her brother caught up. Her father struck him a couple of warning blows with the shaft of a spear.

At nightfall she was weary and hungry but she could have gone further, which seemed to be more than Puntaru or her father could have done. Her mother and brother were exhausted, and they collapsed on the ground and moaned with the pain in their legs. Mayrah ate her share of the kangaroo and drank, then curled up and went to sleep. It was broad daylight when she woke, and everyone else was still alseep. She yawned and curled back up again, then sat up and woke her mother when her father and Puntaru began stirring.

The men began rationing the kangaroo meat and doling out tiny portions for everyone, and she became hungry again, a deep, ravenous, gnawing hunger which made the smell of the remaining meat a torture. The hard pace continued, and her mother and brother became more inured to it. They were much further from their hunting territory than she had ever been, and it was almost like a different world. The temperature was more moderate, and the vegetation had gradually changed from the wiry brush and tall spinifex to stands of large mulghee trees, low, tender spinifex, pardoo bush, canji, and dukarra, the prickly bush with long seed pods which could be eaten. When they were close enough for her to snatch off without breaking her pace, she pulled them off and cracked them open to eat the kernels as she trotted along. Then her father noticed what she was doing, and he made her stop, pointing out that the cracked seed pods she was dropping made a glaring trail behind them. But for the first time in memory, he corrected her in a casual, offhand tone instead of an angry growl.

They ran out of water, but the scent of open water was on every side. Puntaru appeared to have difficulty detecting it, but Mayrah and her family turned toward the nearest water without hesitation, cautiously approached it through the thick stand of pardoo brush around it to fill the vessels and drink, then went on. They ran out of food, and they had only the occasional lizard or snake they saw while running, and the insects, grubs, and edible plants they could find while resting or stopping for the night. Mayrah's hunger was intense, but it was not a hunger which would sap her strength. The days of hard traveling had pared ounces of fat from her and her ribs were beginning to show, but she had just reached her stride.

Her condition seemed to bother Puntaru. He appeared to notice her loss in weight one afternoon while they were resting, and he and her father looked at her thoughtfully as they murmured to each other. They stopped early that night, and Puntaru and her father left them and crept silently away through the thick foliage around them to lay in wait by a water hole. A couple of hours later, they returned with two fat plains fowl, a rare and delicious treat. Mayrah and her mother built a small fire and roasted one of them, and Mayrah's father gave her a large share, much to her brother's dismay. Then they began traveling at a slower pace and stopped periodically along the way to hunt.

The terrain continued changing, the vegetation becoming lush and game and water more abundant. Flocks of birds flew through the tall trees, and there were lizards, fat grubs, and edible plants everywhere they stopped. But they were far out of their tribal territory and proceeded with caution, remaining constantly on the alert for others. They reached an area of rolling hills and wide, open stretches of the low spinifex, and frequently had to go long distances away from their straight line of travel to stay in the cover of trees and skirt around the open places.

It rained steadily for two days and a night, far longer than it ever rained in their hunting territory. The rainwater removed the thin layer of body oil impregnated with dust and dirt from Mayrah, turning her several shades lighter in color and making her skin feel taut and uncomfortable. The flies and mosquitoes were more numerous than in their territory and the air seemed to be filled with them after the rain. They were a constant annoyance because her skin was more tender after its drenching.

When the clouds cleared, a hill with a very distinctive, jagged profile was visible in the distance. Puntaru knew the landmark well, because Mayrah overheard a conversation between him and her father while they were resting. He pointed it out to her father, referring to it as Wayamba.

– 5 –

They passed north of the jagged hill shortly after starting out one morning, climbing across ridges covered with sharp stones which hurt their feet, and by late morning it was behind them and they were going down a sharp slope covered with trees. The breeze carried a strong scent to Mayrah's nostrils, and she lifted her head and sampled it as they trotted along. She had never smelled it before, but she instinctively classified it as that of animals which were *kuka*, flesh which could be eaten. There was also a distant bleating sound which she associated with the *kuka* animal odor. Judging from the dilution of the scent by the smell of the foliage and water around her, and making an estimate of the distance from the sounds, there was an enormous number of the unknown animals. Her hunger intensified, and she wondered if the journey had been for the purpose of traveling to an abundantly rich hunting territory.

The sounds became louder and the odor grew stronger as they worked their way through trees around several low, rolling hills covered with short spinifex, then they were almost upon the animals. Her mother occasionally glanced back at her, her eyes wide with curiosity, and her brother closed the distance between them and tried to see what was ahead through the trees. Puntaru stopped, and her father waved for them to stop. The two men moved away and talked for a moment, and Puntaru turned and trotted on down the hill, disappearing almost immediately among the trees. Her father turned to them and told Mayrah's mother to put a *goomilla* on Mayrah. She looked at him curiously, but his expression and demeanor forbade questions, and she silently rooted in her bag for the *goomilla*. It was a thick, shiny belt made of coarse kangaroo hairs braided together, with a small square of fabric made of woven opossum hair hanging down in front to cover part of the lower abdomen, the pubic hair, and part of the inside of the thighs, a decorative dress women sometimes wore for corroborees and similar occasions. Mayrah looked at her father and at her mother in surprise, and her mother frowned warningly for silence as she took the *goomilla* out of her bag.

Mayrah stepped into the *goomilla* as her mother held it, and her mother slid it up over her hips and into place, adjusting it and tugging the flap down, then she glanced at Mayrah's hair and pushed at it. Her expression reflected something in the nature of a grim acceptance, and Mayrah suddenly had an uneasy feeling that something important was about to happen to her without her knowledge. Her father looked nervous, tense, and worried, and she could hear Puntaru shouting loudly from the foot of the hill, the sound of his voice moving away. The noises made by the *kuka* animals were so loud that they absorbed other sounds and it was difficult to hear Puntaru clearly, but he seemed to be calling out in unintelligible gibberish.

Her mother sat down on her heels, avoiding Mayrah's eyes and looking off into the distance, and Mayrah sat down on her heels by her mother. Her brother sat down under a tree and leaned back against the trunk wearily, his fatigue overcoming his curiosity. Her father paced back and forth, looking through the trees in the direction Puntaru had gone. There was a distant sound similar to that made by dingoes, then it stopped. Long minutes slowed passed. Her mother sat motionless, and her father continued pacing back and forth. Mayrah yawned with nervousness. Then she heard hurried footsteps coming up the hill through the trees, and Puntaru came back into sight, running toward them. She poised ready to respond to a command to flee, then she saw that Puntaru had a pleased, excited expression on his face. Her father trotted toward him and met him, and Puntaru stopped and puffed breathlessly as he motioned with his hands and talked. They exchanged a few words, then her father turned and motioned for Mayrah, her mother, and her brother to follow. Mayrah and her mother began gathering up their things, and he motioned again and barked impatiently. They picked up their sticks and left their other things, trotting down the hill toward the two men, and Mayrah's brother groaned and pushed himself to his feet to follow.

There was every indication that they were in an extremely dangerous situation. Her father was tense and nervous, and there were alien and unknown scents and noises all around. Puntaru appeared less apprehensive, but he seemed least cautious. Near the bottom of the hill, Mayrah caught another strong scent of some kind of animal through the almost overwhelming odor of the *kuka* animals. It was something like that of a dingo, and she automatically associated it with the sound she had heard which had been similar to that of a dingo. Then she caught another scent, an acrid odor. A white man. She hesitated, and her brother almost ran into her. Her mother looked over her shoulder and frowned in warning. She took a couple of quick steps and caught up again.

They left the trees at the bottom of the hill, coming out onto a broad, open field covered with low spinifex. The field sloped upward ahead, and instead of working around the edge of it in the cover of the trees, they went straight across it and up the slope. The scent and sound of the animals became even more pronounced, and she saw them as they crossed the crest of the slope and started down the other side. They were loosely grouped in the next valley, a staggering number of them, and they were standing in the open and without apparent fear as they grazed on the short spinifex. There were four of the other animals, similar to a dingo but larger, with longer hair, and of a different color, and they were scattered around the *kuka* animals. They began uttering their barks, then became quiet again in response to a deep, powerful voice shouting from further up the slope. She looked up the slope.

The man was gigantic, his face above his mustache and beard more red than white even from a distance, and the covers which enveloped him made him appear even larger. Puntaru waved and shouted as he led the way up the slope toward him, calling out unintelligible words which the white man apparently understood, because he replied in a deep, resonant voice. The white man was holding something which appeared to be a short, thick, misshapen spear, then as they approached him she realized that it had to be one of the magical weapons of which she had heard. Her heart pounded heavily, and she shivered with fright as she wondered what had possessed her father to place them in such a hazardous situation. They stopped, and Puntaru continued talking with the white man. Mayrah planted her stick on the ground and leaned on it. The white man's eyes seemed to bore into hers, and she averted her eyes.

The white man turned and walked a few yards away, with Puntaru and her father following him. Mayrah's mother motioned to her, and they followed. There was a large bag of some fabric similar to the white man's coverings on the ground, and he knelt by it and began taking things out of it. They were meaningless to her at first, then she recognized the shape of one of them. It was an axe made of the white man's stone, such as the one Puntaru carried in his belt, and a knife with the blade of the same stone. Then another axe and a knife, and pieces of the stone. The pieces of the stone were a puzzle for a moment, then the significance of them became clear; they could be made into spearheads such as the one Puntaru had. The purpose of the long journey became evident; it was to get weapons made of the white man's stone. Puntaru made a sound of delight, digging among the things, and Mayrah's father knelt and looked at them. They began separating them between them. The white man stood up and took a step back, looking at Mayrah, and she averted her face.

And a chilling thought occurred to her. A good spear with an ordinary point was valuable, as was a good axe or a knife made of ordinary stone. So the weapons made of the white man's stone were enormously valuable, and her father possessed only one belonging of sufficient value to barter for them. Herself. She looked at her mother, trembling with shock and fright. Her mother's face was averted. Puntaru and the white man conversed again, then Puntaru turned to her father and asked if he was satisfied with the bargain. Her father made an affirmative gesture with his hand. They began moving away from the white man, carrying the weapons, and her father looked at her as he passed her.

"You are this man's woman. Remain here, and be obedient to him."

Mayrah felt numb, her mouth was dry, and her knees trembled. She looked at her father in panic, frantically trying to think of something to say to dissuade him. And among the welter of confused thought, a single, coherent concern surfaced; she had left her *wirree* and her bag on the hill. They were highly valuable and her only possessions other than her stick, and it was a disgrace for a woman to be given away without the ordinary possessions of a woman in her hands. Her father passed her, and her mother started turning to follow him.

"My *wirree*, my bag..."

Her mother turned back to her, looking up at her. "You have been commanded. Be obedient." She started to turn away, then she hesitated and turned back again, reaching out and touching Mayrah's forearm with the tips of her fingers in an awkward, fleeting caress of love and of farewell. Then she dropped her hand and turned away, trotting after her husband. Her brother followed her mother. Puntaru passed Mayrah without glancing at her, looking at the things he was carrying with an expression of satisfaction. He began running rapidly, catching up with her brother and mother and passing them, and he trotted along beside her father. They reached the crest of the slope and disappeared over it, none of them looking back.

She had been given to a white man. Her fears had focussed around being given to a man and having to leave the known and familiar territory and her mother, brother, and father, but it had turned out far worse than that. She had been given to a strange and alien being whose odor was sour in her nostrils, and she was surrounded by grotesque animals which emitted a powerful stench and a constant din which made it virtually impossible to hear or smell anything else. And she had been given like one who didn't even have a family, without any possessions in her hands. Not even her *wirree*, which she had labored lovingly to decorate and had made perfectly water tight so

66

that it wouldn't waste a drop. Or her bag, with her fire-making materials and her tribal talisman which identified her as a Knurair of the Arunta. Now tribeless and nameless, she had been given away like an animal, to one who was likened to devils. She was all alone. She leaned on her stick and put her other hand over her eyes, bursting into tears of anguish.

The white man's heavy footsteps moved toward her, almost shaking the ground under her feet, and she looked at him through her tears. His deep voice rumbled, and he reached out toward her shoulder. She squeaked with fright, leaping to one side. Her hands trembled on her stick as the impulse to strike out with it clashed with the conditioning of a lifetime. Her father's command had placed the white man in what had been her father's position, and she was prohibited from attacking him, or making a gesture or movement which could be construed as a threat of attack. But moving away from him bordered on resistance, which was also prohibited, and she dug in her toes to make herself stand still as she looked at him, her teeth rattling together in fright and shivers racing through her. He stood and stared at her, his eyes moving up and down her.

Mayrah felt a stir of instinctive response which almost made her change the way she was standing, to shift her weight to one leg and move her hips to one side and make herself more attractive and desirable. But he was not even a male in her mind, a sexless alien more than anything else, and confusion, fright, and despair churned within her. She stood flat-footed and looked back at him in terrified misery, tears running down her cheeks as she sobbed.

He turned away, looking down the slope at the animals, and he knelt and rested his weapon against his shoulder as he pointed at the ground at her feet. It was an obvious command to sit. She sat down on her heels with the end of her stick between her feet and rested it on her

67

shoulder, automatically huddling down to present a low profile on the ground in the open, exposed place and reflecting on the additional problem which had occurred to her. The lack of communication with him was a serious deficiency. He might want her to take one part of the horizon to watch for danger, but there was no way of knowing. If they were attacked and he wanted her to assist instead of flee, there was no way he could tell her. The animals apparently belonged to him and he might expect her to help protect them. She rested her forearm on her knees and put her chin on it, tears still streaming down her cheeks.

The man spoke again, his voice low and soft and in a tone which could be construed as soothing and reassuring. She glanced at him and looked away again. He rose to his feet and looked down the hill toward the animals, shouted and motioned with his arm, then knelt again. One of the dingo-like animals raced up the hill. It slowed as it approached them, glancing at the man and flattening its ears and twitching its tail ingratiatingly, then it looked at her with the instinctive hostility of one carnivore for another. She looked at it warily, the muscles in her thighs moving as she poised. The man talked to the animal, making a popping noise with his fingers and motioning. The animal approached closer, its nose twitching as it scented her. Her nostrils widened as she scented the animal, identifying its individual smell among its species. The animal's eyes moved over her stick, then met her eyes. There was understanding. She was larger and stronger, easily as fast and perhaps faster, and the stick was a symbol of a crushed skull and instant death. In its proximity to her, the animal continued to live only because of her forebearance.

The creature sat down by the man, its tongue hanging out as it panted, and the man stroked the animal's head. He spoke to her again and motioned, appearing to invite her to touch its head. It seemed a senseless, pointless thing to do. The animal's eyes met hers again and slid away, its attitude reflecting agreement with her. She looked away. The man spoke to the animal and waved his arm, and it ran back down the hill.

Aside from the inviolable command which restrained her from fleeing, there was nowhere to which she could flee. Between her and the territory she knew as her own, there were long miles of dangerous territory she could never traverse alone. She was isolated and far from her people, a condition which approximated her concept of death, but worse than death in that she continued to live and suffer the utter despair of her situation. The comfort of being among those she knew, the comfort which came from the knowledge that she was protected, was gone.

With her family around her, the difference in the feel and aspect of the territory would have been easier to accept, because it teemed with food. The short spinifex produced abundant seed which could be collected, ground, and made into cakes, there were innumerable edible plants and roots about, indications of game everywhere, and the ground was alive with grubs and insects. Her misery was so great that it took her mind off food, and she looked disinterestedly at movements in the grass upon which she would have eagerly and gleefully pounced at other times. The large group of *kuka* animals were all moving slowly in one direction across the slope below, inching along as they ate the grass, and the dingo-like animals sat on the ground around them, occasionally moving a short distance to keep near them. The man made subvocal noises now and then, as though he wanted to communicate something. Her tears stopped.

A locust fluttered through the air and landed almost at her feet, and she instinctively reached out and caught it. Locusts were a delicacy usually present in numbers only during exceptionally rainy times in her territory, but she had absently observed many of them about on the slope. It was a large, fat one, and she automatically offered it to the man, holding it out to him as it kicked and squirmed in her fingers. He smiled, nodding his head up and down and murmuring something. The motion of his head and the sound meant nothing to her, but he didn't appear to want it. She looked away, pushing it into her mouth and poking the legs in with her fingers as it scrambled around frantically, and she closed her mouth on it, crushing the body with her teeth. The man made a sound, and she looked at him again as she chewed it. He was looking away. She spat out the wings and other large indigestible pieces, then swallowed and searched her mouth with the tip of her tongue and spat out pieces of crushed legs and other bits. The man stood up, shouting and waving his arm, and the dingo-like animals began moving about purposefully, crowding the *kuka* animals together and turning them up the slope. He looked at her and motioned up the hill, and she rose and followed him.

From the top of the hill there was a view of miles of surrounding hills, open fields, creeklines, and thick stands of trees in the bright, late afternoon sunlight, the predominant feature the hill with the jagged, irregular outline several miles away. He had made a large *wiltja* for shelter, but some of the bark was placed wrong and would catch rain and allow it to leak into the interior, and it was located in the open where it was more vulnerable to the elements, instead of being in some sheltered spot below the brow of the hill. Numerous things of obscure purpose were scattered around it, a large stack of wood was piled near a firebed in a circle of stones, and a freshly-killed animal was hanging in a clump of trees on the other side of the *wiltja*. It was covered with material similar to the coverings the man wore, and she immediately associated the odor of the flesh with that of the *kuka* animals.

A large enclosure of poles a short distance down the hill from the *wiltja* reeked of the *kuka* animals and was littered with their dung. The dingo-like animals drove them up the slope, and the man dragged some of the poles

70

about and stood to one side, waiting. They came closer, trotting along and making their bleating sounds, and the man spread his arms wide and walked toward them as they approached the enclosure. They turned and poured into it, a few of them hesitating or turning aside and the dingo-like animals darting about to force them back into the main body of the others. A cloud of choking dust arose as they filed into the enclosure, and the noise they made was almost deafening. The man dragged the poles to the opening in the enclosure and put them into place after the last of the animals trotted into it, then he turned and walked toward her and the *wiltja*.

She felt awkward, out of place, and unsure of where to stand or what to do. There was a large container of water, and he filled a smaller one from it and offered it to her. The only thing she could associate it with was the infrequent occasions when her father had commanded her to drink deeply because he knew water would be scarce during the following days. But there was an abundance of water in virtually all directions, and she had drunk that morning. She took a mouthful, and it seemed to satisfy him. He built up the fire and motioned for her to sit down by it. She sat, looking at the dingo-like animals on the other side of the fire as they looked warily back at her. The man went around the *wiltja* and came back with a large piece of the flesh, and he put it over the fire on a pole. He stirred around and did other things, putting a container of water on the fire and a large, flat container of something else on it, then he sat down near her.

In the short time she had been with him, she had already seen enough to tell stories at a gathering of her people which would keep them spellbound for hours. Everything was different, and everything was strange. His control over the animals was miraculous. He had apparently obtained enough of the *kuka* animals to feed him for the rest of his life, and he had settled down on the hill to a life of luxury and ease, killing and eating the *kuka* animals and using the dingo-like animals to help him control them. The containers he had put in the fire didn't burn; they looked like the stone of which his weapons were made and they were very thin and conveniently shaped for handling. She kept waiting for the stick he had used to suspend the flesh over the fire to burn in two, because the flames were licking up around it, but it was some kind of stick which wouldn't burn. He did something with his weapon, then he put it aside and demonstrated his magical abilities, breathing fire and exhaling noxious-smelling smoke from a stick in his mouth.

It appeared that his objective was to burn up the flesh rather than roast it, because the sun set while it hung over the fire on the stick, smoking, hissing, and dripping into the fire as the flames licked around it. Then darkness fell, and the fire glowed in the eyes of the dingo-like animals as they lay and looked at her. Their sense of hearing was very poor. Two dingoes ran around on the slope below, examining the possibilities of a safe approach to the *kuka* animals in the enclosure, but only one of the dingo-like animals appeared to suspect their presence and it wasn't sure, occasionally lifting its ears and looking into the darkness in the direction of the dingoes. The man filled a small container from the container on the fire and held it out to her. He didn't appear to be commanding her to drink it and it smelled revolting. She made a negative gesture with her hand. The gesture seemed to be lost on him, because he continued holding it out, smiling and saying something. She examined his expression again to see if he was commanding her, decided he wasn't, and made an emphatic negative with her hand. He looked at her hand and she wasn't sure he understood, but he put the container aside, dragged the other container out of the fire, and lifted off the top half of it.

He wanted her to eat first or at least with him, something new in her experience and generating a fleeting suspicion that his intention was to use her to assure that the food was safe for him to eat. The contents of the large container appeared to be *bingui*, a type of large fungus, but it didn't smell like it. And it didn't have the astringent odor and taste which immediately identified poisonous substances, so she ate a piece of it even though it was sticky and had an unpleasant lack of taste. The flesh was roasted to a soft, pulpy consistency, and it was extremely greasy and rich. A feeling of nausea warned her that she would regurgitate unless she ate it sparingly and chewed it thoroughly, but he apparently didn't intend for them to eat all of it. He cut off all the burned parts and threw them to the dingo-like animals, and he put a large portion of it into the container with the remainder of the fungus-like substance and put it to one side.

The fire was wastefully and foolishly large, advertising their presence over a wide area as it blazed on top of the hill, but he was apparently confident in the power of his weapon to deal with any danger it attracted. She hoped that the power of his weapon was more effective in reacting to danger than were the dull senses of the dingo-like animals in detecting it. The sounds of the dingoes on the slope below faded as they left, apparently too wary to approach the *kuka* animals. The man drank the odorous liquid he had offered to her and puffed smoke from the stick in his mouth again, then he rose and motioned toward the *wiltja*. She rose and followed him into it.

Much of the interior was occupied by a thick mat of foul-smelling coverings similar to those the man wore. He removed part of his coverings and lay down on the mat, and she lay by him, waiting for him to have his will with her. Her mother had told her about the process in infinite detail, pointing out that part of her body which was involved and explaining what would happen, and much of her mother's time and energy at corroborees and at other times when men had been around had been devoted to assuring that no man had opportunity to undertake that activity before she was given away. Her mother had also explained that it was a matter of crucial importance and a continuing need for men, and it was that need which made a man willing to provide a woman protection and sustenance.

But even that wasn't fulfilled. She waited breathlessly, shivering with fright again. Then he began breathing deeply in sleep. Mayrah put her hands over her face and turned onto her side, weeping quietly.

Her detachment from all previous patterns of life and her bewilderment over what was expected of her increased the following day. Before, Mayrah had felt a constant concern over her whereabouts and what she was doing, but the white man didn't appear to care. And there was nothing to do. There was food everywhere, in addition to the large supply of flesh and bags of other things at the *wiltja*, and there was no need for her to gather any. There was abundant water in all directions, and no need for her to dig for it or store it against future needs. He tended the fire, and he cooked the food. Mayrah felt absolutely useless.

She followed him down the slope as he took the animals to graze and drink, she sat down when he sat down. Being without her belongings still troubled her deeply, and after they sat for a time she rose and went across the hill, down into the next valley, and up into the dense trees where she had left her *wirree* and bag.

The *wirree* was a couple of paces from where she had left it, and it was overturned and the bottom was cracked. Some scavenging animal had chewed a hole in her bag and scattered her things about, and her tribal talisman had been gnawed, the feathers shredded and the opossum tendons which held it together mangled and broken. She wept as she gathered the things up, the torn bag, her fire-making materials, the pretty stones she had found, the ravaged remains of her talisman, and she put them into the broken *wirree* and walked slowly back down the hill.

As she left the trees and started up the slope, she saw his

large form through her tears. He had come looking for her, and he ran heavily to her, his voice rumbling and reflecting a note of concern. She showed him the things, sobbing brokenly and trying to explain. But he didn't understand.

– 6 –

It had been well over a month since Puntaru left, and Garrity had begun to think that he had either failed in his quest, had forgotten it and gone about something else, or had met with some mishap. But time apparently meant little to him, and from his attitude he could have left only the day before as he chattered about the admirable characteristics and qualities of the woman he had found. Garrity listened doubtfully, his reluctance about the entire matter returning in full force. But he agreed to look at the woman, Puntaru left to get her and her family, and Garrity walked to the top of the hill to get the bag containing the axes, knives, and bits of metal from his shelter.

From his first glimpse, he knew he was looking at a

type of aborigine he had never seen before. They were more or less like Puntaru and other aborigines he had seen in general physical appearance, but the similarity stopped there. Puntaru and the others lived on or were at least accustomed to the fringes of civilization, but the man following Puntaru was accustomed to nothing but the bush. The lines of white paint on his forehead, nose, and down his chest and arms added to the overall impression, but his appearance was only a minor part of it. His eyes, expression, and the way he moved and looked about gave him the aspect of a fierce, deadly animal. He was like Puntaru in about the same measure that Puntaru was like a white man. And the reason for Puntaru's long absence was adequately explained. It was evident that he had gone far into the bush on his search.

There was a short, thin woman of about the man's age following him, then a younger woman and a boy, a complete family. Garrity's eyes moved back to the younger woman as they approached, then they became fixed on her. She was taller than the woman who was apparently her mother, and she had long, slender limbs and high, firm breasts. There was a belt around her waist and some kind of rude covering hanging down in front and covering her pubic area, but the scrap of a garment concealed none of her charms. She was beautiful. Her waist was tiny, swelling out to slender hips, and her thighs and arms were thin but shapely. She moved with a natural, feline grace, and pride and confidence in her beauty were reflected in the lines of her chin and mouth and the way she held her head. Her savage nakedness, the short, ragged line where her coarse hair had been chopped off around the sides of her head, and the other things about her which might have detracted from her beauty somehow failed to do so. Her features were small and almost delicate, with high, wide cheekbones, large eyes, and full, wide lips. There was an atmosphere of the distant wilderness about her, something free, wild, and untamed.

She was utterly feminine, and she was very desirable. Puntaru and the man behind him were panting from the rapid pace, and the thin woman and the boy were almost gasping. But the young woman was hardly breathing heavily, and the small, firm breasts moved in deep, measured breaths as she planted the end of the long, heavy stick she carried and stood with a lithe, easy stance which gave the impression that she was poised to move smoothly into motion again. Her eyes met his. She frowned and looked away with a bored yawn which showed the tips of even, brilliantly white teeth.

Puntaru began talking again as they stopped in front of Garrity, pointing to them and rattling their names, and he asked Garrity what he thought of the young woman. Garrity pulled his eyes away from her reluctantly and silently nodded as he turned and walked to the bag containing the things, and he suddenly wondered if he had enough. There were two axes, two knives, and metal for six spearheads, the amounts Puntaru had suggested, but it suddenly seemed nothing. They followed him, and Puntaru exclaimed with delight as Garrity took them out of the bag. Puntaru talked to the other man as they rummaged through them. The other man grunted terse comments, and Garrity became more concerned whether there was enough. Then they began dividing the things between them, and Garrity felt a rush of relief. They continued talking between themselves, making movements to leave. Garrity had expected them to stay, perhaps for some food or to rest, but the other man was clearly uncomfortable and in a hurry to leave and Puntaru apparently wanted to accompany him. The other man walked away, stopping to grunt something to the young woman, then walked on. Puntaru thanked Garrity effusively and grinned widely as he moved away. The older woman murmured something to the younger one and touched her arm, then turned away.

Things had happened with blinding speed. They had

come into sight only moments before, trotting rapidly over the brow of the rise in the field, and they were leaving again, at the same pace, with Puntaru hurrying to catch up with the man. And the young woman was left standing by herself. They disappeared.

The young woman was holding the long, heavy, smoothly-polished stick with one hand and leaning on it slightly, her face averted as she looked in the direction they had gone. She was standing in profile, her back and shoulders straight, the sun gleaming on her dark gold skin, the curves of her slender body looking like the creation of a master sculptor.

And she suddenly began crying. He frowned with puzzled concern. It hadn't occurred to him to even consider what she might think about staying with him. And it was clear that her initial reaction was one of distress. He stepped toward her and spoke to her, reaching out to put his hand on her shoulder and reassure her. She uttered a shriek, leaping away from him. Her movements had the abrupt, blinding speed of a snake striking. He dropped his hand in startled confusion and looked at her. The heavy pole she carried looked dangerous. It was possible that she thought he intended to throw her to the ground and take her. She looked back at him, her features twisted as she wept and the tears streaming down her cheeks. He pondered for a moment, trying to think of something to do, then he rested his musket on the ground and knelt, motioning for her to sit down. She sat down on her heels and leaned the long stick against her shoulder, still weeping.

The lack of communication was a problem, because he had no way of winning her confidence with words. He thought of amusing her with one of the dogs, and he called one of them away from the flock and up the slope. As the dog approached, her behavior and that of the dog was virtually identical to the meeting of two wild animals, both of them wary as the dog's nose twitched and her nostrils flared. And the dog was frightened of her. It was a courageous dog, because it had tried to bite Williamson and other men who had brought supplies, and it hadn't been afraid of Puntaru. But its courage melted as it looked at her. Garrity patted the dog's head and encouraged her to pet the dog, but she didn't appear interested in it. He sent it back down to the flock.

Before, the idea of having a woman had been simply an idea and nothing more, an impersonal and vague, generalized abstraction of having someone around. He had given the matter considerable thought during the time Puntaru had been with him before and after he had left, and the very basic and fundamental omission in his thoughts on the subject had been a failure to consider what the woman involved might think about the situation. Unquestionably she had an emphatically negative reaction to it. She sat with a forlorn expression on her small face and stared into space, occasionally wept for a few minutes, then wiped her tears away and stared into space again. He sat in helpless frustration, trying to think of some way to establish communication with her or make her feel better.

A locust flew through the air and landed almost at her feet. It started to fly again, and her small hand shot out in a blur of movement and snatched it out of the air. She looked at him and showed it to him. Her meaning wasn't clear, but it seemed likely that it had been a demonstration of how quickly she could move, which was amazing. He smiled and nodded, relieved that something had happened to ease the awkward silence between them, and amused that she so casually handled what would be regarded with extreme distaste by some women.

Then she ate it.

His mouth dropped open in aghast astonishment, then he looked away, feeling queasy. He had seen aborigines catching lizards and snakes to eat and had heard that they ate some kinds of large grubs, but he'd never heard of anyone who ate insects. But she was thin to the point of looking almost undernourished. It was somewhat early to take the sheep in for the day, but he decided to take them to the fold and prepare something to eat. He stood and called to the dogs, signalling them to turn the flock up the slope.

When he finished putting the sheep in the fold, she was standing and looking around with a lost expression. He dipped a cup of water out of the bucket and offered it to her in event she was thirsty, and she looked at him and at the cup with an enigmatic expression before she took a sip. There was some moss in the cup, leading to speculation that she might hesitate to drink from it because she considered it unclean, but aborigines he had seen before hadn't appeared to be fastidious. He drank and motioned for her to sit down by the fire, and he began preparing the meal. Before, he had planned to immediately begin teaching the woman how to cook for him, but that intention was lost in the necessity to establish a rapport between them and help her overcome the homesickness, loneliness, fear, or whatever was bothering her. He cleaned his musket and smoked his pipe, and she sat unmoving as the sun set and darkness fell.

She didn't want the tea, and she didn't appear to like the damper but she ate a bit of it. And she ate only a small amount of the mutton, far less than he had expected, considering how hungry she must be. He fed the dogs, put the leftovers in the pan and pushed them to one side, and smoked his pipe and drank the remainder of the tea in the billy. She sat and looked into the fire again.

She went into the shelter with him readily when he motioned her toward it, but she took the heavy stick with her everywhere and she dragged it in and put it by the pallet when she lay down. There was nothing in her attitude which indicated that the stick was in implicit warning against too sudden intimacy or even that she had any reluctance regarding any degree of intimacy, but it was impossible to guess what she was thinking. And she had acted frightened when he started to touch her before. He was confident of his ability to overpower her if he wanted her, but her willingness was important to him. There was a fresh, musky scent about her which was alluring, and the memory of how she had looked in the sunshine was a torture in his mind as he lay within inches of her. But he could almost hear her trembling. It took him a long time to go to sleep.

Her state of mind didn't appear to be improved the next day. She ate a few bites of the food left over from the night before, then listlessly followed him down the slope as he followed the dogs and sheep. He cudgeled his mind for things he might do to make her more comfortable, but he could think of nothing. Williamson kept a few trade goods at the station for giving to the aborigines, and he felt disgusted with himself that he hadn't thought to have some on hand. The sheep grazed slowly down the slope, then across the broad meadow near the bottom of the slope where the trees began, and he sat down on the slope above them. She sat a few feet from him, staring blankly into the distance with a disconsolate expression.

Then she was suddenly gone. He sprang up, looking around. She wasn't in sight. He had observed that she moved silently, apparently making no effort to be stealthy but simply making no more sound than a shadow, never brushing her foot against a clump of grass or rolling a pebble over. He chewed his lip worriedly, something approaching panic rising within him. It wasn't impossible that she had left to rejoin her people, because she was obviously extremely unhappy. He picked up his musket and ran across the meadow in the direction from which they had come. At the crest in the bulge in the hill, he looked down at the line of foliage below. There was no sign of her. He ran down the slope toward the trees.

As he neared the bottom of the slope, she came out of the trees. He stopped, heaving a sigh of relief. Then he frowned with concern and hurried toward her. She was carrying something and sobbing brokenly. He stopped by her, putting his hand on her shoulder and looking down at her as he asked her what was wrong, and she shook with sobs as she pointed to the things and lifted them, showing them to him and murmuring broken phrases in her language. There was a small, boat-shaped container made of bark which had been smoothed down and carved with intricate designs, a woven grass bag, a few rocks, bits of feathers and bones, and other things which appeared to be of little or no value. The container had a split in the bottom and the bag had a large hole in it, and the feathers and bones looked as though they had been chewed by an animal. She had apparently left the things in the trees when she came through them with her people, and they had been ravaged by animals in search of something to eat. However worthless or obscure they seemed to him, they were obviously her treasures and she looked very small and pathetic as she pawed through them, showed them to him, and wept. He put his arm around her shoulders and led her back up the slope, talking to her quietly and trying to soothe her.

They sat down where they had been before, and she sniffled, wiped her eyes with her forearm, and began trying to pull the strands of grass in the bag back together. It was spinifex, but it was the long, coarse type rather than the short variety covering the field around them. She pulled a few blades from clumps around her and tried to weave them in, and she sighed and made womanly sounds of despair when they kept breaking and shredding. There were several taller clumps along the edge of the field, and he walked over to them, cut some of the longer blades out of them with his pocketknife, and brought them back to her.

The result was more than worth the effort. She looked at the grass as he put it down by her and sat down again, then she looked up at him and back down at the grass. A slight frown creased her brow as she pondered for a long moment, obviously puzzled that he had gone after the grass to help her repair the bag. Then she looked up at him again. Her expression had changed. And the atmosphere between them was subtly different. She looked at him with a congenial, pleased expression. He beamed down at her, patting her shoulder. She smiled slightly, looking back down at the bag, and she picked up one of the long blades of grass and began weaving it.

They were still silent, but it was no longer awkward and strained. She was markedly more contented and satisfied as her small fingers moved nimbly, separating the broken blades of grass in the bag and working them loose, then replacing them with blades from the pile beside her. There was a thick ridge at the bottom of the bag where the blades had been woven together, and he took out his pocketknife and cut some of the broken blades for her when she had difficulty in working them loose. The pocketknife and the ease with which he cut the tough grass fascinated her, and he let her look at the pocketknife, warning her with motions to be careful with the blade. She turned the knife over in her hands and looked at it, her lips pursed. He looked down at her, acutely aware of his proximity to her. She was very small and delicate, covered with his shadow as she huddled on her heels by him. Strands of her short, coarse hair fell forward and covered the sides of her face as she looked at the knife. Her skin looked smooth and soft, and there were tiny, almost invisible marks on her shoulders and arms where scratches and small cuts had healed. His eyes moved down to her waist and along her thighs, then up to her breasts. Her head moved slightly, and he lifted his eyes. She was looking at him from the corners of her eyes through her hair. Her lips pursed, her expression becoming arch and coy, and she shifted, folding her legs under her and sitting on them with her hips turned to one side, and she handed the knife back to him. He took it, smiling down at her. She smiled slightly, picking up another blade of grass, and began weaving it into the bag.

She sat in his shadow, but his shadow became smaller as the sun rose toward its zenith and it occurred to him that she might find the sun uncomfortable. He touched her arm and motioned toward the bottom of the slope as he rose, and she gathered up her things, put them in the bark container and balanced it on her head. She followed him down the slope with the long blades of spinifex he had cut for her in one hand and her stick in the other. They walked past the sheep and to the edge of the trees, and he sat down in the shade of a tree and motioned for her to join him. She sat down, sighing with relief and fanning her face with her hand in a comment on the temperature which was much like the gesture he had seen other women use, and he smiled with delight. It was the first clear and distinct communication between them.

He had brought the remainder of the leftover mutton and damper along in his pocket when leaving the shelter, and they shared it. She ate with a much better appetite than she had the evening before or that morning, even eating all of her share of the cold damper. He was thirsty after eating and assumed that she was, and he motioned for her to gather up her things again and walked out of the shade toward the flock, calling to the dogs and waving at them to bunch the sheep. The dogs were accustomed to the daily routine of taking the sheep on down through the forest to where a small stream ran through the valley, and they began crowding them together and turning them toward the forest. Garrity glanced over his shoulder to look for the woman, and she was standing behind him with her things in the bark container on her head and the stick and long grass in her hand. He smiled down at her, then turned back toward the sheep and shouted and waved for the dogs to start them into the forest.

The sheep flowed through the trees, the dogs running along at the sides of the flock and keeping them tightly packed, and Garrity walked along behind them and watched for strays. They smelled the water and began rushing toward it, bleating excitedly, and poured across a small opening in the trees and through the trees on the other side of it to the stream. They splashed into the water, spreading out in the stream, and their motion abruptly stopped as they all got into the water and began drinking. The dogs raced around and crowded a few stragglers closer to the rest of the flock, then they lay down in the edge of the cool water and drank. Garrity glanced around for the woman again. She was still following closely behind him. He led her a few yards up the stream to a shallow pool, motioned her toward the water, knelt down by the edge of it and dipped it up with his hand to drink. She followed suit, then took the things out of the bark container, dipped it into the water, and looked at it sorrowfully as the water ran through the crack in the bottom. At last he understood the purpose of the container.

When the sheep stopped drinking and began picking at the grass and low foliage along the sides of the stream, he shouted and waved to the dogs to start them back into the trees. There was thick, luxuriant grass along the stream, but through experience he had found that sheep which became poisoned frequently did so on something they found near water. The dogs raced back and forth, barking and nipping at heels, and the sheep surged out of the water and back through the trees. He followed them through the trees toward the meadow, and the woman followed him.

They sat in the shade and she worked on her bag while the sheep grazed until an hour before sunset, then he started them back up the slope toward the fold. The atmosphere between them was far different than it had been the night before when they reached the shelter and he began making preparations to cook the evening meal. She put her things to one side and built up the fire, then followed him around and watched closely as he cut a piece of mutton from the carcass in the tree behind the shelter, mixed the damper, and put on water for tea. She had a purposeful, determined expression, as though she demanded to know what to do.

The sun set and the swift darkness fell, and they sat by the fire as the food cooked. She had finished repairing the bag, and she held the bark container on her thighs and tried to fit slivers of bark she had collected in the forest into the crack in the bottom of it. He looked at her as the flickering light played over her features and shone dully on her soft skin, smiling slightly as she clicked her tongue and murmured to herself over the slivers of bark and the container. The fire began burning down, and he put more wood on it. The flames leaped up around the mutton again, boiling heavy drops of grease from it. She lifted her head and looked across the fire into the darkness, turning her head to one side in a listening attitude. During the day, he had observed that she frequently lifted her nose into the breeze in the manner of an animal scenting something and often seemed to be listening to or looking at things that escaped his perception, and he smiled down at her as she glanced up at him. She smiled vaguely, and the smile faded as she looked into the darkness again. One of the dogs on the other side of the fire lifted its head and looked into the darkness with its ears cocked. She looked back up at him, pursed her lips, and indicated the sheep fold with her chin.

"Dingo myrenay nahwandi."

The sheep stirred restlessly in the fold at the same time, a couple of them bleating in alarm, and the sound punctuated the meaning of the single word he understood in the quiet comment, electrifying him into motion. He snatched up his musket as he sprang to his feet, and he leaped across the fire into the middle of the dogs, kicking at them and shouting. "You bloody gets! Lie on your flaming arses while the dingoes kill my sheep, will you? Get out of it!"

They yelped with pain and alarm, scrambling to their feet and racing into the darkness toward the fold, and he pounded after them. The moon and stars were bright, but he was blinded by the fire and he could distinguish only vague and shapeless masses, the dark bulk of the fold with the sheep moving around in it, a nearby tree, and the shadowy forms of the dogs racing around. There was a sudden snarl of anger from one of the dogs on the other side of the fold, then the sound of a fight. He cocked the musket as he ran around the fold, and two of the dogs shot past him. They joined the fray and the sound became louder, vicious growls, gnashing of teeth, and howls of pain, and a dark, writhing mass of dogs and another animal swirled around the corner of the fold and then down the slope. The dingo broke loose and shot away, the dogs in hot pursuit. He let the hammer on the musket back down and whistled for the dogs to return, and almost ran into the woman as he turned back toward the fire. She stepped quickly to one side, and he tucked his musket under his arm, put his hand on her shoulder, and smiled down at her as they walked back toward the fire.

"By God, you're a handy wench to have about. And you have some sharp ears on you and all. It would have had half of my sheep killed before I would have heard it. And I daresay it wouldn't have been many less before those bloody dogs heard it."

Her teeth and eyes flashed in the moonlight as she smiled up at him in response to his tone. The feel of her silky skin and slender shoulder under his hand was very satisfying. The dogs came trotting back up the slope and into the pool of light around the fire, their tongues hanging out as they panted heavily, and a couple of them had flecks of blood on their muzzles and shoulders. He leaped toward them and kicked and shouted at them as they started to lie down by the fire again.

"Now you'll sog down until another dingo attacks my sheep, will you? Some bloody hope you will, you bloody

88

gets! Get your arses down to that fold and lie there tonight! Go on!"

The dogs slunk off into the darkness toward the fold, and he grumbled under his breath as he walked around the fire and sat down. His frown changed to a smile as he looked at the woman, and she radiated satisfaction with his approval of what she had done. He patted her shoulder, smiling at her warmly, then he picked up a couple of sticks to pull the pan of damper out of the fire.

They ate, and the dogs crept back from the fold and hovered hungrily on the edge of the firelight. Garrity cut off burned portions of the mutton and handfuls of scraps, and threw them to the dogs and ordered them back to the fold. They wolfed down the pieces of meat and disappeared into the darkness again, and he put the leftovers in the pan and covered them, poured himself a pannikin of tea, and lit his pipe. The woman was sorting through the slivers of bark and looking at the container again, and she darted wide-eyed glances at the smoke he was exhaling. He chuckled with amusement, moving closer to her, and he held out the pipe for her to take a puff. She looked at it with apprehension, then she smiled slightly and took a puff. Her face twisted wryly from the taste of the pipe and tobacco, and she shook her head rapidly and exhaled with a splutter. Then she looked at the smoke she had exhaled as it floated away and dissipated, smiling widely. He chuckled again, patting her back.

Her smile faded as she looked up at him, her eyes moving back and forth between his. She moved closer to him, curling her legs under her and sitting on them, her face averted as she put the bark container to one side. Desire stirred in him, and he put his pipe down and put his arm around her, moving his hand up and down her side and feeling her soft, warm skin. She put her elbow on his thigh and leaned against him, and she turned her head slightly and looked up at him from the corners of her eyes through the ragged fringe of her coarse hair. Her lips parted in a slow, alluring smile which leaped the language barrier in a single, gigantic bound.

He put his arms around her, lifting her to his lap, and buried his lips in her satiny throat as his hands moved over her to satisfy the throbbing need which swelled within him. She made a sound of satisfaction in her throat, sliding her arms around his neck, and she dug her fingernails into the back of his neck and pulled herself tightly against him, wriggling on his lap. His hands moved over her more demandingly, and he turned away from the fire with her, pushing her down to the ground. She squirmed out of his arms and bounced to her feet, smiling widely, and she walked to the shelter and smiled over her shoulder as she swung her hips provocatively. He clambered heavily to his feet and rushed after her.

He was virtually inexperienced. When he had been at the orphanage and scarcely beyond puberty, he had been running errands from the orphanage one day and had happened upon a weary and mistreated housewife who had identified him as a means of secret revenge for her husband's cruelties, and there had been one encounter with an impatient, drunken whore in Sydney while he had worked on the Nepean. Mayrah was totally inexperienced. But he was inflamed with fiery, passionate desire for her, and her instincts were maximized for race survival in a hostile environment. He was fumbling and awkward, unsure of himself in a delicate undertaking which had been described in his presence in metaphorical rather than practical terms and in which he'd had expert assistance in his limited previous experience. But his driving need was stimulated to a frenzy by her impassioned writhing and whimpering, and he was spurred on by her convulsive surging. What was lacking in finesse was provided by vigor, and if the defloration was less delicate than energetic, he was dealing with more of a tigress than a trembling virgin.

With the housewife it had been a mad race with his trousers down around his knees before the husband had a chance to return, and with the whore it had been a perfunctory coupling on a sward across a dark street from a public house with her skirt hiked up and her two shillings clutched in her hand. But he found himself in a much more demanding situation than before, and when he considered it finished, she considered it barely begun. She pulled at him demandingly, biting at his shoulders and scratching at his back as she wrapped her legs around him and pushed at him, and he responded with a numb, delighted wonder and strength which drew sustenance from her wild, provocative abandon. Her instincts were unleashed and his long abstinence made him a powerful lover, but eventually he became exhausted.

He stumbled out of the shelter and built up the fire, and he put the tea on to warm as he lit his pipe and smoked it, shivering in the unaccustomed touch of the cold night air against his naked skin. She came out of the shelter, yawning and pushing at her hair, and she stood by him and leaned against him, her thigh against his shoulder. He smiled up at her, moving his hand up and down her thigh. She moved around in front of him and knelt, pushing between his thighs, and she leaned back against him as she sat on her heels between his thighs. He put his arm around her, smiling down at her, and held his pipe while she puffed on it and giggled. Her hand moved down his stomach, feeling and groping. His smile faded, and he put the pipe to one side and pulled her closer, feeling her and kissing her. She moved restlessly in his arms, moaning softly. He lifted the billy off the fire, pulled her to her feet, and took her back into the shelter.

7

There were vast differences between them. Garrity's education was rudimentary and his culture was that of the frontier, but his attitudes were based on an upbringing founded on traditions echoing across centuries. Mayrah was basically governed by instincts which dictated affairs from the most mundane to the most vital, from the best place to look for water or grubs to whether the availability of food to sustain life mandated consuming instead of suckling the newborn. Millennia had passed since Garrity's ancestors discovered how to make their weapons of metal. Her father's were of stone. The language barrier was minor compared to the chasm which separated the product of a civilization with roots in Ancient Greece and a child of the Stone Age, but there were points of contact. He was male and she was female. She was totally conditioned to devote all of her waking time and energy to pleasing him. His loneliness had become burdensome. He was an alien in his surroundings, struggling to adapt. She was one with the land, eager to show him the way.

Garrity managed to communicate his name, and he found out hers after some trial and error, because she thought at first he wanted to know her tribe and moiety, which were to her of far greater importance.

He found out by accident that she could outrun all but one of the dogs. He occasionally amused himself by tossing a stick for a dog to fetch, and when he did it again, she watched for several throws, then suddenly sprang into motion, running for the stick and returning it with much the same attitude as one of the dogs, expecting a word of praise. He threw the stick again and the dog perceived the spirit of competition and raced, but the animal was no match for her. She grinned widely in pleasure as he roared with laughter at the dog's chagrin, and she raced the dogs one after the other as he called them away from the flock to match them against her. One of the dogs could pace her and occasionally get ahead of her downhill, but even that one was no match for her running uphill.

He found that it had been no fluke that she had heard the dingo around the fold, that her senses were unbelievably keen. While they were taking the sheep through the forest to water one day, she led him to a den where a female dingo had sheltered a litter of pups. When she understood his intense interest in hunting and killing them, she located and led him to three more dens in the immediate area. Then she discovered his interest in finding all the sources of water in the area, and led him to several which were unknown to him. And he found out that the heavy stick she carried constantly was a much more lethal weapon than he had suspected when they were killing the dingoes.

Much of her time around the fire at night was spent in poring over her belongings. She rummaged through the stones and pebbles she had gathered at one time or other, sorting through them and looking at them, and when a strand in her bag was broken she would promptly replace it. The mangled bits of bones and feathers still caused her distress, and she frequently took them out and looked at them with a forlorn expression. He recognized the feathers as those from a species of small parrot, and he loaded his musket with birdshot and went into the forest and shot one for her. But she didn't associate the bird with the chewed feathers, and when he brought it to her she promptly ate it, thinking that was the reason he had brought it. The crack in the bottom of the water container also continued to bother her, and he helped her with it, shaving down slivers of bark with his pocketknife and wedging them into the crack. Through careful and painstaking work with the sharp knife, he was able to shape the slivers to a close fit, but it wasn't as watertight as it had been when unbroken. Other joints in the vessel had dried out and opened during the days she had been with him, and it was useless from the lack of use. But she still kept it, finding a safe spot for it and her other things in the shelter, because it continued to be an object of high value to her.

Communication between them improved rapidly as they became more accustomed to each other and gestures became easier to interpret. She had a quick, alert mind and rapidly picked up key words of the pidgin English he automatically used in addressing her, and within a few days they had little difficulty in understanding essentials. Their means of communication showed little potential for developing to the point of being able to deal in nuances, but their personalities, activities, and situation were of a more fundamental nature than those of most people in other places and times.

Before meeting her, Garrity's friendship with William-

94

son had been the deepest personal relationship in his life. His indoctrination at the orphanage had included such matters as the appropriate attitude toward parents, and he dutifully regarded his memory of his mother with the attitude he had been taught, but the memory was shadowy and fragmentary, that of a silhouette rather than of a real person. Other people in his life had been separated from him by a wall of impersonal detachment, and most of them had been hostile or self-serving. The relationship with Mayrah was a totally different experience, one which involved him completely and which he regarded with a numb wonder as he tried to analyze and categorize it in the absence of words to define it or past experience to which to relate it. His attitude toward aborigines wasn't unlike his attitude toward other people in general, but he didn't relate her to other aborigines any more than he related her to other people. She was a person unique and apart from others.

This deep and intimate personal relationship with another opened new vistas in his life, ones he had never suspected existed. His life before she had joined him had been one of satisfaction, because he had always compared it to his life in the orphanage, but after meeting her his former life seemed dull and grey in comparison. Each day was different, each day was full. When she explored and found that her freedom was unlimited in relation to what she had known before, her personality expanded and she developed into more of an individual, with occasional outbursts of anger and stubbornness. In the orphanage, cleanliness had been related to godliness, there had been a weekly routine of bathing and washing clothes, and he had continued to bathe and wash his clothes each week when there was water available. Mayrah's reaction to his suggestion of a bath in the stream was at first lack of understanding, then disbelief followed by horror. In her experience, immersion in water was a natural state only for certain frogs, fish and snakes.

Her first bath was a traumatic experience for her and battle for him, with her shrieking in terror and flailing about as he grimly scrubbed her and washed her hair. Then she sat on the bank of the stream, shivering with cold, and glowering at him resentfully as he bathed and washed his clothes. The incident served to emphasize her lack of clothing, and he thought about it as he sat on the bank with her and waited for his clothes to dry sufficiently to put back on. Her natural state was a source of satisfaction for him as he watched her moving about, but he had an extreme reluctance for others to see her nude. And it was nearing the time for Williamson or one of the other men to bring him supplies.

He had other clothes in the shelter, and he sorted through them and found a pair of trousers with holes in the knees and a light muslin shirt. She was eagerly receptive to the idea of wearing clothes, considering them an ornament as well as a means of being more like him, and she quickly learned how to use a needle and thread. The trousers made her a long, wide skirt not unlike those worn by other women when the waist was taken in, the legs cut off at the knees, and the seams in the legs pulled out. Tailoring the shirt was beyond their skill, so he cut the wide sleeves off between her wrists and elbows and she wore it buttoned all the way up to the collar, with the tail hanging down around her knees over the top of the skirt. The clothes were hot and uncomfortable for her, but the novelty didn't wear off and she found the pockets convenient. She gradually became accustomed to them, but they slowed her down when she raced the dogs.

Williamson came a few days later. It was late afternoon. Mayrah had left Garrity sitting on the slope and watching the sheep graze while she went up to start the evening meal, and he turned when he heard the half hiss and half whistle she used to attract his attention. She was running down the slope toward him, her clothes whipping around her and her expression tense and excited, waving her arm in the downward gesture she used for a beckoning motion. He rose, picking up his musket, and hurried toward her.

"What is it, then? A dingo?"

She slowed and stopped, moving her hand in the gesture she used instead of shaking her head, hesitated and thought, then motioned toward him and turned her face back up the slope in the direction of the fold, indicating it with her pursed lips and chin.

He nodded, concluding that she was referring to an approaching man, and he turned and shouted to the dogs. They ran back and forth, bunching the sheep and starting them up the slope, and he put his musket across his shoulder and walked up the slope, Mayrah following along behind him. There was no one at the shelter and no one in sight, but she pointed toward the line of forest below the crest on the other side of the hill, in the direction of the station. He nodded and glanced back at the sheep coming up the slope, then stood and waited, watching the line of foliage. A moment later a man on a horse came out of the trees, followed by a packhorse on a rope. It was Williamson. He waved, and Garrity returned his wave and turned back toward the fold as the sheep neared the top of the hill.

The sheep stirred up a cloud of dust as they swarmed across the trampled ground near the fold, a mass of bleating, bobbing heads and wooly bodies, and Garrity walked toward them and spread his arms, turning them into the fold. The last of them ran in, burrowing into the milling flock as the dogs nipped at their heels, and the dogs turned away from them and began barking at Williamson as he approached. Garrity called them back, sliding the poles into place, and Williamson smiled and nodded as he approached the fold, did a doubletake at Mayrah standing by the fire, then looked back at Garrity and reined up, his smile wider.

"Are you all right, Pat?"

"I'm all right. Are you, Frank."

"Aye." He looked back at Mayrah and chuckled. "And I warrant you *are* all right and all, by God."

Garrity cleared his throat, feeling suddenly defensive. He glanced at Mayrah. She was peering at Williamson through the fringe of coarse hair hanging over her eyes, an expression of wary curiosity on her face. Her shirt and skirt were dusty and soiled, the collar on the shirt was askew, and her arms looked thin as they stuck out of the wide shirtsleeves and hung limply at her sides. The toes of one bare foot were scratching absently at the top of her other foot, a habitual motion when she was puzzled or thinking about something.

"Well, who's this, then?"

Garrity cleared his throat again, looked up at Williamson's twinkling smile, and shrugged self-consciously as he looked away. "Her name's Mayrah."

"Mayrah, is it? Well, that's a comely name. And she's a comely wench and all."

Garrity looked back up at Williamson and nodded, then chuckled and nodded again in response to Williamson's broad grin, suddenly feeling more at ease. Williamson laughed, stepping down from his horse, and slapped Garrity on the shoulder as they walked around to the packhorse. There were two large canvas bags on the packsaddle, and they lifted them off and carried them to the front of the shelter. Garrity pointed to the mutton over the fire, at Williamson, and toward the tree where the carcass was hanging as he turned to walk back toward the horses with Williamson. Mayrah made an affirmative motion with her hand, picked up the knife from the utensils on the wide, flat stone at the side of the fire, and walked around the shelter toward the carcass. Garrity and Williamson unsaddled the horses and hobbled them, and carried the saddles toward the shelter.

"The sheep are looking good, Pat."

"The graze is good."

"Aye, it looks good, but you're a bloody good stockman as well." They put the saddles down by the bags of supplies in front of the shelter, and Williamson took off his hat and wiped his forehead with his sleeve as he looked at Garrity. "I don't suppose you've seen any sign of bushrangers, then?"

Garrity shook his head, motioning toward the fire. "Let's sit down. No, I've seen none. Has anyone else?"

"Aye," Williamson sighed heavily as they walked to the fire and sat down. "They made off with some of Crowley's flock up to the north, and shot Crowley and all. He made it in to the station, and by the time I got some men out to his place most of the rest of the flock had scattered or had been killed by dingoes."

"How is Crowley?"

"He'll be all right."

Garrity nodded, looking at the fire, then looked back at Williamson. "What would bushrangers want with sheep?"

"To drive them over to some of the graziers east of here and sell them, no doubt. There's been a bad drought east of the Darling for the past couple of years, and a lot of the stock has died off."

Garrity nodded again, looking back at the fire. "You'll need to have a care for yourself while you're getting about."

"No fear. I keep a pistol at hand, and beyond that I never have that much with me." He smiled and chuckled wryly. "My age is more concern to me then bushrangers, Pat. The miles are getting longer and harder on these old bones."

Garrity glanced at him and looked away. He was a far different man than the one who had come to the orphanage to look for an apprentice stockman. Hardships and worries had taken their toll, his hair was white, and the flesh seemed to hang on the once burly body. Only the eyes were the same. "You should have sent the rations out by one of the men, Frank."

"No," Williamson said quickly, shaking his head firmly. "You're as much a son as a stockman to me, Pat, and I like to know you're all right."

Garrity scratched his beard and smiled awkwardly, looking down at his boot as he scuffed it against the ground. "It pleases me that you feel that way, Frank."

"Well, I do," Williamson said quietly. He glanced up at Mayrah as she came back around the shelter with another piece of mutton, and he looked back at Garrity. "Do you think you'll keep her, then?"

Garrity nodded. "Aye, I thought I would. No reason why I shouldn't, is there?"

"No, and it's not anyone else's affair, either. But if I'd known, I would have brought something more in the way of rations. Two of my wagons broke down on the last trip from Sydney and I'm short of flour, so I had to give you a short ration on that. But there's extra salt pork and a bottle of treacle there."

"That'll go down good. And we'll do on rations. She doesn't eat much, and I daresay she wouldn't eat any rations at all if I didn't make her. It takes all of my bloody time to keep her from eating beetles, snakes, and such."

"Aye, there's an abo for you," Williamson laughed, nodding. He studied her as she filled the fire-blackened billy with water and bent over the fire to put it on the coals, and he smiled thoughtfully. "But for all that, she could almost pass muster for a white woman if she had more hair and her hide was a cut lighter. Especially with the clothes on her. Whose idea was that?"

"Mine. I don't want any bugger else looking at her arse."

"I can't fault you there, because I'd be the same. Where did you get her?"

"I traded for her. That's why I wanted the axes and knives I had off you a time back."

"Was that it, then? Well, you got a good bargain if that's all you gave for her."

100

Garrity looked up at her. She was moving around the fire, the hem of her heavy skirt brushing the ground and her loose shirt billowing around her. Her eyes met Garrity's, and she smiled slightly and darted a nervous glance at Williamson as she picked up the pan and carried it toward the shelter. Garrity looked back at the fire, nodding. "Aye, it was a good bargain," he said quietly.

Williamson sighed heavily, stretching his legs out in front of him and wincing as he rubbed his knees, and he yawned and dug in his pockets for his pipe. "I brought extra tobacco for you this time, Pat. But I didn't have any rum."

"I can do without the rum, but I'm about out of tobacco," Garrity replied, taking out his pipe.

"I'm pleased I brought the extra, then. You can smoke a piece of this for now."

Williamson took a twist of tobacco and his pocket knife out, cut a piece from the twist and divided it with Garrity, and they rubbed it between their hands and filled their pipes. Mayrah came back out of the shelter with flour in the pan, and she knelt by the fire, dipped water into the pan from the bucket, and put the pan on the ground and mixed the damper with her hand. They lit their pipes with twigs from the fire and puffed on them, both of them silently watching her. Her expression was slightly self-conscious, reflecting awareness of their stares, and she ducked her head and let her hair fall forward as she mixed the batter. She put the top on the pan and put the pan on the fire, then pushed herself to her feet and walked back toward the shelter with her face averted, shaking the batter from her hand.

"Not a mark like other abos I've seen," Williamson said, taking his pipe from his mouth and exhaling smoke. "Where's she from?"

"I don't know, but I have a mind that it's a good distance. Her people acted like they hadn't seen white people, and she can see, smell, and hear better than any dog I have. She knew you were coming when you were over a mile away."

"You don't say? She's worth her keep, then. And she seems to be a good cook and all."

"Better than I am," Garrity chuckled.

Williamson laughed and put his pipe back in his mouth. Mayrah came back to the fire with the bag of tea, lifted the bail of the billy with a stick and took it off the fire, put tea in it and put it back on, then rose and went back to the shelter with the tea, tying the string around the mouth of the bag. She came back out of the shelter and sat down by Garrity, looking up at him with an anxious smile as she tucked her skirt under her. He smiled down at her, handing her his pipe. She took several deep puffs on it and exhaled, and handed it back to him with a wide grin and a quick glance at Williamson.

"I can see why your tobacco is used up," Williamson grinned.

Garrity smiled and nodded, putting his pipe back in his mouth. "She likes her puff."

"I'll leave what I have with you and bring you a double ration the next time, then," Williamson said, gathering his feet under him. He clenched his pipe between his teeth and pushed himself to his feet with a groan, then walked to his saddles. "Let me see if I don't have something for her here. I usually carry a few things around with me on the chance that I'll meet some abos and need to get on their good side." He knelt by his saddle and untied the rolled blanket on top of the bags and pushed it to one side as he opened the flaps on the bags. "Aye, this will please her, no doubt," he said, rummaging in the bag and taking out a couple of things, and he rose to his feet with another groan and walked back to the fire. "Here, give her these, Pat."

He handed Garrity a small mirror wrapped in raw wool to protect it from breaking and a string of bright glass beads. Garrity smiled and nodded in thanks, and he turned to Mayrah, put the beads around her neck, and pulled the wool off the mirror and handed it to her. Her expression reflected a total lack of understanding, her eyes moving down to the beads, up to the mirror, and back and forth between Williamson and Garrity. Garrity lifted the mirror in front of her face. Her eyes moved back down to the mirror, and an expression of stunned shock spread across her face. Williamson laughed, sitting back down and looking at her around Garrity as he puffed his pipe, and Garrity smiled down at her. She turned the mirror in her hands and looked at the back of it, then turned it over and looked at her face in the mirror surface again. A wide, pleased smile spread across her face, and she looked down at the beads and lifted them to look at them, making a sound of admiration in her throat. Garrity chuckled and patted her shoulder, and he put his pipe back in his mouth and glanced at Williamson.

"I'm much obliged, Frank."

"No cause to be. I'm happy that she's pleased."

Garrity smiled and nodded, glancing at Mayrah then back at the fire as he puffed his pipe. Mayrah made small sounds of pleasure as she looked at the mirror and beads for several minutes, then rose and went into the shelter to put them with her other precious things. She came back out and moved the iron rod holding the mutton over the fire to turn the mutton over, then lifted the bail on the billy with a stick, took it off the fire, and poured tea into the pannikin among the utensils on the flat rock. She handed the pannikin to Garrity, then looked at it and at Williamson with an uncertain expression. Williamson got to his feet and went to his saddles, took his pannikin, metal plate, and fork out of the bedroll, returned to the fire and handed them to her. She put the plate and fork on the flat rock, filled the pannikin with tea, and handed it back to him. He smiled and nodded in thanks as he took it, and she smiled shyly, looking away.

"Does she like a drink of cha, then?"

Garrity sipped his tea and shook his head as he put his

pannikin down and put his pipe back in his mouth. "She doesn't fancy it."

"She'll come around to it."

Garrity smiled and nodded, taking another drink and puffing on his pipe again.

Williamson cleared his throat, and he looked at Garrity as he put his pipe back in his mouth. "I'm bringing out more sheep."

Garrity lifted his eyebrows. "More? You're grazing up to twenty thousand now, aren't you?"

"More, and I could graze fifty. The only thing that's kept me back is finding stockmen and the increase of the flocks. But a lot of stockmen are coming over from the stations closing east of here, so I've been hiring a few so I could try them out. I have enough men to take care of five or six thousand more now, so I'm planning on bringing out that many more."

"From the Nepean flocks?"

"No, I'm planning on buying them. Would you like to buy into them?"

"For how much?"

"You have almost five hundred guineas in the bank in Sydney now. That would buy you between two and three thousand sheep, depending on the price at the time they're bought. Right after they're sheared, the price falls by a third to a half, and that's when I plan on buying them. If you want to, we can go together on the flock and split the losses and profits. Or if you want to, you could hire one of my men to help you, and you could buy your own flock and handle it yourself. And you'd have my good will and best wishes, together with a job at any time, if you lose your flock."

"How much does it cost to hire a man?"

"About twenty-five or thirty guineas a year for his wages and rations, depending on how much the rations cost. My head stockman costs me forty or more, and the other odd men around the station cost up to twenty. Abos cost from five to twenty a year, depending on what they do. On top of that, you have to have your washers and shearers in season. If you want to set up your own station, I'll go into all of it with you."

Garrity smiled slightly, looking at him. "Trying to get shot of me, Frank?"

Williamson chuckled and shook his head, then his smile faded and he shrugged. "I'd like to see you with your own station, Pat, and there's ample room here for both of us. But I don't intend to push you into it. Not right at this time, in any event. If you want to buy into a flock with me, well and good. Or we can just continue as we are. But sooner or later I want to see you with your own station."

Garrity looked into the fire in silence for a long moment, puffing his pipe, then shrugged. "I'll have to sleep on it, Frank."

"Take your while, Pat."

The sun was setting, and the light was soft. The stands of deep forest and open pasture blended together in the distance. The slight breeze freshened, making the flames dance and the bed of ashes glow bright red and yellow. It brought an acrid smell of dust from the trampled area around the fold and the strong odor of sheep from the fold. Garrity looked at the dogs lying on the other side of the fire, snapped his fingers and waved toward the fold. They rose and trotted toward it. Mayrah rose and took the iron rod off the fire, put the meat on the flat rock by the fire and began trimming off the burned portions with the knife.

Darkness fell, and she tossed more wood onto the fire. The dogs became visible on the edge of the firelight as they moved back from the fold and waited hungrily for their portion of the meat. Mayrah gathered up the burned portions and a pile of scraps, then rose and walked around the fire to feed the dogs. She divided the bits of mutton among them, and waved them back to the fold, and came back to the fire and dragged the pan out with a stick. She broke pieces of the damper, put them and pieces of the mutton on the plates and handed them to the men, then refilled their pannikins with tea. It emptied the billy, and she looked at Garrity and lifted her eyebrows, pointing toward the bucket. He nodded, and she refilled the billy, put it back on the fire, and went into the shelter for the bag of tea. She put the tea in the billy, took the bag back into the shelter, then returned to the fire and knelt by Garrity and plucked at his sleeve. He looked at her, chewing. She pointed to the bags by the front of the shelter, lifting her eyebrows. He nodded and pointed to the shelter. She went to the bags and opened them, and took out the slabs of salt beef and pork, bags of flour, salt, and sugar, and the other things, turning each one over in her hands and examining it closely. Garrity watched her over his shoulder, and when she took out the jar of treacle he snapped his fingers and pointed toward a broken bottle at one side of the shelter. She put the jug down gingerly and made an affirmative motion with her hand.

"What's that in aid of?" Williamson asked through a mouthful of food.

"She thinks everything is made of iron. She broke that bottle a while back, and I keep it there so I can show her when something can be broken."

Williamson grinned and nodded. Mayrah finished taking the supplies out of the bags and carried them into the shelter, putting the empty bags on the packsaddle. She returned to the fire and took the billy off the fire, refilled the men's pannikins, sat down by Garrity and began eating her mutton and piece of damper.

They finished eating, and Williamson and Garrity filled their pipes and lit them again. Mayrah collected up the utensils and washed them by dipping handfuls of water from the bucket and rinsing them, held them in front of the fire and dried them, then carefully laid them in a meticulously straight row on the flat stone, with the plates turned upside down on the forks. She went into the

106

shelter and came back out with her bark water container and bag, put them down and refilled their pannikins from the billy, then sat down by Garrity and looked through her belongings. The string of beads and mirror were among them, and she looked at the beads and ran them through her fingers with a pleased smile, then picked up the mirror and began closely examining her teeth and eyes, turning it to catch the light from the fire. Garrity touched her arm, pointed to the broken bottle, then pointed at the mirror. Her eyes widened, and he picked up the wad of wool which had been around the mirror and handed it to her, and she wrapped the mirror in it and burrowed into the bag to find a safe place for it.

"She didn't know the mirror would break?" Williamson asked.

"No, she doesn't seem to know anything until I show her. But I only have to show her once, which is more than you can say about most people."

"Aye, I'll not argue that," Williamson replied. "She's a proper little wife for you, and nobody could argue with that either." He knocked the dottle out of his pipe against his heel, then he stood up and yawned, stretching. "I think I'll put my blanket down by the fire, Pat."

Garrity nodded, knocking his pipe against the side of his boot, and he glanced at Mayrah and motioned toward the shelter as he rose. "I'll talk to you again in the morning about the sheep, Frank."

Williamson nodded and yawned again as he walked to the saddle and picked up the bedroll. "All right, Pat. Or I could wait for a few days to give you more time to think about it."

"I wouldn't want to hold you back, Frank."

"Well, we can talk about it in the morning and see if you need to think about it some more."

Garrity nodded, following Mayrah toward the shelter. "All right. Good night, Frank."

"Good night, Pat."

Mayrah disappeared into the darkness of the corner of the shelter and made small, rustling sounds as she put her belongings away. Garrity felt his way to the pallet, sat down on it and took off his boots, and began undressing. Mayrah stepped past him and sat down on the other side of the pallet as she removed her clothes. He pushed his clothes into a pile, then stretched out on his back, looking up at the ceiling in the darkness and thinking about what Williamson had said about the sheep. Mayrah moved closer to him, putting her head on his shoulder and touching his groin with a light pressure of her fingers. He shook his head. She made a soft sound in her throat, moving closer to him and putting her arm around his waist, and she put one leg across his and settled her head comfortably in the hollow of his shoulder. He put his arm around her shoulders and patted her, then relaxed.

It amounted to risking everything he had earned, which in turn had been earned with a high element of risk. Other men worked for wages, which were much less than the profit shares he had received, but were assured. He had been fortunate, and the sheep hadn't been lost in a fire, drought, or through his becoming injured and unable to keep them from straying. The carts transporting the wool had arrived safely in Sydney, and a good price had been received for the wool. So the risk had paid well, and in two shearings from his flock he had accumulated more money than many man did in their entire life. And it could all be lost if he ventured into buying into the sheep with Williamson. Williamson wouldn't be going to Sydney, so the sheep would be entrusted to hired men. And everything could be lost even before the sheep arrived from Sydney if a fire swept across the trail or another of a multitude of possible disasters came to pass. There would unquestionably be some losses along the trail, though once they were at the station much of the danger would be past. But the danger remaining was substantial, and they could still be lost.

But a decision to accept the risk and to buy into the sheep with Williamson wouldn't end it. There was a further decision whether to continue on with Williamson or to take his share of the sheep and strike out on his own. He had never before analyzed his life in terms of long range objectives. Each day had been simply a repetition of the day before, and satisfying because he enjoyed what he did. Since Mayrah had been there it had changed to the extent of incorporating her. The money in the bank at Sydney had been an end in itself, because money was the purpose for which everyone strived. But all that changed with the possibility of having his own station. Suddenly there was an objective, and one which he desired with a fierce, deeply-rooted determination. He wanted his own station. And it was within reach. He knew everything about sheep he needed to know, and Williamson would help him. Within a week or two he could learn the few details of station operation he would need to know. But while two or three thousand sheep could be expanded to large flocks within a few years, it was also such a small number that it would be marginally profitable. He wouldn't be able to buy carts or hire more than one or two men, so he would be dependent upon Williamson for supplies and to haul his wool to Sydney. And a single brush fire or a year of drought would wipe him out. Many of the small stations to the east which had failed had undoubtedly been undertakings such as his would be, and had been unable to last through even moderately hard times.

There was a point at which risk became unacceptable, and it appeared that trying to start his own station with such a small number of sheep surpassed that point. He was reluctant to have someone else tending sheep he owned while he was looking after Williamson's sheep, but Williamson would see that they were tended as well as any of his other sheep. And the profits from his share of the sheep would mount rapidly, because half the lambs would be his. If all went well, within a few years he would have thousands instead of hundreds of guineas.

Williamson uttered a snore, and the sound carried into the shelter. Mayrah woke with a convulsive start and lifted her head, turning it from side to side. Williamson snored again. Mayrah moved away from Garrity and rose from the pallet, and walked silently to the door. The moon had risen, and her slender, naked body was silhouetted against the pale moonlight outside the shelter. She stood in the doorway for a moment, listening to Williamson snore, then she turned and moved silently back across the shelter to the pallet. She leaned over Garrity and looked at him to see if he were awake, then she pointed toward Williamson as she made a snorting sound and laughed softly. Garrity nodded and grinned, pulling her back down by him on the pallet. She breathed a soft sigh, wriggling and settling herself against him again. The memory of how she had looked silhouetted against the moonlight remained in his mind's eye and he searched for some means of escaping the agonizing deliberation over what to do about the sheep, and he reacted as her hand brushed lightly across his groin. She stiffened slightly, and her hand moved back, groped, then moved purposefully. He turned toward her, putting his arms around her. She made a soft sound of satisfaction as she opened her thighs and put her arm under him and around his waist, pulling him toward her.

Afterwards, he lay on his back and looked up at the bark roof in the darkness again, still sleepless. Mayrah lay against him with one leg over his and her arm across his chest, breathing soundlessly with a low, deep rhythm which was detectable only by the movements of her breasts against the side of his chest. He thought the entire proposition through several times, and each time it seemed foolish to jeopardize everything for which he had worked. But the money was basically worthless to him in

110

a bank. And it wasn't unknown for banks to fail and lose all the money deposited in them.

Given the fact of risking the money, the next point which represented a stumbling block was entrusting his sheep to another stockman. He had never seen a flock tended by another man which satisfied him. To others it was a job. To him it was life itself. But the point was easily and logically satisfied. Beyond the fact that he would make far more money by continuing with Williamson and taking shares from the other sheep at the same time, he would be constantly entrusting his sheep to the care of other stockmen if he ever did have his own station.

And he intended to have his own station. By continuing on with Williamson and taking shares from the other sheep at the same time, he would be in a position to stock a fully profitable station within a few years, if things went well. He decided to do it, and when he had made the decision he was filled with a seething impatience to complete the details and be done with it. He moved away from Mayrah and sat up, groping for his trousers. She looked at him in the darkness, making an interrogative sound. He pulled his trousers on and walked toward the door in his bare feet.

Williamson was a dark shadow on the ground, rolled tightly in his blanket by the dead fire. Garrity knelt by the fire and stirred the ashes with a stick, dropped splinters of wood on the red coals under the ashes, and leaned lower to blow on them. They burst into flame, and he stacked several pieces of wood on the blaze.

"Frank?"

Williamson jerked, then sat up and looked around with a dazed, startled expression, automatically reaching for the pistol on the ground beside him. "What is it?"

"On the sheep, I'd like to go halves with you on them."

Williamson looked at him in the flickering firelight, blinking his eyes in a sleepy bewilderment, then nodded.

He yawned, looking up at the stars, then put the pistol down and sat up straighter, rubbing his face with both hands. "Well, all right, Pat."

"How can I transfer the money in the bank over to you?"

"You can write me a draft on the bank. I brought along paper and ink on the chance that you would want to do it."

"Let's make the paper out now, then."

Williamson looked up at the stars again, then looked back at Garrity. "Just this minute, Pat?"

"I'd like to be done with it. I'll build up the fire so we can see to do it."

Williamson scratched his head and nodded, pushing the blanket down and gathering himself to rise. "All right, Pat."

Garrity broke up more sticks from the pile of wood and tossed them onto the fire as Williamson yawned widely and stumbled toward his saddle. Mayrah came out of the shelter, looking from one of them to the other with an expression of curiosity as she buttoned her shirt, and she walked to the fire and knelt by it, nudging Garrity away from the wood with her shoulder and selecting more sticks. Garrity sat down by the large, flat rock by the fire, moving the utensils to one side. Williamson searched in one of his saddlebags and came back to the fire with an oilskin wrapper containing paper, a small phial of ink, and a stubby, bedraggled quill.

Williamson put the phial of ink and oilskin wrapper on the flat rock and took out his pocketknife, and he held the end of the quill up to the light of the fire and carefully sharpened it. Mayrah yawned and scratched her head as she filled the billy from the bucket of water, and she stood up and moved around the men to put it on the edge of the fire. Williamson put his knife away, took a sheet of paper from the oilskin wrapper, and flattened it on the rock, and looked at Garrity as he took the cork from the phial of ink.

"Do you want to write it out, Pat?"

"You've done this before, haven't you?"

"Oh, more than once."

"You do it, then."

Williamson nodded as he put the phial down, and he smoothed the paper on the rock and cleared his throat as he picked up the quill. A couple of the dogs came to the edge of the firelight and lay down with their muzzles between their paws, watching the men. Williamson dipped the end of the quill in the ink, and smoothed the paper again, then he began writing laboriously. Mayrah moved closer to the two men and leaned over them, peering over their shoulders as Williamson wrote on the paper in the ruddy, wavering light of the fire.

8

Garrity was following the dogs and sheep back out of the forest after watering them, and he stiffened with surprise as one of the dogs suddenly broke away from the flock and raced toward a thick stand of acacia a few yards away, snarling and gnashing its teeth. A musket cracked and a puff of smoke billowed from the acacia, and the dog squealed with agony as it fell to the ground. A ripple passed through the sheep, and they were suddenly in a headlong run toward the meadow. Garrity froze for an instant, then lifted his musket and pulled the hammer back as he picked out the barrel of the gun against the dark green of the acacia leaves. He started to sight down the barrel, and another puff of smoke blossomed in the acacia. A powerful force struck his right thigh, knocking his legs from under him. His musket discharged into the ground in front of him as he fell.

He looked dully at the two men riding out of the acacia thicket. It had happened so rapidly that his mind was reeling. At one moment he had been engrossed in the daily routine of bringing the sheep back from the stream, with no thought that anyone else was within miles of him, and in the next moment he and the dog had been shot. And the shrill yelping of the wounded dog was deafening, adding to his confusion. The pain in his leg was moderated for a moment by stupefaction and numbness, then the pain descended in full force, in fiery, seething waves which centered in his thigh and raced through him. Understanding came at the same time as he looked at the men, bringing an empty, hollow feeling which was as intense as the pain. They were bushrangers.

His first thought was of Mayrah, and he lifted his head and looked through the edge of the trees and up the slope. They had run out of flour a few days before, and she had spent several hours each day in collecting tiny, barely-visible spinifex seeds which she ground in a stone basin and turned into a flour-like powder from which she made small cakes. Earlier, when he had followed the sheep into the forest to take them to water, she had been kneeling in the spinifex halfway up the slope and patiently gathering the seeds. But she wasn't in sight.

Then he thought of the sheep, and in the back of his mind there was a fleeting surprise that he had thought of her before the sheep. They had run out into the pasture, their panic short of the fright which would have sent them into a wild, headlong rush, and the remaining three dogs had answered their own instincts and training and had gone with them. They were turning the sheep in a wide circle to drive the leaders back into the rear of the flock and start them milling. It wasn't the smooth, effortless control the dogs usually exercised, because their attention was divided between what they were doing and the squealing of the wounded dog thrashing about on the ground and biting at its hindquarters in mindless agony.

He looked back at the men. They reminded him of the chained lines of incorrigible prisoners he had occasionally seen being taken from one place to another through the streets of Sydney. They were hard and predatory, cruel and totally depraved. One of them looked deformed, his head too large for his body and one side of his face covered by a brownish-red birthmark, and the other was tall and thin. They wore filthy rags, and their horses were thin and weary, coated with sweat-streaked dust. The tall one dismounted by the dog and clubbed it with the butt of his musket, and the dog's yelps became a deep, hoarse sound as the heavy weapon slammed against its head with a solid, meaty thud. He lifted the musket and slammed it down again, and the sounds faded into gargling. The one with the birthmark rode on over to Garrity, looked down at him with impersonal, detached disinterest as he dismounted. He picked up Garrity's musket and stepped a few feet away to batter it against a tree. The tall man pounded the butt of his musket down on the dog's head a few more times, then put his musket across his shoulder and led his horse toward Garrity, looking down at him.

"You just winged him, Cummings."

"It did the job, didn't it? And you didn't do too good on that dog."

The name was tantalizingly familiar, one which he felt he should recognize immediately, and it took it a second to surface through the confusion and pain. His mother had worked for a man named Cummings. He looked up at the man. The line of the birthmark ran down the center of the man's forehead, nose, and lips, and it emphasized the abnormally large size of the man's head. It gave his face a strange aspect, as though two faces had been crushed together to make one.

The man looked down at him with a sardonic sneer, lifting his eyebrows. "Do you know me?"

Garrity looked back down at the ground and silently shook his head.

"Well, you do now," he chuckled. "And not many forget me once they've seen me. What's your name?"

"Garrity."

"Garrity? Would you be kin to Sheila Garrity? Her that worked as a charwoman in Sydney?"

"She was my ma."

"Aye, you're the one she had in the orphanage, then," Cummings laughed dryly. "My dad caught her stealing to bring to you, and a bloody good hiding she got for her trouble and all. Old slut that she was." He looked back at the tall man, dismissing Garrity. "Do you want to see how many of them we can handle?"

"There's no hurry. We'd do well to eat while we have a chance, because we'll have to keep going until we reach the pen, once we get started. What do you want to do about him?"

"Leave him—he'll be no pother with that pin, and it'll take him all of his time just to get back to his station. You go ahead and pick out a good one, then, and I'll build a fire."

The taller man nodded, handing his reins to Cummings, and he charged his musket as he walked toward the edge of the meadow. Cummings led the horses to one side and tied them to a tree, and began gathering up twigs from the ground. The dogs were confused and afraid, and they had let the sheep scatter over the lower stretch of the slope. The sheep were milling around, also confused and apprehensive, some of them grazing and others darting back and forth to push their way into clusters in their instinctive search for safety in the middle of the herd.

Garrity was lying at full length, and he dug his elbows into the ground and lifted himself to look over his shoulder at his leg. The pain intensified, and he winced and gasped weakly, bracing his elbows and lifting himself higher. His loose, thick trousers were plastered to his leg

117

with blood. He clenched the muscles in his right leg to move his foot. The pain became excruciating, but his foot moved. His arms suddenly went weak, and he stiffened them with an effort and turned his head to scan the slope again for Mayrah. She wasn't in sight. He sagged back to the ground, panting breathlessly.

The knowledge that his flock was lost was a devastating weight, as painful in its own way as the wound in his leg. They would probably kill the rest of the dogs, then they would take as many as they could drive on their horses. The rest would scatter to be killed by dingoes. A furious resentment toward the men rose within him, a galling anger that the result of his labor was to be taken by those who preyed on others, who produced nothing and subsisted on that produced by others. And he was angry at himself for his failure to be watchful.

But along with the anger, there was fear. They had assumed that he was alone, because stockmen were always alone. But the flock had scattered almost halfway up the slope, and they might see Mayrah at the shelter if they went near the top of the slope in collecting those they wanted to drive away. Then reason intervened even as the chilling fear began gripping his mind. Mayrah would have been able to hear the musket shots and the wounded dog's howling from the top of the hill. She was warned. The loss of the flock was a staggering blow, but all wasn't lost. It didn't feel as though the musket ball had hit a bone, and the leg would heal in time. As long as Mayrah was safe, life would continue.

Cummings built a fire and took a billy, a pan, and other things from the packs behind the saddles on the horses. A musket shot sounded in the pasture, and the sheep darted about, scattering further apart. The dogs raced back and forth uncertainly, crowding some of the sheep back together and looking around aimlessly for him to give them instructions. The tall man dragged a young ewe into the edge of the trees, propped his musket against a tree, and took out his knife and bent over the ewe, slashing and ripping the skin open. Garrity had killed many sheep to eat and felt no compunction in doing so, because it was a harvest of his labor and a necessity in order to sustain himself. But always there was a consciousness that he was taking life. There was no such awareness in the man's attitude. He was callously indifferent, intent only upon satisfying his need of the moment. And totally unconcerned with waste, because he separated a foreleg and carried it toward the fire with blood dripping from it, the remainder of the ewe forgotten on the ground behind him. The odor of the blood and flesh was heavy in the still air among the trees.

They hung the joint of meat over the fire as they talked quietly. There was a cake of cold damper in the pan as well as a pot of rice heating on the coals, indicating that they had either robbed someone else of food or the rewards of their lawlessness were greater than their ragged appearance reflected. From their conversation, they had a pen some miles away that they had used before, and they planned to drive as many of the sheep as they could handle without dogs to the pen and then find someone to buy them. It was the same unconcern with waste as leaving most of the ewe on the ground to spoil and to be eaten by wild animals. They would be able to drive only a small part of the flock without dogs, and many of those would scatter and be lost along the way. Others would die in the pen while they were finding someone whose need for stock and desire for gain were great enough to make them willing to buy what they would know to be stolen animals. The largest part of the flock would scatter to die of thirst or to be killed by dingoes. And four good and faithful dogs would be dead.

The rich, fecund odor of the soil was strong in his nostrils, and the ground was soft and cool against the side of his face. He felt his strength ebbing, and a gnawing impatience for them to be done and leave replaced the anger and depression. His leg was bleeding badly, and when they left Mayrah would come to help him. Perhaps one or two of the dogs would be frightened away instead of being killed and he could even muster a few of the scattered sheep after they left, if they left before his strength deserted him entirely. The pain seemed to be less severe, the sound of the men's voices seemed to rise and fall, and he felt a hazy detachment from his surroundings.

Three green-breasted parrots flashed through the air and started to alight in a bush further back in the trees, then fluttered their wings rapidly and flared away from the bush. Garrity lay with the side of his head resting on the ground and looked absently at the bush. There seemed to be something strange about it. Then he suddenly stiffened and his eyes widened. He was looking at Mayrah. She was naked, and her slim body was stretched out along the ground under the lowermost branch in the bush, and supported on her left hand and her knees. The long, heavy stick she always carried was in her right hand and parallel to her body, an inch off the ground. She was completely motionless, completely invisible against the mottled pattern of the ground and foliage and at the same time in plain sight once the lines of her body were picked out. There was a flowing movement, a couple of leaves on the lower branch of the bush stirred slightly as though a breath of wind had touched them, and she was gone, disappearing behind a tree.

His eyes were riveted on the tree, and he almost missed the movement. A dusky shadow flicked from the tree to an adjacent tree in the space of time it took the eyes to blink. He looked from the second tree back to the first, still not positive he had seen her. Then there was a sinuous movement along the ground by the second tree as she disappeared into another bush. And he realized what she was doing. She was stalking. Fear exploded within him, and he gripped himself to keep from crying out and warning her away. It would serve no purpose to call out, because she probably wouldn't understand. And they would be warned. But she was only a small, thin woman, and they were two armed men. And all would be lost if he lost her.

There was a shadowy movement from the bush to another tree. Then there was an open space of thirty or forty yards between the tree and the fire where the two men were sitting and talking as they waited for the mutton to broil. The route he always used to take the sheep to and from the stream was where the trees were thin so he and the dogs could see any breaking away from the flock, and all of the bushes had been trampled down by the sheep or he had pulled them down for better visibility. There was absolutely no concealment between the ghostly, pallid grey trunk of the large whitegum behind which she was hiding and the fire.

Then it occurred to him that she might have only come to investigate, to see what she could do. And seeing the two well-armed men by the fire, she would wait until they left to come to his assistance. He gathered his strength and lifted his head so she could see that he was only wounded.

And she was darting across the open space. Her first step was a full stride in a headlong dash at the men, and it seemed that she was halfway across the open space before what his eyes were seeing registered in his mind. She was running upright, her legs a brown blur, and her slender body was bowed backwards with her right arm back and the muscles in it knotted, holding the stick to throw it like a spear. The coarse hair was blowing back from her face, her eyes were wide and glaring, and her lips were drawn back from her teeth in an expression of wild fury. He gathered himself to go to her assistance.

The stick flew through the air toward Cummings, and the tall man glimpsed her at the last moment and snatched at his musket on the ground beside him. The end of the stick slammed into the side of Cummings' head and knocked him sprawling, and Mayrah launched herself

121

through the air in a long bound, her hands grasping claws and her bared teeth gleaming. Excruciating, searing pain shot through Garrity as he lurched up off the ground, trying to hobble forward as his right leg kept collapsing, and the ground seemed to come up and slam into him with a stunning blow as Mayrah landed on the tall man. Her fingers clawed at his eyes, and she bit at his throat. He lifted the musket and brought the butt around, slamming it against her head, and she bounced away from him, blood pouring from her forehead. She scrambled back toward him. Panic exploded within Garrity, releasing reserves of strength, and the pain was only a fleeting sensation on the edges of his awareness. His feet were under him again, and he hopped on his left leg, dragging his right one. The man lifted the musket to slam it against Mayrah's head again as she scratched and bit at him, and Garrity threw himself at the musket.

His breath burst from his lungs and grey clouds of unconsciousness closed in as he hit the ground with a shattering impact, and he blindly clutched at the musket and the man's arm. He felt the cold metal of the musket under his hands and a thrashing movement of the man's arm as he lifted it, and he heaved himself forward to hold the musket down with his weight. His last dregs of strength were rapidly ebbing, and he held onto the man's arm grimly, hoping that Mayrah would be able to blind him. The man's arm lifted him and he threw his weight downward, and his face ground into the dirt as he flattened the man's arm again. Then he felt the muscles in the arm become rigid and knotted, jerking convulsively but not pushing up against his weight, and a hoarse, ragged scream burst from the man's throat.

Garrity lifted his head, shaking it to clear his vision. The man's body was bowing up off the ground, his mouth wide open and his long, yellow teeth bared, and his tongue thrust far out as he screamed again. Mayrah's fingernails were still probing and digging at his eyes, but her purpose had already been accomplished. His eyesockets were bloody, pulpy holes, surrounded by deep scratches. She had her face buried in his beard and was uttering muffled, growling sounds as she shook her head rapidly like a dog worrying a small animal, and his other hand was jerking at her hair.

She lifted her head as Garrity reached for the man's hand to drag it out of her hair, and he froze, looking at her in shocked horror. It looked as though the man had torn half of her face off with the butt of the musket, because there was nothing but raw flesh from her nose to her chin, with blood streaming down from her forehead and covering her eyes and cheeks. Then he saw the blood spurting up from the man's throat, and she spat out the ragged piece of flesh. She had ripped out his throat with her teeth. The man made a choked, gargling sound, and his arms and legs began jerking in a throbbing rhythm as the thick stream of blood gushed from his throat.

She wiped the blood out of her eyes with her forearm as she turned away and looked at Cummings. Garrity pulled himself around on the ground and lifted his head higher to look at him. The end of the stick had made a depression an inch or two deep in his temple on the side with the birthmark, killing him. But Mayrah wasn't satisfied. She crawled to him and crouched over him with his head between her feet and the stick in both hands, churning it and pounding the side of his head until it was soft and pulpy. The blood continued running down her face from her forehead, dripping off her chin to disappear into the mass of blood, hair, and brain tissue. Then she dropped the stick and fell onto her side, wiping feebly at her eyes and forehead with her arm.

The tall man's limbs quivered and twitched for a moment longer, then he was still. The wood on the fire crackled, and the mutton hanging over it hissed and popped, dripping grease into the flames. The water in the billy on the coals boiled with a gurgling sound, and the horses moved their feet restively. Birds called in the trees and darted back and forth. Everything was suddenly still. Mayrah lifted her head and blinked the blood out of her eyes, and smiled weakly at Garrity as she pulled herself along the ground and crawled toward him. He lifted himself shakily to one elbow and reached over the tall man's body toward her, and she put her small hand into his, sliding toward him.

The edge of the metal plate on the butt of the musket had cut a three inch gash almost to the bone above her left eye, and it was still bleeding freely. It seemed impossible that she had remained conscious after such a blow, and she was obviously weak from exertion and loss of blood. She kept trying to pull away from his hands to look at his leg, but he snapped at her and made her sit still as he took out his pocketknife, cut a strip from the tall man's trousers, and tied it around her head. Then he motioned for her to help him sit up, and he cut his trousers open and looked at his thigh. The musket ball had gone all the way through the fleshy part of his thigh without hitting a bone, and it was still bleeding heavily. He cut strips from the tall man's trousers and bound it tightly, then he used the man's musket for a crutch and tried to get up, Mayrah straining and lifting at him. His head swam giddily and his arms went weak, and he fell back to the ground.

There was a muddled, detached feeling of unreality, and the pain in his thigh came in waves, swelling to a wracking intensity, then subsiding again. He felt weak and lifeless, and his mouth was dry and sticky. Cummings had taken a couple of leather-covered water bottles from the horses to fill the billy, and he pointed to them. She brought one of them to him, and he pulled the cork out of it and drank. The water was musty and bitter, tasting of mud, and it didn't satisfy his thirst. He handed it to her so she could drink, and he pushed the cork back into it, looking around and thinking. The sheep had once again become the most important consideration. He put the bottle to one side, looking at Mayrah and motioning her toward the horses.

Williamson's horses were the only ones she had ever seen before, and she was wary of them. And the horses were frightened of her. But they had been mistreated, overworked, and poorly fed, and they had little spirit. They flared their nostrils and cocked their ears at her as they stamped nervously, but they were docile enough as she approached them. It took her a moment to figure out how to untie the knot on the reins, then she got one of them untied and led it toward Garrity. He lifted himself to one elbow and motioned for her to bring the horse closer, and the horse rolled its eyes at the dead men on the ground and at him as it wheeled about skittishly. She worked the horse around until he could reach one of the stirrups, and he gripped it and began pulling himself up from the ground. The horse moved sidewards and dragged him a few inches, and he gripped the stirrup and held onto it with all of his strength as the fiery pain in his leg seemed to envelope him and the threatening grey clouds of unconsciousness hovered close. Then the horse stood still again, and cold sweat broke out on his face as he summoned his energy and pulled himself higher, reaching for the side of the saddle. It sagged to one side as he gripped it and pulled himself higher, then he was leaning against the side of the horse, almost upright. He slowly dragged himself up onto it. The horse moved and he almost fell over it headfirst, then caught himself and balanced his weight as he lay across the saddle.

It was impossible for him to swing a leg over, so he slowly turned, lifting himself to a sitting position with both legs on one side. Sweat streamed down his face and he panted hoarsely as he sat with head drooping, fighting the giddiness and unconsciousness which kept trying to close in on him. Then he swallowed dryly and lifted his head, motioning for her to hand the reins up to him. She handed up both of them on one side of the horse's neck and he had difficulty communicating to her what was wrong, until she finally figured it out and put the reins over the horse's head. He turned the horse toward the edge of the meadow, slumped on the saddle.

The sheep were spread all over the slope, and the dogs were wandering about aimlessly. Garrity's mouth was so dry that it was hard to whistle, but as soon as he attracted the attention of one of them they all raced toward him, eager for the reassurance of instructions. He held onto the front of the saddle with his right hand and lifted his left arm with an effort, sending them up the left side of the slope to gather the sheep back to the right. Then he slumped, his chin on his chest. The grass looked soft, and it was tempting to slide off the saddle and lie down. He sighed heavily, lifting his head. The dogs had swept the left side of the slope, and all the sheep were moving toward the line of forest on the right side. He drew in a deep breath and tried again, and managed a weak whistle. One of the dogs hesitated and looked at him. He lifted his arm and beckoned. All three ran down the slope toward him. His chin dropped back to his chest again, and he closed his eyes. The darkness of unconsciousness hovering at the back of his mind seemed alluring instead of threatening, inviting and promising warmth and comfort. He gathered his strength and lifted his head again. The dogs were standing in front of the horse and looking at him. He braced himself and lifted his arm, and sent them up the right side of the slope.

The dogs perceived his intention to cluster the flock in the center of the slope. They raced about purposefully, driving the sheep away from the line of forest along the right side of the slope and darting into the trees to chase out a few which had wandered into them. A few of the sheep on the left side began to wander away again, and one of the dogs leaped from one sheep's back to another to get to the left side of the flock and drive them back again. A movement on the right edge of his vision attracted his attention, and he turned his head. Three sheep were running out of the trees at the bottom of the slope, and Mayrah was stumbling slowly along behind them, waving her stick at them. They saw the flock and ran toward it to join it. Mayrah planted the end of her stick on the ground and leaned on it, holding her head. Then she slowly lifted her head and stumbled back into the trees again. Garrity's chin dropped to his chest again.

His mind floated drowsily in a state between consciousness and unconsciousness. There were urgent concerns which gnawed at him demandingly, but they seemed very distant and he regarded them with a placid nonchalance. Then his surroundings intruded, sound and movement registering on his awareness. He opened his eyes. Mayrah was standing by the horse and tugging at his left foot as she spoke his name over and over. The rag around her forehead was saturated with blood, the blood on her cheeks was dried and cracked, and her small face was drawn and pale with pain. One of the leather-covered water bottles hung from her shoulder by its thong, and she unslung it, pulled the cork out, and handed it up to him. He lifted it with an effort and took a drink, then handed it back to her. She replaced the cork, then motioned toward the slope and said something in her language. He looked toward the slope. The sheep were a blur in front of him. It took a long time for her meaning to penetrate. She was suggesting taking the sheep to the fold. He lifted the reins and moved in the saddle. The horse began walking forward. Mayrah walked ahead of the horse through the spinifex, whistling shrilly between her teeth and waving her arm. The dogs were distant, shapeless blurs in front of his eyes as they began moving around the flock.

It seemed to take an endless time to get up the slope. As he neared the top, it occurred to him that he should be in front of the flock to turn it into the fold. He guided the horse around the left side of the flock, and through the thick cloud of dust he saw Mayrah standing with her arms spread apart and waving her stick, turning the sheep into the fold. A couple of them broke away, and she waved her arm and whistled sharply. A dog darted around and turned the sheep back into the flock.

The horse stopped near the shelter. The bark bowl she used for gathering the spinifex seed and the crude mortar and pestle she used for grinding were by the large, flat rock by the fire. Her skirt was near the rock, and her shirt a few feet away. Apparently she had correctly interpreted the sound of the shots as trouble and had shed her clothes to be unencumbered as she ran toward the trees. The dogs sat down between the shelter and the fold and looked at him, their tongues hanging out as they panted. Mayrah went to the fire, put the leather-covered bottle and her stick down, then walked to the side of the horse and reached up to help him down. He looked down at her. She blinked, then smiled and moved her fingers in a beckoning motion. He turned and gripped the saddle, and began easing himself down. When his right foot touched the ground there was an instant of unbearable pain, then unconsciousness.

Confused, fleeting impressions registered on his awareness. There were sensations of movement, of cold, and of heat. And always there was pain, a continuing torture which seemed to be the fabric of existence and from which there was no escape. Distorted images moved about him at times, and at other times there was only a cold and lonely darkness. Then moments of consciousness came and went, brief periods when he thought he was in the orphanage and terror gripped him because he had fouled himself in his bed, then longer periods when the fever gripping him and the struggle of his body to recover from the massive loss of blood wiped his memory away and he had nothing to which to relate what he saw around him. Time was warped, an instant stretching for an endlessly long period while a single twinge of pain jangled along his nerves for an eternity. Impressions crowded together in rapid sequence and periods of light and darkness flickered by in a dizzying swirl.

Lucid moments came. At times he was alone in the shelter, and the bright sunlight flooded through the doorway and the interior of the shelter was hot. He was naked, sweat forming and trickling down his face and the sides of his body, and he was lying on blankets he had never seen before. The two muskets and the pistol on the floor by the doorway were a puzzle for a time, as were the blankets and a stack of clothing in the corner, until he figured out that she had collected all of the dead men's belongings, including the clothing they'd had on them. And he wondered where she was and what had happened to the sheep.

The moments of lucid thought faded into darkness and others came, when the light in the shelter would be more diffuse, it would be cooler, and Mayrah would be there. She looked different because she was wearing one of the men's hats, a dusty and sweat-stained felt with a wide brim and crumpled crown which almost swallowed her small head. At times she was holding him up and giving him drinks of water or feeding him, putting bits of spinifex seed cake dipped in treacle into his mouth or chewing pieces of mutton and spitting them in his mouth for him to swallow. At other times the pain was severe because she was moving him off a blanket he had fouled and washing him and putting him on another blanket, and at yet other times it was dark and she was asleep beside him.

Full consciousness and awareness returned late one afternoon. He lay for several minutes and thought about what had happened and tried to figure out how long he had been lying in the shelter. Concern over the sheep was an imperative worry gnawing at him. He lifted himself to a sitting position and braced himself on one arm, pushing the blanket down. A wide, thick bandage of woven grass was tied tightly around his thigh, and it was impregnated with some kind of poultice which looked like a mixture of dirt and bits of leaves. He was very weak, sweat breaking out and his arm trembling from the effort of holding him up in a sitting position, but his head was clear. And he was ravenously hungry. He made an abortive attempt to rise, then turned around and crawled toward the doorway.

The pain had subsided to a dull ache, and his movements started sharp, stabbing twinges lancing through his thigh again. But they were nothing compared to what he had suffered before, and only a minor annoyance compared to the weakness. He had to stop twice to rest, panting with exhaustion as he lay on the dirt floor of the shelter, then he crawled on.

The sun was hot against his naked skin, the pebbles on the ground in front of the shelter were coarse and rough, and the light breeze blowing across the hill smelled fresh and clean. The fold was empty, and the poles removed from the section used as a gate were placed neatly to one side. A grey tendril of smoke was rising from the ashes in the circle of stones. Everything around the fire was meticulously neat, and there was an abundance of pans, plates, and utensils, things which had belonged to the men. Blankets she had washed were hanging on one side of the shelter to dry and air out. He crawled closer to the fire and looked in a covered pan on the large stone. It contained a joint of cold, roasted mutton and most of a cake of damper. He pulled off a piece of mutton and chewed it, and absently wondered where she had got the flour to make the damper as he broke off a piece of it. Then he remembered the men's packs.

His ribs were showing and his arms and legs were thin compared to their previous muscular size, and he felt cold even though the late afternoon sun was warm. He ate, drank from one of the leather-covered water bottles by the fire, then he reached over to the pile of wood for a stick, uncovered the hot coals in the bed of ashes, and tossed slivers and bits of bark on them. They burst into flame, and he tossed pieces of wood onto them and moved closer to the fire. Then he heard the horses and sheep coming up the hill.

The bobbing heads of the horses came into sight first, then Mayrah between them and in front, leading them. The large hat, her shirt, and her skirt were covered with dust, and her face was dusty, streaked with sweat, and lined with fatigue. Her eyes widened with surprise as she saw him sitting by the fire, then a brilliant smile spread across her face, her teeth gleaming in the shadow cast by the wide brim of the hat. She began running with the horses, dragging them along behind her, tied them to one of the poles in the fold and ran to him with her arms outstretched and her skirt and shirt billowing. He put his arms around her and kissed her, the warm, familiar scent of her body filling his nostrils, and her hands moved over him in light, caressing touches. She also had lost weight and she looked very weary, and there was a thick, wide scab on the cut across her forehead. Dust began billowing up at the brow of the hill and the sound of the flock approaching became louder, and she patted him and slid out of his arms as she rose to go turn the flock into the fold.

It was two days before he could get around the vicinity of the shelter with the assistance of a long stick, and several more days before his strength returned sufficiently for him to venture further. But there were things to do. She hadn't known to take the saddles and bridles off the horses, and they had both developed saddle sores and become even more gaunt from the insufficient graze they had been able to crop with the bits in their mouths. He hobbled them and doctored the sores with sheep tallow, and they grazed and watered with the sheep and stayed in the fold at night. By the time they became spirited enough to kick at the sheep at night, he had regained his enough strength to go around to the line of forest at the side of the hill and cut poles to make a separate pen for them.

131

There were only thirty-two fewer sheep than there had been before the bushrangers struck, a negligible loss all things considered. The packs behind the saddles had contained substantial amounts of rations, flour, rice, sugar, dried peas, and beans, and Mayrah had collected all the other belongings, the weapons, utensils, and the clothings and boots the men had been wearing. And in their pockets she had found three gold ten-guinea pieces and a Spanish doubloon, which she had confiscated and put with her stones and other treasures in her grass bag.

As soon as he was able to mount one of the horses, he rode down to the stream to bathe and change into clean clothes, and he began taking the sheep out to graze and leaving Mayrah at the shelter so she could rest and recover from the grueling labor of taking care of him and of the sheep while he had been disabled. He carried one of the muskets as well as the pistol, and he was cautious and watchful when he was in or near the forest. In taking the sheep back and forth to the stream, he frequently stopped and looked around for any remains of the two men who had ambushed him. After several times of looking, he finally found a single bone which had been gnawed by small animals and which looked like it might be from one of them. Or it might have been from the ewe they had killed.

Williamson came three weeks later, and he frowned darkly and shook his head as Garrity told him what had happened. He looked at Mayrah with a smile of respect when Garrity told him what she had done. Garrity didn't want even a vague and indirect association between him and the bushrangers, and he didn't tell Williamson that one of them had been named Cummings.

They ate, and Williamson and Garrity sat and smoked their pipes and drank tea as Mayrah rummaged through her belongings in her nightly routine of examining them. Williamson had sent men to Sydney for the sheep he and Garrity were buying on shares, and they talked about them and where Williamson anticipated pasturing them. When Garrity gave Mayrah his pipe to let her puff on it, Williamson rose and went to his saddlebags, dug around in them, and returned to the fire with a new pipe for Mayrah.

- 9 -

The station houses and pens were in the center of a broad, level stretch which extended for miles in all directions, its single distinctive feature a tree-lined creek which slashed across it. Garrity's first glimpse of the houses and pens was from the top of a low bulge in the ground some six or seven miles away, and what had once been a rude collection of shacks, sheds, and hastily-erected pens among scrubby trees and brush had changed, reflecting the expansion of Williamson's flocks and income, to become a sprawling complex of buildings and large, sturdy pens which covered acres. The trees had been girdled and cut down and the brush had been cleared away. The plain was a sea of thick, rich grass which stretched as far as the eye could see, broken only by the creek and an area of bare, hard-packed earth around the houses and pens.

All of the houses were on piles to help keep out termites, snakes, and poisonous insects, and to elevate them above the ground when it became a sea during downpours of rain. They were all of unpainted wood, and in a line along the creek. Williamson's was the largest, six or seven rooms with a broad veranda in front, and tall pepper trees around it provided shade. Four large wooden catchment tanks for storing water were further along the creek, then was a house of three or four rooms for the head stockman and a row of several smaller houses for other married men. The shearing shed, barrack buildings, storerooms and workshops were scattered around in an area fifty yards from the houses, and behind them the pens began, large squares which covered the bare area out to the edge of the grass.

Several flocks were already in, because some of the pens were full. And two men had a flock out grazing. The two men began circling their flock and waving at their dogs as they moved further away, and Garrity whistled at his dogs and sent them racing along the long, wide, undulating ribbon of trotting sheep in front of him to straighten a couple of slight curves in it. If two flocks approached each other in the open, the most experienced stockmen and the best of dogs would be unable to keep them from flowing together like quicksilver. A ripple in the line of sheep ahead of him straightened, then the other one disappeared. Garrity relaxed in the saddle again.

Mayrah was riding along behind him on the other horse, perched on the saddle with both of her legs on one side and the stirrips dangling loosely, and she carried the other musket and her long stick across her lap. Large packs behind the saddles carried all of their belongings, and they had dragged poles for a fold along behind them until the previous night, when they had left them to pick them up on the way back. It was March and the weather had turned cool with an early autumn. Garrity wore a long sheepskin he had made, and Mayrah wore one which had been in one of the bushrangers' packs, a worn, ragged, man's wool coat with baggy pockets which hung almost down to her knees and with the sleeves cut off to fit her arms. Her hat was pulled down tightly on her head, almost hiding her face, and she smiled wanly and nodded when he looked back at her and pointed to the buildings and pens, indicating their destination. In other circumstances she might have been curious, but the trek to drive the sheep in for the shearing had been hard on her because of the continuing nausea which had troubled her since she had become heavy with the child she was carrying.

Several men were moving about the pens and buildings, and a man on a horse rode out from the buildings toward the flock. A couple of other men ran on foot toward a corner pen. Garrity reined his horse away from the rear of the sheep and motioned for Mayrah to take up her position, and she nodded as she flipped her reins and nudged her horse closer. He rode several yards away from the sheep so he wouldn't deflect them from their path, then kicked his horse into a fast trot and rode toward the other rider. It was Iverson, the head stockman, a burly man somewhat older than Garrity who always treated Garrity with a cordiality tinged with wariness because he knew Garrity had been offered the head stockman job several times. He waved and called out cheerfully as they approached each other.

"Are you all right, Pat?"

"I'm all right. Are you, Jim?"

"Aye," he replied, reining his horse around by Garrity's. "Frank said you had a spot of trouble with bushrangers."

"I did, and I have these horses and such for my trouble."

"And thanks from all of us for being shot of them," Iverson said, standing in his stirrups and looking toward the rear of the flock curiously. "Frank said you have a woman. That'll be her, I expect?"

"Aye, that's her."

"Frank said she was an abo. From here she could

muster for a white woman."

"Aye, and closer still."

"I'm sure she does. Is she all right, then?"

"She's a little off her feed because she's carrying a nipper, but she'll do."

"With a nipper, is she?" Iverson chuckled. "By God, it didn't take you long to finish that chore, did it? Well, she'll feel better when she's had a sit-down. There's an empty house and Frank said you're to have the use of it while you're in. And I'll have your sheep done for you tomorrow so you can leave the next day if it suits you."

"It suits me. Is Frank all right?"

"He's a little off his peak, because he has his years and he still thinks he's a yearling. But he's all right. I'll just go on up and give the boys a hand with the gate, Pat, and I'll talk to you again in a few minutes."

"Right, Jim."

Iverson jabbed his heels into his horse's ribs and cantered away toward the corner pen, where the men were opening the wide gates. Garrity reined his horse around and looked at the rear of the flock. A few sheep were trying to break away and snatch mouthfuls of grass, but Mayrah was handling them easily enough, reining her horse around and driving them back into the flock. Iverson reached the pen, and he leaned down from his horse to take one side of the gate and drag it open as the two men opened the other side. The long line of sheep was guiding slightly to the right of the gate, and Garrity kicked his horse into a trot and rode along the side of the line, shouting and waving at a dog to turn the front of the line back to the left.

There was a large water tank in a pen to the left of the corner pen and the sheep had been without water all day. They began veering toward it as they approached and smelled it. Iverson was sitting on his horse at the side of the gate and the two men were sitting on the top rail of the pen, and other men had come out of a pen further along the line of pens and were looking at the sheep approaching. It would be easy to lose control of the sheep because of their thirst, and it was a matter of pride in his ability with sheep to drive them smoothly into the pen, without the help of the men who were watching and who would assist him if he called them or if the sheep began scattering on him.

The only way to keep them from breaking toward the water was to make them run so their momentum would take them into the pen. He reined his horse closer to the sheep and kicked it into a canter, whistling and whooping at the dogs. The dogs began darting back and forth and barking, and a ripple ran along the line of sheep as they began trotting more rapidly. He cantered along the line of sheep, shouting at them, and they began running as he neared the front of the line. It was pointed directly at the gate, and he rode back along the line toward the rear of the flock to keep the line straight.

Mayrah cantered along at the rear, whistling and jabbing her stick at stragglers and keeping them up with the rest of the flock. Fine dust rose from the grass as the sheep ran through it, and a thick cloud rose at the pen as the first of the sheep ran through the gate. A bulge in the line suddenly formed near the rear of the flock as some of the sheep veered toward the water, and another one formed near the middle. He charged his horse toward the nearest one, and through the dust he saw Mayrah's horse running around the end of the flock and forcing the others back into line. They straightened out again, and he wheeled his horse around and rode back toward the pen. The sheep streamed smoothly through the billowing dust around the gate and into the pen at a dead run. It was over when the dogs began peeling back from the front of the line and ran back along the sides to keep the line straight and the sheep running into the pen. Mayrah reined back around to the rear again, forcing stragglers into the flock, and the dust boiled up in a choking cloud as the remainder of the flock flowed inside.

"That was a good job, Pat," Iverson called, riding

toward Garrity through the dust. "We were chasing sheep over half of the station yesterday, because every flock that came in scattered."

Garrity smiled and shrugged, glancing back at Mayrah as she followed him out of the boiling cloud of dust. "I have my horses and my woman to help me."

"And did it more neatly than the whole station mob could have and all," Iverson chuckled, reining his horse up and wiping the dust from his face with his sleeve. "The house on the end is the empty one, and you can put your horses in the stock pen down at the other end—there's ample fodder and water for them there. And Frank's in the shearing shed, if you want to speak to him."

"I'll stop in and speak to him on my way over, then."

"You might want to stop in at the rouseabout barrack, too," Iverson said, smiling widely. "Most of the stockmen are over there, and Frank sent over some rum to keep everyone company."

"Aye, I'll stop in and have a sip."

"Have one for me as well," Iverson laughed, turning his horse away. "It's good to have you in, Pat."

"It's good to be in, Frank."

Iverson rode back toward the pen, shouting at the two men to open the inner gates and divide the sheep, and Garrity rode along the long line of pens toward the buildings, with Mayrah and the dogs following him. Some of the sheep in the pens had been washed and were ready for shearing, and others had been shorn, thin and pink-looking and covered with red nicks from the shears. There was always a momentous feeling associated with arriving with the sheep to have them shorn, and after the quiet solitude of the bush there seemed to be enormous numbers of people about and a constant scurry of activity. Most of the activity centered around the shearing shed and the smaller holding pens behind it, and he turned his horse toward it. Men occasionally passed as Garrity rode along at a slow walk, nodding to him and looking curiously at Mayrah.

It was a long, open shed, with four shearers working at the end adjacent to the holding pens, rapidly stripping the wool off as handlers scurried around them and gathered it up to take to the sorting tables, dragged out sheep which had been shorn, and pulled in other sheep from the pens. Men worked at the sorting tables, grading and piling the wool, and other men carried the piles to the press in the other end of the shed. The press clanked and rattled, forming large bales of compressed wool. Men dragged them out and covered them with canvas, and they were rolled out the back of the shed. Sheep bleated, and men cursed and shouted as they ran back and forth. Williamson sat on a tall stool near the middle of the shed where he could see everything, and he occasionally bellowed at shearers who injured sheep, sorters who graded the wool too hastily, and at the men at the press when the wool began piling up.

Garrity dismounted and tied his horse to a rail at the corner of the pens. The dogs clustered around him, nervous and excited by the unaccustomed noise and activity around them, and he snapped his fingers at them and ordered them to lie down. They obeyed and Mayrah edged her horse closer to Garrity's and relaxed in her saddle as Garrity turned toward the shearing shed. Williamson smiled widely and stepped down from his tall stool to shake Garrity's hand and slap his shoulder, but their conversation was brief. The interior of the shed was bedlam, and Williamson was constantly distracted by the bleat of a sheep scraped by the sharp edge of a pair of shears or by a handler scattering wool as he carried it to a sorting table. It was some months before the sheep they had bought together would arrive and he didn't have any more information about them, and he reiterated what Iverson had said about using the house and about the rum at the rouseabout's barrack. They shook hands again and he told Garrity he would come to see him when the day's work was over, and Garrity left.

The rouseabout barrack was a long, narrow building of

rough, warped boards and was canted to one side on its short piles. It had gaping, uneven, odd-sized holes for windows, a small, sagging porch in front, and a rickety, odorous privy at one side of it. The door was hanging loosely open with one of its hinges broken, and Garrity could see several men inside as he approached. He reined up and dismounted, and the dogs sat down around his horse and panted and sniffed curiously at the hut as he tied the horse to the pole. Mayrah moved her horse up beside his and relaxed in the saddle again as he climbed up the worn, dusty steps to the porch.

There were half a dozen stockmen sitting around on the heavy, crudely-made cots, along with a couple of new men who had come to talk to Williamson about jobs, and the cook the shearers and washers took with them as they went from station to station. Garrity knew all of the stockmen from when they had worked together on the Nepean, and he shook hands with them, with the newcomers and the cook as they introduced themselves, and took a drink from one of the bottles being passed around as he sat down on the edge of a cot. Someone asked him about the bushrangers, and he gave them a terse, brief description of what had happened. The talk turned to bushrangers in general and other matters of common concern, and Garrity listened and took drinks from the bottles as they were passed around. Most of the stockmen had spots of scurvy on their hands from their steady diet of damper and mutton, pork, and beef, and there was talk about Williamson's efforts to get lime juice to cure it. Garrity had suffered from it before and one of the stockmen asked him how he had cured it, and he shook his head and shrugged. He suspected that it had been cured by things Mayrah had collected, a root which tasted like a small yam, a fruit which she called a quandong, and other wild berries and fruits, but he didn't want to expose himself to ridicule.

Reality always fell short of expectation. He'd had Mayrah use his knife the night before to trim his mustaches, beard, and hair, and he had cut her her hair in a short, even line all the way around her head. And they had both washed their clothes. It was something he had done for as long as he had worked for Williamson, answering some vague and ill-defined need he felt to prepare for his arrival after a year of grazing the sheep, a need which found its satisfaction in the rules of cleanliness and appearance ground into him at the orphanage. And one which others apparently didn't experience, because most of them had ragged, unkempt beards, mustaches, and hair, and some of them wore clothes which were stiff with the accumulated soil and sweat of months. But the anticipation of arriving at the station had always generated the urge to make some appropriate gesture in recognition of the event. And the arrival was always anticlimactic and disappointing.

The hut was cluttered and dirty, and the air was hot, stuffy, and heavy with the strong odor of sweat, unwashed clothes, and the stockmen's uncured sheepskin coats. He was tired and concerned about Mayrah, but the gathering upon arrival to share the bottles Williamson provided was routine for the stockmen, married and unmarried. It was aggravating, but it was what everyone did. One of the newcomers kept looking out through the doorway at Mayrah with what seemed to be more than courteous interest, which was also aggravating. One of the men went to the window and vomited out of it, and another one lay down on one of the bunks and dozed off. A couple of bottles were emptied, and more were opened.

When the cook got unsteadily to his feet and weaved toward the door, talking about starting the evening meal for the shearers and washers, it seemed like a good opportunity to leave. The men laughed and joked with the cook as he staggered to the doorway, then began talking among themselves again. Garrity took a drink from a bottle and passed it on, then rose and glanced around, moving toward the door.

142

"I'll be going along as well. I'll see all of you again before we leave."

"There's ample rum here yet, Pat," one of the stockmen said.

"I'll give up my share. I've got my dogs and horses to see to, and Frank has given me the use of a house and I think I'll have a look at it."

The newcomer who had been looking through the doorway at Mayrah looked up at him and laughed. "For my part, you could make free to stop in the barrack if you bring that woman with you."

The drunken smile faded from the man's face as Garrity's expression changed to rage, and he scuttled away. Garrity seized the front of his shirt and coat and jerked him to his feet, and brought his right fist around in a powerful blow, lifting himself to his toes and putting the strength from his legs, back, and arm behind his knuckles as they crushed into the man's nose and mouth. Blood exploded from nose and mouth, his shirt and coat were jerked from Garrity's grip, and he reeled across the hut and slammed into the wall with a force which shook the building. Garrity took three quick steps, his long, heavy sheepskin coat swaying, and as the man bounced away from the wall he drove his fist into the man's stomach. He doubled over, and Garrity brought his right around again and hit him in the side of the head. Blood splattered on the wall as he careened into it again, and he slumped to the floor.

There was sudden silence in the building. Garrity stood with his fists clenched, looking down at the man. The man moved his limbs weakly, and he moaned hoarsely as thick, heavy streams of blood trickled from his nose and lips to the rough, grimy floorboards. Garrity stepped forward and cocked his foot to kick the man in the side, and Campbell, a tall, heavyset stockman with long, white mustaches and beard, stepped in front of Garrity, leaned over the man and gathered him up by an arm and a leg,

143

and threw him out a window.

"There, Pat, that does him. You have him, and it'll do you no good with Frank if you kill him. Let's have another drink. Give us a bottle here."

The other newcomer was on his feet, his fists clenched and his face white and trembling with anger. "By God, my mate was only having a bit of fun, and there was no need for you to—"

"There's no need for your mouth in it, either," Campbell said, stepping between Garrity and the other man and glaring down at him. He put his hand against the man's chest and pushed him away. "I don't know how it is in bloody Sydney and I couldn't care less, but that sort of remark about a man's woman here will get someone killed. Now let's have a drink and have an end to it. A lesson's been taught and learned, and there's the end of it."

"By God, I'll not stand aside and see my mate—"

"An end to it, I said!" Campbell bellowed, shoving the man down on a cot and glaring at him warningly. "Another bloody word from you, and you'll be out there with him! Because I'll put you there!" He straightened up and glanced around, then reached for a bottle a man was holding. "Here, give us that. Now have you a sip, Pat."

Garrity took the bottle and drank from it, then handed it back to Campbell and nodded as he turned toward the door.

"We'll see you again directly, then, Pat," Campbell said.

"Aye," Garrity replied shortly as he went out the door.

Mayrah was looking at the doorway with a dark frown, on the point of sliding down from her horse, and she settled herself on the saddle again and looked at him interrogatively. Garrity forced a smile and nodded to her as he jerked his horse's reins loose from the post, and he turned the horse and led it toward the houses by the creek. The dogs began trotting along beside him, and Mayrah's horse clopped along behind his. He glanced over his shoulder at the rouseabout barrack. The other newcomer and one of the stockmen had gathered the man up and were carrying him around to the steps to take him inside.

A dim roadway ran along in front of the line of houses, and aborigines had built shelters along the creek a few yards from the houses. Two small children stood on the roadway and looked at them curiously as they approached. Both of them were naked, one an aborigine and the other a white child. The house had two small rooms, with a stone firepit and a solid, heavy homemade table and pair of chairs in the back room. A bedframe was built against the wall in the front room. The bedframe was covered with a canvas bag filled with raw wool for a mattress, there were candles on a shelf in the back room, and firewood had been cut and stacked under the porch. The house was neat and clean, and it had apparently been unoccupied for some time because grass had grown up on the path to the privy, a tiny structure which overhung the creek on shaky stilts.

Mayrah prowled through the house with intense curiosity as Garrity carried in the packs and saddles from the horses and stacked them in the front room, then she began taking things out of the packs. Garrity led the horses to the stock pen and turned them into it, then returned to the house and took the bucket to the water tanks and filled it. When he came back, Mayrah had a fire going in the firepit and was cutting slices of salt pork into a pan. He put the bucket on the table and filled and lit his pipe with a twig from the firepit, looking at her. Even the odor of food seemed to bother her at times, and she looked pale and drawn. But she nodded tightly when he asked her if she was all right, and he went back through the house and sat on the steps, smoking his pipe. Presently he heard her vomiting out the window in the back room.

She was unable to eat. He ate while she sat on the bedframe in the front room, and she went back in to put the leftovers away and wash his plate when he took his pannikin of tea through the front room to the porch. The

145

food and hot tea had dissipated the mild euphoria from the rum he had drunk, a headache throbbed in his temples, and he felt a dull, unfocussed dissatisfaction. There seemed to be activity all around him, the sounds of other people moving around in the other houses and men moving about the buildings across the open area, a ceaseless, churning motion. He felt as though it involved him but he had no control over it. Anger toward the man at the barrack remained, becoming resentment toward the other men by association, and he was worried about Mayrah.

Mayrah came out with the billy and her pipe, and she refilled his pannikin and sat down on the steps by him, puffing on her pipe. She had taken off her hat, washed her face, and dusted her clothes, and her small, smooth face still looked very pale, making the deep, wide scar on her forehead stand out in relief.

"Are you all right, then?"

She exhaled a puff of smoke, spat, and nodded as she put the pipe back in her mouth. "'Right."

"I don't bloody understand how. How can someone be all right when they can't bloody eat?"

"*Birrahlee* big and strong, samesame you. Bimeby him like tucker."

"All the same, I'm going to get someone to look after you."

She took her pipe out of her mouth and exhaled and spat again, then gave him a cool glance and looked away as she put her pipe back in her mouth. From the time she had first become pregnant, he had been worried about her delivering the baby with only him to help her. But it wasn't unknown for aborigines to have more than one wife, and she had been darkly suspicious about his suggestion that he get another woman to help her. He sighed heavily and looked away, puffing on his pipe. During the months they had been together, she had shown an increasing capacity for independent thought, which made her companionship more of a pleasure. But she had also shown an increasing willingness to express opposed opinions, which was occasionally irritating.

Men began dispersing from the shearing shed near sunset, the shearers and washers leaving in a group and others wandering about between the buildings. Aborigines living in the shelters further along the creek crossed the open space toward their shelters, and some of the men who lived in the houses waved to Garrity as they walked toward their houses. Smoke eddied along the creek from cooking fires and the mosquitoes and flies became thicker as dusk approached, then a breeze stirred and dissipated both the smoke and the insects. Fires burned brightly among the aborigines' shelters and candles and lanterns glowed in the windows of the buildings as darkness fell, and the sounds of the insects and frogs along the creek became louder. Several lanterns burned in the shearing shed, where men were working late.

A lantern crossed in the open space toward the end house, casting a yellow glow on the dusty ground and dimly illuminating the baggy trouser legs of the man carrying it as it swung back and forth. It was Williamson's characteristic tread, and he was carrying a bucket in his other hand. The dogs under the house growled as he started across the road. Garrity spoke sharply to the dogs, and Williamson called out.

"Pat?"

"I'm here, Frank."

He held up the lantern as he approached the steps, and he smiled at Mayrah. "Are you all right, Mayrah?"

"'Right."

"We butchered an ox, and I thought I'd bring you over a ration of it."

The bottom of the bucket was covered with fresh meat, gleaming a dark red in the dim light of the lantern and spotted with clusters of flies crawling around on it, and the odor of the blood and meat was rich and heavy.

"That'll go down good," Garrity said. "Take it on in and bring his bucket back, Mayrah. Have a sit-down, Frank."

"Aye, I will for a minute, then," Williamson said, handing the bucket to Mayrah, and he put the lantern down on the bottom step and sat down with a heavy sigh as she crossed the porch with the bucket. "It's been a long day, Pat."

"I suppose I've done by bit today to add to your burdens and all. I clouted a man around over at the barrack."

"That?" Williamson snorted. "I heard about that, and I don't bear you any ill will for that, Pat. And his arse will be off this station as soon as he can walk. I'm short of men, but not that short."

Garrity looked at him and shrugged as he looked away. "That's no reason not to hire him if you need men, Frank. He might make a good man when he learns to keep his damper hole closed."

"Aye, it could be that I'll think about it again, then," Williamson said, then he chuckled. "He wouldn't be able to eat me out of rations, in any event. They said you belted about half of his teeth out."

Garrity laughed and nodded, tapping his pipe against the side of the steps, and he took out his tobacco and knife and cut a small piece off the tobacco. "Is your wife all right, then?"

"As far as I know. She's in Sydney."

"Sydney?" Garrity replied in a surprised tone.

"Aye," Williamson replied heavily. "She said she'd had as much of the bush as she wanted, and she left with the boys the last time the carts brought supplies. Jim went along to help her get fixed in Sydney and to look at the stock on the Nepean, and he said she's well situated and all."

Garrity divided the tobacco with Williamson, and they rolled it between their palms and filled their pipes. Williamson's tone had been despondent, and it was a subject Garrity wasn't sure how to address. "Would you

148

like a bite of tucker? There's ample left, because Mayrah is off her feed."

Williamson shook his head as he opened the mantle on the lantern and lit his pipe, and he puffed on the pipe and handed the lantern to Garrity. "No, the cook goes over and fixes for me. Jim said that you had told him Mayrah has been off her feed."

Garrity lit his pipe, closed the mantle on the lantern, and put the lantern back down on the step as he puffed his pipe. "Aye, she has, but she says she'll be all right. That doesn't bother me as much as the thought of what's going to happen when she drops it, and I've been thinking of finding a woman to help her."

"That might be wise, because you've some size to you and the baby might be big for her. There are a few old women among those down the creek, and I could talk to my handlers tomorrow and see if you could get one of them."

"That would be good as long as she's old and ugly. I don't want Mayrah cutting off my cod piece."

Williamson laughed uproariously and stamped his foot on the step as he slapped Garrity's shoulder, and Garrity chuckled and nodded as he puffed his pipe. Mayrah came back out of the house with the bucket, a pannikin, and the billy full of tea, and she filled the pannikins and sat on the edge of the porch as Garrity and Williamson drank the tea, smoked their pipes, and talked. Williamson's moment of hilarity faded as they discussed the sheep they had bought, and he talked about the difficulties the stockmen would have in driving the sheep from Sydney to the station and about the possibilities of profit. The drought in the area to the east was continuing, and the wool market had been fluctuating rapidly. He sounded weary, depressed, and morose, as though the problems of the station had become almost too much for him, as though they had become so burdensome that they obscured his vision of what he possessed.

When Williamson left, Mayrah took the billy and

pannikins into the house, then there was silence. Garrity sat on the steps and chewed the stem on his pipe, thinking about what Williamson had said. The lights in the buildings across the open space went out and the fires among the shelters further along the creek died down. The place was quiet, but it still had a feel of a seething undercurrent of poised energy ready to burst into motion. He tapped his pipe against the side of the steps and put it in his pocket as he rose to go inside.

Mayrah's tempetuous and demanding passion of their first weeks together had changed into a ready willingness which had lasted through the time when she had become pregnant. Then she had become more demanding again, conveying the impression that she sought a kind of reassurance provided by the merging of their bodies. When her stomach had become inconveniently large, it had seemed to him a symbolic barrier to gluttony when the purpose of pleasure had been fulfilled, and she had shown an inventiveness in devising positions to circumvent the awkward size of her stomach which to him was suggestive of decadence. The dim light coming through the window made her brown body seem darker and his seem lighter as they lay on the coarse canvas cover over the lumpy wool, and her fingers moved restlessly, gently insistent, keeping him from sleep and stirring a response from levels which bypassed his will. She turned her back to him and opened her thighs wide to fit him to her, and he was hesitant and cautious, afraid of injuring the life within her. Long minutes passed as he moved slowly, and the bright light of the moon streaming through the trees outside and coming in the window crept across them, subduing the difference in the colors of their skin and making them much the same as their limbs entwined. Then he was satisfied in his way and she in hers, and she turned in his arms and put her arms around his neck and her head on his shoulder to sleep. Her breath was sour from vomiting, but it wasn't unpleasant to him and he went to sleep with his lips touching hers.

She was up well before daylight, moving around in the back room in the flickering light of the firepit and yawning and buttoning her shirt as she filled the billy and put it on the fire and began warming the leftover pork, rice, and damper from the evening before, and her teeth shone in the firelight as she smiled at him and touched his arm with a light pressure of the tips of her fingers in a silent reference to the night before. There were sounds of activity outside as he ate, men who lived in the other houses shouting at each other as they went to work and hoarse cursing and shouting from the washers as they took a flock to a waterhole on the other side of the aborigine shelters, and there was a seething bustle of activity around the shearing shed when he put on his coat and went out into the chilly grey of early morning.

The dogs came from under the house, yawning, stretching, and shivering in the frosty air, and they started to follow him away from the house. He ordered them back and crossed the open space to the stock pen to check on his horses. They were munching contentedly on a pile of fodder in the corner of the pen with the station horses and a few span of oxen, and he returned to the house, gathered up the saddles and bridles, and carried them to the harness shed to oil them and replace worn and rotted pieces of leather. As he was working on them, a couple of aborigines who worked for Williamson as handlers came in to talk to him. Williamson had told all the aborigines that Garrity was looking for an old woman, and both of the men were prosperous enough to have two or three wives each, some of whom were relatively older women. One of them also had an older female relative whose specific relationship to him was of a nature which was beyond the scope of the men's pidgin English to describe.

Garrity walked over to the cluster of shelters in the trees and brush along the creek, and the two men shouted and summoned their wives. The activity also drew other women, a crowd of children of various ages, old men, and men who weren't working, and they gathered around.

151

When other men found out what was happening, they also began producing women ranging in age from children to grandmothers, angering the two men Garrity had accompanied and producing confusion, heated arguments, and pushing and shoving. Garrity became irritated and shouted and cursed at the other men to leave him alone, feeling resentful and self-conscious because of the suggestive tone of the giggling and comments around him. The men got the women lined up, and they were all unprepossessing in appearance to him, but he was unsure of how Mayrah would view them. Then the older relative joined the line. She was of indeterminate but substantial age, with bony arms, shanks, and shoulders, a pot belly which almost concealed the scrap of pubic hair, and long, flat dugs which hung down on her thin ribs. Some kind of infection or disease had made most of her hair come out, and the rest was cropped off in uneven patches. She appeared to be completely toothless, and her face was a maze of crevices and wrinkles, with a single, glaring, red-rimmed eye. She didn't look very strong or healthy, but her appearance would unquestionably eliminate any doubt Mayrah might have of libidinous intent on his part. The man wanted ten shillings for her, and Garrity argued him down to five and told him to tell the old woman to collect her belongings and go to the house.

He returned to the harness shed and finished the work on his saddles and bridles, and when he carried them back toward the house the old woman was coming along the road toward the house, carrying her stick, a bark water container balanced on her head, her other belongings in a piece of ragged canvas hanging down her back and slung from a flat rope of braided grass across her forehead, and her single eye fixed on him. Garrity carried the saddles and bridles into the house and told Mayrah about the woman, and she glared at him in speechless outrage, snatched up her stick, and stamped outside. He followed her outside, and her anger evaporated when she saw the old woman. She looked at the old woman with a mollified

152

expression, shouted at the dogs as they came from under the house and growled threateningly, and beckoned her inside. Garrity was mildly surprised that Mayrah and the old woman apparently spoke languages which were somewhat different and had a degree of difficulty in understanding each other. But it was sufficient for communication. The old woman's manner was ingratiating and Mayrah's imperious as she stood over her and presumably explained what her duties would be, occasionally punctuating her comments with a rap of her stick on the old woman's forehead.

During the afternoon Garrity took his horses to the farrier's shed and had them reshod, then he returned them to the stock pen and went to the storeroom to draw his rations. It took several trips to carry them to the house, and he stacked them against the wall in the front room while Mayrah sorted through them with the old woman helping her. In Mayrah's conversation with the old woman, he picked up the fact that she was called Doolibah, a reference to her lack of hair.

Mayrah had indeed been troubled by his intentions to get another woman and was relieved by the outcome. She was in an exceptionally good mood. She also seemed to feel better than she had for the past days, because she ate with him. The beef had boiled until it was soft and tender, and they sat at the table in the back room and ate beef, peas, and damper as the old woman huddled near the warmth of the firepit. After they ate, Mayrah fed the old woman and the dogs, then filled her pipe and they sat on the steps in front of the house and smoked as Garrity finished the billy of tea.

Williamson came by and sat and talked with Garrity again. The shearing was almost over and the yield of wool had been exceptionally high, and he was in a more optimistic mood than the night before. They talked again about their sheep, and Williamson speculated on plans for the coming years. The land policies which had been established in Sydney and London were confused and contradictory, but it was beginning to appear that a situation might eventually develop which would result in legal ownership of the land they possessed. Williamson's latest information on land policies had come from a Captain Charles Sturt, an explorer and surveyor who had traveled through the area some months before and had stayed at the station for a few days to rest his animals and complete details of his maps of the area. The man had apparently traveled near Garrity's grazing area, because he had designated the district on his maps by a name he had derived from a topographical feature which he had observed and with which Garrity was familiar. He had seen the mountain the aborigines called Wayamba, and he had called it the Broken Hill.

– 10 –

Doolibah's appearance was deceptive, because she had a wiry strength and a tenacious grip on life. She trotted effortlessly along for hours each day on circuits to each side of the trail with her belly bobbing and her dugs flopping, her single, glaring orb sharper than most pairs of eyes as she spotted lizards, snakes, insects, and grubs, snatched them up and gummed them with relish. Each night she did her chores, devoured her share of the meal, looked after Mayrah, then curled up in her blanket in a deep, soundless sleep which could immediately change to alert attention with the bulging, bloodshot eye staring around at the slightest movement around the camp. And her skeletal appearance had been the result of starvation, because her bony body filled out somewhat during the leisurely trek back to the grazing area.

The last pasture Garrity had used prior to taking the sheep in for shearing had been grazed down, and when they returned he picked out a place near the broken hill to build the shelter. It was more arid and the graze was poorer, but the hills would provide shelter from the frigid winter winds, and he planned on moving the sheep through the area during the winter and working them into the better graze on the rolling terrain to the north and east in the spring. The area was rich in heavy concentrations of minerals, and the stretches of claypan left by rains were streaked with white, red, and ocher. Mayrah and Doolibah found many signs of temporary camps made by their people, and Garrity was at first concerned over having his sheep in a place heavily traveled by aborigines. Then Mayrah explained that the camps had been made by small parties which had traveled surreptitiously across tribal lines, and such trips were ordinarily undertaken only in late spring and early autumn, when the weather and availability of game would provide optimum conditions. The colored clay was what drew them to the place, and from the scattered artifacts and signs of camps in the area, aborigines had been coming from long distances away for centuries to mine the colored clay and carry it off to use for body decorations and to decorate utensils and implements.

Garrity was still apprehensive about remaining in the area and was pondering moving back to the north until Mayrah and Doolibah found a cairn of stones with a stack of carved sticks in it at the foot of the broken hill. The structure had some sort of religious or supernatural significance for them and they regarded it as a highly auspicious place for childbirth, so he decided to stay until Mayrah delivered the child.

She was in labor for almost thirty-six hours, and it was late afternoon on a grey, wintery day when he saw the smoke rising from the direction of the tiny shelter they had built by the cairn, the signal that the child had been born. He was breaking the ice on a shallow, muddy pond so the sheep could drink when he noticed it, and he finished watering the sheep, took them back to the fold, and walked across the field of scrubby mulga to the narrow, rocky cleft in the side of the hill where the cairn and shelter were located. He had slept poorly the night before and had eaten little that evening and nothing during the day, and he felt numb and dazed as he pushed his way through the brush. Doolibah looked like a grotesque apparition as she crouched by the fire in which she had burned the afterbirth, a blanket clutched around her shoulders and the muddy white of her eye a solid red from her many hours without sleep and from the smoke of the fire. She lifted off a section of bark from the front of the shelter so Garrity could crawl inside and look at the baby. Mayrah was asleep, looking pale and drawn. The baby was very large, a brawny boy, wrinkled and red and spotted with dried blood and slime, and he was bawling lustily. Garrity tucked the blankets back around Mayrah and the baby and backed out of the shelter. Doolibah moved back to the fire and tossed more sticks and green twigs on it, her bulging eye swiveling around and glaring up at him. Garrity pulled his sheepskin coat closer against the chilly wind and looked up at the grey clouds scudding across the sky. It seemed that there was something that he should say or do, but he couldn't think of what it might be. He walked back toward the fold, thinking of what to call the baby, and he decided to call him Colin.

Because the birth had been difficult for Mayrah her recovery was slow, and it was almost a month before she was moving freely about with something approaching her former energy. The baby was very much like Garrity, with his blue eyes and indications of his brown hair, and even at a month he showed promise of growing rapidly to develop Garrity's large build. Garrity noticed spots of colored clay on the baby and found that Mayrah and Doolibah had been drawing designs on him. Mayrah was unable to communicate the precise reason for the designs, but from her attempt to explain it was clear that they had

157

some supernatural function, which Garrity found distasteful. He ordered her to stop, and he decided to begin moving the sheep to the north and east and remove her from the temptation of the clay.

He moved the flock slowly, picking an area of pasture among the fields of scrub and low, flinty hills to spend a few days, then dismantling the fold and moving on again. Doolibah took care of the baby most of the time, carrying him in a canvas sling on her back which was lined with wool they pulled from the sheep and bringing him to Mayrah several times daily to be suckled. When Garrity observed that Mayrah and Doolibah were beginning to feed the baby bits of mutton and damper which they had chewed up, he told Mayrah firmly that the child was not to be fed pieces of snake, lizard, or other vermin.

The weather began to moderate as the terrain changed to rolling hills covered with spinifex and patches of forest. He found a good area with ample water a few miles from where the bushrangers had been killed, and they erected a semipermanent shelter which was large enough for all of them. Mayrah had by now recovered completely from childbirth, and it took him some time to develop her nonchalance about having Doolibah in the shelter with them at night when they made love. But Mayrah's returning demands overcame his modesty, and by the time Williamson came on his first trip of the new year, she was pregnant again.

Williamson was delighted with the baby, playing with him and jogging him on his knee with an enjoyment which was surprising to Garrity. He spent two days with them instead of the usual overnight visit, holding the baby as he and Garrity talked by the fire. The sheep they had bought had arrived, making the trek with very few losses, and Williamson had put them with a couple of good stockmen to graze. There had been more indications that land ownership would devolve upon the one who had possession, and Williamson had hired extra men and had started a major project to fence in as large an area as possible. A home paddock consisting of several thousand acres had already been enclosed, and Williamson intended to do the same to other paddocks to the north and as far south as the broken hill, if possible.

Her second pregnancy was hard on Mayrah because the summer was exceptionally hot and dry, and it became apparent that the baby would be due at about the same time that the sheep had to be driven in for the shearing. Williamson was deeply concerned about it and wanted to send out men to bring the flock in so Mayrah wouldn't have to make the trek, but she was adamantly opposed to the suggestion for reasons she had difficulty in communicating to Garrity. But the baby was stillborn several weeks before the time came to drive the sheep in, and Mayrah was barely able to make the trek because it had been another difficult delivery for her.

The men Williamson had hired to clear and fence the land had worked their way far to the south of the home paddock, and Garrity began seeing signs of their work two days before he reached the pens. Trees were being ringed to kill them and brush was being cleared so spinifex would grow. Fences were being constructed of log rails and of piles of brush staked into place where no timber was available. On the last day before he reached the station, he traveled across a fully-enclosed paddock which stretched for miles. The station looked much the same except that more barrack buildings had been built and the aborigine settlement along the creek was larger.

Mayrah had attributed the stillbirth to the inauspicious character of the place where they had been camped, as opposed to the more favorable climate for producing life at the broken hill. Garrity was more inclined to attribute it to fate, but his upbringing had provided him with the expectation of the wrath of God for living in sin, which made him fearfully suspicious that more misfortune might lie in store for him unless his relationship with Mayrah received divine sanction. He was on the station for four days, waiting for the flocks in which he owned a share to come in so he could look at them, and while he was there a traveling missionary passed through the station. The missionary married Garrity and Mayrah in a brief ceremony, with Williamson, Iverson, and Iverson's wife as witnesses, and the missionary gave Mayrah a small Bible and instructed Garrity to read to her from it.

When Garrity returned to his range with his flock, he waited anxiously for Williamson's first visit to find out how much wool the sheep had produced, but Williamson was ill and a rouseabout brought his first supplies of the new year. Williamson came the next trip, and he had already received word back from Sydney on the sale of the wool. The sheep had produced well, and Garrity's combined share from the flock he tended and the flocks he owned with Williamson was over fifteen hundred guineas. Garrity was satisfied, but Williamson was less pleased. The wool market had declined to an extent, and there had been economic problems in Sydney and a couple of banks which had overextended on credit had gone bankrupt. Wages had been going up since the cessation of convict assignments, which had increased Williamson's expenses to the extent that he had stopped fencing. Williamson suffered from a stomach complaint which lasted most of the summer, but he came twice more to bring supplies and told Garrity that the labor situation was becoming steadily worse.

Mayrah was pregnant again when they took the flock in for shearing that autumn. Garrity wanted to stay at the station until the flocks were sheared so he could find out how much wool they had produced, but Mayrah was apprehensive about going into labor early and they left to return to the grazing area as soon as Garrity had seen to his horses and rations, and his flock had been sheared. Mayrah wanted to have the baby at the same place Colin had been born, and they drove the flock on through the gently rolling hills to the rugged terrain in the vicinity of the broken hill. They made a semi-permanent camp and built a secure shelter, Doolibah and Mayrah built a small

160

shelter of sticks and bark near the cairn, and Garrity prowled the area with his flock again, finding good graze and working out his paths to the watering places. It overlapped the area where he'd had his flock two winters before, and at first he disregarded the signs of sheep he found, thinking that they had been left by his flock when he'd been there before. Some had, but he also began to find dung from sheep which had been in the area the previous summer. He began searching more closely, and he found clear evidence that a small flock had been pastured in the area for several months the preceding year. It came as something of a shock to realize that there were finite limits to the vast stretches of grazing land, and he felt an automatic, instinctive hostility toward those who had encroached upon what he regarded as his grazing territory.

They had been in the area something less than a month when Garrity was awakened early one morning by Mayrah and Doolibah hastily gathering up Mayrah's bag, bark water container, and other belongings. The boy started to follow them when they left through the scrub to go to the tiny shelter by the cairn, Mayrah clutching her belongings and bent over from the pains gripping her and Doolibah helping her along, but Garrity ordered his son back into the shelter. He took Colin with him when he drove the sheep out of the fold, and that afternoon he saw the smoke rising from the direction of the cairn and being whipped about by the keening wind, and he returned the sheep to the fold and left the child at the shelter as he went to the cairn. Mayrah had given birth to a girl. He thought about a name for her as he walked back toward the fold, and he decided to call her Sheila, after his mother.

Colin had become even more like Garrity from the time he had learned to walk, with a trace of his mother's dusky coloring and an aborigine cast to his features, but he was exceptionally large for his age and had clear blue eyes and finely-textured brown hair. By the time Sheila was a few weeks old, it was apparent that the mixture of bloods had

161

taken a different course in her. Her eyes were a sparkling black and her skin was dark, but the modeling of her features was Anglo-Saxon. She was also a large baby, not as large as Colin had been, but larger than average.

Garrity began taking a more personal interest in Colin after Sheila was born. His first words had been in his mother's language, and Garrity was concerned that aborigine might become the boy's primary language. When they started moving back to the north with the flock, Garrity began keeping Colin with him most of the time, talking to him, letting him play with the dogs, and carrying him or putting him on one of the horses when he became tired.

Williamson brought sweetmeats for the boy when he came, and he was delighted with Sheila, holding her and chuckling over her admiringly as Mayrah smiled proudly. He also brought a bag of potatoes among the rations, the first ones Garrity had seen for years, and Mayrah baked some of them in the coals to eat with the damper and fried pork. They were more tasteless than Garrity remembered, and he found himself comparing them unfavorably with the yam-like roots that Mayrah and Doolibah dug to bake in the fire.

The flocks in which Garrity owned a share had multiplied well the previous year and had produced an abundant amount of wool, but Williamson hadn't received word back from Sydney on the sale of the wool. And he also seemed strangely disinterested, willing to discuss it with Garrity but having a detached attitude as he did so. Garrity had seen Williamson in various moods, but this was one he had never before seen, a resigned indifference which Garrity found disturbing. And Garrity found that Williamson didn't share his concern that someone else had been grazing sheep in the vicinity of the broken hill.

He showed no indication of leaving the following morning. When Mayrah and Doolibah rose in the pre-dawn darkness and began warming up the leftover

162

potatoes and pork from the night before, he rolled up his blankets and tossed them on his saddle in the front of the shelter and sat down to eat with Garrity. They ate, then walked down to the fold to turn the sheep out, with Colin stumbling along behind them, and they walked along together in silence as they followed the flock and dogs to pasture. They reached the pasture where Garrity had been grazing the sheep for the past few days, then sat down in the shade of a clump of trees as the sheep scattered into clusters and moved slowly across the pasture, cropping the spinifex. Williamson chewed the stem of his pipe as he looked at Colin trotting busily back and forth and amusing himself with sticks and stones, and he smiled fondly.

"He'll do you credit in his time, Pat."

"Aye, if he's as good a man as his mother is woman. I've had my moments of doubt about getting children of mixed blood, but she's been a good wife to me."

"She has that, and she's less of a savage than a lot of white women I've known. And there's a lot the abos can teach us, if we'll but learn."

"I'll not debate that. Is your family all right?"

Williamson was silent for a long moment, and Garrity looked at him. He was holding the bowl of his pipe and chewing the stem, looking blankly across the pasture with an inscrutable expression. There had been times since Williamson's family had left to live in Sydney that he had seemed bitter about them, and Garrity looked away again, conscious that he might have broached a subject Williamson didn't want to discuss.

"My oldest boy was out for a while last summer."

"For a while?"

"Aye, a short while. He's been working with my wife's brother in Sydney, who's a businessman there, and it appears that he's more suited to that sort of work. The flies and mosquitoes tormented him a lot and he was sick all the time he was here. So I sent him back."

"It could be that your other boy will have something

more of the nature of a grazier."

Williamson shook his head, spat to one side, and wiped his mouth with the back of his hand and put his pipe back in his mouth. "His mother keeps writing me that this is no place for him, just like she did about the other one. And now that she's had her way with them for a time, she's probably right." He sighed heavily, chewing his pipe stem, then he smiled slightly and looked at Garrity. "You've been more of a son to me than my own, Pat."

Garrity looked down at the ground and scraped at it with his heel, then took his pipe out of his pocket and put it in his mouth. "I don't know what might have become of me if you hadn't taken me out of the orphanage, Frank."

"Aye, well, it could be that you've done as much or more for me than I've done for you, Pat."

Garrity wasn't sure of his precise meaning, but the comment didn't seem to call for a reply. He nodded silently, chewing his pipe, and Williamson became silent again, looking out across the pasture with a musing expression.

Williamson was silent much of the day, and his absent replies to Garrity's occasional comments indicated he was deep in thought. He walked around with Garrity as Garrity took the sheep to water and drove them to another pasture during the afternoon, and part of the time he amused himself with Colin, chuckling and talking to the boy as he looked at the things Colin found to play with, but most of the time he stared into the distance with a thoughtful, withdrawn expression. A few times he seemed on the point of talking about something, but he remained silent.

Late afternoon came, and they followed the flock back to the fold. Mayrah and Doolibah had the meal prepared, and they all sat around the fire and ate. Garrity and Williamson finished the tea and smoked their pipes as the sun began to set and the shadows gathered, and Mayrah and Doolibah stirred around the fire, putting the leftovers away, feeding the dogs, and cleaning the plates.

Williamson puffed on his pipe, staring into the fire, then glanced at Garrity.

"I'm thinking about packing it in, Pat."

It took a long, dragging second to assimilate the meaning of the quiet comment after the long silence, then a moment to analyze its impact on him. And then he felt a stab of wrenching despair. The number of sheep he owned was still too small to build a profitable station around. In a few years they would have been, but not now and he didn't have enough money to buy more. And he probably never would have, because it was unlikely that another grazier would be as generous as Williamson had been. At the same time that he was thinking about the sheep, his mind reeled at the thought of working for someone else. His years at the orphanage had collapsed together into dim and faded memories in his mind. It seemed that he had always worked for Williamson.

"A man should do what he feels he should, Frank."

"Aye, or what he has to. My health isn't what it was, and it's getting worse. I still have the selection on the Nepean, and the manager I have there is robbing me blind. And it's more of a size I can manage. Moreover, I'd be wasting my time and killing myself for nothing if I went at it to build something for my sons. All I have in mind now is providing for my old age, because I've come around to thinking that they've picked their own ways."

Garrity nodded, puffing on his pipe and looking into the fire. "What will you do with this place, then?"

"You could manage it for me, if you want to."

A gleam of hope suddenly penetrated the gloom. It would provide an interim for him to build his flocks and save his money so he would have enough to be independent. He nodded again. "Aye, I'd like to. But it wouldn't be honest of me to let you think that it would be permanent."

"I wouldn't want it to be. I've told you before that I want to see you with your own place. So if you want to, you can buy this place instead of managing it."

165

Garrity looked at him in surprise. "You know I don't have enough money to buy this station, Frank."

"I wouldn't demand ready money from you. The stock I have and the improvements I've made are worth well in excess of ten thousand guineas, and from you I'll take ten thousand. You should have something over four thousand after this year's wool is sold, and I'll take two thousand ready money and promissory note from you to pay off the remaining eight thousand at a thousand a year."

Garrity looked away into the distance, his eyes shining, the muscles in the sides of his face moving as he chewed the stem of his pipe, and a wide smile spreading across his face. "I'll do it," he said quietly, nodding.

"You should have a mind to what you're getting into, though, Pat. I can see some hard times coming for graziers, and many who don't have the burden of an eight thousand guinea debt will be failing. And I'm not selling you land, mind, because that's yet to be settled. I'm selling you buildings, stock, and a grazing license, because that's all I have. And some of those bloody sods in Sydney and London think an acre in New South Wales will graze fifty sheep like it will in England, when it's more like two acres for one sheep. You'll have them to fight, along with floods, fires, dingoes, thieving stockmen, bushrangers, and God knows what all else."

"I'll fight," Garrity murmured in a quiet, emphatic tone, looking at Williamson. "And I'll bloody win."

Williamson looked at him, a wide smile spreading across his face, and he slowly nodded. "Aye, I believe you bloody will and all." His smile suddenly disappeared and his lips tightened as his eyes became bright, and he looked away, clearing his throat. "If you were my boy, Pat, I'd stay here and we'd cover New South Wales with sodding sheep, head to arse," he said softly, his voice cracking.

Garrity looked away, silently nodding and puffing on his pipe.

Williamson cleared his throat again and wiped his nose with the back of his hand as he blinked rapidly. "Well, there it is, then," he said gruffly. "It's settled and done. And if you have a bad year and can't pay the thousand, I'll have seven percent interest instead. But if something happens to me and my wife's brother is looking after her affairs for her, you'd better have the thousand ready to put in his hand."

"I'll have it."

Williamson nodded, puffing on his pipe, and it made a wet, sucking noise. He tapped it against the side of his boat, then put it back in his mouth and chewed on it. "I'll send a stockman out to take your flock as soon as I get back, and you can come on in and find out what you're about. And I'll stay on for a couple of months to make sure you have your feet on the ground before I take myself on back to the Nepean and see if I can find cause to put that thieving manager in jail. After that, it'll just be a matter of people learning to call this Garrity Station instead of Williamson Station. Unless you have a different name in mind for it."

Garrity looked into the distance again as the last rays of the sun touched the tops of the hills and etched them in sharp outline against the sky, and the jagged peaks of the broken hill stood out in bold relief. "Aye, I do. I'll call it Wayamba Station."

Part Two

The Pommie

– 11 –

At some deep, distant level beneath the slough of despair
of experience, there was a vague, fragmentary memory of
the first sheep she had ever seen. It was a childhood
memory, a picture from the swirling scene around her
which had been captured and preserved by her mind from
a trip to the outskirts of Sydney, probably when she had
accompanied her father somewhere. It was a scintillating
jewel from a time when the mind had been unsullied and
had built soaring crystal palaces from the stones along the
road of life, a picture of a fresh, green pasture with the sun
beaming down from a clear, blue sky on wooly animals
gamboling about in the sheer joy of life.

But reality was a mockery of the memory. Instead of
fresh, green pastures, there was only a sprawling, limitless
stretch of brown, dessicated brush and hillocks of dry
grass, with occasional stands of trees, an empty, lonely,

desolate wasteland. The sun didn't beam down from a clear, blue sky. It blasted down from a brassy, pale sky with a torrid intensity which sapped the strength and heated the air until it burned in the throat and lungs. Sheep were scabrous instead of wooly. And instead of gamboling about in the sheer joy of life, they simply struggled to survive, like every other living creature.

They also stank. And they had fungus infections which were frequently so severe that they disintegrated as they trotted along. Others were so sunburned after shearing that the entire back from the neck to the rump became one gigantic blister, sometimes rupturing and drenching the sides with fluid which dried to a crusty brown, peeling back in a flap to hang over the rump and drag along the ground until another one stepped on it and ripped it all the way off, exposing glistening layers of tallow and muscle tissue. Some had ruptures, baggy swellings on the sides and stomachs, and others had worm infestations which made their necks so grotesquely swollen that they could hardly walk. Almost all of them were mulsed, the skin around the anus and over the stump left from the tail amputation stripped off so dags, or clots of manure couldn't gather. On a few dags had collected and had become fly-blown, and their rumps were masses of maggots. On others the mulsing had been hurried and they had been mutilated so badly that it was difficult to see how they still lived. Some were blind on one side, missing ears, or dragging a hamstrung leg from hurried shearing.

There were other diseases and deformities among them, some which stirred an agony of anguish at the sight of the dumb, grim struggle to finish the day's trek so sustenance could be gathered to provide energy for another day's struggle in a meaningless treadmill cycle of torture. But none were killed out of mercy. Life could at times continue under almost unbelievable circumstances, and they might live to finish the trek and endure until time to be sheared again. For the sake of man's desire for wool, they had been doomed to birth and condemned to live.

And even as she looked at the mass of bobbing bodies through the cloud of fine dust stirred up by their trotting hoofs, the time for the moment of respite in the long night of life came. Richardson, the head drover, a distant figure at the head of the column and dimly-seen through the cloud of dust, stood in his stirrups and motioned with his arm, and the drovers began shouting at the dogs and wheeling their horses around. The sheep began moving to one side and circling into a wide field of the short, silvery-brown grass as the dogs darted around and snapped at their heels. The wagon in front stopped. Her husband pulled back on the traces and shouted at the horses as he stepped on the brake lever, and their wagon lurched to a stop. He put the whip in the socket by the seat and wrapped the traces around it, and glanced at her as he started climbing down.

"Now get up there and see if you can make yourself of some benefit."

Elizabeth silently nodded and gathered her skirt, then stepped over the side of the wagon, placed her foot carefully on a spoke in the wheel, then lifted the other foot over the side of the wagon and stepped down to the ground. She was unwanted. Drovers were reluctant to allow women to accompany them because of the restrictions feminine presence placed on speech and behavior and because of women's lesser capacity to bear hardship, which had been explained to her in excruciating detail by her husband before the trip began as an example of the burden she represented to him. But it seemed to her that their speech and behavior had to be coarse beyond belief if her presence had inhibited them. And it also seemed to her that she and her husband had probably been permitted to join the drover and his men on the trek because her husband was taking up a position as head stockman of the station where the sheep were being driven, a position where he might be of future benefit to the drover. But there had been other concessions. It was

172

part of the agreement that she would help the cook, and her husband helped with the sheep. And still it appeared that her husband had misrepresented her to the drover. Her lack of knowledge about camp cooking had been the subject of a heated argument between her husband and the drover. And when she had been frightened by a snake in the wagon, there had been another argument between them and her husband had been enraged at her for screaming. There had been other things since, but the drover had been grimly silent, accepting the situation and apparently not wanting to make things worse for her. He was a hard, brusque man, like most, but he wasn't cruel, as many were.

The dust settled when the motion stopped. And the flies and mosquitoes gathered. The flies clotted around the eyes and the mouth and crawled into the nostrils in search of moisture, not biting but creating a maddening feeling of revulsion, and it was almost impossible to open one's mouth without getting one or two in it. The mosquitoes gathered in shrilly droning clouds, attacking all areas of exposed skin and even biting through clothes, raising lumps which itched constantly. She fanned them away from her face as she walked toward the cook's wagon, feeling an urgent need to relieve herself. But there was only a single small, thin stand of trees a hundred feet from the wagons. She would have to wait until dark, as she usually did. The men stared and smirked, and they scarcely bothered to conceal themselves from her when they relieved themselves. And when she went she would have to count them to make sure they were all around the fire, or there might be a coarse chuckle in the darkness. At best there would be the chilling fear of stepping on a snake and possibly the sickening disgust of walking where one of the men had been before.

Sweat seemed to be oozing from every pore, it had been weeks since she had bathed, and she could smell herself. Her hair was stiff with sweat and dust, and her head itched. She stood in abject misery and fanned at the flies

173

and mosquitoes as the cook and the man who took care of the horses unhitched the team from the cook's wagon. The man led the horses away and the cook walked around to the rear of the wagon. He was a short, thin man of forty or so with brooding eyes and a bitter line to his mouth, and like the drover he seemed to be simply callous rather than cruel. And, strangely, like so many men, his callousness seemed to extent even to himself. There were raw splotches of scurvy on his hands which he scratched at habitually, and it was common knowledge that it was caused by dietary deficiency. A potion of bark infusion from a chemist in Sydney or even a basket of fruit for a few coppers would cure it, but he simply didn't bother. Like a diseased or infected sheep, he continued along his path.

He dropped the tailgate on the wagon, pulled a bag of flour out, lifted a couple of large pans down from a hook on one of the bows supporting the canvas cover on the wagon, then turned away. Those were the things she couldn't lift or reach. She pulled out the bag of salt, then picked up the bucket and went around to the side of the wagon to dip water out of the barrel. One of the other men had separated a sheep from the flock and dragged it over to the side of the wagon near the water barrel, and the cook was looking at it. It was a ewe, and it had some kind of infection of the vulva which had swelled its organs grotesquely, and its rear legs were stiff and spread wide apart. It was standing with its head hanging, chewing a bite of grass it had snatched as it had been dragged away from the others. The cook motioned toward the other side of the wagon and walked behind Elizabeth as she carried the water to the rear of the wagon. He took a large knife from the rack of utensils on the sideboard of the wagon and went around to the side where the man had dragged the ewe. The ewe uttered a single, gagging bleat. But it was more a sound of relief than of pain and fright.

Elizabeth's task was to prepare the damper, a tough, flat, doughy bread made from flour, salt, and water. Two large panfuls were prepared, one to be used as bread for the evening meal and the morning and noon meal the next day, and the other to be drenched with tea thickened with brown sugar and called pudding for the same three meals. The damper, roasted mutton, pudding, and large buckets of tea boiled over the fire was the steady diet, with peas or rice perhaps once a week. She dipped out the flour, spooned the salt into it, and poured in the water and began mixing it with her hands. The flies and mosquitoes swarmed around her face, and she tried to shrug them away with her shoulder. It was impossible to keep them out of the sticky damper mixture, and it soon became speckled with dark spots.

The cook and the man helping him carried the carcass of the ewe around to the other side of the wagon to hang it up, and the stench of blood and death was heavy in the hot, still air. A cloud of flies followed them, and the gleaming red of the warm, raw flesh was spotted with flies. The cook cut off the forequarters, carried them around to the rear of the wagon and put them on the tailgate, and rummaged in a pile of rags and clothes in the corner of the wagon, taking out an odorous cloth bag which was stiff with blood. He shook it out as he walked back to the carcass, dragged it up over the carcass, and gathered the top of it tightly around the small hoof above the tendon impaled on the hook on the side of the wagon, the hoof to which bits of dirt and dung still clung from the last steps before that which had been alive changed to that which sustained life. And then he tied it, entrapping hundreds of flies in a warm, dark prison which tendered its prize of a rapturous and orgiastic feast on thick, rich clots of blood and moist flesh still warm with life before exacting its toll of sure death, in some measure collapsing the full scope of the grand design of all creation and reducing its gigantic scale to flies, a soiled bag, and a hurried and impatient motion of tying knots in a bit of dirty cord.

The carcass would last three days, the portion roasted on the second day dusted with curry and the portion roasted on the third day coated with curry, and her pattern of eating followed the same cycle, with her consuming a relatively substantial portion on the first day, eating on the second day when she was hungry enough, and starving on the third day. The cook took a bundle of wood gathered from the last forested area they had passed through and built a fire, and he threw handfuls of green boughs on the fire when it began burning hotly. Thick clouds of smoke billowed around the wagon from the green boughs on the fire, making it difficult for her to breathe and bringing streams of tears from her eyes, but the smoke more or less fulfilled its intended purpose of driving away the flies and mosquitoes and it was less of a discomfort than the insects because it was discomfort of a different nature.

The cook impaled the forequarters on an iron rod and suspended them over the fire. Elizabeth finished the damper and he put the pans on the fire, and she took the bucket used for making tea around to the barrel, filled it, and put it on to heat. Richardson rode up and dismounted, removing his hat and fanning the flies and mosquitoes away from his face with it as he glanced around.

"Are you all right, missus?"

It was a gruff kindness of the sort he had begun displaying after the first few days, a rhetorical and meaningless question, and she forced a slight smile and dropped her eyes, nodding.

He grunted, turning toward the cook. "See if you can get that mutton hot all the way through this time."

"If it don't suit your bloody fancy, the flaming gut pile is on the other side of the wagon."

"You hold your bloody tongue, sod. Do you want my fist along the side of your bleeding ear hole?"

"Do you want a dollop of saltpeter in your cha?"

The drover grumbled in his throat, slapping his hat back on his head and seating it with a hard tug as he glared at the cook, then turned back to his horse, mounted, and rode away. The cook glared after him, then grunted and knelt by the fire, putting more sticks and green boughs on it. Some of the relationships among the men were a mystery to her. Since her marriage, she had been among people whose questions of precedence and of right and wrong were usually resolved on the basis of who was most capable with his fists, and for the most part that seemed to hold true among the drover's men. But the cook, possibly the smallest man of the entire group, stood apart. He was the object of a certain amount of rough joking, such as when a wagon wheel had been broken and one of the men had suggested that the cook bake a damper to use for a wheel instead of repairing the one which was broken, but he was the only one who would stand up to the drover. And when their rough joking stirred the cook's anger, the men became silent in the face of his vitriolic response. The reference to saltpeter was lost on her, beyond the fact that she knew it to be a component of gunpowder, but the threat of putting it in the tea seemed to be his weapon over the men and there were vaguely lewd implications associated with it from the comments and laughter she had overheard among the men talking around the fire at night.

The need to relieve herself became an agony. The sheep were settled for the night, and the men began coming to the wagon. The dogs fought over and ate the entrails on the other side of the wagon, then went back to the sheep. She stood at the tailgate of the cook's wagon where she would be out of the way and noticed least, and where part of the smoke swept over her to keep the flies and mosquitoes away. The cook knelt at the side of the fire where the smoke was heaviest, moving the damper pans about, putting tea in the bucket of water, and turning the mutton, and the men gathered on the other side and talked and laughed as they swatted at the flies and mosquitoes. Her husband walked around their wagon and looked it over, and he glanced at her coldly as he walked to the fire to sit among the other men. On the first couple of days of the trip she had sat by the fire, then her husband had ordered her to stay away from the men. He'd had two fights with men over comments they had made about her and which he had interpreted as an insult to him, one which he had won and one which had been stopped by the drover because it had continued to the point of becoming dangerous.

The light deepened as the sun started to set, the sky becoming a bowl of red which darkened to a thick carmine in the east and spread toward the west, and the fields around the wagons were flooded with the crimson glow, the men, dogs, horses, wagons, and sheep becoming tinted with varying shades of red. Then darkness fell, and she counted the men around the fire and walked across the field to the stand of trees. When she returned, the cook was cutting portions of the mutton and handing out pieces of the damper. She took her share, ate the mutton, shredded the damper, picked out the flies and ate it, then climbed into the wagon.

The temperature fell rapidly after dark, bringing welcome relief from the stifling heat. She took off her dress and settled herself on the pallet at the side of the wagon in her petticoat and pantaloons, trying to ignore the sticky feel of the fabric against her and the sweaty odor of her body. The wooden sideboards were two feet high, and she lifted the canvas covering above the edge of the sideboard a crack to let in enough light from the fire to make out the words in her prayer book and Bible. Her eyes were still burning from the smoke and they filled with tears and blinded her as she strained to make out the words, and she could read only a few lines from each of them. Cruel fate guided her fingers to open the Bible at Job, leaving her with the poor comfort of a snatch of Job's wailing lamentation and railing against injustice, because it was too dark to read further. Then she prayed for strength, patience, and endurance.

The men's voices were clearly audible as they sat around the fire with their pipes and pannikins of tea, laughing and talking. Their conversation frequently made her cover her ears with her hands or withdraw into her memories or into extended prayer so she could ignore it, but she had a burning, hopeful, and fearful curiosity about their destination. There had been women on the places adjacent to the selection her husband had owned on the Georges River outside of Sydney, women who had been common and uneducated by the most generous standard and whose resentful diffidence toward her had represented a barrier too substantial for her wisdom and understanding to overcome, but their presence had eased the loneliness, disappointment, and hardships to an extent, and their grudging advice had frequently been valuable. But she had heard that there were few women in the far Outback.

The semiliterate note her husband had received in response to his query about employment as the head stockman had contained no mention of those matters important to her. She hoped there would be other women, she hoped there would be a comfortable house, she hoped for many other things. She had asked her husband to inquire, and his response had been a silent, affronted glare for her presumption in attempting to involve him in trivia and make a fool of him. But sometimes the conversation between the men was about their destination. Most of the men had never been there, and that led them to ask questions of the drover, cook, and the few other men who had seen the place. There had been mention of one woman, a daughter of the owner. The focus of interest in the questions and replies about her had been her attractiveness, but side comments had established that she worked as a stockman, and there had been other remarks which made it seem doubtful that she might turn out to be a friend. Other things said about the place had been largely disappointing. But once there had been a remark about flowers someone had planted, a sarcastic comment which had brought laughter from the others around the fire. That had been a nugget of information

179

which gave her food for thought to while away the grueling hours, starting visions of flower gardens in her mind. And there was a house of sorts, because there had been mention of it, and it was near a creek.

She put her prayer book and Bible away, and she settled herself on the pallet again, waving her hand at a mosquito which was whining around her face in the darkness. They were talking about the place again. She listened, hoping to hear something which would feed her timid and fervent expectations of what the place might be like. The cook was talking about the owner of the place in a tone of boasting familiarity and admiration.

"....rum old bugger he is, and he'll outlive the youngest one here. He's as blind as a bat and as old as sin itself now, but there's still no sod who could have him, because he's the size of a bleeding mountain and as mean as a flaming stud brumby."

"He's got to have some years on him," another man said. "I was hearing of him when my ma was wiping my arse, and even then Wayamba was again the size of any other station west of the—"

"It's how it came to be that bloody size is what makes the difference," the cook interrupted with a chuckle. "Old Pat Garrity took what he wanted, and any sod else could take what was left. There was three other squatters who planted down to the south of him in the hills, and it was told to me that he sent them word by Colin to move their bleeding arses to the south of some hill that he had taken as his boundary. Well, they bloody didn't, and then there was a frigging fire that spread smoke from the Gibbers Desert to the junction of the Darling and Murrumbidgee. When the smoke lifted, forty thousand sheep had roasted. And some say up to six men died in that fire. But after that, any other sodding squatter who wanted to set roots west of the Darling and between Tibooburra and Mildura went to see old Pat Garrity about it first. And then there was the business about the surveyers. When the pommies in Sydney started sending out surveyers to settle the squatters' boundaries, three surveyors went out and was never heard from again. The fourth one came back, and the lines of Wayamba Station were put on his map just where old Pat Garrity bloody wanted them."

There was a roar of laughter around the fire, and another man spoke as it began dying away. "How many kids does he have?"

"He had four," the cook replied. "But his boy Frank was killed a while back down in—"

"He had three," the drover interrupted him. "Colin, Sheila, and Frank. And Frank's dead, like you—"

"There's four of them!" the cook shouted heatedly. "By God, I've seen them, and I can bloody count as high as —"

"And you didn't know what you were looking at, sod!" the drover shouted back. "Don't you know that old woman of Garrity's is too old to have a kid as young as that youngest one? That kid is Sheila's!"

"Sheila's?" the cook replied in a surprised tone. "I don't know Sheila had ever been married."

"Since when has that kept a woman from whelping?" the drover retorted. "In case you didn't know, it's not the parson's talking that gets a woman with child."

There was another outburst of laughter, and the cook's bemused voice was barely audible through it. "By God, I didn't know that. It had to be some stud of a man who topped that one, because she's as spiny as the one who got her."

"Sheila's all right when you learn her ways," the drover said. "Colin and Sheila are both half abo, and you have to bear that in mind."

"She's well set up, I'll say that," the cook said. "It would take a pommie not to want to have a look when her strides are down."

"A few have pawed the ground around her, for all the good it's done them," the drover chuckled. "She's as good a stockman as any man who ever walked, and that's all she has on her mind."

"She must have had something else on her mind at one

time or another," another man commented.

There was more laughter, and the drover replied in a laughing voice, "I won't debate that."

"Wonder who it was?" a man asked.

"Old Harry Robinson who used to work on Wayamba told me it was a shearer named Jim Campbell," the drover replied.

"Old Harry Robinson that died up at Cooper Station four or five years ago?"

"That's him. He was working there at the time, and he told me that it was about two or three months after shearing time that old Pat found out she was in a family way. He said that old Pat beat her all over the home paddock whith a stock whip trying to find out who had done it, and she wouldn't tell him. Then he tied her up and sent for a big ram from the ram paddock, and he killed that ram, skinned it out, and sewed her up in the hide with the flesh side out and left her in the mustering yard in the sun for three days. About the time the worms ate their way through to her, she started talking. Then old Pat cut her loose, saddled his horse, and rode out. They said that Campbell had gone down toward Menindee with a shearing mob, and that's where old Pat headed. And no one ever heard of Campbell again."

"Old Pat had him?" someone asked over the chuckles around the fire.

"I didn't say that," the drover said firmly. "Old Pat Garrity's gone blind and he don't get out anymore, but I'll not put my mouth to him, his, or what he does. All I said was that Campbell was supposed to be down around Menindee, old Pat went down that way, and Campbell was never seen again. Campbell was working on Loxton Station at the time, and old Coober Cockburn was alive and owned it then. Old Coober sent for a constable, because they found Campbell's clothes out in one of the paddocks with blood all over them and there was some talk about what might have happened. But the constable didn't find out anything, and he didn't feel like traveling up to Wayamba to talk to old Pat. I say he must not have felt like it, because he bloody didn't and all."

"Old Pat Garrity must have been a real ram in his day," a man commented as the others laughed.

"Aye, he had to be to get through the hard times," the drover replied. "When other squatters were leaving and going back to Sydney, Wayamba Station was growing."

"How did he do that?"

"Bloody tallow!" the cook shouted triumphantly over the drover's voice. "All the other squatters were still trying to sell bleeding wool to sods who didn't want it, and old Pat was slaughtering sheep and rendering them. When sheep were selling for a bloody shilling a dozen, factors in Sydney were paying old Pat fifteen shillings for the tallow from every frigging sheep he rendered. And he started the first bloody tallow plant on the Darling."

"There was that, and he drove sheep down to the gold diggings and sold them," the drover said. "And made bloody good money at it and all. But he had the stock to be able to do things like that, where others didn't, and he had the sand to deal with any trouble that came up while he was about it. When he started driving meat to the gold diggings, a bunch of merchants out of Sydney and Parramatta got their wind up because they'd been having a fair time of it and old Pat came in with his flocks and showed them up for the bloody cheating sods that they were. Well, it was told to me that three of them got together and told old Pat that he would have to sell to them instead of to the fossickers, and I have an idea what he told them back. Then the three hired some men to rush the next flock he drove down. That's the last anyone has ever heard of the buggers that were hired, and a few days later the three were found hanging in their stores down at the Pinnaroo field with a meat hook through their necks. And no bloody merchant ever found any need to talk to old Pat Garrity again."

There was an explosion of uproarious laughter. It slowly faded, and there was more conversation in the same vein. There had been similar conversations on other nights, the drover and cook talking about the legendary Patrick Garrity and his fiefdom of Wayamba Station, a sprawling sheep empire more expansive than the lands ruled by many of the crowned heads of Europe. They had talked about his aged aborigine wife, and they had told the story of when his son Frank had been killed in Adelaide and he had gone to wreak vengeance on those who did it. The previous references to Sheila Garrity had been libidinous comments about her beauty and admiring remarks about her skill with a stock whip and as a horsewoman, a kind of awe in their voices which was unlike their normal attitudes when speaking of women. And all of the stories had been much the same in that they were tales of violence and cruelty by those who were folk heroes because they were as violent and cruel as the vast desert wasteland over which they ruled. Elizabeth sighed heavily, looking up at the canvas covering over the wagon in the darkness. What she had heard had been as disappointing as what she had gleaned from other conversations about the place.

The conversation around the fire began dying away presently as the men sought their blankets, because the days began early. The drover sent four of the men to watch over the sheep, and a few minutes later those who had been relieved by them came to the fire for their food. The cook grumbled at men to move out of his way as he banked the fire for the night. Other men moved around, taking their blankets out of the cook's wagon. She heard her husband exchanging quiet comments with a couple of the men.

And then the moment of terror came. He climbed heavily into the wagon and sat down on the edge of the pallet. She silently moved her arm to her sides and lay on her edge of the pallet, motionless. He smelled strongly of sweat, sheep, and sour breath, and he grunted and sighed as he took off his boots and clothes and dropped them in a pile at the side of the pallet. Then he lay down, heaving a gusty sigh and clearing his throat. She steeled herself to keep from trembling and forced herself to breathe with a slow, steady rhythm. He cleared his throat again, then licked his lips and swallowed noisily. The seconds dragged by, each one an eternity long, and she could hear the men moving back and forth around the wagon and passing within inches of her as they settled down for the night. He turned toward her and put his heavy hand on one of her breasts. Her face twisted with anguish in the darkness, and her lips opened in a silent wail of hopeless desperation. His hand tightened on her breast, and he shook her impatiently.

"Please," she breathed. "Please, no . . ."

"You'll not deny me," he grumbled. "If I'm to have the trouble of you, I'll have the use of you."

She started to protest again, then stopped herself. His tone had contained a threat of becoming louder, and he seemed to derive some perverse enjoyment from the other men knowing. His hand was squeezing her breast painfully hard. She numbly gathered up the skirt of her petticoat and unfastened her pantaloons, and he released her breast as she sat up to push them off. Then she lay back down, and he moved towards her.

His skin felt greasy and dirty against hers, and the odor of his body was overpowering as he hovered over her, fumbling and probing at her. Then he penetrated her with a painful thrust, and he lay down on top of her, grunting and sighing heavily. She reached out with her hand and groped for her Bible in the darkness. He pushed at her thighs impatiently and spread them wider, and he began making animal-like noises as he moved. Her fingers found the Bible, and she clutched it. There was a coarse chuckle from somewhere near the wagon, and she cringed inwardly with shame and mortification. His hands slid under her, and his fingers dug roughly into her hips and lifted her as he moved more rapidly. Something in the wagon made a metallic sound in rhythm with his movements. There were other sounds of rude amusement outside the wagon. She tightened her fingers on the Bible until they ached. He lifted her higher, his movements becoming frenzied. Then he gasped, and he lowered her again and relaxed on top of her, a heavy, suffocating weight. Presently he lifted himself and moved off her, lying down by her again and sighing.

Her hand was numb when she released the Bible. She pushed the skirt of her petticoat down and drew in a long, shuddering breath, swallowing dryly. The tears began welling up. She tried to hold them back, but they burst through and she turned her head to one side, weeping quietly.

"Aye, have a cry for what other women have had a smile, you bloody pommie get. But it's all the bloody same to me. The more you bleeding cry, the less you'll frigging piss."

– 12 –

Elizabeth's mother had always been abundantly and proudly aware that she had married well above her station, a fact which had always been fundamentally apparent to all who met the plump, red-faced merchant's daughter and the sage, withdrawn, ascetic churchman with honors from Oxford.

They were both from Wexford, but similarities ended with origin, because he had been years older and destined for the cloth from childhood, and had been writing learned tracts on religious minutiae when she was still a child working in her father's shop, destined to be wife of some small tradesman or mechanic. When a chaplain at Eton, he had been advised by doctors to emigrate to Australia for his health, and he had traveled back to

Wexford to finalize his few affairs where he had met the chubby eighteen year old Mildred Haley at a town reception in his honor. And for some obscure reason, he had asked her father for her hand.

The birth of their child had been even more of an enigma. Somehow the Reverent Andrew Willoughby in his mature years was difficult to associate with carnal impulses, but none could imagine his industrious and dedicated wife dishonoring his bed. After years of childless marriage, a seed had become implanted in the receptive womb, nature took its course and in due time Elizabeth Willoughby was born.

She always felt herself something of a bridge between her father and mother, blending elements of both natures. Her father always regarded her with a kind of bemused wonder, as though his surprise at her existence was unending, and he appeared to think of her as something more than a vessel for sin and piety, as he regarded others. He was fond of her and even found tolerance within himself for her, and she regarded him with a love and respect short of the adoration rendered him by her mother. Her mother regarded her with an affection which was tempered with impatience with Elizabeth for drawing her attention away from the major purpose of her life, attending to the needs of her husband. Her mother punctually and grudgingly saw to her physical needs until she achieved a minimum capability to see to them herself, and that age coincided precisely with the age at which her father undertook her education, a matter he viewed as far too delicate to be entrusted to public schooling establishments.

They were poor, because there was only a small annuity from Eton, a pittance from the George Street church where her father was accorded a position of emeritus pastor, and an occasional gift from the Willoughby and Haley families in England. On Christmas a devout parishioner would frequently donate a fat goose or other choice meat for their table, and her father would promptly give it to the poor, as he did all gifts from his family, and they would have fish. It was a characteristic her mother regarded without thought of criticism and as an immutable fact of existence which had to be dealt with, such as rain on washday, and she was frugal with what they had, silent about money she received from her family, and thrifty with tradesmen. The tradesmen were understanding and willing to achieve the self-satisfaction of helping when it was at little or no cost to themselves. A boy from the fish merchant would frequently bring remnants from the day's trade with a message that they were for Elizabeth's cat, and there would always be a nice perch or sea bass suitable for the table in the bits. When Mildred went to the green-grocer for a potato, he would always silently stuff her basket with vegetables which were a little wilted. The sundries merchant saved bits of cloth suitable for facing clerical collars and making ribbons and aprons for Elizabeth.

They had few friends, because her father's station and profession placed them within a limited circle and her father had an unfortunate propensity to point out sin among the well-placed as quickly as among the common people. He also had an eccentric egalitarianism and a bland disregard for placing himself and his daughter in what others regarded as unlikely situations. Elizabeth always walked abroad with him from the time she was capable of full locomotion, trotting along with her crisply starched skirt sweeping the cobblestones, her apron bow standing out neatly behind her, the brim of her sun bonnet in a neatly curved line and the bow of the strings in precise symmetry under her chin, and her tiny reticule clutched in her hands, while her father's freshly-blacked boots marched along in the slow but sure and steady pace with which he pursued sin through life, his threadbare black suit lovingly sewn, pressed, and brushed, his collar snowy from boiling, his pale face drawn and lined with age, ill health, and concern for humanity, and his pale blue eyes mistily regarding the scene about him and seeing what was invisible to others.

At times they went to Government House to see to details of an undertaking for some unfortunate of the city, with a harrassed clerk or minor official wincing and sighing over the difficulty of bending government regulations to God's will as her father spoke in his soft, crisp, precise Oxford accent. They went to the orphanage, where the boys looked at her from under their eyebrows as her father led the prayer. They also went to the homes of the sick. More often than not, it would be a small, shabby, dirty house of a lower priority to other clerics, where her father knelt by the bed and prayed quietly and insistently while the rest of the family stood about and Elizabeth stood at the foot of the bed with her head bowed and her folded hands tucked under her chin. But they also occasionally went to more prosperous houses and, more rarely, to the best houses in the city, and on those occasions Elizabeth was under a firm and unwavering dictum of a practical nature from her mother that a copper slipped into her pocket or reticule need not be mentioned to her father, or a pastry tied into a serviette for her to take away was to be handled carefully to keep it from crumbling and was to be brought home for dinner.

Their progress along the streets was marked by tipped hats and curtsies, and it was frequently interrupted as her father stopped to talk about some matter. Sometimes it would be someone who had been ill, occasioning a brief and impromptu prayer of thanksgiving which would interrupt the normal flow of traffic as her father closed his eyes and prayed with the aplomb of long practice and absolute lack of self-consciousness in any situation, while the red-faced object of prayer would shuffle and dart uncomfortable glances from under his brows, and passing tradesmen, mechanics, and shoppers would adjust their mien and attitude to the nature of the communication taking place as they edged past. At other times it might be a government clerk or official who had managed to evade her father on some problem, forcing a sickly smile and nodding in resignation as he agreed to see what he could do. She and her father also went into shops, where tradesmen would be gently but firmly compelled to send food or goods to some poor family by the one they helped support. Their routes included all the streets of the city, including some where the clerical collar and the presence of the small girl of immaculate appearance caused a shock wave to travel along ahead of them, and they stopped outside public houses for her father to talk to clusters of sailors, porters, and apprentices who knuckled their foreheads respectfully and glanced about in alcoholic confusion. On occasion they would be present in the area when a fight or knifing in one of the places along the street would occur, and they would enter some dim, odorous interior for her father to pray over a bleeding, groaning man on the grimy floor or stretched across battered tables, asking for divine intercession to the processes of nature until the barber arrived, while stupefied customers stared open-mouthed and the owner hovered about and glared warningly at the customers.

And there were other places they entered when her father would be told that an ill woman was inside, places which were dim and ornate where the heavy, musky scent of incense masked more pervasive odors, and where the wide, toothy smile on a woman's face would dissolve into consternation when she saw who was there. The woman would leave, and they would wait as a bedlam of racing through hallways, doors slamming, and the sounds of men climbing through windows spread through the place. Then another older woman would come and take them to the room. And Elizabeth would stand at the foot of the bed with her head bowed and her folded hands tucked under her chin as her father prayed fervently for the health of the body and for the casting out of seven devils, his bland blue eyes not perceiving an essential difference in worth between the diseased or injured whore and the best citizen of the city.

Other portions of Elizabeth's education were undertaken in her father's study in the modest house at the foot of Harrogate Street, where the cleric reverted to the schoolmaster and he lectured ponderously as she sat on a hard chair at a small table by the window and tried to absorb an avalanche of history, geography, and philosophy. Her small fingers were bent to the task of cyphering the intricacies of calligraphy. She learned the art of shaving a quill to a fine point and exercising a light pressure to keep it from wearing unduly, and her fingers became ink-stained from practicing on precious sheets of foolscap, covering every inch of both sides with her exercises.

And she learned. From a sounding board for his sermons, she became the scribe who committed his thoughts to paper so they would be preserved for future use, and as the years passed she became less of a pupil and more of a disciple and companion, delighting him with critical evaluations and suggestions.

Her range of acquaintances was wide. She came into contact with those of her age of both sexes at church and activities associated with church, and she was invited to parties and similar functions as she progressed through her teenage years. The traits of her mother and father were mixed in her; shining blue eyes and a rosy complexion from her mother; a tall, slender frame from her father, and his delicate, patrician features. She was more attractive than most, but her background had given her a precocious dignity which was distinctly unpopular in her age group. There was a shortage of women in general in Australia, but not in Sydney and Parramatta. Family connections in England were closely maintained, sons were usually educated in England, and eligible young women in Sydney and Parramatta were in competition with those in England. Elizabeth was more disadvantaged than most in marriage prospects. Her family was poor and she was without dowry, and while social association with her family was politic, closer connections were undesirable because of her father's eccentric disregard of class distinctions. Young men were drawn by Elizabeth's attractiveness, but their fathers and mothers discouraged them. Elizabeth regarded the situation with total equanimity as she approached twenty, secure and happy in her life.

The Reverend Willoughby was something of a hobbyist in gardening, and in the absence of money for seed or plants, he and Elizabeth frequently prowled through the common above the Battery or in the fields around Fort Macquarie for plants to grub up and transplant to their garden. On one such outing on the common, they found a small pepper tree they decided to dig up and take home, and the exertions of the digging combined with her father's age and caused a fainting spell. A man crossing the common between the stock trader's market and the entry to George Street came to their assistance. He was a quiet, well-built man of forty or so in plain, durable, and not particularly neat or overly clean workman's clothes, with a silent, determined manner. There was something impersonal about his offhand attitude, but he was capable and effective, and he took charge of the situation, tying up the roots of the tree, putting it on his shoulder, and giving her father his other arm to lean on as she followed along behind.

He came to their house in late afternoon the following day in a baggy wool suit and clean, wrinkled shirt, his beard and mustaches trimmed and his boots freshly blacked, carrying a hindquarter of mutton wrapped in canvas on his shoulder. He left the mutton in the kitchen with Elizabeth's mother, who was stunned by the windfall of fresh meat, and he removed his coat and rolled up his sleeves as he went out into the back garden to plant the tree. The tree was planted by the time dinner was ready, and he came back in from the garden with her father, washed his hands and put his coat back on, ate with them, and left.

Frank Cummings was a grazier, the holder of a small selection a few miles from Sydney and the owner of a few hundred sheep. He was the son of a free settler, and one of three brothers. One was George Cummings, a trading factor in the city and also a bachelor, a state which seemed to satisfy many men in the working and small trade class. His older brother, Cain, had been convicted of murder and transported to a colony for felons in Van Diemen's Land years before, but had escaped from the colony and had been seen once in the vicinity of Phillip Bay, after which he had disappeared and had never been heard from again. Frank Cummings had apprenticed to a grazier and had eventually worked his way up to owning a few sheep, but he had been plagued by poor fortune most of his life and his progress had been slow and faltering.

It was through her mother's attitude toward Cummings that Elizabeth realized that she was what brought him to the house. The disparity in their ages was greater than usual in their circle, even though it was common in the working and trade class, and he acted almost indifferently toward her and directed most of his attention to her father. Her father accepted his presence graciously, as he would have that of the Governor or the owner of a bordello, and he seemed to find Cummings an interesting man. They talked about sheep, farming, and similar matters, and he neither accepted nor rejected Cummings as a suitor for Elizabeth but accepted him readily as a guest. Elizabeth wasn't consulted, but she had no intention of marrying him. She regarded marriage in general with reservations, she considered Cummings far too old for her, and there were characteristics about him which she found highly undesirable. He was uneducated and unpolished, his indifference toward her clashed with her pride and a mild vanity other men had created in her; he drank, and she suspected that his quiet manner concealed dark, hidden depths in his personality. Elizabeth's mother made him welcome because her husband accepted him, and he frequently brought highly practical gifts; a flitch of bacon, a bag of flour or sugar, a quarter of mutton, or a large bundle of lamb chops, presenting them with a blunt directness which somehow by-passed subtlety and made them less embarrassing and objectionable than a gift left on the doorstep.

He came frequently for a period of several weeks, like one surveying a situation in the same way as he had assessed the situation when her father had become faint on the common. Some young men who had been visiting Elizabeth suddenly stopped coming, and Cummings began visiting twice each week. He came on Sunday to accompany them to church, and he came on Wednesday to have dinner with them. To a casual observer he was visiting with her father and was a family friend, and Elizabeth became accustomed to his presence, as did her father and mother. And once the routine was established and accepted, Cummings appeared to be content with the situation, as he was in watching his sheep to see what return the season would bring, or as a cat watching a mouse hole.

The illness which had brought her father to Australia was a weakness of the lungs, and the generally hot, dry summers and mild winters had been beneficial for him. He had lived to an age considered substantial for the most healthy, and his wife, though years younger and of sturdy stock, was beginning to feel the effects of her age. But her father's weakness had only been diminished and it remained, evidencing itself in the flushed spots on his cheeks, occasional breathlessness, spasms of coughing, and a susceptibility to respiratory ailments during winter. Elizabeth and her mother were both familiar with and watchful for the first indications of one of his bouts of respiratory illness. They had developed a smooth routine of medicating him with infusions and vapors and putting him to bed at the onset, beginning the cure even before the ailment was fully developed.

There was nothing unexpected or out of the ordinary about his cough and a slight hoarseness one night at dinner, because he and Elizabeth had spent much of the day on the common and the weather had suddenly turned much cooler. When they finished dinner, Elizabeth prepared the infusion and the hot water for the vapor while her mother washed the dishes and cleaned up, then her mother took them up to administer them to him and Elizabeth crushed more herbs to have them ready to prepare the medication the following morning. But the following morning he was dead.

Elizabeth was numb with shock. The main focus of her life was suddenly gone and her mind reeled as she tried to assimilate her loss. Her mother was prostrate, deprived of the very reason for her existence. Elizabeth went to the rector of the George Street church, who came home with her to talk to her mother and appointed an assistant pastor to help them with their affairs. Her father died on Tuesday, and Cummings came on Wednesday. He went back to his place and made arrangements for someone to look after his sheep, then he returned and stayed.

Much of Sydney turned out for the funeral, clergy of all denominations, the Governor and his senior staff, and hundreds of acquaintances. Cummings was in the background at the funeral and burial, and when friends took Elizabeth and her mother home in a carriage, he followed on foot. Elizabeth's mother went to her room and Elizabeth sat in the parlor, her eyes red with weeping and her mind dazed and confused with a turmoil of emotions. Cummings saw to the wood and the fire in the kitchen to prepare tea, and he talked to the friends who remained about and held the door for them when they left. Other friends came to bring food, and Cummings met them at the door, took their offerings, and thanked them. When darkness fell, Elizabeth went to her room, and Cummings put out the candles, locked the doors, and slept on the floor in the parlor.

Cummings was still there the following day, building up the fire in the stove and heating water for tea, moving silently about and ignoring Elizabeth as he took care of what had to be done. The assistant pastor came and Cummings talked to him on the step, and people who had brought food came for their dishware and Cummings gave it to them. Elizabeth made soup for her mother and it remained untouched on the nightstand, while Elizabeth ate some soup and drank a cup of tea. Then she sat in her room and looked sightlessly at a book on her lap, trying to read, but the tears kept returning every few minutes. Cummings moved quietly around downstairs.

By Saturday her mother was moving about the house in a silent stupor of grief, and she was beginning to eat some of what Elizabeth prepared. Cummings was still there, taking care of tasks around the house and occasionally disappearing along the street for an hour or two to get something which was needed or on some errand of his own. On Sunday he took them to church and returned home with them, and he left during the afternoon to check on his sheep. He returned before dark.

On Monday Cummings talked to Elizabeth about marriage. It was one of the few times he had addressed her on any subject and it took her somewhat by surprise. His approach to the subject was that it was a foregone conclusion. She was stunned for a moment, then collected herself and told him firmly that she didn't intend to marry him. He went to her mother's room and brought her downstairs, and Elizabeth found that he had already discussed it with her, and she was in agreement. Her mother had written to her family in England about what had happened, and it was possible that they might have received financial assistance within several months, but their immediate situation was one of urgency. They had no savings and no income, and Cummings had agreed to support them if Elizabeth married him. And Cummings hadn't been rejected as a suitor by Elizabeth's father, which was the ultimate recommendation in her mother's mind. Some of the atmosphere of sorrow in the house disappeared in the conflict as Elizabeth argued stormily with her mother and Cummings for the next two days, during which Elizabeth saw the edge of Cummings' temper for the first time. Then Elizabeth's mother went to the bishop and brought him home to talk to Elizabeth, and he told Elizabeth that her father would have been disappointed by her disobedience. There were more arguments, and Elizabeth finally gave up and the banns were posted.

Their state of mourning eliminated an elaborate wedding and Elizabeth didn't want one. There were a minimum number of witnesses present, along with Elizabeth's mother and Cummings' brother George. After the wedding they returned to the house for a brief and awkward breakfast. Cummings had left his cart with the bullock hitched to it in front of the house, and he loaded the things Elizabeth had packed. Elizabeth climbed in, and they rode away in silence.

It was late afternoon when they reached the selection, two hundred acres of overgrazed hillside with the narrow, winding Georges River at the bottom of the slope. A worn path where his cart had traveled back and forth led from the dirt road to the house, a small, shabby structure of unpainted slabs, spotted with pieces of bark where boards had rotted or fallen off, with a couple of rickety sheds and a tiny privy behind it. There had been flies and mosquitoes in the city, but the offshore breezes from the bay had made them only a minor nuisance during winter, less than a warning for the swarms which had gathered around her as the cart jolted along the rutted road. She felt sick from hunger and nauseated from the lurching of the cart, and the cold wind sweeping across the hillside and stirring the stubby brown grass made her shiver uncontrollably. Cummings climbed down from the wagon to open the gate and lead the bullock through it, then he closed the gate and climbed back onto the seat as the bullock started along the path across the field to the house. He hadn't looked at her or spoken to her since their exchange of vows.

There were two sagging steps leading up to the door, and the door dragged against the floor as he shoved it open with his shoulder, carrying in part of her things. The house had two rooms. In the front room there was a firepit full of dead ashes in the corner, a deal table and a couple of chairs against the wall, and a rough wooden shelf over the table for dishes and utensils. The floor was caked with mud and sheep dung, dirty clothes hung from pegs on the walls, and dishes on the table had dried remains of food on them from days before. In the other room was a bedframe built into the corner and covered with dirty sacking for blankets, and the only other thing in the room was a shelf on the wall with dirty clothes piled on it.

He finished carrying in her things from the cart and stacking them along the wall in the front room, then went out to unhitch the bullock and turn it loose. She walked slowly from one room to another in a daze. It didn't look like a human habitation to her. She took off her coat and looked around for somewhere clean to hang it. When he came back in, he took it from her and hung it on a peg, then led her into the other room. At first she did not understand when he began unfastening her buttons and ties. Then understanding came, bringing panic. She tried to get away from him, but he held her effortlessly as he stolidly continued loosening her clothes. She began screaming and thrashing frantically about, but he ignored her screams and held her more firmly. He undressed her, lifting her, turning her, and changing her from one arm to the other to peel her garments off, then took her to the bed, pushed her down on the dirty sacking, and climbed on after her, unfastening his trousers and pushing them down.

She had only the most vague idea of the mechanics involved, and she was in a frenzy of mortification and fear as he pushed her thighs apart and crouched between them, moving closer to her and guiding himself. The pressure was painful and she shrank from his touch. He began cursing at her to lie still and pinching the tender skin on the inside of her thighs, and the pain of his pinches became agonizing, greater than the pain of the thrusting pressure. She forced herself to lie still. There was an instant of excruciating pain, and he seized her thighs and gripped them with a crushing pressure as he fell forward on her and began moving rapidly. It took only a moment, and he uttered a loud gasp as he dug his fingers into her thighs with a force which made her cry out in protest. Then he moved off her and slid off the bed.

He walked toward the doorway to the other room, pulling his trousers up and stuffing his shirt into them as he fastened them. She was dazed by what had happened, but her nakedness was an imperative, overriding concern and she tried to cover herself and reach for some of her garments at the same time as she sat up on the bed. He turned in the doorway.

"You stay as you bloody are, you. I'm going for my flock and I'll have it again when I get back, and that's how I want to find you. In Sydney you were the fucking parson's daughter and looking down your flaming nose at me, but now you're my wife and from now on you'll be looking *up* your bloody long pommie nose at me."

– 13 –

The abrupt transition was traumatic, and Elizabeth
stumbled about for days in utter confusion, trying to
please him as he cursed at her and pushed her into the
back room two or three times each day to take her. She
burned her hands on pans and the open flames in the
firepit trying to cook, her back ached agonizingly from
carrying water from the river to wash the floor and
clothes, and her hands became raw from the lye soap. The
flies and mosquitoes were a constant torture, mice and
snakes got into the house from the field, and the walls
crawled with insects. She itched from insect bites, the
insides of her thighs became blue from his pinches when
she involuntarily tried to draw away from him when he
took her, and the poor food made her ill. He cursed at her,

occasionally made her go about the house naked to punish her, and came home drunk when he made his weekly trips to Sydney.

Then there was an adjustment of sorts. She missed church, but her prayer book, Bible, and daily prayers were a comfort, lifting her out of her surroundings and giving her a periodic respite from her circumstances. She became accustomed to the flies and mosquitoes to an extent, developing a habit of constantly waving them away without thinking about it, and she began to ignore the filth. Her hands and muscles hardened, and she became inured to the labor. His desires consisted of food three times each day, obedience, and her immediate readiness for sex when he wanted her. He began to accept her lesser strength and endurance compared to his, and when they began to fall into a pattern he cursed at her less and ignored her more.

Six weeks after he brought her to his selection, he took her with him on his weekly trip into Sydney so she could visit with her mother while he was attending to his affairs. Elizabeth was candid with her mother about the circumstances to which her mother's insistence had brought her, but her mother offered little sympathy. Cummings had taken several pieces of the furniture from the house and had sold them, and he was seeing to her affairs after a fashion and taking care of her, so she wanted no trouble with him. And she had been exceedingly fortunate in her own marriage, because Elizabeth's wasn't unlike the situation she had been reared to expect. She explained to Elizabeth that men who had been bachelors for years frequently made difficult husbands for a time, and she advised Elizabeth to be patient and obedient. Elizabeth suppressed the impulse to respond with some of the words she had learned from Cummings, then felt ashamed of the impulse. Presently Cummings returned with the cart, his eyes bleary and his breath smelling strongly of rum, and he had a bottle under the seat from which he took sips. As the cart rumbled along the high street, a carriage crowded with half a dozen young men and women Elizabeth knew from parties and church socials passed in the other direction. They were laughing and talking, and they looked very clean, fresh, happy, and carefree. She averted her face so they wouldn't see her, but they didn't appear to notice the cart.

The selection was fenced with brush which had been cut and staked in windrows with poles. A strayed cow or ox from another selection would occasionally wander through and tear a gap in it, and sometimes gusty winds would scatter a stretch of it, but it more or less contained the sheep. The sheep still had to be watched so none of them would get through the holes in the fence and so they wouldn't break into a rush and trample each other if something frightened them, and Cummings liked to keep them grouped in one part of the selection for several days at a time to allow the rest of the overgrazed pasture to regenerate as much as possible. In the past it had been his practice to take the flock to an adjacent selection when he was going to be absent, where the owner had a large boy who would watch the sheep for a few coppers. A couple of months after their marriage, he began showing Elizabeth some of the essentials of controlling the dogs and flock so she could watch them on the days he went into Sydney and save him the money he had been paying to have them watched.

There were three dogs. None of them had ever experienced affection, and they responded with suspicious growls when she tried to pet them. One was a pregnant bitch and Elizabeth began feeding her extra bits of food to build up her strength. She gradually worked her way into the dog's confidence, and eventually stirred a responding affection when she petted her. When the dog had the litter, Elizabeth made a bed of straw and bits of wool under the corner of the house for her, and she allowed Elizabeth to handle and pet her pups. Cummings

203

paid no attention to the pups beyond kicking them out of his way as he went in and out of the house, then he showed interest in them for the first time on a morning when he was preparing to go to Sydney. The five pups were almost three months old, sturdy and healthy from what Elizabeth had been feeding them, and he looked them over, gathered them up, and took them down the hill to the sheep. Elizabeth watched from the doorway, puzzled for a moment, then she saw that he was seeing how they reacted to the sheep. He walked back up the hill, carrying two of the pups, and put them in the cart. The other three had failed the test. He took each of them by the hind legs and slammed their heads against the corner of the house to kill them, threw the bodies down the hill, and climbed into the cart. Elizabeth came out to watch the sheep as the cart rumbled away. The female dog bit Elizabeth's hand when she tried to pet her.

An area behind the house and to one side of the privy was used as a vegetable garden, and when spring approached Cummings took rusty, battered gardening tools out of one of the sheds, brought the gardening tools from the house in Sydney, and told Elizabeth to dig up the ground and prepare it for planting. He helped part of the time, but mostly she worked alone. The ground was full of rocks and had been only scratched up instead of properly turned before, and it was grueling, tedious work. It seemed ironical that some of the tools she used were those she had used in the flower gardens around the house in Sydney from early childhood. Then when she had finished turning the ground, she had to carry water from the river at the bottom of the hill to water the seeds.

Owners of two adjacent selections were married, and one of the women came to visit Elizabeth while she was digging in the garden plot. She seemed to be a woman of forty or so, prematurely aged by hardship, toil, poor food, and ill treatment, and she was profane, worn, and drab. She was carrying a baby of six months or so and a small boy of about eighteen months, and both of them were crying dreary, monotonous, tearless sobs. Solitude had become a hardship, but Elizabeth's pleasure and gratitude for the woman's visit was tempered because of the woman's intense, gossipy curiosity. And the woman seemed surprised and then suspicious of Elizabeth's speech and mannerisms. But they had things in common. There was an automatic and unspoken understanding that the visit couldn't interfere with work, and the woman put her children down at the edge of the turned ground, took a mattock, and made token gestures of helping as they talked. She could stay only a few minutes, and presently she gathered up the children to leave, telling Elizabeth to come and visit her if she could.

The other woman came a few days later. She was much the same as the first one, and the visit was similar. Then they both came together some two weeks later, on a day when Cummings had gone to Sydney and Elizabeth was watching the sheep. The visits broke the monotony, but they were also depressing. Both women had husbands much like Cummings, and their visits back and forth had an element of surreptitiousness to them, something which would result in punishment if it happened too often or interfered with their work. They both grimly accepted their situation, and both had secret ways of striking back at their husbands. There were selections adjacent to theirs which were owned by bachelors, whom they also visited when their husbands were in Sydney.

They were too different from Elizabeth for contact on any level except the most superficial, but they provided sound and motion in a bleak and hopeless world, other human beings in a vast wasteland where human beings were few. She didn't understand them and they didn't trust her, but they continued calling occasionally. One of them showed Elizabeth how to soak the clothes in the lye soap before washing them, which saved her hands to an extent, and the other one showed Elizabeth how to make a yoke out of a piece of wood to enable her to carry water from the river with less strain on her back. And Elizabeth prayed for them.

Some six months after Elizabeth and Cummings had been married, Elizabeth's mother received passage money from her father for her and Elizabeth to come to England. She booked passage for herself and gave part of the remaining money to Cummings as a belated dowry, and she also gave him the house and the remainder of the belongings in the house. It appeared that Cummings had been anticipating something of the sort, and it put him into an exceptionally good mood, motivating him to tell Elizabeth he would take her to Sydney on the day her mother left so she could see her off.

Elizabeth's wardrobe had never been extensive, and the few clothes she'd had when she got married had deteriorated rapidly from the hard work on the selection. She washed, patched, and sewed her best dress, but after she had done all she could, it was still far below the standard of appearance her father would have required. It was a dark blue muslin, and the heavy scrubbing and boiling which had been necessary to get out the dirt and grass stains had turned it a muddy grey. There were patches on the elbows and a couple of sewn places on the bodice she couldn't hide, and the collar, cuffs, and hem were threadbare. She tried to sew up the worst places in the hem, ran out of thread, then gave up and hung it on one of the pegs.

The boy who watched the sheep before was ill, and for a time it appeared that Elizabeth wouldn't be able to go to Sydney to see her mother off, but Cummings found someone else at the last moment. It cost more than it had before and it delayed their departure, and Cummings was irritable and impatient, shouting at her to get into the cart, beating the bullock viciously with the whip, and cursing all the way along the road to Sydney. Her mother had already left the house when they reached it.

Cummings remained at the house, and she hurried to the high street, then down the wide thoroughfare to the docks.

The breeze carried the strong, familiar odor of sea and tar along the thoroughfare. A forest of masts jutted into the air, bristling with spars and draped with their shrouds of cords and furled sails, looking like a tangled mass at a distance then separating into different ships as she drew closer. People were moving along all the wharfs, but a crowd was clustered among the stacks of bales, boxes, and barrels on one of them and activity seethed on the deck of a ship moored to the wharf. Elizabeth ran along the causeway and turned onto the wharf, weaving her way through the shouting, waving people, looking for her mother among those jammed along the rail of the ship. The gangplank was up, men were climbing about in the rigging, orders ringing out on the ship were audible over the sounds of the people around her, and she realized with a sinking feeling that she was too late to be able to speak with her mother. She looked along the rail again, moving from side to side. The people were crowded together, waving and gesticulating and moving about in a confusing mass, but her mother didn't appear to be among them. Elizabeth frowned, standing on tiptoe and craning her neck to look around at the other ships to see if any others appeared to be leaving. There didn't seem to be any unusual activity around any she could see, and she turned and looked at the people on the ship again.

Then she saw her. She had looked at her several times and hadn't recognized her. It was the first time she had seen her mother with rouge on her lips and cheeks and with rice powder on her face. And her clothes were loud, expensive, and in an extreme style compared to how she had dressed before. She was wearing a short, pale grey linen coat trimmed with pink, a pink muslin dress with white lace facing on the bodice, and a wide, pink hat with a large pink feather trailing back from it. It had been weeks since she had seen her mother, but the transition from her mother to the woman she saw was of a scope which had nothing to do with time, unless eternity could be spanned in terms of a calendar. She appeared to notice Elizabeth at the same time, and she smiled and waved. Even her stance and gestures seemed to be different. Elizabeth lifted her hand and waved back. Her mother said something to a man standing by her, pointing to Elizabeth, and he looked at Elizabeth and smiled and waved as her mother waved again. Elizabeth numbly continued waving.

Gulls circled overhead, swooping gracefully and screaming. The ship edged away from the dock, ropes chattering through pulleys, and the shouts and waving between the people on the ship and along the wharf became frenzied. A sail spilled downward from a spar, and it filled with air with a solid crack which echoed along the docks. The ship began moving more rapidly, bobbing in the swell rolling across the harbor and edging to the right as another sail spilled down. Elizabeth felt the stitching in the armpit of her dress tearing, and she dropped her right arm and lifted her left arm to wave. More sails unfurled on the ship and the men climbing about on the spars and rigging became tiny figures as the ship moved further into the harbor and began riding the higher swell. It swung into a shallow tack toward the roadstead, edging to the left, and the people crowded against the rail on the deck became hidden behind the tall stern of the ship.

The gulls followed the ship, white dots circling through the air and swooping down toward the masts and sails in turns and loops. The wharf was suddenly quiet after the shouting and flurry of excitement, and people murmured among themselves as they walked back toward the causeway along the waterfront. The breeze whipped across the wharf, stirring Elizabeth's hair, and she lifted her hands to tuck it in and tighten her ribbon, keeping her right elbow close to her so no one could see the torn stitching in the armpit of her dress. She glanced around, and saw two women with whom she had been casually acquainted, both of them about her age and daughters of Government officials. They were with two well-dressed men she didn't remember having seen before, and they looked attractive in their bright dresses, and wide hats. She felt suddenly vulnerable in her shabby dress and without a hat and gloves. One of them was looking at her, and Elizabeth smiled and waved. She turned away, and she said something to the other one as the four walked along the wharf to the causeway. The other one glanced over her shoulder at Elizabeth and looked away.

Elizabeth looked at the ship again. It had tacked back to the right, and it was in the harbor roadstead and under full sail, white foam boiling under its bow as it plowed into the waves rolling in from the open sea. The people on the deck were tiny spots of color in the distance. She didn't see a spot of pink among them, but she lifted her hand and waved again in farewell.

A cart was leaving the house with the bedding piled on it and roped down, the bulging mattresses and ticks looking like formless animals trying to escape the confines of the ropes as the cart bounced on the cobblestones, and Cummings and another man were loading the kitchenware into another cart. They were in the kitchen gathering another load as Elizabeth walked along the path, and she went in through the open doorway, glanced around the parlor, and walked into the study. The house looked and felt like somewhere she had never been before, totally strange and unfamiliar. The study was in disorder, the furniture moved around and stacks of books piled on the floor. Drawers were standing open and empty and the shelves where papers had been were empty; Eton had requested his papers, and presumably the bishop had seen that they were packed and shipped. She began picking out the books she wanted to take.

Cummings stopped in the study doorway and looked in

at her with a suspicious frown, then walked on. An iron-bound chest in the corner which had contained paper was empty, and she dragged it outside and up into the cart, then carried the books out and stacked them in it. The only other thing she wanted was the set of Wedgewood that some relative of her father's had given her parents for a wedding present, and she went around the house to the shed to look for a box. There were a couple of heavy wood boxes and straw in the shed, but either of the boxes would be too heavy for her to lift with the china in it. She gathered up an armload of straw, dragged one of the boxes around to the cart and pushed it up into it, then began carrying out the pieces of china and packing them into the box. Cummings and the other man had finished carrying out the kitchenware and were standing by the man's cart talking as they took drinks from a bottle, and Cummings looked at her a couple of times as she brought pieces of china out of the house. He looked vaguely dissatisfied by what she was doing, but he didn't say anything.

Another cart came along the street and stopped in front of the house, Cummings went inside with the man who drove it, and the cart with the kitchenware left. Cummings and the other man began carrying out tables, chairs, and other pieces of furniture and loading it onto the cart. Elizabeth finished packing the china in the box, covered it with a thick layer of straw and put the top on the box, then sat on the seat and waited as the men finished loading the cart with furniture. The man gave Cummings some money and left, and Cummings locked the house and climbed onto the cart.

It was late afternoon when they got back to the selection, and Cummings left the cart in front of the house and went after the sheep. Elizabeth took the books out of the chest and the dishes out of the box, dragged the chest and box inside, then carried the books and dishes in, repacked them, and pushed the box and chest under the

210

bedframe where they would be out of sight. Cummings returned with the sheep and left in the cart. He returned two days later, after selling the house and the rest of its contents.

He bought more sheep, but Elizabeth saw no other evidence of the money. The sparing amounts of tea, flour, salt, and sugar he bought didn't increase, and they continued to live on mutton and damper, an occasional bit of pork or beef, and the vegetables from the plot behind the house. Elizabeth's clothes continued to get more ragged and tattered and her shoes became so worn that they were falling apart, but when she mentioned her needs to Cummings he only glowered at her in silent warning or made a sneering comment about the necessity for her to become accustomed to her changed station in life.

A letter to her from a cousin of her father's was shuffled from one clerk to another and lay in stacks of unclaimed mail at Government House for a time, then it was sent to the bishop's office by a clerk who recognized the name. Inquiries were made by an assistant at the bishop's office, Elizabeth's whereabouts were determined, and a young minister dispatched out of the city on other business was given the letter to deliver. He was a young man of good family, a recent graduate in divinity from King's College and a recent arrival from England, and not overly familiar with the conditions of the working classes in England or in the colonies. But treatises and sermons delivered by Elizabeth's father at various times during his career had been scattered through the curriculum at King's College and the young minister was familiar with the Willoughby name. The letter he carried was from a good address in London and was from a Willoughby who was a barrister. He came on a day when Cummings was in Sydney and Elizabeth was dividing her time between watching the sheep and carrying water from the river to the garden patch behind the house. And when Elizabeth finally convinced him that he had located the adressee of the letter, he was speechless with horror.

The bishop made allowances for the young minister's youthful idealism and lack of experience with the hard facts of life, but there still seemed to be cause for concern. He dispatched his assistant to the Cummings selection the following day, where he found Elizabeth carrying water to do the washing and Cummings sitting and watching the sheep. The assistant was an impatient, ambitious man who had found himself at a dead end in a colonial office under the jurisdiction of a decrepit and backward bishop who had sent him on what he considered a fool's errand because of the ravings of a youthful hysteric, and he had also known Elizabeth's father well and had regarded him with a mixture of amusement and contempt. But he felt an intense admiration for Elizabeth's silent endurance, and was aware of the bishop's influence in forcing Elizabeth into a marriage and felt a satisfying anticipation over confronting the bishop with how the marriage had turned out for her. He found an outlet for his frustrations and dissatisfactions in Cummings, and he gave him a severe tongue lashing and left him quaking with the threat of being summoned to the assizes.

Cummings was brought up sharply against the fact that he had married into a class where there were minimum standards of maintenance, support, and care. He was enraged, and he was also powerless. His entire arsenal of weapons against Elizabeth had been expended in casual, thoughtless cruelty, and she was so accustomed to his cursing and shouting that they meant nothing to her. And he was restrained from thrashing her because of his fear of the bishop's assistant. He took her with him on his next trip into Sydney to buy her shoes, fabric for clothes, and other necessities, cursing and haggling loudly with each of the merchants, and left her sitting for hours in the cart while he entertained himself in a public house.

The letter, from a Stephen Willoughby, mentioned the

fact that Elizabeth's mother had remarried. An uncle had died and had bequeathed the sum of fifty guineas to her father. Her mother had rendered herself ineligible to receive the money by remarriage, and Elizabeth was heir to the money. The letter included belated condolences on her father's death, remarking on the loss to the clergy and to humanity at large as a result of his death. It requested an acknowledgement and the name of the bank against which she wished the draft to be drawn, and it also invited her to communicate any matters in which the writer might be able to assist her and to advise him of any necessities which she was unable to obtain in Australia and which he might be able to send her.

It was a brilliant beam from a world outside the dark and dreary pit of despair in which she dwelt, a link with life beyond the suffocating walls of shabby, tawdry poverty which surrounded her. The tone of friendly cordiality was a poignant reminder that there were those who were motivated by characteristics other than selfishness, cruelty, and bestial desires, and the matter discussed in the letter was evidence that there were activities of a broader scope than the dreary, deadly routine of existence into which she had fallen. The letter satisfied a need more vital than that for shoes and clothes, and it provided gratification at a level impervious to Cummings' cruelties.

The promise of fifty guineas made Cummings distinctly agreeable to the purchase of writing materials. She sat at the rude table with half a dozen sheets of foolscap and trimmed a fine point on the quill, and he hovered over her in suspicious, illiterate incomprehension as she wrote, staring at the flowing lines of the letters as though trying to discover some universal pattern which would give an insight into their meaning. Her hands were calloused and her fingers stiffened by labor, and the months which had passed since she had effortlessly formed letters with thoughtless precision seemed years.

She began slowly and carefully, composing the sentences in her mind and tracing the letters in the delicate, spidery calligraphy which her father had taught her, and within a few lines it had all come back and she was writing with accustomed ease, as though sitting in her father's study. She replied in the same tone as the letter, thanking him for his efforts on her behalf and for his offer of assistance, and through some lingering feeling of pride she repressed any hint of the circumstances which had befallen her. She used the bishop's office as her return address, writing that her husband's lands lay at some distance from Sydney and the mail service was time consuming and unreliable, and she ended the letter with repeated thanks and cordial wishes.

The weather began turning cool as autumn approached, and in March Cummings took the sheep to be sheared. He was in an ill temper for days afterward, because the wool market was in one of its frequent slumps and he had received a very poor price for the wool, less than it would cost them to live through the winter. He railed and cursed at Elizabeth for what he had to spend on her, and he became even more miserly than before with money for food. But she had new shoes for winter.

In early winter, Elizabeth received another letter from Stephen Willoughby which contained a bank draft for fifty-two guineas, twelve shillings, and sixpence, the sum she had inherited plus seven percentum interest from the time he had received the money until he had drawn the draft. The letter was as long as the first one, far more than the polite remarks of a barrister concluding a transaction. It commented on Australia and the wool industry and included news of other family members of whom she had heard from her father, and it called for a polite response. Cummings was adamantly against spending the seventeen shillings and sixpence it cost to send a letter to England until Elizabeth suggested that there might be more endowments coming at one time or another, when he grudgingly assented.

By spring the fifty-two guineas had long since been exhausted, and they were living on the money Cummings had realized from the sale of the house in Sydney and its furnishings. There was a quit-rent on the land to pay. The bullock died and Cummings had to buy another one. He limited his trips into Sydney to one every two or three weeks, and they had only mutton for days at a time until the vegetables in the garden plot began to mature. The additional sheep Cummings had bought had diminished the money he had received from the house and furnishings, and the season was unusually dry, reducing the graze on the selection until it was too sparse to support the number of sheep on it. He had to pay to graze some of the sheep on other pasture during the summer, and Elizabeth eked out the meager supplies of food, hoping for a good price for the wool come autumn.

It was another year of low prices for wool, and the yield from the sheep was less than it had been the autumn before. There was still money left from the sale of the house and furnishings, but it was questionable if there was enough to last through another bad year. Several neighboring graziers with small, marginally-profitable selections of land and flocks were selling their belongings, intending to try their luck in the gold fields or to join the bands of itinerant stockmen and swagmen who roamed between the stations in the Outback, and Cummings pondered doing the same thing himself. Elizabeth examined her situation, considering what she would do if Cummings left, and she decided she would ask the bishop for his assistance in obtaining a position as a school mistress or governess if possible, or as a domestic if necessary.

Then Cummings returned hurriedly from Sydney one afternoon, shouting for her to leave the sheep and come to the house as he whipped the sweating, exhausted bullock along the path to the house. He had gone to the market to sell half a dozen sheep for a few shillings, and had stopped in a public house where he had met a man who was in charge of a large convoy of wagons bringing wool from a large station in the Outback. The head stockman at the station had recently left, and the owner of the station was looking for a replacement.

The station was well known, one of the largest in New South Wales, and Cummings had a tenuous relationship with the owner. The owner, a man substantially older than Cummings, had been the natural son of a woman who had worked for Cummings' father, and Cummings thought there might be a chance that the relationship could be used to his advantage. The wages would be good, and once established in the deep Outback he might have a chance to buy or settle on another place with his own flock.

Elizabeth wrote the letter for him, emphasizing his experience as an owner of a selection and flocks and working in subtle comments on what Cummings could remember of the woman who had worked for his father, then Cummings hurried back to Sydney with the letter to give it to the man in charge of the wagons to deliver when they returned to the station with supplies.

He was garrulously cheerful for a few days about the possibility of getting the job, then the weeks passed and things became much as they had been before. The winter was unusually severe, and when he had to buy Elizabeth yet another pair of shoes he cursed viciously and reminded her that if they went into the far Outback they would be away from the watchful eyes of the bishop's assistant. The bleak, wintery days followed one after another and some of the sheep began to sicken and die. Cummings became bitter about the job, cursing the station owner, making disparaging remarks about his mother, and accusing Elizabeth of having written something other than what he had told her to write.

Then Cummings returned precipitantly from Sydney on a cold, grey day and came running down to the river where Elizabeth was breaking the ice to dip out water. He had a letter, and he waited impatiently as she opened the packet with numb, blue fingers to read it to him. The letter was short, in an ill-formed scrawl and without proper capitalization and punctuation, and it was bluntly to the point. Cummings was requested to come as soon as possible to speak with the owner about taking the position as head stockman at Wayamba Station.

– 14 –

The sheep and the selection sold for enough to buy a
wagon and team of horses, with an ample amount of
money left over, and the new owner gave them permission
to remain in the house until they could complete their
arrangements. Cummings shopped in Sydney for things
they would need which were scarce in the Outback, and
on one of his trips into the city he tried to sell Elizabeth's
chest of books and box of china at the market. But they
weren't the sort of commodity which sold well at any time,
and as the poor prices for wool had made it a time of
scarcity for everyone, no one would buy them. He
returned with them, grumbling and cursing about the
amount of space they would take up in the wagon.

Numerous unattached men traveled about in the

Outback, but it was considered an extremely hazardous undertaking to travel with a woman without being in a group. There was a delay while he found a group, during which time he frequently reminded her of the burden she represented to him, then he found a drover who was taking five thousand sheep to Wayamba Station. The arrangements were finalized, and they left early one morning and met the drover and his crew at Camden, a moderately large settlement on the Nepean.

The transition between living at the selection and traveling in the wagon was almost as great as the transition she had made when she married Cummings. At the selection there had been times when Cummings had been away, giving her moments of privacy. But Cummings was with her constantly in the wagon, and she was surrounded by profane, uncouth men virtually all of the time.

It became a living nightmare which she endured from one day to the next. Blistering days alternated with frigid nights, and she became ill from time to time. But she endured.

The road was a series of connecting links made by people traveling between adjacent stations, and therefore it changed direction frequently during the first weeks as it went from one home paddock to another. They occasionally stopped overnight and the owner of the paddock or some of the stockmen came to sit by the fire and talk to the drover and his men, starved for the sight of new faces and news from the outside world. A few times they stopped at a place where there was a woman, and the owner went back to get her when he heard that Elizabeth was with the group. The women were almost pathetic in their loneliness. They also became more rare as the miles passed.

The first stations were well established and had obviously been there for many years, and many of them had large, comfortable-looking houses with an aura of having been passed through generations. Large garden plots were enclosed by sturdy fences, and chickens and cats wandered about. They were homes instead of shelters, with flower beds and lawn furniture under spreading pepper and wilga trees. The fences enclosing the paddocks were dark and well-seasoned with age, with spots of brighter wood where repairs had been made, and the land they enclosed was cleared of brush. The first stations seemed enormously large places after the selection on the Georges, but they became even larger further on and the road became a straight track across them to the west. As the stations became larger, the countryside seemed more remote and unsettled, with broad stretches of grassland, low, stony hills, and areas of deep forest. In some places the trees had been ringed and had died, and they were waiting to be cut down. In the meanwhile, they were white, ghostly skeletons with groping fingers stretching upward to the sky and providing perches for flocks of staring crows.

Some of the stations had tiny settlements of aborigines, clusters of huts along a creekline or in a stand of trees near the houses and sheds on the home paddock. The ratio of aborigines and people of mixed blood to white people seemed about the same as that in Sydney at first, and the aborigines looked much like those she had seen in Sydney. Then there were many more aborigines as they traveled further, many of them apparently coexisting independently with the grazing activities on the stations, and there was an even greater increase in the number of people with mixed blood, most of them stockmen or other station employees. And the aborigines showed fewer influences of civilization, going about scantily dressed in cast-off rags or clothing or wearing nothing.

Then the stations became massive, taking several days to cross, and many of the houses were smaller and built of unpainted wood, with a naked, unfinished look about them, an air of impermanence, of tenuous existence in a hostile environment. The terrain became more arid and the heat more intense, the flies and mosquitoes more voracious. Elizabeth became numb as the weeks passed, going through the motions required of her in a daze. At some level it seemed that she had become trapped in the cycle of activity around her and was participating without conscious volition, and that she was doomed to continue in the tortuous routine through eternity. Yet, at another level, she didn't want it to end. After what she had endured, a deeper disappointment in what she found at the end of the journey would be too much to bear.

It came as a shock when she found that they were on Wayamba Station. She was lying on the pallet in the wagon one night in the dull, detached state which had become a defense of her sanity, and a comment by one of the men brought her sharply back into full contact with her surroundings. They were on Wayamba Station, and apparently had been for at least a couple of days. It was the ultimate anticlimax. After the effort and the hardships of the trek, it seemed that their arrival should have been announced by something more than a continuation of the daily routine, but they had arrived and she hadn't even known it. She tried to separate what she had seen during the day's travel from the memory of what she had seen on other days, but it was all much the same in her mind. And on the following day she looked around with more interest, but all she saw was a plain of deep grass spotted with clumps of low scrub stretching away to the horizon in all directions. If there was anything about the vast expanse which distinguished it from the rest of the terrain they had crossed on the trek, it was that it was less distinctive.

The next night there was talk about entering another paddock soon, and just before noon the following day there was another fence of three rails which disappeared into the distance in both directions as though it were a line which cleaved the earth in two. The rails in a section were

221

dropped and they went through, paused for the noon stop, then went on. The fence disappeared into the haze of the heat behind, and the open terrain stretched out ahead again. The breathlessly hot hours of the afternoon passed, and the blazing sun began descending to the west. The long column of sheep finally formed into a circle, and the wagons stopped.

A sheep had been slaughtered the day before, and the cook dragged the odorous, blood-soaked, fly-encrusted bag containing the carcass out of the back of the wagon and hung it on the side of the wagon, and he began building a fire as Elizabeth started mixing the damper. A drumming thud of approaching hoofbeats penetrated her daze, and she glanced over her shoulder. The drover was riding from the sheep toward the wagons, and Elizabeth's husband was trotting back toward the wagons after putting the team with the other horses to graze. The cook came around to the rear of the wagon, hesitated at the corner of it and shaded his eyes with his hand as he looked into the distance ahead of the wagon, then took a knife out of the rack on the sideboard and walked back around the corner of the wagon, looking in front of it with an expression of curiosity. Elizabeth shook the flour off her hands, stepped to the corner, and looked. A rider was approaching at a steady trot, rider and horse moving as one at a pace which swiftly covered miles. All of the transients they had seen had been on foot and in less isolated places, so it was apparently someone who worked on the station. Elizabeth felt curious, but strange men usually misinterpreted curiosity. Richardson and her husband were nearing the wagons, and her husband had warned her repeatedly about calling attention to herself. She stepped back behind the wagon to the pans and began stirring the flour with one hand as she poured in water with the other.

The hoofbeats of the horse approaching from the front of the wagon became louder, then the horse slowed as it neared the wagon. The drover reined up at the same time, a wide smile of greeting on his face as his horse moved past the rear of the wagon at a walk.

"Are you all right, Richardson?"

Elizabeth stiffened with surprise as the drover replied in a cheerful, ingratiating tone. The voice had been a ringing contralto, a woman's voice.

"Aye, I am now. Are you all right, Sheila?"

"I'll do. How many did you lose?"

"Not more than twenty. Would you like to go over and take a look at them?"

"I can see all I bloody need to from here, sodding scruffy lot that they are."

"Scruffy lot?" the drover replied in a defensive tone. "They've come a bloody good way, you know."

"Have you brought them from China, then? But it's naught to me, in any event. I just came over to tell you not to venture south of the track. There's a mob no more than three miles to the south with two jackaroos on it, and we'll have it bloody fair if this lot gets within a mile of them."

"Aye, we'll stay well to the north, then. Will you be at the home paddock when we get there?"

"No, I'm settling this pair on this mob out here, and it'll take another while. Colin's at the home paddock, and he'll take your tally and give you your pay."

"Aye, and I'm ready for it . . ." The drover's voice faded as Cummings approached, puffing breathlessly as he ran past the rear of the wagon. "This is Cummings, your new man."

"Oh? We were about to give you up, Cummings."

"I had trouble finding others coming this way," Cummings replied, breathing heavily.

"Aye, it's the wrong time of year and all, isn't it? Well, you can see Colin at the home paddock, and he'll talk to you and take you to meet my dad."

"I have the job, don't I?"

"You're asking the wrong one. I'm a stockman on

223

Wayamba, and that takes me all of my while. Colin and my dad do all the hiring, and they can bloody have my part of it. But they haven't hired anyone else for the job, or they hadn't when I left the home paddock three days ago."

Cummings made a dissatisfied sound, and Elizabeth felt suddenly weak with fear. The letter from the station hadn't specifically promised the job, but it had strongly implied that Cummings would be hired on the basis of the qualifications in the letter she had written for him. He had been more than satisfied with what the letter from the station had said, and she had assumed that his interpretation had been correct. But what if they had misinterpreted things? If he weren't hired, they would be in an impossible situation. The woman's voice had been reserved and brusque when she replied to Cummings, possibly a bit more so than when she had addressed the drover. A haughty, impatient voice, thick with the accent of the Outback. It was less than a friendly welcome. The drover asked something else about the sheep, and Sheila replied in the same cool tone and with a note of dismissal, referring him to her brother Colin. Elizabeth felt a sudden surge of helpless anger, and she scraped the dough off her hands on the side of the pan and moved to the corner of the wagon.

The woman and Richardson were sitting on their horses facing each other on the other side of the fire, the cook was by the fire looking up at them, and Cummings was standing near the horses. Richardson was inviting her to stay and eat, and she was shaking her head in a curt refusal as she gathered her reins and started turning her horse away. She glanced around, then did a quick doubletake when she saw Elizabeth and jerked her horse back around with a snap of the reins that made it toss its head and stamp its feet.

It had been easy to mistake her for a man from a distance because of the dusty, wide-brimmed stockman's hat, the wrinkled, faded shirt and trousers, and the heavy boots. And because of her size, because she was easily as tall as Richardson, a man of something more than average height. But at closer range there could be no mistake. She was an exceptionally tall woman, but distinctly a woman, far too slender and slight of build to be mistaken for a man. Her shoulders and back were straight, but there was the subtle softness of feminity about them rather than even a suggestion of masculine brawn. Her shirt and trousers were loose and shapeless, but the front of the shirt had the fullness of a woman's bosom, and her small waist and slender hips were differently proportioned to those for which the trousers had been made. The large brown hand held the coiled stock whip with the ease of long familiarity, but the fingers were long and graceful, if somewhat grubby.

The aborigine blood wasn't reflected in her size, enormous for an aborigine, or in the way her features were modeled. Her nose was classically British, long and thin, and she had the British short upper lip. But the aborigine came through clearly in her coloring. The brim of the hat shadowed her face and she obviously spent most of her time in the sun, but her face had a smooth, walnut sheen, far too dark for a white, and her lips and skin were the same color. Her hair was coarse and black, caught in a loose, careless clutch which hung below the back of the hat brim, and stray hairs hung around her ears. The eyes were a solid, gleaming black. She was devastatingly beautiful.

Her voice had sounded unpleasant, but upon seeing her it fell into perspective with the rest of her which made it natural and expected rather than rude or discourteous. Elizabeth remembered the arrival of the new Governor's wife, an extremely overbearing woman, and when she had mentioned it to her father, he had replied that everyone would have been disappointed if she had been otherwise. And while it had been an instance of his oblique and sometimes surprisingly dry wit, it wasn't untrue.

Characteristics which were unpleasant in isolation became more acceptable or even expected when an integral part of a whole which fit the circumstances and situation. Sheila Garrity had a regal air about her, the straight, thin line of her mouth and almost belligerent thrust of her chin reflecting overweening pride and self confidence. It would have been surprising if she had been otherwise. Her family's vast lands stretched in all directions for distances which staggered the imagination, and their flocks were too numerous to count. The marriage which had given her the dark coloring and delicately etched features had also blended the land and the sheep in her veins. She was a princess in this domain, on lands ruled by her family, doing what her family did.

And while the expression was withdrawn, the large, black eyes were open and questing, reflecting curiosity. They shone with a penetrating light which was difficult to look into and at the same time was intensely pleasant. Elizabeth suddenly became aware of absolute silence, the three men looking between them as they looked at each other. And she felt a flush starting to steal up her cheeks. Cummings was characteristically gauche, staring lumpishly instead of breaking the silence with an introduction. Elizabeth nodded and spoke politely.

"How do you do? I am Elizabeth Cummings."

Sheila lifted her head slightly, her eyes widening. Her features remained fixed in rigid lines of hauteur, reflecting something between surprise and affront. Then the thin line of her lips relaxed. A smile spread across her face, slowly widening until her brilliantly white teeth were gleaming against the dark color of her lips and face. "I'll be wiped! A bloody pommie!"

The tone was one of friendly humor rather than condescension, light and warm. Elizabeth felt the flush rising to her cheeks, her smile widening in response to Sheila's gleaming smile. "No, I'm from Sydney."

"Oh?" she chuckled. "Give me no mind, then. To be

from east of my east paddock is pommie to the likes of me. Are you all right?"

"Yes, I'm very well, thank you. How are you?"

"I'll do."

Her smile remained for a lingering second longer. Then she seemed to remember the presence of the men, and her smile disappeared with a sudden, startling abruptness. She glanced at the men and nodded shortly to them as she tightened the reins and turned her horse to ride away.

"Goodbye," Elizabeth said.

Sheila reined her horse back again, turning her head and looking at Elizabeth. She nodded and lifted the whip in a slight motion. She nudged the horse with her heels, and it sprang into a trot which carried her rapidly away. Elizabeth watched her moving effortlessly with the horse, then she looked at the men. She cleared her throat self-consciously and turned and walked back to the pans.

"Did you hear what that bloody black slut said?" Cummings snarled angrily. "I've not come all this fucking long way for naught, and I can tell you that."

"She didn't say you had," Richardson said. "She's not mucking about in what don't concern her, that's what she said."

"She bloody well knew more than what she told me, and we both know that. It's just that the bloody black whore didn't want to give me any of her flaming time, that's all. That, and the fact that her bloody heart is as black as her bloody hide."

"That may be, but don't let her hear you say it. She's had a whip in her hand since she was ten, and she can take an eye out of a man's head at twenty feet without stirring his eyelashes."

Cummings grumbled wordlessly in his throat, and Elizabeth heard him stamping back along the side of the wagon. He stopped at the corner of it, glaring at her. "And you putting on your bloody pommie airs will do me no fucking good here, you. I've had my lot of trouble with you, and I'll have the hide off your pommie arse with my belt and leave you here if you do me out of this job."

Elizabeth felt her face flushing with resentment and mortification, and she continued looking down at the pan, kneading the dough with her hands.

"Do you bloody hear me?" he bellowed at her.

"Yes," she replied in a quiet, controlled tone, still looking down at the pan and working the dough with her fingers.

He snarled wordlessly in his throat, wheeling away, and he stamped off in the direction of the horses. Elizabeth bit her lower lip between her teeth and blinked her eyes rapidly to hold back the tears. It had been a long time since his raging and cursing had bothered her, and she wondered what had made her suddenly vulnerable.

"I don't know what he has his bleeding wind up about," the cook grumbled. "I would have been satisfied with what Sheila had to say, and there wasn't any reason for him to charge his woman that way."

"You're not him, and what goes between him and his woman is between them, unless you want to fight him for her."

"I'll fight for rum, but not for a woman. But he'd be well off if Sheila had been as well taken with him as she was with his wife, pom or no."

"Aye, and you'd be well off to mind your own bloody flock."

"Then fuck off and leave me to it," the cook shouted in sudden anger. "How am I to cook with you here underfoot?"

"You mind how you speak to me, you bloody get!" Richardson stormed back at him. "You'll have my fist along the side of your fucking head!"

Elizabeth tried to blot their profane shouts out of her awareness as she looked down at the sticky dough and the flies embedded in it, but they kept intruding. Then the cooked stormed his final threat, that of putting saltpeter in the tea, and Richardson left and rode off toward the sheep. And Elizabeth thought about Sheila.

She thought about her the next day as the wagon jolted along and she sank into a dull reverie from the suffocating heat, and she thought about the promise that Sheila represented to fulfill her need for a friend. The need was an agonizing longing within her, which had never been truly fulfilled, but had at least been satisfied to an extent by her father while he lived. And the need which Sheila undoubtedly felt, because there had been some kind of communication between them as they looked at each other. A mutual response at some deep and complicated level, something she had never before experienced, a glowing, living spark of contact which had been delicate and precious. And Sheila's groping search for friendship was utterly pathetic, because she had unquestionably been subjected to the most brutal circumstances all of her life—a hard, cruel environment which shriveled the finer impulses as the burning sun dried the fluids from the body. She had been surrounded by men like Richardson, Cummings, and the rest of them all of her life, and the constant object of their lecherous desires, because she was breathtakingly beautiful. And she had been taken advantage of in her youth and inflicted with the shame of a child out of wedlock, if what Richardson had said was true. She was ruled by a tyrannical father, and brutalized by being put to work as a stockman. And through all of that, she still retained a timid eagerness to have a friend, an impulse revealing a sterling character.

Sheila was at the home paddock when they reached it. There was a flurry of activity, the exhilarated excitement of reaching their destination gripping everyone as riders raced out to meet the sheep, and Elizabeth caught tantalizing glimpses of the place through billowing clouds of dust raised by the sheep as they broke into a rapid trot. Dogs barked, stockmen shouted, whips cracked with explosive sounds, and Cummings whipped the team into a lope behind the shadowy bulk of the cook's wagon lumbering rapidly along through the thick haze of dust. There was a headlong rush and an uproar as the noise and activity rose to a climax, and Elizabeth saw the outlines of mazes of pens, buildings, sheds, and distant trees through the dust as the wagon careened along. Then the cook's wagon was sliding to a stop in front of them, and Cummings hissed curses as he slammed his foot down on the brake lever and dragged the traces back to pull the team to a stop.

They were near the gate through which the milling sheep had gone when the breeze began moving the cloud of dust away and Elizabeth could see around them. The men were moving around the wagons on their lathered, panting horses, laughing and shouting, and Sheila was further along the pen, standing in her stirrups and leaning toward a man as she shook her whip at him and shouted in anger. He was a younger man who worked at the station, and he was looking at Sheila with a chastened expression as she raged at him. There was too much noise and confusion for Elizabeth to hear what Sheila was saying, but the ringing sound of her voice carried over the noise in an obviously profane tirade about something the man had done or failed to do. She turned away from him, jerking on her reins and glaring at him over her shoulder, and moved her horse toward the wagons. She and her horse were covered with a thick coating of dust, and streaks of sweat down the sides of her face made dark lines where her skin showed through the dust.

Richardson reined his horse around the side of the wagon, moving toward Sheila as she approached the wagons. "I thought you were going to stop in the back paddock for a while, Sheila."

"I needed to speak with Colin, not that I have to explain myself to the bloody likes of you," she replied shortly. "You get your men around to the other side so we can pass this lot of scurvy goats through a tally run, and then you can explain where the rest of them are." She started to turn away, then hesitated and looked at Cummings. "You can go on over to your house. It's over by the creek, the one next to the big house. When you're set there, you can go over to the mustering yard and talk to Colin."

She kicked her horse with her heels and slapped its shoulder with her whip as she spoke, and rode rapidly along the line of pens toward another gate. Richardson looked around with a dissatisfied frown, and followed her. The cook's wagon turned away from the pens and moved toward a long, narrow building across the open space by the pens. Cummings released the brake and snapped the traces, and the wagon began rumbling along the line of pens toward clusters of trees and houses on the other side of the broad expanse of bare, hard-packed earth beyond the pens.

"If I do have this bloody job, I'll not be at the flaming beck and call of some sodding black slut, I can tell you that!"

The remark was a deep, low grumble, a means of relieving his surly resentment rather than a comment directed at Elizabeth. She wiped the dust from her eyes, looking at him, and made a rare, gratuitous comment to him as she looked away.

"She would have hardly have told us to move into the house unless the position were yours, would she?"

The simple, logical conclusion had escaped him. He looked at her with a thoughtful frown, then nodded and looked away with a mollified expression. Her lips tightened with disgust as she glanced at him again from the corners of her eyes, then she looked away again, thinking of how Sheila had acted. She had seemed very cold and impersonal, not even glancing at her, but she had been angry about something. But she had returned to the home paddock to talk to her brother, and upon arrival, Cummings suddenly had the position of head stockman instead of having to talk to the Garrity men about being hired.

231

- 15 -

A critical eye would see that the houses of Wayamba
Station were located at a less than genteel distance from the
activities with the sheep, the pens being at a distance of
less than two hundred yards and in plain sight from the
verandas, but the most discriminating taste could find
nothing else wrong. It was like an oasis. The three houses
stood along the edge of the creek with a verge of grass
between them and the road, overshadowed by massive,
ancient ghost gums along the creek and clusters of dense,
pale green pepper trees which made deep, cool shade fresh
with the moisture of the creek and fragrant with the scent
of the foliage. Flights of birds flashed between the trees,
tiny finches and sparrows and brilliant parakeets, galahs,
and cockatoos, and the air was alive with their constant
motion and their cheerful calls.

The houses were on piles, and chickens clucked and scratched in the cool space underneath. Stretches of closely-scythed sward fifty feet or more wide lay between the houses, wide enough to provide a measure of privacy without isolation. Eight large wooden water tanks stood in a row by the main house. Between the water tanks and the house there was a small graveyard looking calm and serene in the deep shade. Beds of wallflowers, marigolds, and dahlias around it had gone untended and grown wild. Roses, climbing wisteria, and native vines grew around the water tanks and all the houses, making them look cool, comfortable, and inviting.

Cummings stopped the wagon on the road in front of the center house, climbed down, and walked off across the open space toward the pens. Elizabeth climbed down from the wagon, walked rapidly along the path to the house, and went in. It was luxurious. There was a large parlor, a dining room, kitchen, and two bedrooms, all of them spacious. The furniture was homemade by a craftsman from native woods—chairs and a settle on the veranda, and in the parlor chairs and a settle with sheepskin cushions, corner tables with lamps on them, sets of shelves, and a fireplace. The dining room had a table and four chairs, a long sideboard, and an occasional table in the corner. Both bedrooms were furnished with beds, dressing tables, occasional tables, and chairs, and in one of them there was a mirror on a shelf. There was a stove in the kitchen, as well as a large workbench, a wall cupboard, and a food safe. The back door opened onto a small porch where a tub, buckets, and scrubbing board were stored for washing, and steps led down from the porch to the path leading to the privy which overhung the creek. Elizabeth walked back and forth through the house, looking at things and touching them to assure herself that what she was seeing was real. It was dusty from being unoccupied, but it was neat and the floors had been pumiced to a dark glow. The furniture had a

233

gleaming, satiny finish. A cool breeze swept through the house. It was far more than her most optimistic expectation, almost too good to be true.

A stout, plain woman of forty-five or so crossed the sward from the smaller house as Elizabeth went back along the path toward the wagon. She was warily friendly, introducing herself as Bessie Marshall and eyeing Elizabeth curiously as she responded to the greeting.

"Elizabeth? They don't call you Bess or Bessie, do they? I have my mark on that name here."

"No, I'm usually referred to as Elizabeth."

"Aye, it seems to fit you more and all. Is that what your man calls you, then?"

"I can't recall his ever having referred to me by my name."

"Just like mine," Bessie chuckled wryly. "Wants his tucker and his bit in bed, but he could ration with the jacks and have a sheep in bed for all the difference it would make to him. I could die, and he wouldn't know to bury me until I started stinking. I'll give you a hand unloading your wagon, then."

"That's very kind of you, but I wouldn't want to keep you from things you have to do."

"I have ample to do, and there'll be ample when I finish that. And it'll be for somebody else to see to when I die, because there'll be ample left. So I'll give you a hand with unloading your wagon to keep you from breaking your back. Not that you look weak, but I've seen stronger-looking and all."

Elizabeth smiled and nodded as they started walking toward the wagon. "Thank you very much, Bessie."

"It's no more than I should do. I had a look at your man as he was crossing the yard, and I was hard put to say whether he was your dad or your man."

"He is a few years older than I am."

"Aye, and then some, for you. And he'll have a job keeping the men in their place around you, or I'll be fooled. Pommie, are you?"

"No, I'm from Sydney."

"Sydney, is it? You sound proper posh to me, not that I think you don't know where you're from. The last woman in this house was from Sydney, and she wasn't a mark as posh. Their name was Hobart, and she went raving mad. The man had to take her back, and he wasn't that much better from what I could see. The job done him, and the Outback had her. I hope the same doesn't happen to you."

"I'm more or less accustomed to isolation, and this seems to be a very pleasant place to live. And I'm sure you and I will be fast friends, and we will be able to visit. There is Sheila as well, so I'm sure the time will pass very pleasantly."

"Aye, I'd like to be friends with you. And Sheila is all right, but she's not what I'd call friendly. Not that I've had that much to do with her, as far as that goes. You'll be all right if you can bear the Outback. And if your man can bear the job. If you had been much longer, it could have been that they would have asked my man to take it. But he told me he was going to refuse it if they did."

"I'm sure it is a very difficult position."

"Not as far as I can see, but my man's shy about telling people to do things. But the bit they give him for me to cook at the big house brings it even enough, don't you see? So it's all the same and still easier for him. Well, let's see what you have in here . . ."

She was an enormously strong woman, effortlessly carrying one side of the chest of books and the box of china and chatting while Elizabeth struggled with the other side. When they had finished unloading the wagon and carrying the things in, Elizabeth led the team and Bessie went along with her to show her where to put the wagon and horses. Elizabeth had only glimpsed the stations along the way, but Wayamba was easily the largest and most complex she had seen. The area was dominated by the huge maze of pens on one side of the open space and the shearing shed and somewhat smaller pens associated with it on the opposite side. There was a mustering yard at some distance beyond the shearing shed, a single, huge enclosure where most of the grass had been trampled down, and at one side of it there was another large enclosure with cattle and horses in it. Most of the buildings were between the main pens and the shearing complex, barrack buildings for rouseabouts and stockmen, a building used to quarter itinerant shearers and washers, a smithy, storage sheds of various sizes, and a cook house, where the cook who had accompanied the drover had parked his wagon. At one side of the main pens was a pigpen and a holding pen with a couple of cattle in it, with an adjacent slaughter yard and shed for processing and salting meat. Kennels for dogs filled a large space between two storage sheds, and there was also a large poultry yard, from which the chickens under the houses had apparently escaped.

A large garden plot ran along the creek from the houses, where potatoes, tomatoes, cabbage, beetroot, onions, carrots, and other vegetables were grown, and on the other side of the garden plot was an aborigine settlement. A couple of aborigines were hoeing in the garden plot, others were moving about around their shelters, and still others were crossing the open space between their shelters and the buildings on tasks and errands. Men moved about between the buildings and pens, and a large cloud of dust rose on the other side of the main pens, where sheep were being moved about. A rider was driving a herd of fifty or more cattle across the mustering yard toward the pens, and other men were catching horses in the stockyard. There were more people about than there would be in a large village, and considerably more activity. The buildings were spread out over an area much larger than a village would encompass, a visible symbol of the relatively low value of land where holdings were counted in hundreds of thousands of acres.

Several wagons were parked by the smithy, and Elizabeth and her new friend parked the wagon among the others, unharnessed the horses, and led them to the stockyard where they put them in with the others. Several of the men moving about between the buildings stopped and stared at them curiously, and one turned and walked toward them as they walked back from the stockyard. He was a tall, heavyset man in his twenties with a thick, dark beard and mustaches, and he had a wide, impudent grin on his face. Elizabeth glanced at him and looked away, moving closer to Bessie and she nudged her to change direction slightly. Bessie was pointing to the garden plot and talking about the difficulties with the opossums and rabbits eating the vegetables, and she glanced at Elizabeth, looked at the man approaching, and groaned.

"That bloody Tom Stapleton," she sighed heavily. "I might have looked for trouble from that bloody get."

"Act as though you don't see him," Elizabeth said quietly, her face averted from the man and nudging Bessie again to turn at a sharper angle away from him. "What were you saying?"

"Saying? Saying about what? Oh, I was—"

"Here now," the man laughed in a jeering tone, striding toward them and stopping in front of them. "Not so bloody fast—I'll have a look at the pommie mort." He laughed again and moved to one side to block Elizabeth as she started to walk around him. "Aye, and it's worth the trouble of looking and all. They said she was a comely bit, and they didn't lie."

"Leave be, you bleeding lout!" Bessie snapped. "We've no bloody time for the likes of you."

"And I've none for you, you old sow," Stapleton retorted, taking Elizabeth's arm as she moved to one side again to go around him. "Stay and let me have my look, pommie. That'll suffice me for now, no fear."

Elizabeth lifted her eyes and glared into his, trembling with anger. "Take your hand from my arm," she hissed indignantly.

He released her arm and stepped back with an

237

expression of exaggerated astonishment, and he took off his hat and bowed mockingly. "Oh, she's the grand lady and all," he crowed. "I do beg your pardon, m'om."

"She's better than you, dag face," Bessie snarled. "Not that I'd compare her to the likes of you."

He looked at Bessie then back at Elizabeth with a sour smile, putting his hat back on and turning away. "I'll find out how good she is when I have a bloody mind to," he sneered. "No bloody fear about that."

Bessie sighed heavily and shook her head, looking at him as he walked away. "Aye, your man is going to have a job keeping them in their place, Elizabeth. And that sod will be the worst of the lot—he's a real trouble maker, he is."

Elizabeth bit her lower lip, struggling to maintain control. Tears of anger and indignation were struggling to burst forth, and her heart was pounding heavily. But she felt an almost overwhelming rush of relief that he was gone, that a hostile, threatening force surrounding her had dissipated, mixed with a sense of foreboding from the threat he had left hanging in the air. Her arm felt unclean, as though she could still feel the touch of his heavy, hard hand. She drew in a deep, trembling breath and released it in a sigh as she silently nodded, and she rubbed her arm as they started walking again.

"We can go over by the storeroom and get your week's rations on the way back, and I'll help you carry them to your house."

Elizabeth cleared her throat to control her voice and shook her head slightly. "No, thank you, Bessie. I believe I'd rather just go on back to the house and—"

"No, you'll have to have your rations," Bessie interrupted in a firm tone. "You can't stop living because of the likes of that bleeding get, Elizabeth. And if anyone else gives you any pother, I'll kick his cod piece up his arse. Your man will see them right soon enough."

Elizabeth felt a warm rush of gratitude as she looked at

Bessie's homely, smiling face, and she forced a smile and nodded as they angled toward the long, low building Bessie indicated. Bessie began talking about the garden plot again, and Elizabeth listened to her absently, thinking about what she would tell her husband. Judging from past experience, his reaction would be far different from the unqualified support and assistance Bessie anticipated.

The incident had taken the sparkle from the day. Before, the abundant rations the old, crippled storekeeper weighed and counted out would have inspired delight, but now they only served to lighten her depression somewhat. There were vegetables from the garden, generous portions of flour, salt, sugar, rice, dried peas, tea, pepper and curry, salted pork and beef, fresh mutton, candles, oil for the lamps, soap, and even eggs, a rare delicacy under any circumstances. Bessie helped her carry the things to the house, went back to her house for a shovelful of hot coals to start a fire in the stove, then left to start the evening meal at her home and the Garrity house.

Elizabeth had been looking forward to a bath and clean clothes, but the dread of having to tell Cummings about the incident with Stapleton and the lingering anger and resentment from the incident had taken the pleasure out of it. Now it was simply something else to do. She started the evening meal, carried water and washed all the dirty clothes, then disrobed in the kitchen and stood in the tub to bathe and wash her hair. Part of the clothes had dried enough to wear when she finished her hair, and she put on clean underclothes and a dress and finished cooking the meal. The golden light of late afternoon was filtering through the foliage overhead and filling the house by the time the food was ready, and she covered the pans, put them on the back of the stove and began cleaning the house.

When Cummings came in, it was immediately obvious that she didn't have to tell him. She had just finished dusting the parlor, and stood with the rag in her hand looking at him as he stood in the doorway and glared at her in rage. His left eye was puffy, and his knuckles were battered.

"We don't even get settled before you start bloody trouble for me," he snarled angrily. "The first bloody thing you do is set about displaying yourself and enticing the men here. If there's one thing I don't need, it's fucking trouble. So you have a bloody mind to your flaming work, and you stay away from the men here. Now do you understand me, slut?"

"If you are referring to that Stapleton man, I can assure you—"

"And I want none of your bloody pommie speeches! You do as you're told, or you'll be bloody sorry, I can tell you!"

"I don't know what he told you, but what happened was no fault of mine. I tried to avoid him, but he pursued me."

"He told me enough to get his sodding arse stretched on the ground, is what he told me. And if you'd been at your work instead of bloody displaying yourself about, he wouldn't have had a chance to *pursue* you, as you say, and get me into a fucking fight with him."

Prudence warned her to be silent, but the utter injustice of the situation made her anger flare. "I was seeing to the horses and wagon, which might possibly be attending to your work instead of mine. Be that as it may, if you chose to fight with him instead of discharging him for insolence to your wife, then you have only yourself to—"

"I'll have a bloody end to this!" he stormed at her, walking toward her with his fists knotted. "I'll listen to no more of your flaming scavey!" He stood over her and glared, his face working with rage. "You'll do as you're told, and I'll bloody decide what's your work and what's mine without having your long bloody pommie nose in it! And I didn't..." He hesitated, his tone changing to a mocking imitation of her accent, ". . . *discharge him,*" he sneered, then leaned closer to her, shouting in her face, "because I don't come to a job and start by getting shot of people! And it's not mine to say who will work here and who won't! Now you get your flaming pommie arse in there and get my tucker, and be done with your bleeding sauce!"

She steeled herself and looked up into his eyes with an unwavering stare for a long second. His nostrils flared and his face flushed to a dark crimson at her silent defiance, and he uttered a strangled sound in his throat as his fists clenched harder and he began trembling. She slowly turned and walked through the dining room and into the kitchen. He was motionless and silent for a long moment, then he growled in his throat and stamped into the dining room, jerked a chair away from the table, and dropped into it.

He sat with his fist on his chin and looked down at the table with a stony expression as she brought in a lamp and the dishes and silverware. He began wolfing his food down and spoke in a deep grumble through a mouthful as she sat down. "We've been called to Mr. Garrity's house tonight. Why he would want *you* there I can't say, unless he's already heard of what you've been up to and he wants to tell you to stop displaying yourself about and causing trouble. And if you put on your bloody pommie airs and shame me while we're there, you'll bloody have it from me when we get back here."

She silently nodded, looking down at her plate and chewing slowly.

"Answer me!"

She swallowed and lifted her eyes, looking into his. "Very well," she said quietly. "There are clean clothes on the rail on the porch. Perhaps they will allow us to come inside if you will change."

His face darkened with rage again and his knuckles turned white as he gripped his knife and fork with a force

241

which made his hands quiver. She looked back down at her plate, took another bite, and slowly chewed. He snorted and grumbled in his throat, and began wolfing his food again.

There had been a few instances of Elizabeth's hesitant, faltering rebellion against his cruelty and unreasonable demands during the early months of their marriage, but he had crushed them into a passive lack of resistance. Circumstances had somehow changed with the ending of the trek and the arrival at the station. Her defiance had been only a token resistance, but it had been defiance. And the atmosphere between them was different. It was that of adversaries rather than of the dominating and the submissive. There were houses on each side of them and people were near, which placed limits on the degree of cruelty he could inflict on her, particularly since the Garrity family was in one of the houses. He was less sure of himself than he had been on the selection. But beyond those things, there was a subtle change in Elizabeth which eluded her when she attempted to isolate it, but one which had given her the will to resist. She felt a calm, serene satisfaction which brought back something of her earlier pleasure over the house and the station, and a hopeful sense of anticipation glowed within her as she thought about going to the Garrity house. She wondered if Sheila would be there.

Darkness had fallen, and the damp air off the creek was cool as they walked along the path and turned onto the road toward the Garrity house. The insects in the grass chattered in a wavering blur of noise which rose and fell, frogs chorused along the creek, and there was the occasional mournful call of a night bird. The yellow glow of candles and lamps shone in the windows of the houses, as well as in several of the buildings scattered about between the pens and shearing complex. An atmosphere of tranquility hung over the station.

The soft light coming through the front windows and

242

open doorway of the Garrity house outlined a man sitting on the edge of the veranda at the top of the steps, and he stood up as they walked along the path toward the house, looking enormously tall in silhouette against the lighted doorway.

"Is that you, Colin?"

"Aye. Are you settled in?"

"Well enough. Taking the air, are you?"

"A bit." He moved to one side as they walked up the steps, looking down at Elizabeth. "This will be your wife?"

"Aye, her name's Elizabeth."

Her husband's tone was as careless and perfunctory as Colin's had been courteous, pointing out the obvious to indicate the necessity for an introduction. He was an exceptionally tall man, and he looked neat and clean, his beard and mustaches cropped short and his hair combed straight back. In the dim light coming through the doorway, his features appeared to resemble Sheila's closely, those of a strikingly handsome man.

"I'm pleased to meet you, Mrs. Cummings. Are you all right?"

"It's my pleasure, and I'm very well, Mr. Garrity. Are you well?"

"Yes, thank you. Please come on in."

His tone and manner weren't polished, but they were sincere and were reminiscent of years past, when handsome young men had smiled at her in admiration and stepped quickly to hand her down steps and open doors for her. But her longing was for a time and place where gentility had been a pattern of life rather than a desire for admiration and attention, for a time and a place where rude approaches by uncouth men had been unthinkable and social order had been based on adherence to custom rather than on the weight behind a fist. Cummings hesitated as Colin stepped back for Elizabeth to precede him across the veranda, and she

243

entered the house with the two men following her.

Sheila was there, looking very comfortable and relaxed with the cuffs of her faded trousers tucked into her boots, her collar open, and her sleeves rolled up. She was even taller in close proximity than she had looked on her horse, almost as tall as her brother. Elizabeth was so pleased upon seeing her that she lost control over her polite smile and it widened into a grin, and Sheila's smile became dazzling in response, her dark eyes becoming warm and soft and her teeth gleaming in the light from the lamps. Then she suddenly looked away, her smile moderating, and as the lamplight shone in her hair Elizabeth noted with mild surprise that there were touches of grey in the coarse dark strands.

Her mother's wrinkled skin was somewhat lighter in color than Sheila's, although she was clearly unmixed aborigine, and she was a thin woman of average height whose back and shoulders were unbowed by her years. She wore a man's shirt which was much too large for her spare frame and which hung down to her thighs, a heavy, shapeless, skirt-like garment which had been made from a pair of men's trousers, and her gnarled, calloused feet were bare. And she was puffing on a large pipe. But somehow the clothes she chose to wear and the pipe didn't appear ridiculous or even eccentric, because she had a serene aplomb and air of total harmony with her surroundings which placed her outside the pale of judgement by others. Her hair was almost completely white, very thick and the texture of Sheila's, cut almost as short as a man's. There was a deep, long scar from near the center of her wrinkled forehead to a point over her left eye, a creased ridge of lighter color against her dusky skin from what had obviously been a severe injury sometime in the past. The most startling thing about her was her eyes. They were young, clear, bright, and inquisitive, the windows of an exceedingly alert mind.

Sheila and Colin had inherited their size from their father. He was sagging with age, his face splotched and a maze of wrinkles, his lips collapsed on his toothless gums, and his scalp showing pinkly through his thin, white hair. But when he had been in his prime he had obviously been of a size which matched his lands. His eyes were sightless masses of cataracts and he cocked his head to one side to be able to hear the activity around him, but the gnarled, wrinkled hand holding the pipe was steady and his features were set in hard lines of imperious authority.

There were introductions, to which the old man and woman responded with nods and murmurs and Cummings with gauche heartiness, and Sheila sat back down in her chair. Elizabeth and Cummings sat down on a settle, and Colin went to a sideboard and poured watered rum for his father, Cummings, and himself, and sangaree for Sheila and Elizabeth. The old woman drank nothing. Elizabeth looked up at Colin with a polite smile as she took her glass, and she observed that his eyes were a dark blue. And he was even more handsome than she had thought.

The atmosphere was strained and awkward at first, because Cummings was painfully ill at ease. Then the old man expressed some interest in the Cummings family, and Cummings began talking at length about the old man's mother, attributing to her angelic qualities and superhuman virtues which were patently untrue. When he began to run out of superlatives, the old man again referred to the Cummings family in a quiet murmur, puffing on his pipe and staring sightlessly at Cummings. Cummings talked about his father and his brothers, the one who had been an escapee from a penal colony and the one who was a shipping factor in Sydney. The old man listened silently and expressionlessly, and there was a short silence when Cummings finished. Colin and Sheila maintained a respectful silence. The old man asked Cummings about the selection on the Georges. That turned the conversation to sheep and related matters, and all three men began discussing the station.

Elizabeth listened absently, glancing around the room.

It was about the same size as the parlor in the head stockman's house, and the furniture was more or less the same. The house was almost austere, larger than the head stockman's house but no more luxurious, and the Garritys dressed in the plain and sturdy clothes of stockmen.

There had been sheep station owners who lived in Sydney and left their holdings under the management of overseers, and while she had no specific knowledge on the size of properties they had owned, most of them had to be smaller than Wayamba. But the station owners in Sydney had been among the most wealthy people of Sydney and Parramatta. Their children were educated in England, they lived in the finest houses, and they traveled about the city in the most exclusive circles, always in expensive, stylish clothes and in carriages drawn by a matched four.

But the Garritys were different, and the differences ran deep. From sly gossip Elizabeth had heard at one time or other, it wasn't unknown for stations to be managed by children of mixed blood fathered by the owner, far removed from sight in the Outback while he lived respectably in Sydney or Parramatta with his white wife and children. But the old man had made the aborigine woman his wife and it had been an act he had never foresworn. The entire family spurned the comforts of the city for the hardships of their lands, apparently from choice. But the choice was wise, because the old woman with her unusual clothes, bare feet, and pipe would hardly be accepted at the level their wealth would place them in the city. And Colin and Sheila wouldn't be accepted either. Some of the best families had roots which went back to the time when Australia had been a dumping-ground for felons and had covered the fact with manufactured family histories, but visible evidence of unfortunate parentage was regarded with disparagement, because of widespread sensitivity on the matter. So they wouldn't be accepted because of their mixed blood, and their lack of education and polish. And Colin, with his strong, handsome features, blue eyes, and short beard would be considered far too dashing and rakish by fathers concerned about their daughters' virtue. And Sheila with her wild, dark, sultry beauty would appeal strongly to men, but men of the wrong sort.

Most of all, the old man wouldn't fit in the city. The reasons why were less tangible than for the others, but Elizabeth felt a firm, unwavering conviction that they were even more definite and unyielding. It had to do with the way he sat, with his huge boots sprawled out in front of the oversize chair which had been built to accomodate his frame, with the way he held his head, and the volume of his voice, soft yet filling the room when he spoke. He was on too large a scale for the city. Blind, hard of hearing, toothless, and shrunken with old age, it still took the vast expanse of his own lands to accomodate him.

So they lived, consuming modestly and spending generously on their lands. It appeared that what represented a means to others had become an end for them. Their purpose in life was the land itself, not the yield. It wasn't ignominious, as greed and other unworthy motivations were, and it had an element of dignity. But it also clashed strongly with accepted values and traditional concepts of the purpose of labor in a way which evaded rather than violated them, much as the old woman's appearance eluded comparison with other standards of appearance.

They were different, people who would have fascinated her father, and their motivations in general seemed obscure. When Cummings had applied for the position, she had given little thought to his qualifications, but it had seemed that a man who had owned a flock and his own selection would be fully qualified as a kind of overseer on another place. But after seeing something of Wayamba Station, she had strong doubts. Cummings wasn't an intelligent man and he had little insight into others, characteristics which appeared crucial for the head stockman in view of the large number of employees at Wayamba and the scope of the activities. But he had been hired. And Elizabeth was still puzzled over the way he had been hired. When Sheila had met them enroute, she had been clearly noncommittal about his prospects of having the job. She had also said she intended to remain out in the paddock for a time. But she had gone at the home paddock instead and had told the drover that she had come in to talk with Colin. It seemed an inescapable conclusion that the meeting out in the paddock with its strange but gratifying feeling of intimate affinity had motivated her to ride in and ask Colin and perhaps her father to hire Cummings.

Elizabeth became conscious that she was looking absently at Sheila as she pondered, and Sheila was looking back at her. Her chair faced the end of the settle on which Elizabeth sat, with her mother and the three men to her left and to Elizabeth's right, and they were isolated from the others in their silent regard of each other. She was sprawled in the chair in careless ease, sitting much like a less than socially conscious man would, her knees apart, her legs stretched out in front of her, and her glass of sangaree resting on her thigh. Her features assumed a somewhat sullen, withdrawn expression when in repose, and her black eyes were neither warm nor cold, simply staring. She seemed to be engrossed in thought.

Her eyes suddenly focused. She took a sip of her sangaree. "Is the house all right?" she asked in a quiet murmur below the men's conversation.

Elizabeth's utter delight with the house returned as she thought about it, and she smiled and clicked her tongue. "All right? It's absolutely lovely, Sheila, far more than I expected."

Sheila nodded and smiled, her eyes moving away as she took another sip of her sangaree, and her eyes moved past

248

the hallway to the bedrooms then returned to it. "Come on, then," she said quietly, motioning.

A boy of six or seven who had been standing in the hallway out of Elizabeth's line of vision came into the room, glancing around with a diffident expression. He was wearing trousers and small boots, but he was bare from the waist up, the lamplight gleaming on his smooth, tanned torso, and he shyly returned Elizabeth's smile as he crossed the room. There was apparently at least some foundation for the story Elizabeth had heard the drover telling, that the boy was Sheila's child out of wedlock. He was older than Elizabeth had expected, and his father had apparently been a fair-complexioned man. His features were Anglo-Saxon, his eyes large and pale blue, and his hair light brown with streaks of sun-bleached blonde. He went to Sheila, and she moved her glass to her other hand and put her arm around him, her features softening into a smile as she spoke to him.

"Where's your bloody shirt, then?" She hissed sharply and cut him off as he motioned toward the hallway and began replying in a soft murmur, and she glanced at her father and looked back at him. "Speak in English, you little sod. You bloody know that your granda' gets his wind up when you speak in *Daen*, and the old bugger will have me leathering your arse for it again if he hears you. Now where's your flaming shirt?"

He whispered a reply, pointing toward the hallway again.

"Is that where it's supposed to be, you lettle get? Are you supposed to leave your bloody shirt in your room and go about like a sodding abo whelp when visitors are in the house? Never mind, it's done now. Give us a kiss, then. Aye, there's a good lad. That's Mrs. Cummings—go over and pay your respects."

The blistering profanity was obviously an element of her normal vocabulary, because her tone was caressing. Another facet of her personality showed as her long, graceful fingers lingered on his arm and shoulder and she looked at him with the soft, loving maternal eyes. The boy walked toward Elizabeth, and Sheila's eyes followed him, a proud smile on her face.

"My name is James Garrity, and I'm pleased to meet you, m'om," he whispered shyly in an uninflected rote of memorized words and a heavy brogue.

"The pleasure is mine, James, and I am delighted to meet such a handsome young man." His eyes looked enormous in his tanned face, and his small, delicate features were very attractive. She took his arms and pulled him closer to touch her lips to his cheek. He felt warm and silky, and there was a scent of sun and the cool breeze along the creek about him. She looked at him again, feeling a warm empathy, and she wanted to pull him closer and embrace him but restrained the impulse because of the impropriety of a too-ostentatious show of affection. But he was grinning widely, apparently perceiving her warm regard for him. "How old are you, James?"

His shyness made him stumble over the answer. "He was seven in December," Sheila said, putting her glass down, and she snapped her fingers at the boy and motioned him toward her as she stood. "Let's take the air, Elizabeth. This bloody tobacco smoke will have to be cut out of here with an axe."

The boy trotted toward Sheila, and Elizabeth glanced at the others to excuse herself as she put her glass down and stood. Cummings glanced up at her absently, his attention on what he was saying to the old man. Colin looked at her and smiled politely as he nodded. The old man's attention wandered toward her and Sheila then back to Cummings again. The old woman was staring at Elizabeth fixedly, and Elizabeth suddenly had the impression that the old woman's attention had been on her all the time but she hadn't noticed it. The old woman's eyes moved to Sheila then back to Elizabeth without a change of expression as she put the end of the pipestem between her lips and puffed on it. Her eyes were inquisitive and probing. Elizabeth smiled at her and turned toward Sheila as Sheila effortlessly scooped the boy up on one arm, and they walked toward the door.

They walked along the path and out of the shade of the trees into the bright moonlight on the road. The air was fresh and cool, and over the sounds of the insects and frogs there was a soft chanting from the aborigine huts, a rhythmic rise and fall of voices which blended naturally with the other sounds of the velvety night. The boy shivered in Sheila's arms, and she put her other arm around him and held him closer, kissing his forehead. "Aye, you'll learn to wear your shirt, you little beggar," she murmured.

Elizabeth looked at them, wrapping her arms around herself against the chill. The boy was clinging to Sheila and huddled against her for warmth, and she held him tightly, her smooth, brown arms blending in color and texture with his bare back in the bright moonlight. "He's a lovely boy, Sheila."

"Aye, he's a sweet nipper. And a lot of his dad in him, he has. I suppose you know he came on the wrong side of the blankets?"

Elizabeth looked up at her uncertainly, disconcerted by Sheila's bald approach to the subject. "Oh, you mean... well, no, I had no idea... no, that isn't true. But it is true that it's none of my concern, nor is it mine or anyone else's place to judge. And he is a very lovely boy and a great joy to you, I'm sure."

"But you did know how he was got?"

Elizabeth cleared her throat uncomfortably, looking away. There was a possibility that Sheila might conclude that Bessie had talked about it, which wouldn't be fair to Bessie. She nodded. "Yes. I wouldn't listen to malicious talk about anyone, Sheila, and particularly about you now that I've met you, because I consider you an admirable person. But I was interested in what this place would be like, and I listened at times to the men when they talked at night. There was mention of it among them."

"Aye, and I'll wager the story you heard was twice as good as what happened," she chuckled.

"I'm sure it was. People who are given to irresponsible talk are also given to exaggeration."

Sheila looked down at her thoughtfully, then smiled and nodded. "I hadn't thought of it that way, but I wouldn't debate it." She looked away, sighing softly and shrugging. "Well, it happened and I wish it hadn't, but I wouldn't be without the boy now. The bastard was a shearer, James Campbell by name, and a better looking man you never saw. Nor a better talker, because he talked me out of my strides when my dad had told me he'd nail them to my arse with a spike if I ever pulled them down for a man. And I thought the old sod was bloody going to when he found out that my regularity had stopped. I told my ma, and I should have bloody known better because she was pissing herself to tell him as soon as she found out. She's always thought of no bugger but him, and when you speak to her you're talking to him. But she told him, and this whole station was on its bloody ear while he was having at me to find out who had done it. I suppose the drovers had their piece to say about that?"

The conversation was discomfiting, but it was also satisfying. Sheila clearly wasn't a person given to discussing herself or her affairs, but a feeling of trust had come quickly and naturally. "Sheila, they talked constantly about things which are none of their concern, and subjects of that nature are continually on the minds of people of their sort."

"Aye, no doubt. What did they have to say about it?"

"Only foolishness, Sheila. The boy will probably be an excellent stockman, won't he? His background is—"

"No, he won't, and it's good that he's a lad because a dog that doesn't show any more interest than he does in

252

sheep gets knocked on the head. What kind of foolishness did they have to say?"

"Sheila, I don't really recall . . ." Her voice faded as she stopped herself from lying, and she looked up at Sheila and looked away again. "Oh, something about . . . ah, punishing you with a whip, and . . . ah, tying you up in a ram's skin, but I'm sure that they—"

"Aye, well, that was a bloody lie."

"Of course it is, Sheila. As I said, they were given to foolish—"

"It was a ewe's skin."

"Pardon me?"

"A ewe's skin. He was as mad as a wild boar with a thorn in its cod piece, but he'd never kill a ram that was doing a proper job of servicing. He staked me out in the mustering yard in a ewe's skin, and I found my tongue after a couple of days of that, I can tell you. I haven't been able to eat mutton since, either. All I have to do is put a piece in my mouth, and I'll chunder my gorge." She chuckled softly and shook her head, her teeth shining in the moonlight. "I was the daft one of the lot to think I could keep it from him. He's a rum old bugger, my dad is. When he has his mind set, nothing will turn him aside. He's blind, half deaf, and toddles around like a weaner, but I'd curse God before I'd go up against him."

There was a clear note of admiration in her voice as she talked about her father and what he had done to her, revealing a side to her nature which was cruel and coarse. But many of the influences which had formed her nature had been brutalizing, forcing callousness to develop in defense, and there were other sides to her nature. There was the side which made the movement of her long, thin fingers in the boy's hair seem a living symbol of love, the stern lines of her face in repose dissolve into a sweet, friendly smile, and gave her dark eyes a hollow and lonely look. She was a very complicated person. Strangely, it seemed that they knew each other well although they had just met. And in another way it seemed unlikely that they would ever truly know each other. Elizabeth felt confused.

The boy wriggled in Sheila's arms and murmured, and Sheila put him down and ruffled his hair, telling him to go to bed. The boy trotted along the path to the house, and Sheila folded her arms and looked up at the sky, yawning.

"It's very pleasant here, Sheila."

"Aye, it's quiet when the rabble has sogged for the night."

"No, I mean the station in general. It's a very beautiful place, and a lovely name, by the way. Who named it Wayamba?"

"My dad. He bought it from a man named Williamson years back when it was a small place, less than a hundred acres. Dad worked for Williamson, and his range was down to the south, by a place called the Broken Hill. The abos call it Wayamba, and Colin and I were born there. Dad's always had a feeling for the place, so he gave the name to the whole station. If I had my say, we'd pull the boundary back to the north of there. The place is full of mineral outcroppings and draws a lot of fossickers who tear the fences down, and it's more trouble than it's worth. It won't take more than twelve thousand, and that's on a good year. But my bloody say goes for nought here."

"I'm sure that's an exaggeration, Shiela. I'm confident that both your father and brother have a great deal of confidence in you."

Sheila tossed her head back and laughed softly. "You've a pretty way with words, Elizabeth, although you confound me as to what you mean half of the time. Did you go to college in Sydney?"

"No, my father was a minister and he tutored me."

"Minister? Then how did you come to be married to— well, that's none of my flock. Would you like to teach the nipper? Colin and I can read and write well enough to do a fair job on the station books and such, but we're not up to teaching anyone else. And it could be that the lad would find that sort of thing to his liking. He's shown no ability in anything else, and sooner or later he'll have to do something to earn his rations. It would be worth five shillings a week for you to teach him to cypher and to read and write."

"You could be judging him too hastily, Sheila, because he's still a very small child. But he should unquestionably be taught to read and write and to do sums, and I'll be more than glad to do it for nothing."

"No," Sheila said flatly, shaking her head. "It'll be five shillings a week."

"Well, I certainly don't want to seem ungrateful, and that's very generous of you. In speaking with Bessie, I understand that she does the cooking for your household and other things. Shall I share the work with her?"

"That's a chore her husband got for her, and you won't have time to do anything more than take care of your house and teach the lad, because I want him taught properly."

She obviously wanted her son tutored, but it also appeared that she had thought of a way to satisfy Cummings with additional income, as Bessie's husband was receiving, while putting herself in a position to interpose an objection if Cummings searched for ways to get even more. If it were true, it revealed a shrewd mind, and a flattering concern. Elizabeth thought again about Sheila's return to the home paddock when she had said she was going to remain in an outer paddock, and of the way in which all questions about whether or not Cummings would be hired had disappeared.

"Sheila, I heard you tell the drover that you were going to stay in the other paddock for a time. Why did you come in instead?"

Sheila looked down at her, her lips pursed and an aloof expression on her face. "To speak with Colin," she replied quietly. "Why do you ask?"

255

"Was it to ask Colin to hire my husband?"

Sheila's brows abruptly drew together and her chin thrust out in a dark frown. "Now why would I do a bloody thing like that?" she snapped.

Elizabeth was taken aback by the sudden change and by the disappearance of the cordial atmosphere between them, and she looked up at Sheila and shrugged uncertainly. "I thought it might have been a gesture of kindness to me, Sheila. And the reason I asked is so I can thank you, if that is indeed what you did."

Sheila's frown faded into a wooden expression, and she looked away and nodded slightly. "Aye, well, I did," she said quietly.

"Then words can't express my appreciation. But I can't understand your sensitivity. Surely an act of kindness and consideration for another isn't a cause for shame."

"That's as may be," Sheila murmured, shrugging slightly. "But the first thought in my mind is Wayamba Station. I don't put myself in front of this station, and I'll do it for no bugger else. And I wouldn't have put my mouth into it if I hadn't thought he could do the job. To me, Wayamba comes first, last, and always." She looked down at Elizabeth again, smiling slightly, and her tone softened. "And don't forget that, little pom."

"I shan't," Elizabeth replied, smiling warmly and taking Sheila's hand between hers. "Nor will I forget what you did. I am very grateful, Sheila. I am grateful because this is a lovely place and I know I am going to enjoy it, and I am grateful for the opportunity to be near you. I do hope we'll be fast friends."

Sheila looked down at her in thoughtful silence for a long second, a slight, absent smile on her face, then she nodded and chuckled. "Aye, we shall be, then." She took her hand from between Elizabeth's and put it on Elizabeth', shoulder, turning her toward the path. "Let's go back in before the chill has us."

Elizabeth smiled and nodded, gratified that the feeling

of harmony had been restored. They walked back along the path, up the steps and across the veranda, and Sheila nudged Elizabeth through the door ahead of her and dropped her hand from Elizabeth's shoulder as they entered. Colin and Cummings glanced at them and the old man's head turned slightly, then the conversation between the three men continued. The old woman chewed on the stem of her pipe, looking at Elizabeth as she crossed the room to sit down. Elizabeth smiled at her politely. The old woman nodded slightly and continued puffing.

– 16 –

Life at Wayamba Station was like a golden, joyous dawn after a long and dreary night. Each morning began with the lively chatter of birds in the trees surrounding the house and the crowing of roosters. The cool, fresh breeze along the creek swept through the house, and there was a distant bustle of activity around the buildings and pens as the station began another day.

Mornings were deliciously leisurely, because Cummings was gone for days at a time in one or another of the paddocks. The house was a continuing joy with its comfort and conveniences, and it was a pleasure to keep it clean. The variety and abundance of food was greater than she had ever known, providing a kind of entertainment in planning and preparing meals. James was an alert and perceptive child, as much a companion as pupil. Bessie's homely face and wisdom provided pleasant interludes. Pruning and tending the vines and flower beds and cleaning off the graves in the small graveyard was a labor of love which brought back memories of childhood.

There was ample privacy, but a sufficient presence of others. Bessie stopped to chat for a moment now and then. James came during the afternoon, and Tom, Bessie's boy of nine who helped the cook, came for two hours. Even in moments of solitude there would be the sound of the aborigines hooting to each other along the creek and shouts betwen the men among the buildings a hundred yards away. While working on the vines and flowers, she occasionally saw the old man and old woman. Sometimes they would be sitting on their veranda in silence and smoking their pipes, the old man's blind eyes staring into the distance at visions only he could see and the old woman holding the long, heavy, polished stick she always carried with her when she was out of the house. The old man never left the house without the old woman.

At other times Elizabeth would see the old woman leading the old man along the path to the privy behind their house, the old man's hand on the old woman's shoulder and the old woman taking slow, measured steps, sometimes carrying her stick and at other times resting the end of it on the ground. They never seemed to talk, but Elizabeth had a distinct impression that there was a kind of comunication between them at a deeper level than conversation. Elizabeth smiled and waved when she saw them, and the old woman always responded with a dignified nod.

And there was Sheila. She would be out in one of the paddocks for two or three days and even longer at times, but most of her time was spent at the home paddock in overseeing the multitude of activities which took place, seeing to repairs on buildings, wagons, and other equipment, counting, weighing, and measuring the foodstuffs and goods in the storeroom, picking out sheep, cattle, and swine to be slaughtered, and prowling restlessly about on other details of the station operation.

The first time Elizabeth tried to draw Sheila into the civilized ritual of afternoon tea, the result was symbolic of the nature their relationship was to take. She truculently insisted on having her tea in a pannikin instead of a Wedgewood cup, polite conversation was difficult because of her long silences, and she abruptly rose and left without saying goodbye. Sheila was totally different from anyone Elizabeth had known before, and her conduct fit no established pattern. She was a moody woman, occasionally serenely placid but often either affectionately friendly or withdrawn. It was puzzling, but Elizabeth struggled to accept her as she was and understand the influences which had made her who she was, and Sheila's darkest mood was preferable to her absence. And Sheila at her most distant was always interested and concerned in Elizabeth's welfare.

Their divergent backgrounds gave them little in common, and most of Sheila's conversation was about the station. At first Elizabeth's interest was motivated solely by courtesy and a wish to keep some kind of conversation going with Sheila when she visited, then she found herself developing a growing curiosity about the station and a concern with its affairs. Each of the paddocks had a name, Bulloo, Windorah, and Oldea to the north, Penong and Wilcannia to the east, Tanami, Wayamba and Barrow to the south, and Maralinga and Tambo to the west, and the references to them began to be more meaningful as Elizabeth learned about them and where they were.

But meaningful only to an extent. They were all divided into sections, and a reference might be made to a section or to a whole paddock, depending upon the conversation. The names of the sections could be derived from the geographical position of the section in the paddock, from some unique tree or feature of the terrain in the section, or from some historical event associated with the section. And, to Elizabeth's utter confusion, a single section could have more than one name as well as both English and aborigine names. Sheila would at times refer to Bulloo North and Bulloo Wilga and mean the same section, Oldea West, Oldea Moora, and Oldea Boar were different names for the same section, and the sections in Maralinga Paddock were particularly confusing because it was also called Widgie Paddock. The division into sections had been made on the basis of the availability of water or the condition of the graze, usually into four or more sections for each paddock, and in some instances the fences dividing the paddocks had been moved because of changing conditions through the years. In other cases the names had inexplicably remained unchanged. Tanami Paddock was relatively small and was divided into only two sections, and at one time the fence had stretched to the east and west, dividing it into north and south sections. The fence had been changed so it ran north and south, but the sections were still called Tanami North and Tanami South, the one referred to as north being the nearest to the home paddock. And Sheila was puzzled and remotely amused when Elizabeth insisted that it was illogical.

Elizabeth also acquired an insight into the activities at the pens and into the duties of the various employees. The relatively large number of employees at Wayamba was another instance of traditional lack of thrift which was rarely found at other stations, where more work was done by fewer people, and some of the employees had what was almost a sinecure. The storekeeper was a former stockman of many years who had been injured, and there was a hired cook for the men instead of having them share the duty. Another former stockman who had been on the station many years and who had become frail and undependable was kept on the payroll to wash clothes for the men, and others did odd jobs. The aborigine settlement on the station was enormous in comparison to the aborigine settlements on other stations. Some of them worked at the station in jobs ranging from stockmen through working in the garden plot and on fencing, and others simply lived there. There were many young men on the station learning the trade, and there were a few boys, sons of employees, who accompanied their fathers about. Most of the men were out in one or another of the paddocks at all times, but they were frequently changed about according to need and their desires, and they had occasional days off.

The number of men at the home paddock at any one time appeared even larger because of the number of transients wandering through the station, swagmen who roamed the tracks between stations on foot and had a sort of symbiotic relationship with the stations. Rations of flour, tea, sugar, and mutton were routinely issued to them by the storekeeper, and a fiction of searching for work was maintained on both sides. In practice they would draw their rations, spend a night in one of the barrack buildings, then wander on with their swag rolled in one of the blue wool blankets which were popular among them, a rope tied to each end and the blanket swung over their shoulder. But they would also look for and repair breaks in fences along the way, and they would find help when stretches of fences were down. They looked for dangers to stock and signs of dingo activity, and they picked up and distributed news and gossip from one station to another. During shearing and other periods of heavy activity, they worked for a time to get clothes, boots, tobacco, and other necessities, which was of vast benefit to small stations with limited numbers of employees, and they broke the dull monotony of the solitary work at the smaller stations and in outlying paddocks of large stations. And when a grass fire or other cataclysm threatened a station where the rations were generous, they flocked to help.

A feeling of involvement developed as Elizabeth's interest and knowledge of the activities broadened, adding a new dimension to her life. The grey misery of her life before coming to Wayamba faded into an unpleasant, dream-like haze in her mind, and each day was rich and full. Teaching James was a continuing pleasure. There were characteristics about him which reminded her of Sheila and gave her a feeling akin to having a more amenable and obedient Sheila with her, but he had a personality of his own which she found congenial. Elizabeth had never taught before, but she found that his intelligence and interest more than made up for what she lacked in technique. Teaching Bessie's boy Tom was a more difficult process, but James absorbed knowledge hungrily.

Within the first few days of knowing him well, she began to agree with Sheila's assessment that he would never make a stockman. He was inclined to be small for his age, somewhat spindly and frail and vulnerable to sicknesses. But more than his physical characteristics, his personality didn't fit into a stockman's life. Somehow, and under the most unlikely circumstances, he had turned out to be a thoughtful, introverted, and sensitive child. But he had a mind like quicksilver. He had been roaming the creek and searching for things to amuse himself, and through personal observation he had accumulated an organized and comprehensive knowledge of the habits of the native reptiles and animals which was extraordinary considering his age. And he had effortlessly learned the aborigine language and was totally bilingual, to his grandfather's extreme displeasure. When Elizabeth started teaching him, he learned the alphabet within hours and the basic fundamentals of the numerical system within a few days, then rapidly progressed into reading and copying simple sentences, and went through the processes of addition and subtraction and into the intricacies of multiplication and division. As he progressed and Elizabeth began to evaluate him and plan ahead, she gradually came to the realization that he was learning in weeks what it had taken her painful months to learn at an age somewhat older than his.

There were minor problems, because he had something of his mother's impatience. He was inclined to skip steps in his cyphering and do sums in his mind, which was fraught with the possibility of error, and he tried to rush through exercises in calligraphy, not understanding the necessity of developing ingrained habits of forming letters which displayed the writer's education as well as conveying information. But he was obedient, instantly contrite when she made him repeat an exercise or recast a column of figures with the neat marks of computation and proof at one side. Sheila regarded his progress with motherly satisfaction, but when it eventually dawned on Elizabeth that she might be working with a potential scholar and she talked to Sheila about sending him to boarding school in Sydney, Sheila was darkly doubtful.

Life at Wayamba exceeded her most optimistic expectations, but it still had its deficiencies and its unpleasant moments. The nearest church was at Menindee, miles to the south and far too distant to attend services, and prayer and reading from her Bible and prayer book fell as short of providing the renewal of faith and the inspiration of congregational worship and sermons, as they had while at the selection on the Georges. And Cummings was at home for a day or two every two weeks or so. It was a time Elizabeth dreaded, but it was ameliorated by the fact that they were invariably invited to the Garrity house when he was there, giving her an additional opportunity to chat with Sheila unless she was off in one of the paddocks, and allowing her to bask in the courteous attention of the handsome Colin.

She was less helpless with Cummings than she had once been. The misery of the trip across New South Wales had been something of a trial by fire for her, and she found herself strengthened by it. It had given her confidence in herself, and knowing Sheila had given her courage. At the same time, Cummings knew of her close friendship with Sheila and was less sure of himself. There were confrontations, during which she found a potential for rage within herself which surprised her, and he became more cautious in dealing with her.

One of the men had made a comment about his lack of children which he had interpreted as a slight against his manhood, and he took her frequently when he was at the home paddock, snarling and puffing at her to become pregnant as he thrust into her viciously. She accepted it stoically, as she had accepted his wider range of cruelty in the past. He revolted her, but she interpreted Biblical injunctions literally, as she had been taught.

Stapleton was another problem. Several of the men stared and grinned impudently when she found it necessary to cross the road and go to one of the buildings on an errand or task, but Stapleton was the only one who was aggressive. She tried to tell Cummings about it, and he cut her off brusquely, blaming the situation on her. Then she found a partial solution in closely watching the men come and go at the stockmen's barrack so she could tell when Stapleton was out in a paddock and when he was at home, and adjusting her activities so she could remain in the vicinity of her house while he was about.

The situation came to a climax when she had been at Wayamba just over three months. She went to the storeroom to draw rations for a week, thinking Stapleton was gone, and as she started to leave she saw him standing in the doorway of the storeroom, grinning down at her sourly and blocking her way. The anger which might have enabled her to face him down was mixed too heavily with fear, and he had the advantage, jeering at her as he kept her from leaving. The old cripple who worked in the storeroom took her part, but he was afraid of Stapleton and could only give moral support. Bessie saw what was happening from her house and ran to help, but Stapleton roughly pushed her aside and seized Elizabeth, kissing her and handling her roughly. Then he left, taunting her and promising to do more the next time.

The incident left a feeling not unlike that she had experienced the first times Cummings had taken her, one of invasion and degradation. Her dress was torn and one of her breasts ached from being squeezed viciously. She sobbed with rage and shame as Bessie and the storekeeper helped her pick up her scattered things. Bessie was almost weeping with outrage herself and the storekeeper was angrily sympathetic, but there was nothing they could do. If Stapleton had offered to do physical harm, the weight of opinion would have been against him. But what he had done would be broadly interpreted as rough horseplay and a source of amusement among the other men, and it was a matter between him and Cummings. But even if Cummings would do anything about it, he was off in one of the paddocks.

Sheila was also in one of the paddocks. Elizabeth returned home and got rid of Bessie and her indignant snorting, then tried to collect herself as she put her things away. She felt soiled and greasy, the stench of his sweaty, filthy clothes and body still lingering in her nostrils and the feel of his rough, hard hands still burning on her skin. She carried water and took a bath and put on clean clothes, then washed the clothes she had taken off and went about the rest of her tasks. James came for his lessons, and she was still so wrought up and distracted that she snapped at him, bringing tears to his eyes, so she held him and kissed him until he began smiling again. Then she sent him to play along the creek, while she sat in the parlor and watched for Sheila.

It was beginning to seem that Sheila was going to

remain out and the torture of helpless anger would drag through a sleepless night and into the next day, but during late afternoon she saw Sheila walking through the buildings from the direction of the stockyard, her coiled whip in her hand, her clothes dusty and sweaty, and her pace slow and weary. Elizabeth waited impatiently until Sheila was halfway across the open space, then she went out, crossed the veranda and went down the steps, and walked along the path to the edge of the road to wait for her. Sheila saw her and changed her direction, walking toward her.

Sheila cross the road, her dusty face in the hard lines which indicated a bad mood as her eyes moved over Elizabeth's face. She stopped, looking down at Elizabeth with an inscrutable expression and tapping her whip against her leg. "Aye, I smelled something in the wind," she said quietly. "What is it, then?"

Elizabeth felt suddenly confused and flustered, wishing fervently that Sheila's mood had been better, and she smiled weakly and nodded. "How are you, Sheila? Did you have a—"

"Let's leave that," Sheila interrupted impatiently. "What's amiss?"

Elizabeth hesitated, then smiled apologetically and made a helpless motion with her hands. "Sheila, as much as I dislike having to do this, I find that I must ask your assistance. I have given this matter considerable thought, and I see no other recourse but to ask for your help. So it is with great regret that I—"

"Elizabeth, I didn't think you were out here taking the bloody air," Sheila interrupted, taking off her hat with her left hand and wiping her face with her sleeve. "Now will you tell me what's amiss?"

Part of her hair had come loose from the string she tied it back with and was hanging in untidy strands around her ears. The dust was caked in the lines and hollows of her face, and the upper half of her forehead was the clean, smooth brown of her skin where her hat had protected it from the dust. Her black eyes were hard and cold. She held her hat in one hand and her whip in the other, looking down at Elizabeth with her lips in a thin, impatient line. Elizabeth cleared her throat, folding her hands in front of herself and composing herself. "Perhaps I should wait until another time, Sheila. I can see that you're weary and that you—"

"I'm bloody mad," Sheila snapped. "I've just come from where a dagworm of a stockman let thirty fucking sheep get killed by dingoes, and I'll still be bloody mad come Saint Geoffrey's. Now have an end to this and tell me what you want of me, Elizabeth."

It was consistent with how she had been before. She could be painfully abrupt and rude, but she was always interested and concerned. Elizabeth bit her lip nervously, then sighed and nodded. "Very well, Sheila. It's the Stapleton man. He attacked me today while I was at the storeroom, and I have no recourse but to ask you to speak with him and—"

"Aye, I've been waiting for that," Sheila sighed in a morose, resigned tone as she put her hat back on and seated it with a tug, and she turned to walk back toward the buildings. "I'll have him roll his swag, then."

"Discharge him? No, I don't wish to put you in a position of exceeding your authority, Sheila, and I have no particular wish to see him—"

"To do *what?*" Sheila barked irritably, wheeling back around and frowning darkly. "When I have a mind for some bleeding sod to leave this station, then he'll bloody bluie, no bloody fear!"

"Well, I don't understand . . ." Elizabeth's voice faded as Sheila glared at her, her black eyes snapping, and she shrugged weakly and shook her head. "It's just that I thought that your brother and father were the ones who engaged and discharged employees, and I wouldn't want to place you in a—"

"That's none of your bloody flock!" Sheila snarled, her face dark and flushed with anger under the mask of dust. "You can tell me what's amiss, but you'll bloody well not tell me how to repair it! Not on bloody Wayamba you won't, nor Colin, by God! The blind old bugger who got me is the only sod who'll tell me fuck all about Wayamba! I said the shit sack will roll his swag, and there's the end of it! Not that I have any bloody stomach for it, because he's a sodding good stockman and all! Now have an end to it!"

Elizabeth's lips began trembling and the tears welled up in her eyes as she wrung her hands. "Sheila, I wish I hadn't even mentioned this to you. But I've talked to my husband about it, and he won't do anything. There was nothing I could do but ask you to help me, but now I wish I hadn't even—"

"Nothing else you could do?" Sheila hissed in a low, furious tone, walking slowly toward her. "Do you think you're the only bloody cunt on this bloody station? You're bloody not, you know. What do you think I do? This lot of bloody rams would be swiving me in my flaming ears if they thought they could, but they know what they'd have in its bleeding stead." She stopped inches from Elizabeth, her lips pale and tight and her black eyes narrow and gleaming, and she tapped the heavy whip against Elizabeth's chest. "There's bloody ample you could have done. You could have scratched his fucking eyes out. You could have kicked his cod piece so hard he'd have to swallow twice to have it back between his fucking legs. And if you had, he would have let you be because he daren't lay the weight of his hand against you in a fight. And Wayamba wouldn't be shot of a bloody good stockman. So you have a mind to that, because I'll tire bloody quick of getting shot of men on your account. You can be bloody assured of that and all."

Sheila wheeled away, and her heavy boots stirred small puffs of dust as she crossed the road and walked toward the buildings, with long, rapid strides, slapping the whip against her leg. Elizabeth was frozen motionless for an instant, her mouth open, then the tears came in a sudden flood. She turned and ran back along the path toward the house, weeping wildly, and ran up the steps. Her toe caught in the hem of her dress on the top step and she sprawled heavily at full length on the veranda, and she climbed back to her feet and stumbled blindly into the house, shaking with sobs.

It was a long night. The chatter of the insects, croaking of the frogs, and the mournful calls of the night birds echoed through the dark house as Elizabeth lay on the bed and wept until she had no more tears, then sobbed dryly. There was no guarantee of justice in life, but the gross unfairness of the situation was a searing torment. And the memory of Sheila's face twisted in fury as the scathing tirade spilled from her tight lips remained in her mind's eye, torturing her. Dawn came, blurred to her swollen eyes, flooding in and lighting all the dark and hidden corners, and she struggled out of bed and grimly set about another day. She drank some tea and vomited it back up, then began going through the motions of preparing to do the wash. Bessie came, having heard from her husband about Sheila's violent confrontation with Stapleton when she ordered him off the station the evening before, and her triumphant gratification changed to bewilderment when she saw Elizabeth. Her hesitant, worried concern met with a cold, tight-lipped silence, and she left.

Elizabeth was bent over the tub rinsing her dress from the day before when she heard footsteps coming through the house, the solid thudding of heavy boots in a light, quick rhythm, the sound of a man's tread and a woman's stride characteristic of Sheila. It was a step to which her ears were attuned and which had always made her heart leap with pleasure, but which now only stirred a painful memory of that pleasure and gave fresh sustenance to the dry, angry ache of resentment and made it swell anew. She concentrated on the heavy mass of wet broadcloth, scrubbing the collar and sleeves between her knuckles to make sure all of the strong lye soap was out. The footsteps crossed the kitchen. She dipped the dress in the murky water and stirred it, then pulled it back up onto the scrub board propped in the tub and searched for the collar and cuffs again. Sheila stepped out of the back door onto the porch. On the edge of her vision, Elizabeth could see that Sheila wasn't wearing her hat and her sleeves were rolled up, which was unusual for the time of day on a workday. She dipped the collar and cuffs and scrubbed them between her knuckles again.

"I've never bloody said I'm sorry to a living soul for anything I've ever done, Elizabeth. But I've come to tell you that I'm sorry. I'm ashamed of what I said, and I'm sorry for saying it. It was that I was so . . . well, it makes no bloody difference. I'm ashamed, and I'm sorry, Elizabeth."

It was easy to believe that she had never apologized before. The words sounded stiff and awkward, in a strangely strained, taut, and muted tone, but more than that, contrition simply wasn't a part of her. It was much more natural for anything in her path to be tossed ruthlessly aside without a second thought and with hardly more than a disdainful glance from the shining black eyes down the long, haughty nose. Gratitude for the apology swelled, blending with the bittersweet desire to forgive, to apologize herself, and to make peace. But the wounds of the deep hurt were still raw and sensitive, generating an angry, vicious need to inflict pain. She dipped the dress and pulled it back up onto the board again, straightened up, pursed her lips primly and looked at Sheila from the corners of her eyes.

"There is no need to apologize, Sheila. You were more than correct in saying what you did. And it is I who should apologize and thank you for teaching me a very valuable lesson. The lesson that I have only myself to depend upon. As I shall in the future. I shan't bother you with my concerns again."

Sheila recoiled, almost as though she had been struck,

and her dark face looked haggard and grey with hurt. Then color suddenly flooded back into her face and her nostrils flared with anger. She stepped to Elizabeth and took her arm, pulling her around and away from the tub, and she gripped Elizabeth's shoulders and shook her. "If there's aught that concerns you, then I'll bloody know about it and I'll have no different! Now I'm sorry for what I did, and I'll do what it takes to put it aright! And if leathering your arse is part of it, I'll do that as well! Do you bloody hear that?"

Elizabeth's control began crumbling, and she fought to hold back the tears and to keep her lips stiff as she looked up into Sheila's angry, pained eyes, struggling to say something without bursting into tears.

Sheila dug her fingers into Elizabeth's shoulders harder, shaking her again. "Do you hear me, you little sod?"

The tears broke through, and Elizabeth's features twisted as the tears began streaming down her cheeks. "You hurt me, Sheila," she wailed, sobbing. "You hurt me."

Sheila made a choking sound, putting her arms around Elizabeth and pulling her to her, and she sighed heavily, holding her tightly. "Aye, I know, Elizabeth," she whispered. "And I couldn't be bloody sorrier. And that's God's truth."

Elizabeth buried her face against Sheila's shoulder, her arms around Sheila's waist. The pain was gone, and in its place there was a wrenching relief that the conflict was over, that the incident which had been the cause of such grief had turned into evidence that she had the firm and unwavering affection of this strange, tall woman. She controlled herself, pulling away from Sheila and wiping her eyes with her hands. "Making a fool of myself..."

"I think not. But if you are, it's your bloody turn because I've had mine. Come on and we'll have some tea, then."

Elizabeth nodded, turning toward the tub. "I'll hang this over the rail to dry first."

"Here, I'll do it for you."

Sheila stepped around Elizabeth and lifted the dress out of the tub, wringing it with quick, deft motions of her hands. Elizabeth sniffled and wiped her eyes with the back of her hands, breathing in the quick, shuddering breaths of the aftermath of tears. Sheila looked at her and smiled as she wrung the dress, and Elizabeth smiled back. The old woman was standing in front of the privy behind the Garrity house, leaning on her stick and looking at them.

"There's your mother."

Sheila looked at her and nodded as she looked back down at the dress, gathering the bottom of the skirt and wringing it. "Aye, taking my dad for his movement, it appears. She's taken a fancy to you, you know."

"What do you mean?"

"She likes you. She's never had a thought about the others who came and went here, but she's forever asking me what you're doing and all."

Elizabeth smiled and nodded, wiping her eyes again. "Well, I'm very flattered, but she . . . well, she hasn't said much to me, and I had no idea . . ."

"She's a bloody abo," Sheila chuckled, shaking the dress out and turning to drape it over the rail. "She likes you, but don't wait for her to come calling for tea. She's my ma, but she's still a bloody abo for all of that. Forever standing about with her queer bloody black looks at everything just like the rest of them." She pulled the dress straight on the wooden rail at the side of the porch, then turned back toward Elizabeth, smiling. "Come on and let's have that tea, then."

Elizabeth smiled and nodded, and glanced at the old woman again. She was still standing in front of the privy, unmoving, both of her hands on the long, heavy stick as she leaned on it. The strange clothing she wore hung slackly on her thin frame, and the short thatch of greyish-white hair on her head was a splotch of lighter color against the verdant green of foliage behind her, contrasting with her dusky face. Sheila put her arm around Elizabeth's shoulders, turning her toward the door, and Elizabeth smiled up at her as they went inside.

The surface ripples caused by the incident passed away within the next few days. Bessie had her say and expressed her gratification, then other events and pressures claimed her attention and became a topic of conversation. The vacancy created by Stapleton's departure was filled by a man wandering along the track and looking for work. Cummings knew about the incident when he returned, and he limited his conversation on the subject to a few dark grumbles about the loss of a good stockman. There was no mention of the incident in the conversation at the Garrity house, when he and Elizabeth were invited there on the evening he returned.

But below the surface there were deeper and longer-lasting effects from the incident and the way it had been resolved. There was another subtle shift in the relationship between Elizabeth and Cummings. An event of major importance concerning her had taken place outside his control, her ties with the Garrity family were more obvious, and the result was a strengthening of her independence of him and a diminishment of his authority over her. The change in the relationship between Sheila and Elizabeth was less subtle. It appeared that Sheila had become aware of the possibility of a serious rift between her and Elizabeth, and she went to greater pains to make herself more congenial. She was still moody at times, but she was consistently more amiable and she stayed away when she was angry about something. Their friendship deepened, but Elizabeth still found Sheila unpredictable, her grasp of Sheila's personality remaining vague and fragmentary.

The men also treated Elizabeth differently. There were no more open and impudent stares and grins. Some surreptitiously stared or watched from a distance when she was among the buildings, but when she passed near them most of them either looked away or nodded warily. Some of the younger ones grinned and spoke to her in a friendly manner mixed with admiration which approached flirtation, and the storekeeper and some of the other older men regarded her with friendly, fatherly attitudes.

Christmas came a few weeks after the incident with Stapleton, and the maximum possible number of employees were at the home paddock for a traditional celebration, along with a large number of swagmen who had timed their arrival at Wayamba to be present for the celebration. On Christmas day, the cook and most of the younger employees labored over large fires built in a circle near the shearing complex, roasting a hog and cooking large pots of potatoes, peas, and apple dumplings, and near evening trestle tables were loaded with the food and with bottles of rum from the storeroom. Elizabeth ignored Cummings' dark looks and surly grumbles and joined the celebration, something which would have been unthinkable weeks before.

The feast began after darkness, when the cool of night replaced the torrid heat of the day. The old man sat in a straight chair in the edge of the light of one of the fires, his clothes freshly washed and flatironed, his boots freshly blacked, and his white, thin hair neatly combed for the occasion, his presence a symbol of hospitality because he didn't eat and drank only a token pannikin of watered rum. The old woman stood by him with one hand on his shoulder and her other on the stick planted on the ground by her, her shirt and skirt-like garment also freshly washed and flatironed and her bare feet dusty. Men stood around the old man to pay their respects, some of the older swagmen hovered around and reminisced, while the old man murmured toothless monosyllables.

Colin moved between clusters of men, towering over

them and looking darkly handsome in the firelight as he laughed and talked. Sheila was very much a part of the scene around her, eating and wiping her fingers on her shirt, frowning in disagreement with a comment, laughing in response to a joke. The hypnotic groaning of digereedoos, clatter of rhythm sticks, and rise and fall of chanting came from the aborigine shelters as they moved around their fires in a celebration of their own.

The men around Elizabeth shouted, laughed, and argued as they consumed great quantities of food and watered rum. It was far different from the Christmases since she had been married to Cummings, which had passed much like any other day in work and misery, and it was just as different from the Christmases she had known in her father's house, more like a pagan bacchanal than the subdued celebration and worship which had marked Christmas when Elizabeth was a child. She enjoyed it, chatting with Bessie, Sheila, and Colin, and drinking watered rum until late into the night.

In January Elizabeth suspected she was pregnant, and in February it was confirmed. Cummings was exultant, and he lost no time in spreading the news. Bessie was delighted, and she fussed over Elizabeth with an attitude of seasoned experience. Sheila was involved in preparations for the shearing. For the first time, the old woman displayed something of the interest Sheila had mentioned. She produced a greasy string made of some kind of woven animal hair for Elizabeth to wear around her neck under her dress. It looked and smelled revolting, but Elizabeth wore it to keep from offending the old woman.

The tempo of activity increased as the time for shearing approached, and it reached a climax as the shearers and washers arrived, filling up the barrack buildings. Their cooks established their working areas, built their fires, and set up their equipment between two of the buildings. Hordes of swagmen arrived, and the wide stretches of open space between the buildings suddenly appeared too small to contain the seething activity which began at daybreak and ended at nightfall. Choking clouds of dust swelled into the air and hung over the home paddock as tens of thousands of sheep began arriving from the outlying paddocks to be mustered, washed, sheared, then driven back out again. Lanterns glowed around the shearing shed late into the night each night as Sheila supervised a crew of men sorting and baling the backlog of wool which had built up during the day, and Colin and Cummings worked crews of men in filling the holding pens with sheep for the shearers the next day.

The stacks of large, canvas-covered bales of wool at one end of the shearing shed became higher, growing into small mountains. The first of the drays arrived, low, stout wagons built of massive beams and drawn by multiple span of powerful oxen, and the area around the pens and shearing shed became a mass of congestion and confusion. Then the drays began leaving with heavy loads of wool, and their places were taken by others. Cummings was sullenly irritable all the time, getting home late at night and leaving before dawn, and Elizabeth felt resentful of his continued presence in the house when she had been accustomed to having it to herself most of the time. She occasionally saw Sheila walking between her house and the shearing shed, dusty, sweaty, and slumped with fatigue and lack of adequate sleep regardless of the time of day, and she always waved and smiled tiredly in response to Elizabeth's greeting.

Elizabeth glimpsed the old man and old woman a few times. They crossed from their house to the shearing shed each morning at dawn, when the swagmen rolled in their blankets around the buildings would be stirring, the old man's hand on the old woman's shoulder as she led him along. The old man sat all day on a tall stool in the center of the shearing shed, silent and motionless as the frenzied activity swirled around him, and the old woman leaned on her stick and stood at the side of the stool. They returned home each day at dusk.

When the shearing was finished, the home paddock

seemed strangely deserted and quiet after the activity ceased and the people left. The weather remained unseasonably hot, and towering, black thunderheads moved across from the horizon and filled the sky. They blotted out the sun and the days were strangely dim and blue, but the temperature remained high and the air was torpid. There had been talk about the low rainfall during the past couple of years, but Sheila looked at the clouds and shook her head morosely when Elizabeth asked her if it was going to rain. The clouds thickened and seemed to hang lower daily, and the atmosphere became taut and stifling, as though forces of awesome power were poised and about to be unleashed.

Suddenly, shuddering claps of resounding thunder battered eardrums as sizzling arcs of lightning flashed between the clouds and the ground. The home paddock seethed with activity again as crews of men were formed to go out and fight the grass fires started by lightning, taking tools to cut open swaths in the brush and grass and light backfires. Swagmen came, groups of two and three becoming groups of half a dozen or more rushing to help as the pall of smoke thickened over the home paddock, and they dropped their belongings in the storeroom where they drew their tools and hurried on along the track toward the center of the smoke. The acrid smoke became choking in the breathlessly still air, but the lack of wind was a godsend. Crews of exhausted, smoke-blackened men returned to eat and sleep, then went out again to move sheep and fight more fires. Then the clouds began rolling away, the crews encircled the fires, and the smoke dissipated.

Winter was belated but frigid. Elizabeth's dresses were worn and thin and she had let them out and pieced them as her hips, breasts, and stomach swelled. She wore her coat as she hurried about her tasks and spent as much time as she could by the stove in the kitchen. Then Sheila brought Elizabeth a large, shapeless sheepskin coat similar to the one she wore, and on another visit a bolt of heavy wool cloth and shrugged off Elizabeth's mention of payment. Elizabeth made herself dresses and a pair of gloves from the cloth, and she began enjoying going out into the crisp, fresh air on her tasks, bundled in a warm dress and the heavy coat.

The old woman's interest in Elizabeth became more intense as she became heavier with the child. It was flattering, but in her sixth month of pregnancy it took a form which Elizabeth found disconcerting. When Elizabeth and Cummings visited the Garrity house, the old woman began taking Elizabeth into another room, along with Sheila to translate because Elizabeth had difficulty in understanding the old woman's laborious, heavily-accented pidgin English. The old woman asked questions about what she was eating, her bowel movements, and other things of an extremely personal nature, discomfiting Elizabeth and amusing Sheila. When James came for his lessons, he always asked Elizabeth if she had slept well and was feeling well and other things which were obviously questions from his grandmother. On one occasion when Elizabeth tried to evade the situation by remaining at home while Cummings went to the Garrity house alone, Sheila was at the door within minutes, chortling with amusement and taking Elizabeth's arm to lead her over to her house so her mother could ask her questions.

In Elizabeth's seven month of pregnancy, the old woman's interest took an even more personal form. She cornered Elizabeth in the bedroom, pulled up her dress, and thrust her withered, claw-like hands down into Elizabeth's pantaloons to feel her stomach. The old woman was surprisingly strong, and Elizabeth stood in red-faced and embarrassed silence as the old woman probed and squeezed over her stomach and Sheila leaned against the door and held her sides, convulsed with laughter.

Sheila's amusement abruptly disappeared as the old woman pulled her hands out of Elizabeth's clothes and turned away from her, murmuring something in her language. Elizabeth pulled at her clothes and adjusted them in flustered confusion, barely conscious that Sheila had stopped laughing. The old woman muttered quietly as she crossed the room, and Sheila looked at her with a startled, thoughtful frown as she moved away from the door and opened it for the old woman. She closed the door behind her, still frowning, then her frown changed to a smile as she looked at Elizabeth.

"What did she say?"

Sheila shrugged and chuckled wryly. "I can't understand that bloody gabble as well as James can, Elizabeth, but she thinks your delivery will be easy enough. Which will be more than mine bloody was and all."

"Sheila, I've seen and heard you speaking in the aborigine language any number of times, and even though I can't understand it, you obviously speak it as fluently as James and your mother, as far as that goes. She seemed to think that something was wrong or that—"

"She's a bloody abo, for all that she's my ma," Sheila interrupted impatiently. "And they're forever bleating about foolishness that will curdle your blood in your veins, if you'll but listen to them. There's naught wrong, so leave it be."

"Sheila, I could tell by her expression that she thinks something *is* wrong."

"Then you're a bleeding witch, because it would take a witch to tell aught from an abo's expression. She said your delivery will be easy enough, and there's an end to it. The nipper will come when its time comes, and there's no bloody more to be said about it. And if we could say the same about the rain, I'd be bloody thankful. If we don't have rain soon, we'll be rendering sheep to thin the flocks."

Elizabeth tugged at her dress and adjusted the waist. "Is it that bad, then?"

"Aye, it is and all," Sheila said, opening the door and putting her hand on Elizabeth's shoulder to guide her through the door. "We had four good years in a row and built the flocks to all the land would take, buying sheep from everywhere and keeping all the lambs, but now we're going to have to start thinking about thinning them so we don't ruin the land if we don't get rain." She chuckled and patted Elizabeth's shoulder. "But that's none of your flock. You just think about taking care of yourself, that's all you need do. And if you've a mind to worry about something, you can worry about what my ma's going to want to have a feel of next. You've seen bloody naught yet."

Elizabeth froze in the doorway, her face flushing and her mouth dropping open, and Sheila exploded into hearty laughter, pushing her on through the door and closing it behind her.

- 17 -

The rain came down in a steady deluge, as though the heavens had split open and were dumping oceans to scour the earth clean, and it poured down on the roof with a thunderous roar. The discordant, monotone groaning of digereedoos, rattle of rhythm sticks, and droning chant of voices came through the floor from under the house, blending with the pounding of the rain on the roof in a volume of battering sound which went beyond sound and closed in around Elizabeth as a physical force, a suffocating, crushing pressure. There was a pattern to it which seemed to match some cosmic cadence which was understood rather then perceived, which by-passed the senses and vibrated through the very fibers of her body, a cadence on which the cycles of nature and of life and death were based, one to which the stars were attuned and to which the tides responded in their flow and ebb, and one to which her heart was synchronized as it labored heavily and drove the blood through her veins. The all-encompassing rhythm seemed to throb in and all around her with its measured beat, rising and falling with the sound of her voice which came to her ears as though from a very long distance away, pulsing in time with the waves of seething agony which swelled, enveloped her, then subsided and left her numb and dazed.

The light in the room was dim, filling the room with a grey, flat, and lifeless monochrome in which there were no highlights and everything faded into graduated degrees of shadow. The air was cold and clammy against her skin and she was exposed to the eyes of others in her nakedness, but the touch of the air and of fingers registered only dimly, and modesty and other sensibilities had fled to cower in a tiny recess in her mind to escape the torture. The two aborigine women nodded their heads in time with the sound of the digereedoos and rhythm sticks and their lips moved slightly in a token of mouthing the chant, but the flat, dim light distorted them and exaggerated their movements as her tortured senses tried to place the images transmitted by her blurred vision into some frame of reference, and they seemed to be two priestesses of some pagan sect, their primitive beauty barely concealed by the scraps of clothing they wore, weaving and bobbing in the movements of a heathen rite of which she was the victim. Her fingers were laced firmly through the old woman's, gripping the shriveled claw as the old woman sat in the chair by the head of the bed and leaned over her, and the strangely young eyes embedded in the maze of wrinkles and lines were dark, shining pools of wisdom and understanding of the agony of life. Bessie's voice was loud and strong, the only sound making a distinct impression through the mists clouding her awareness, and it struck a responsive chord with the clamoring, instinctive urge to push, thrust, eject, and discharge the source of the searing, excruciating agony.

Time collapsed, consciousness becoming something less but at the same time something more than itself as it slipped into a different plane to protect itself, and awareness of existence became measured in terms of effort rather than in reference to the passage of minutes. Energy ebbed, but both the voice without and the voice within called for continued exertion, and she persisted, joining with and guiding the flow of forces forming in her body at a level which was just within reach of control. Then the end approached, requiring one final surge along a series of shelving plateaus to reach the summit, with a promise of relief on the other side. Each one was more difficult than the last, and something seemed to be rushing her along from one to the next before she had time to gather herself. The last one approached, and there was a note of triumph in Bessie's voice, loudly urging her on. She grasped for it, abandoning her reserves of energy and throwing herself into it. There was an instant of teetering on the verge, then she slipped over. And it was finished.

Consciousness returned slowly. The roar of the rain beating on the roof filled her ears. The chanting dirge of the aborigines under the house had stopped. There was a peaceful, soothing absence of pain and a feeling of expansive well-being. She felt rested and refreshed, as though she had slept for hours, but the room was still filled with grey daylight and it couldn't have been more than minutes. There was a restless stir in the bundled blanket resting in the crook of her arm, a thin mewling, and joy and satisfaction flooded through her. Sheila was standing at the foot of the bed, her shining wet slicker dripping on the floor and her soaked hat in her hand. Her hair was mussed and damp, the feathery touches of grey at her temples standing out in sharp relief against the utter blackness of her hair, and her brown face looked clean

284

and bright, gleaming and wet with rain. She was smiling slightly, her eyes strangely soft and bright. The two aborigine women were gone. The old woman had her hat and slicker on, ready to leave, and was standing by Sheila and leaning on her stick. Bessie was standing on the other side of Sheila. Her face was pale and drawn, unsmiling. A dark stab of apprehension raced through Elizabeth as she glanced between their faces again, and she turned her head and lifted the edge of the bundled blanket.

At first there was a numb lack of understanding, a feeling that some mistake had been made and could be put right as soon as she called their attention to it. Then there was a dazed kind of comprehension, mixed with shattering disappointment. The head was abnormally large, and the dome of the forehead almost hid the tiny eyes. The eyes and the tiny knot of a nose were compacted closely together, and the mouth was a grotesque gash which curved down at the ends and was low on the chin, like that of a carp. The skin was shriveled and red, that of a newborn, but one side of the distorted features was of a darker color, almost a purple, a blighted discoloration of a massive birthmark with a well-defined edge which ran down the center of the face and covered one side of the head.

Elizabeth looked up at them again. Bessie's lips were trembling, and she was fighting to hold back her tears. The old woman's features were neutral. Sheila was still smiling slightly, looking into Elizabeth's eyes in warm regard. The old woman turned and walked toward the doorway, her slicker rustling and her bare feet soundless on the floor. A sob escaped Bessie's control, and she pressed her lips together tightly as a tear ran down her cheek. Sheila stepped around the corner of the bed, moved along the side of it, and bent over Elizabeth. The smell of the outdoors and of the fresh rain wafted around her, and Sheila's lips were cold and damp against her forehead.

"My ma says you've come through it well."

"But Sheila, it's... it's..."

Sheila frowned slightly, her face close to Elizabeth's, and she shook her head impatiently. "To buggery with aught else. You've come through it well, and there's a bloody end to it." She smiled and kissed Elizabeth again, then she straightened up and turned away from the bed, looking at Bessie. "Let's get some broth in her gullet, and a drop of rum wouldn't be amiss."

Bessie nodded and turned toward the door, wiping her eyes with the back of her hand, and Sheila followed her. There was a sound of heavy, hurried footsteps on the steps and veranda over the pounding of the rain on the roof, and they stopped, Bessie looking back at Sheila. Sheila turned and stepped to the side of the room, and she put her hat back on, folded her arms, and leaned back against the wall, her lips pursed and her expression one of readiness for trouble as she looked at the doorway from the corners of her eyes. Bessie sniffled, wiped her eyes again, and moved away from the doorway as the footsteps crossed the front room. Cummings hesitated in the doorway, looking at the bed, then walked rapidly toward the bed.

"By God, I'll just have a look at my nipper, then..."

Elizabeth looked up at the ceiling. On the edge of her vision she could see him bending over the bed, his hand plucking at the bundled blanket. Then he stiffened. A choked, wordless sound of revulsion came from his throat. He started to move back, leaned closer and looked again, then shoved the blanket closed and stood back from the bed. Elizabeth turned her eyes toward him, looking up at him numbly. His face was twisted with disgust. He shook his head, turning away and walking slowly toward the doorway.

"I should have bloody looked for it," he growled. "You're no bloody good for anything else, and now your bad blood has come out in your whelp."

"Aye, here's our grand thoroughbred," Sheila sneered softly. "Him who was got by some old ram goat polluting his cod piece in a slime pit."

He wheeled toward her with an angry snarl, pointing his finger at her. "This is none of yours, and you'll keep your bloody mouth out of it!" he barked. "Or I'll speak to your brother about you!"

"Speak to my brother of me until you have to draw wind through your sodding arse, for all the bloody good it'll do you," Sheila replied in a quiet, angry tone. "And there's room in this for me when you might be getting Wayamba ewes with lambs what'll have bristles instead of wool. My ma said it had naught to do with Elizabeth's generation, and you might bear that in mind when you're speaking of bad blood."

"What does she bloody know of white people?" he bellowed, trembling with fury. "Or you, as far as that goes? And who had the bloody thing? I bloody didn't!"

"Who put it there?" Sheila snarled, pushing away from the wall and moving toward him menacingly. "You've had bloody sheep's heels in the front of your boots until you don't know how to get a woman with a proper child! And you keep your flaming shit hole of a mouth off my ma, or I'll have you sliced before my brother and dad can get to you! Her liver's a far measure whiter than yours, and there's God's truth!"

His face worked with rage as he looked at Sheila, his fists knotted, then he wheeled toward the door with a wordless growl, his slicker swirling around him. He stopped in the doorway and turned, looking back at the bed. "But I'll not bloody claim *that*, and I have a mind to be shot of the bloody worthless pommie that whelped it. And what's more, I'll not stop in the house with it. I'll stop in the bloody barrack while I'm deciding what to do with this lot."

"Aye, well, I'll tell the jackaroos to sleep on their arses, then," Sheila sneered.

His eyes bulged with fury and his face turned crimson as he looked at her, and he lifted his fist and shook it at her. "You bleeding black slut!" he choked. "You'll bloody get yours and all!"

She moved toward him again, her lips pale and tight and her eyes narrow and sparkling. "Give it me now, then," she hissed. "I'm bloody ready for you and all, sod, and ten more of you. So give it me now."

He almost sprang toward her, leaning toward her and trembling, then he spun and barged through the doorway with a snarl, stamped heavily across the front room and out of the house, and slammed the front door behind him with a crash. Bessie was pale with fright, clutching her hands in front of her, and she looked from the doorway to Sheila with wide eyes. Sheila smiled sourly, taking off her hat and tossing it into a corner, and she unfastened the buckles down the front of her slicker as she walked back toward the bed.

"Good bloody riddance, I say. Go fix the broth, Bessie, and I'll have a sit-down and stop for a while."

Bessie silently nodded, walking quietly out of the room. Sheila pulled her slicker off and dropped it on the floor as she walked around the foot of the bed. One of her boots scraped on the floor as she crossed her legs, then she was still. The roar of the rain pounding on the roof filled the room again, absorbing incidental sounds and isolating the room from the outside world. Elizabeth looked up at the ceiling, crying silently. She could sense that Sheila's eyes weren't on her; she was simply sitting and looking into the distance, giving the comfort of her presence. Elizabeth moved her left arm across the covers, blindly reaching out toward Sheila. The legs of the chair scraped on the floor as Sheila moved it closer to the bed, and she took Elizabeth's hand, lacing her fingers through Elizabeth's. Then she was still again, her features neutral and her eyes staring blankly into the distance.

The full extent of the deformity hadn't been evident at

first. The feet were misshapen, formless knots of flesh. The arms above the elbows were connected to the trunk with loose webs of skin, making the arms look like the wings of a bat, and there were webs between the tiny fingers. And it was very frail and sickly. It uttered sounds more like the whimpering of some kind of small, newborn animal than the crying of a baby, and the tiny, carp-like mouth worked weakly as it tried to suckle. Elizabeth wept with anguish as she squeezed her breast gently to help it, and despite her grief her milk flowed freely in her eagerness to sustain it. Fierce love and protectiveness sprang from the very core of her being to envelop it, partaking of the intense pleasure of the feel of the small mouth on her nipple, and she cuddled it closely in her arm and held it with her lips touching the smooth surface of its small, bulging forehead, breathing its fleshy odor.

Most of the milk seemed to spill from its mouth or come back up in a whitish, stringy vomit, but it was quiet again, breathing with a wheezing sound. There was no consciousness of time passing, but the yellow glow of a lamp was filling the room when she opened her eyes again. The baby was moving and making sounds again, and she pulled it closer and put her nipple in its mouth, then looked around for Sheila. Sheila was still sitting in the chair, her features neutral and her eyes smiling. Elizabeth reached out for Sheila's hand.

The night passed in a blur of waking, feeding it, and neither sleeping nor being fully awake, and it was suddenly another grey, lifeless day, the rain still falling in a steady deluge. The old woman was there, her hat soaked and her slicker gleaming with water. She looked at the baby, her wrinkled fingers moving the edge of the blanket, then she moved around to the end of the bed and talked with Sheila in a murmur. Sheila looked weary, and there were furrows of concern on her forehead. She turned away from her mother and looked at Elizabeth, and a smile spread across her face.

"Awake, are you? And about bloody time and all. My ma says it's time you were off your arse as well, and there's some broth in the kitchen. Come on, and I'll give you a hand."

"How does she think my baby is?"

"I don't know. For all that she's my ma, I can understand her bloody gabble little better than you. Come on, then. Just hold the baby, and I'll help you up."

It felt strange to be on her feet, and the floor felt cold and damp against her bare feet. She held the baby tightly in her arm, and Sheila held her up as she slipped her feet into her shoes. The lingering pain and soreness were less than she had expected and the feeling of well-being remained under the cloud of depression. She walked weakly but without assistance through the house to the kitchen. Sheila walked with her, her arm resting loosely around Elizabeth's shoulders, and the old woman followed. The kitchen felt warm and dry, and it was bright and cheerful, with a roaring fire in the stove and a steady hissing of rain boiling into steam inside the hot stovepipe. There was a strangely distant familiarity about it, as though it had been a long time since she had been there.

She ate a bowl of the broth and drank some tea and a spoonful of bitter liquid the old woman insisted that she have, and they went back into the bedroom. The bed felt warm, soft, and comfortable as she settled herself in it again with the baby in the crook of her arm. The old woman murmured something to Sheila, then left. Sheila sat back down on the chair, folding her arms and crossing her legs.

"Sheila, I'm very grateful that you're here, but I know what your work means to you and I wouldn't want to keep you from it."

"The sheep are all out of the low places, and there's bloody little that I can do while every ditch on the station is running a banker. Not that I'd have it otherwise, because we can bloody use this."

"Are you sure? I'll be all right by myself now."

"I'm sure."

"But you haven't had any sleep."

"I have and all."

"I mean proper sleep."

"I can get proper sleep sitting in a chair, lying on the ground, riding a horse, or standing on my bloody head if need be."

Elizabeth nodded, looking down at the baby as it made a sound and moved, and she lifted her breast out of her nightgown and put the nipple in its mouth. "I'm very grateful, Sheila."

"And I'm not sorry for the chance to help. I'll be here as long as you might need me, little pom."

The baby seemed even weaker when it tried to suckle, keeping less of the milk in its stomach, and there had been no bowel movement. It was much like a diseased or injured sheep in its numb, instinctive struggle to survive, the small body clinging tenaciously to the life force within it. She fed it, then it lay still and breathed slowly and steadily with a harsh, wheezing sound in its throat. The slight exertion of walking into the kitchen and back had tired her, and the drumming of the rain on the roof was soporific. She dozed off, then woke and fed the baby again. Again she dozed off. A stir in the room awakened her. The light was fainter, and Sheila was bringing in a lamp. She helped Elizabeth out of bed again, and they went into the kitchen. Bessie was there, her face flushed with the heat of the stove and smiling brightly, but her eyes darkened when they moved to the bundle in Elizabeth's arms and she didn't ask to see the baby. She fussed around Elizabeth busily, settling her in a chair and dipping out a bowl of broth from the pan on the stove, and she talked too rapidly and too much. Elizabeth ate the broth and drank the tea, and Sheila walked back into the bedroom with her. She settled herself in bed again, pulling the baby to her to put her nipple in its mouth, and

Sheila settled herself on the chair again.

Consciousness returned abruptly. One instant she had been sound asleep, and in the next she was fully awake. Her eyes moved around the room, looking for what had awakened her. Sheila was slumped in the chair, her feet stretched out in front of her, her arms folded loosely, and her head drooped forward, sound asleep. The rain continued to fall on the roof. The lamp on the dressing table filled the room with a soft, yellow light, and the window was black. Everything looked the same, but something had changed. She rested her head back on the pillow, a puzzled frown on her face, then shrugged slightly and turned toward the baby. The soft, wheezing sound of its breathing had stopped. She dug at the bundle frantically, screaming at the top of her voice.

Sheila was suddenly on her feet, bending over the bed and pushing Elizabeth down on her back. She looked at the bundle, blinking the sleep from her eyes, then put both hands on Elizabeth's shoulders and held her down firmly, shouting for Bessie. Bessie stumbled in from the kitchen, her face bleary with sleep, then she turned and went back. Sheila spoke soothingly in a low, soft voice, trying to calm Elizabeth, but Elizabeth kept screaming, trying to twist away, and trying to reach the bundled blanket. Bessie trotted in with a pannikin. Sheila bent lower, putting her elbows on Elizabeth's shoulders and holding her down, and she took Elizabeth's face in her strong fingers, opening her mouth and pinching her nostrils closed as she snapped an order at Bessie. Bessie bent over the other side of the bed and emptied the pannikin into Elizabeth's mouth. It contained a couple of spoonfuls of bitter liquid. Elizabeth tried to spit it out, but Sheila held her head straight and blocked off her breath from her nostrils, choking her as the liquid ran back into her throat. She swallowed, gagging from the taste, then breathed deeply through her mouth. Sheila released her head and held her shoulders again. The liquid burned a trail of fire down to her stomach, and it spread a glowing warmth through her body as a hard knot of nausea formed in her stomach. She started to scream again, and it was suddenly very difficult to work her mouth and tongue. Everything became blurred, and she felt numb. An overpowering fatigue settled over her, and her eyelids became very heavy. Darkness closed in.

A headache throbbed dully in her temples, and she felt feverishly lightheaded. Contact with her surroundings was flimsy and tenuous, requiring a concentrated effort to make what she saw meaningful. Bessie was asleep in the chair by the bed, and it was day again. The rain was still pouring down. Something vitally important was missing. She frowned with thought, pondering, then began searching frantically for the baby. It was gone. She lifted her head, then sat up. There was a small wooden box just inside the door, freshly made, the wood damp from the rain. She pushed the covers back, slid her feet to the floor, and crossed the room to the box. Bits of damp sawdust still clung to the ends of some of the boards, there was a heavy hammer leaning against the wall behind it, and the top boards were loose. She moved the boards. The bundled blanket was in it. She lifted it out and straightened up, looking in it. The color was darker, the side of the head covered by the birthmark almost black, and the small mouth was open, gaping vacantly.

There was a clammoring, demanding imperative to escape, to evade what the box meant and its utter finality. She moved back toward the bed, looking at Bessie, who was snoring softly, a heavy coat clutched around her. Elizabeth put the bundle down on the edge of the bed, slipped her feet into her shoes and quickly fastened them, then picked up the bundle and walked quietly to the door. Voices became audible over the sound of the rain beating against the roof as she approached the door. Sheila and Cummings were on the veranda and were arguing violently. Elizabeth cradled the bundle in her arms and walked quietly across the front room to the kitchen, then crossed the kitchen to the back door. She opened the door, slipped through it, and closed it behind her.

The sudden drenching from the rain made the vertigo intensify, staggering her. She stopped, recovering her balance and clutching the bundle to her, then began walking carefully down the steps. The downpour soaked her nightgown through to her skin in an instant. It plastered her hair to her head and streamed down her face in rivulets which made it hard to see and to breathe. The cold began penetrating, and she was shivering by the time she reached the bottom of the steps. The ground had disappeared under an inches-deep sheet of muddy water which was a boiling mass of miniature waterspouts which lived for their instant as the large, heavy drops struck. The rain was a grey, blinding curtain on all sides, fading into the muddy water covering the ground without a clear line of delimitation, surrounding her with featureless grey. The loss of visual references, the water all around her, and the rain pouring down her face and blinding her made the lightheadedness and lack of contact with her surroundings more pronounced, and she stumbled from side to side as she stepped off the bottom step and waded across the path toward the creek.

Her general objective was the area along the creek on the other side of the aborigine settlement, an unused area covered with scrubby brush and grass which would offer many places to hide, and the perceived danger was the road in front of the houses, where others passed back and forth frequently. The low-hanging branch of a pepper tree weighted down with wet leaves and the force of the rain beating against it suddenly appeared out of the rain in front of her and swept across her face, then she almost ran into a huge ghost gum tree, its trunk invisible in the rain and dim light until she was inches from it. She knew each bush and tree, but she felt an almost total loss of orientation, as though everything had moved around.

The water was well above her ankles, almost up to her knees in places, and the mud sucked at her shoes. She struggled along, her nightgown sagging wetly, tangling around her feet, and clinging clammily to her legs. There was a faint sound over the steady beat of the rain, a roaring rumble which was as much a vibration all around her as a sound, and she identified it as rushing water, the creek with its banks flooded. She angled to her right, trying to see the edge of the creek, but all she could see was the water a few feet around her, boiling as the rain struck it. The water was suddenly above her knees and had a strong current, and she started to angle further to the right as she took another step. The ground abruptly disappeared as her feet were swept from under her, and her scream was a thin wail lost in the pounding of the rain and the gushing roar of the swollen creek.

Utter panic possessed her mind as the water enveloped her and filled her mouth and nose, and she was spinning, being swept rapidly along, and tumbling as the cold water crushed in around her. She clutched the bundle tightly in her arm, flailing with her other arm. Her head broke clear, but her mouth and nose immediately filled with water as she started to take a breath, and she was tumbled over again. There was a crushing blow as she slammed into something then a mass of brush was around her, the current pressing her into it. She struggled frantically, fighting to get her head out of the water, and pulled herself higher in the brush. She raised her head, and gulped deep breaths as she clawed to pull herself higher. There was a large lump in the brush by her, and she dragged herself toward it, gripping the bundle under her arm. It was a drowned sheep. It slipped and slid sidewards as she tried to climb onto it, but one of her feet found a solid limb among the brush. She planted her other foot on it and pulled herself higher, choking and vomiting water she had swallowed.

It was a mass of debris caught in an eddy around three

large ghost gums, swaying and bobbing in the current, on the point of breaking loose and rushing along the creek. She worked her way along the limb toward the ghost gums, coughing, choking, and gasping for air. Her nightgown snagged on the groping, clinging fingers of the brush, and long rents ripped in it as she pulled it loose and clambered along the limb. A drowned cow was wedged firmly in a branch of the limb in front of her, and she climbed over the cold, stiff, hairy body to the trunk of the tree. It had been washed out of the ground and was caught between the ghost gums, and its roots were an interwoven mass of twisted tendrils, dimly seen through the rain and moving slightly as the tree moved from the current pushing against its upper branches. She climbed past the ghost gums, and shifting, muddy ground was under her feet again. She climbed over another dead sheep and into the shallow water.

Clumps of brush were ghostly shadows through the rain around her, and the wet grass clung to her as she staggered from side to side. She sank to her knees and cradled the bundle in her arms, bending over it, then after a time she struggled back to her feet and went on. The only objective in her mind was a vague and ill-defined impulse to continue onward. Her torn nightgown hung in rags around her, and she shivered uncontrollably. She sank to her knees and rested for a time again, then pushed herself to her feet and went on once more. The water became almost knee-deep, and her steps were tediously slow as she pused her way through it. Then it became shallow again, barely above the tops of her shoes. Low, bulky shapes moved around in front of her and turned into three sheep as she approached them. One of them had a broken front leg. It and the other two were cropping the wet grass, and they pulled mouthfuls and chewed rapidly as they edged out of her path.

The rain beat down on her head and back as she slumped on her knees and cuddled the bundle close to her.

The gnawing imperative to move onward still nagged at her, but the effort of rising seemed insurmountable. A sudden, ear-shattering whoop exploded behind her, and she twisted around and looked. An aborigine was standing ten feet from her, his face turned slightly away from her and his eyeballs fixed on her. He drew in a deep breath, his chest expanding, and he pursed his lips and expelled the air in a shrill, hooting sound again. His only garment was a belt which held a knife and an axe, and he clutched a sheaf of spears in his left hand. She looked at him in fright, stumbling to her feet. He uttered another hoot. She weaved weakly from side to side as she began walking again, and he followed her at a distance of ten feet, hooting every few seconds. She collapsed to her knees again, and he stopped behind her. He stood with the rain beating against his naked body, drawing in his breath and hooting. She managed to get back to her feet again and go a few steps further, and he followed. When she sank to her knees once more, it was too much of an effort to get back to her feet, and she crawled for a distance, using her left arm and holding the bundle to her with the other. He still followed, uttering the hoots at regular intervals. Then it was too much of an effort to move, and she huddled on the ground with the bundle pressed against her breasts. After a time she was less frightened of him and of the shrill sounds he made.

Something stirred on the edges of her awareness, tugging at her attention. It seemed remotely threatening, and she contemplated trying to get back to her feet again. Her mind drew further out of her reverie, and she realized that the hooting had stopped. A large, dark shadow in the rain turned into a mounted rider. The horse stopped in front of her. The rain beat against her face as she lifted it. The blurred outline was well known, warmly familiar. It was Sheila. Sheila bent over her, taking her arms and lifting her, and she looked toward the aborigine and shouted something in his language over the noise of the rain. The aborigine turned and melted into the rain.

Water streamed from the sagging brim of Sheila's hat, and she held Elizabeth up with one arm and pushed her hair out of her face with the other, her eyes moving over Elizabeth's face. "Now look at you. Aren't you the bloody mess and all?" Her features twisted, and she held Elizabeth in both arms, squeezing her tightly and bending down to kiss her. "Why did you ever have to come here, you silly little sod?" she murmured, her voice breaking. "Why couldn't you have stopped in bloody Sydney?" She kissed her again, then sighed heavily, bending over and lifting her. "But you're here, and I'm glad you are. Come on, then, little pom."

She lifted Elizabeth onto the saddle and held her on it with both legs hanging off one side as she climbed onto the saddle behind her, then unbuckled her slicker and pulled it around Elizabeth. The horse turned and began plodding along at a slow walk. Elizabeth held the bundle to her, and Sheila held Elizabeth. The warmth of Sheila's body penetrated her, and she stopped shivering and dozed off, slumped against Sheila.

Sheila woke her lifting her down from the horse, and she began shivering violently again as the rain beat against her and the cold gripped her. They were at the creek, the rumble of the rushing water filling the air around them. Sheila put her arm around Elizabeth's waist, half carrying her and half dragging her as she shouted at the horse and waded into the deeper water beside it, holding onto the saddle. The water became deeper, then they were swept to one side and Sheila was clinging to the saddle with one hand and holding Elizabeth up with her other arm as they were carried along the creek by the swift current. The horse's eyes were glazed with fright as it held its head high and swam frantically toward the mottled blur of the other shore shooting past. The dark shapes of the trees on the other shore were suddenly gone and there was only a sheet of water spotted with clumps of brush, then solid ground was underfoot again. Sheila stumbled and almost fell, and her arm around Elizabeth's waist becoming painfully tight as she recovered her balance. Then they were wading in shallow water, and Sheila stopped the horse and lifted Elizabeth onto the saddle again.

The sound of Sheila's voice woke her again. It sounded deeper, raised over the pounding of the rain and coming through her ear pressed against Sheila's chest. "... go down to the south fork and bring back the lot that went down there. And you go to the north and bring that lot in. You go back by the abo village and make sure they're calling in their searchers, and then you go on out and check the west edge of Wilcannia and make sure it isn't getting too deep."

The three riders and their horses were dim, distorted shadows through the rain, their hats low over their faces and their slickers pulled up around the lower part of their faces. "Why did she bloody do it?"

"That's none of your bleeding flock, you. You do as you're sodding told, and you don't worry about aught else. All three of you get fresh horses if any are left, and you watch yourself down that south fork, John. You'll be in the creek before you see it if you don't have a care."

The three riders turned their horses and faded into the rain. The horse began plodding along at a slow walk again. Sheila pulled the slicker tighter around Elizabeth, and Elizabeth nestled closer to Sheila and dozed off again. It seemed only seconds later that the cold rain was beating against her once more and jarring motion was arousing her as Sheila pulled her down from the horse. They were in front of her house. Sheila was staggering with fatigue, and Elizabeth struggled to keep her knees from collapsing and tried to support herself as Sheila led and pulled her along the path and up the steps to the veranda. The rain stopped beating against her as they went under the overhang of the veranda. It seemed

299

strange to have only the sound of the rain around her. The old woman was standing in the doorway, and she moved out of the way as Sheila brought Elizabeth in. They went on in to the kitchen. It was cozily warm, with a roaring fire in the stove. Sheila lowered Elizabeth into a chair.

"Are you going to drink this, or do I have to choke it down you, little pom?"

The old woman was holding a pannikin, and Sheila bent over Elizabeth and looked into her eyes as she reached for it. Sheila's face was lined with exhaustion, but her eyes were warm. Elizabeth held the bundle with one arm and reached for the cup, and she drank the black, bitter liquid. The taste exploded in her mouth, making her want to retch, and she fought it and swallowed hard as Sheila took the cup. She looked down at the bundle, pulling it close to her, then at her torn, ragged nightgown. The heat of the kitchen seemed to become more intense, and her neck was suddenly too weak to hold her head erect. She was dimly conscious of the old woman taking the bundle from her arms and of Sheila lifting her from the chair.

There was a steely, frozen quiet. She opened her eyes, looking around, then she realized what it was. The rain had diminished to a soft patter. And there was sound, the birds in the trees, insects, and voices on the veranda. She started to turn over in bed, then relaxed again, wincing and gasping with pain. An excruciating headache was pounding in her temples, every muscle in her body seemed sore, and scratches on her arms and legs tingled and burned. The voices became louder, and she turned her head slightly and listened. It was Sheila and Cummings.

". . . going to be shot of her, and you can be bloody assured of that. She's never been worth her bloody rations to me, and now she's bloody mad. I'm not going to—"

"Aye, well, that's your affair and it's naught to me. My concern is the sheep in Bulloo South. Franklin is by himself up there, and it'll take more than the two of us to move them before they drown."

300

"Bulloo South? Bloody hell, that's as high as any ground for fifty miles in any—"

"Not when Burrundie Creek runs a banker, and it's still rising. It's rising while we're standing here slapping our tongues, so come on and let's get those sheep moved up to—"

"Am I the only bloody man on this station? And I'm supposed to be the head stockman and all, not at the bloody beck and call of anyone who points to me. I've just come in from Penong, you know."

"Aye, and Colin left here not more than two hours ago with every man he could muster, including the bloody cook. The sheep in Widgie South will be swimming before nightfall if they're not moved, and he couldn't spare a man to go with me. But now that you're here I need your help, by God. So come on and help me."

Sheila's voice sounded strangely conciliatory toward him, almost banteringly friendly. He grumbled resentfully, agreeing to go with her, and their voices became a distant murmur as the front door closed. Their boots thumped against the veranda and down the steps. The light coming in the window was much brighter, and the chattering of the birds sounded cheerful and lively, as though the world had awakened from a long sleep. Elizabeth's arms and legs ached, and she still felt very weary. She cautiously turned to a more comfortable position and relaxed again, and she thought about the baby. She felt a deep sorrow, but the agony of grief was gone, as though dulled by the passage of years. She closed her eyes and went back to sleep.

Afternoon sunlight was streaming through the window when she woke again, and she got out of bed. The house was full of mud which had been tracked in, and the open area across the road between the buildings and pens was a sea of mud. There was a small spot of fresh earth in the small graveyard near the water tanks, and she stood at the window and looked at it for a long moment. She was ravenously hungry, and she built up the fire in the stove, started potatoes boiling and a pan of pork slices frying, then dressed and began washing the floor with water from the tub on the back porch. She ate when the food was cooked, then continued washing the mud off the floor, working her way from the kitchen through the dining room and into the front room.

Footsteps came up and crossed the veranda as she was on her hands and knees in the front room, scouring the boards with a heavy brush, and she lifted her head as the door opened. It was Bessie. Bessie looked at her with a stunned expression, then it changed into a smile, spreading across her chubby face and becoming brilliant.

"Why... are you all right, Elizabeth?"

Elizabeth sat back on her heels and brushed her hair out of her face as she smiled and nodded. "Yes, I am now, Bessie."

"And after that mud and all, I see. I have a houseful myself that my man and brats tracked in on me, and it looks like I'll have to take a shovel to get it out of the big house."

Elizabeth smiled and nodded again. There was a moment of awkward silence, and she leaned forward and began scrubbing the floor again. "I'll have to see about a gravestone."

"Aye, well, there's no trouble there. Several of the abos are skillful at that, and they'll do it for a shilling or two. They made the ones you see out there now. And there's ample time to take care of it without fear of it being lost, because I put a little stick down to mark it. I did that because the grass grows fast and tracks are soon lost here, you know."

"Yes, I see."

"Well, I'm on to the big house to start cooking, then. I thought I'd look in on you."

"Thank you, Bessie. Thank you for everything."

Bessie smiled and nodded, backing away from the door, and went back across the veranda and down the steps. Elizabeth pushed her hair back from her face with her forearm, dipped the brush into the wooden bucket and splashed more water on the floor, and continued scrubbing.

The first scrubbing removed the surface mud and left dark stains on the boards which were clearly visible even in the dim light of the lamp. She ate again and went to bed, then rose early the following morning, cooked breakfast and ate, and started scrubbing the floor again. As she was pouring a bucket of water out the front door onto the veranda, she saw Sheila and Colin walking up the steps to their house. She stepped out onto the veranda to call out to Sheila, but they were already inside. Elizabeth went back inside and through the kitchen to dip another bucket of water from the tub on the back porch, then she came back into the front room, poured part of the water on the floor, and got down on her hands and knees and began scrubbing again.

There was a movement on the edge of her vision, and she lifted her head, looking through the open door. The old woman was walking along the road, and the old man was following her, his hand on her shoulder. Sheila and Colin were following the old man. They turned onto the path to her house. She dropped the brush and wiped her hands on her skirt as she went to the door. Colin looked solemn. The old woman looked as she always did. Sheila's expression was wooden, her eyes hooded. There was a hollow, sinking sensation in the pit of Elizabeth's stomach; bad news. The old woman climbed the steps one at a time, her eyes on Elizabeth's, and the old man followed her with the cautious tread of the blind. Colin and Sheila waited, then walked up the steps behind them. They crossed the veranda, then stopped in front of the door.

"Are you there?" the old man murmured in his deep voice, his lips slack and shapeless over his toothless gums and his blind eyes fixed on a point somewhere behind her.

"Yes, I am here, Mr. Garrity."

"Your man is dead. A boar killed him."

Elizabeth put her hand on the doorjamb to steady herself. The dread suspicion had been hovering in the back of her mind, because there was nothing else which would have brought all of them. But the shock completely unnerved her. It was utter disaster. Cummings had been a cruel, ruthless man. He had been a poor husband, and he had mistreated her. But he had also represented support. She looked out at the buildings, where the sun was drawing a thin mist from the wet ground. It was a place where she had found sorrow and happiness, but most of all it was a place where she had found a home. And now it was in jeopardy.

The old man spoke. "You're to stay here as you are. And you're to consider yourself as one of mine. I'll speak with you again after a time."

It took a moment to fully assimilate his words. And then it was difficult to maintain an attitude appropriate to having just been told that her husband was dead. She cleared her throat and nodded. "Thank you, Mr. Garrity," she said quietly.

He nodded and turned around with slow, cautious steps. The old woman stepped in front of him, took his hand and put it on her shoulder, and slowly led him toward the steps, her stick thumping hollowly against the floor. Colin looked at Elizabeth as though he were about to say something, then glanced at Sheila and turned to follow his mother and father. Sheila stood with her arms folded, watching them walk down the steps, then walked slowly toward Elizabeth.

"I was there when it happened, Elizabeth, and I couldn't get a shot into the boar in time. Both barrels of his musket misfired, so he didn't have much of a chance against it. High ground is a dangerous time during a flood, because the boars go there just like everything else does."

Her tone was flat and matter of fact, not even hinting at sympathy, because she knew that it would generate more relief than sorrow. Elizabeth nodded, looking away. The memory of the conversation between Sheila and Cummings was fragmentary, but she could clearly remember Sheila's tone as she had talked him into going with her. There was a possibility that Sheila had decided he had to die and had seen to it. She could have done something to his musket and then got him in the vicinity of a boar, because Sheila's intelligence and cunning was on an entirely different order than that of Cummings. It wasn't beyond her. And it didn't bring automatic condemnation, as it once would have. There was a distance between Sydney and Wayamba Station which was too vast to be measured in miles. The rules were different.

But it wasn't a matter which could be addressed directly in conversation. One who forced a person into a situation where they might have to lie was more guilty than one who lied. But it could be addressed indirectly. Elizabeth stepped down to the veranda, taking Sheila's hand between hers. "I'm very thankful you weren't injured, Sheila. I don't know what I'd do if something happened to you."

Sheila looked down at her and smiled fondly, squeezing Elizabeth's hand. "I'm glad to see you're better now."

"I wouldn't be if it weren't for you. Where is it?"

"It?"

"What's left of him."

"Oh, that. Well, the boar got his horse too, and I couldn't handle him by myself. I sent a couple of men after him, and they'll have him back before nightfall. The cook and his mob are making a box, and I sent another man to Menindee for the constable and the vicar. They should be here tomorrow, so we can keep him here tonight and bury him tomorrow, if that suits you."

"Very well. I know it is through you that your father is permitting me to stay, and I'm very grateful, Sheila."

Sheila made a sound of amusement in her throat, squeezing Elizabeth's hand again and releasing it, and she turned away, lifting her hat and pushing her hair under it. "Don't ever think you can count my dad's flocks by the sheep you can see, Elizabeth."

"What do you mean?"

Sheila turned back and looked at her with a thoughtful smile, then looked away again and shrugged. "It isn't the proper time to talk to you about it, but there's nothing amiss in letting you know there's something to talk about. Colin, my dad, and my ma have cast about all the stations around here for a wife for Colin, but they've found no one who satisfies them. They're all satisfied with you, though."

The realization that she was again free to marry came with something of a mild shock. And a warm glow formed in her as she thought about what Sheila had said. She smiled and lifted her eyebrows, chuckling wryly. "That's very flattering. And somewhat amazing, considering what has happened the past couple of days."

"Aye, well, any creek will run a banker when it rains hard enough, little pom," Sheila said, walking slowly toward the steps. "I'll tell them to bring him on over when they get him boxed, and I'll go get some sleep so I can sit with you tonight. And when a proper time has passed, I'll talk to you on the other matter so I can let Colin, my dad, and my ma know if you're of a set of mind that they can talk to you about it. That way no one has to get their wind up, do they?"

"Yes, that's quite right, Sheila. We can discuss it day after tomorrow."

Sheila chuckled, glancing at her and nodding as she turned back toward the steps. "Aye, no bloody reason to waste time, is there? I'll be back when I've had some sleep, then."

"Very well, and thank you, Sheila. Thank you for everything."

Sheila glanced over her shoulder again and nodded as she walked down the steps.

– 18 –

Elizabeth and Colin were married at the church at
Menindee, one of a dozen ramshackle buildings in the
small settlement by the Darling River, and he was
everything Cummings hadn't been. His attitude toward
her seemed to be influenced strongly by the mutual
respect between him and Sheila, and he was gentle and
considerate with her. He was a quiet man, but he also had
a good sense of humor and he seemed to never tire of
hearing about Sydney and her childhood. He was also an
extremely handsome man, and he awakened impulses
within her which she had never realized she possessed.
When he was considerate to the point of being hesitant to
make love to her, she was aggressive. And then she was
shy and blushed when he smiled at her over breakfast.

The old man procrastinated about hiring another head stockman, so they lived in the head stockman's house. Elizabeth was allowed to spend what she wished, and after she had ordered a few pieces of furniture, material for clothes, silverware, china, and some other things, she found herself in the strange position of having a basically unlimited source of money and nothing on which to spend it.

She was ecstatically happy. The work in the house seemed less laborious than before, and she enjoyed washing his clothes and planning meals for when he would return from the paddocks. She carried cow manure from the stockyard and mulched the flower beds, occasionally cut flowers and put them on the baby's grave, and fertilized and pruned the vines on the verandas around the houses until they grew into thick, shady screens. She received another letter from Stephen Willoughby, her relative in England, and she wrote a long reply about Cummings' death, her remarriage, and the station.

Sheila and her father came to the decision to send James to a boarding school in Sydney, and Elizabeth wrote to the headmaster of the school and to the bishop, asking him if someone among his staff could act as a sponsor for James. A reply from the headmaster of the school came back on the next trip the supply wagons made, accepting James as a pupil, and the bishop's reply was just as prompt. It was a long, enthusiastically warm and friendly letter in the bishop's hand which took due note of the change in her name and status on the station, and it communicated his high regard and best wishes for her and assured her that James would receive his personal attention.

James had progressed to the point that teaching him had involved a considerable amount of time and effort in preparation and her undivided attention to his lessons during the afternoons. A major activity was eliminated when he left, and it brought into focus a nagging feeling of uselessness. Colin looked for ways to be pleasant to her, and he complimented her on the attractiveness of the flower beds and on other things she did, but she had a firm conviction that his interest was limited to being pleasant to her and that he really didn't care. He wasn't a demanding man, and the housekeeping required little of her. They began going to the Garrity house for dinner when he came in from the paddocks so he could talk to his father and Sheila if she was there, and the meals she cooked were for herself.

Even that diminished as time passed, because Sheila insistently invited Elizabeth to have dinner at the Garrity house when she was at home, and she was at the home paddock much of the time. The old man and old woman were stolidly uncommunicative most of the time, and they made Elizabeth welcome at their home for dinner and at other times by treating her precisely as they treated Colin and Sheila, a general lack of notice except for stares from the old woman and questions from the old man when he wanted to know something. The old woman chewed the old man's meat for him, a subject for comical comment and pantomime by Sheila when she was well away from them, and their abrupt manner in leaving the table was similarly contrary to polite custom. When they finished eating and the old man had finished asking questions, they would immediately leave the table and go to the parlor or veranda to smoke their pipes.

The grate in Elizabeth's stove burned through, and for three nights she ate dinner with them while another grate was being made in the smithy. Sheila and Colin were both in the paddocks at the time and the old man's interests centered around the sheep, and there was no conversation until the third night. Then the old man asked her if she was pregnant, she stammered a confused and startled negative, and he grunted with dissatisfaction.

310

She had brought out all her books in the process of teaching James, and she had found that her interest in them had strangely waned; they were concerned with academic minutiae, while a vital and active world existed around her on the station. Sheila and Colin included Elizabeth in their conversations when they were talking together, sometimes with painfully obvious effort, because most of their conversation was about sheep, cattle, or other things regarding the station. She found herself learning more about the station and its affairs, and her interest in it increased as her knowledge grew.

At the same time, she became less interested in other activities. Time began to hang heavily on her, and in addition to the guilt she felt about not using her time constructively, she became bored.

When she approached Sheila about learning to ride, she expected some good-natured banter, but she found that Sheila had been waiting for her to ask. The slop chest at the Garrity house provided all the clothes she needed. The old man had always insisted that all of his children be fully clothed and wear boots from the time they were very small, and there were several pairs of boots in various sizes which Sheila had outgrown and which had been carefully preserved with tallow against possible future needs. There were many outgrown shirts and pairs of trousers, soft and bleached from many washings and carefully folded and put away in a cedar chest. Elizabeth felt almost naked in trousers, accustomed as she was to the bulk of clothes around her, and she worried that the outlines of her hips and legs were immodestly revealed. The boots felt heavy and cumbersome on her feet, and her hair was bulky under the hat. But the reaction of the men was more mild surprise at the clothes rather than a specific interest in how she looked in them. And after the first day, the painful soreness in her thighs, back, and buttocks took her mind off her appearance.

311

Lambs were being grouped and tight ties were being put on the base of their tails to cut off the blood circulation so the tail would deteriorate and fall off. She worked with Sheila in the mustering yard, learning to control the dogs and driving bunches of lambs into the pens for the ties to be put on, then worked in one of the pens for a time, breathing the choking dust composed of dirt and sheep dung as she clutched wriggling lambs between her knees and put on ties. Then there was another bunch of hundreds which had to be castrated. She worked again in the mustering yard for a time, then in one of the pens, an uproarious melée of bleating lambs, smoking tar buckets, and dogs darting about. Two of the men worked with unbelievable rapidity, snatching up the lambs and biting the testicles off and grinning widely at her with blood-stained lips, and for a heart-stopping instant she thought she might be expected to do the same. But Sheila laughed softly and shook her head as she took out her pocketknife, and she motioned for Elizabeth to watch as she snatched a lamb by its rear foot and dragged it to her.

She worked from dawn until dusk, and after the second day she began sleeping in an empty room at the Garrity house to keep from walking the few yards to collapse into bed after dinner and so Sheila could awaken her. She was sunburned, her hands were blistered, she was a mass of aching muscles, and the nights seemed to pass in a flash, Sheila calling her impatiently after what felt like only a few minutes of sleep. There were a couple of mornings when it was almost impossible to get out of bed, then suddenly the agony of soreness was gone and she was awakening at the same time as Sheila. There was a warm camaraderie in early morning in the kitchen, the windows black and the lamp filling the room with a yellow light, the fire roaring in the stove and Bessie bustling around it, and Sheila looking bleary as she stamped her feet into her boots, stuffed her shirt into her trousers, and chewed a mouthful of damper and fried pork. And there was a glow of self-congratulation when she saw a riffle of motion which meant that some of the sheep were breaking from the group, sent a dog racing to stop them, and basked in Sheila's approving nod and smile.

Colin returned from the paddocks, and his approval was gratifying. Elizabeth felt a sense of belonging and of being an essential, integral part of the activity around her, and a growing confidence in her ability to learn further and do more. The sense of camaraderie was even more pronounced while Colin was at the home paddock and the three of them ate a hasty breakfast and walked together to the stockyard to catch and saddle a horse in the first light of dawn. She felt completely accepted a few nights later when the subject of hiring a head stockman came up over dinner. The old man said that a head stockman wasn't needed with three members of the family working with the stock.

There was a mass of older lambs which had lost their tails and which had to be mulsed, the skin around the anus and the tail stump stripped off to eliminate the wool where clots of manure could collect and become fly-blown and full of worms. It was delicate, painstaking work during which a slip of the knife could injure a lamb beyond recovery. Her squeamishness changed to a remote distaste and a desire to be finished, and she worked with Sheila, driving a group from the mustering yard into a pen, mulsing them and daubing on tar to keep flies away until the raw flesh healed, then driving them into another pen with others which had been finished and going after another group from the mustering yard.

Colin left for an outer paddock and returned while the mulsing was going on, and over dinner one night the conversation turned to the sheep which were being mulsed. When they were finished they were to be taken to Wilcannia East, on the easternmost edge of the station, and the old man silently nodded when Sheila said she would drive them to the paddock and take Elizabeth with her. Instead of working in the pens the following afternoon, Sheila took Elizabeth along the creek on the other side of the aborigine settlement to begin teaching her how to use a stock whip and fire and reload one of the short, heavy, double-barreled muskets which were carried on the saddles for protection against wild boars.

They left early one morning, saddling their horses and tying their rations and equipment to the saddles in the pre-dawn darkness and chill, then driving the flock out of the mustering yard and to the east in the first grey light, whistling and shouting at the dogs and forming the sheep into a long, thick column. Elizabeth rode ahead at a swift trot to drop the rails in a section of the fence, and a few minutes later the flowing column of sheep came into sight in the growing daylight, bleating and trotting rapidly along as they rippled smoothly through the open section of fence. The sun peeked above the horizon, and the straight line of the track to the east was clearly visible, a swath where the hoofs of many animals and the wheels of many wagons had crushed the grass and brush. It was the same point at which she had crossed into the home paddock in the wagon with Cummings, long before.

Elizabeth revelled in the sense of freedom which corresponded to the feel of the expansive stretch of the rolling land around them. The sheep had to be driven slowly because they were young and still recovering from the mulsing, and they rode leisurely along behind the sheep, whistling and signalling a dog when some of the sheep started to break away to graze along the side of the track. Dust rose and flies were stirred from the grass, but they were a minor discomfort, as was the heat when the sun rose higher. A kangaroo or an emu occasionally raced away from the bustle at the head of the column of sheep, and they moved along the track and up a gradual bulge in the rolling hills from which the pens and buildings of the home paddock were visible, a shadowy blotch distorted by rising heat waves. Then they crossed the bulge, and the

314

home paddock was lost from sight behind them.

They ate cold damper and salt beef for lunch as they rode along, keeping the sheep moving along at a steady pace. The sheep began to tire during the afternoon, all of them slowing and more and more stragglers falling back, and in late afternoon Sheila rode to the head of the column and turned them off the track to the north, where a creekline stretched along the base of a hill. The sheep rushed to drink and began grazing, and Sheila watched over them to keep them from scattering while Elizabeth made a camp for the night in a small cluster of trees, unsaddled and hobbled the horses, and began cooking.

At sunset the sheep finished grazing and began settling down to chew their cud, and Sheila sent the dogs racing around the edges of the flock and herded them close together for the night, then came to the fire. Elizabeth had roasted a large piece of mutton for the dogs and cooked pork, rice, and damper for her and Sheila. They fed the dogs, sent them back to the sheep, then sat by the fire and ate as darkness fell. They put the leftovers away for breakfast and lunch the next day, shared the remainder of the tea, rolled in their blankets and lay down by the fire.

The breeze stirred the trees and rippled through the grass, keeping the flies and mosquitoes away, and it freshened and became colder as the heat of the day faded into the chill of night. Elizabeth huddled in her blanket, thinking longingly of her warm bed at the home paddock. The ground was hard and cold under her, and the blanket and her clothes felt thin with the breeze blowing against her back. The fire made a soft sound as the ashes settled, glowing dark red and then yellow as the breeze swept across it. She reached out of her blanket and threw a couple more pieces of wood on the fire, then pulled her arm back into the blanket and plucked the edge of it up over her ears, shivering and sighing.

One of the sheep made a quiet sound and stirred, and Sheila lifted her head, listened, then lay back down, tugging her blanket closer and looking across the fire at Elizabeth. "Are you all right, then?"

"Aye, beyond freezing my bloody arse off," Elizabeth replied.

Sheila laughed softly, moving her shoulders to a more comfortable position and pulling her blanket tighter.

"Laugh, then, blast your eyes. You're on the windward side of the fire, but it'll burn down and then you'll finish laughing."

"No," Sheila chuckled. "I was thinking that you're getting a proper peppery tongue. Are you cold, then?"

"No, I'm bloody shaking for practice so I'll know what to do when I get cold," Elizabeth replied in a dry tone, shivering.

Sheila lifted herself on her elbow, looking at Elizabeth across the fire. "Shall I keep you warm, then?"

"Aye, unless it pleases you to lie there and watch me freeze to death."

Sheila chuckled again, unwrapping her blanket and standing, and she walked around the fire with her blanket and nudged Elizabeth's boots with her toe. "Unwrap, then, and I'll lie with you and keep you warm, you bloody sickly lamb."

Elizabeth unwrapped her blanket, and Sheila lay down by her on the edge of it, pulled it around her, then put her blanket around both of them and settled herself comfortably, putting her arms around Elizabeth and pulling her closer. Her warmth enfolded Elizabeth, the frigid tension from the cold changing to a soothing relaxation as her body absorbed the warmth of Sheila's, and she pressed her cold nose into the hollow of Sheila's throat and pushed her hands up under Sheila's arm. "You're lovely and warm, Sheila. And now I've found some use for the huge, great cow you are."

"You keep on driving at me like a ram at stud until you push me into the fire, and you'll find out that I'm big enough to leather your arse and all."

316

Elizabeth chuckled, nestling closer to Sheila, and immediately began dozing off.

Sheila pulled the edge of a blanket up around Elizabeth's ears, then relaxed, sighing softly. "I've never slept with anyone before, you know," she murmured in a musing tone. "Not even that sod who got James on me. Every time he did it, he was there and then gone. And most of the time it was during the day. So I've never slept with anyone properly."

Elizabeth grunted drowsily. "You'll not be able to say that tomorrow."

Sheila made a sound of amusement in her throat, pulling the blanket higher around Elizabeth's ears and patting her head. "Aye, that's true enough. But let's not tell anyone, lest they take it amiss."

"Aye, and then you wouldn't keep me warm again. I won't."

Sheila chuckled softly, patting Elizabeth's back. "Good night, then, Elizabeth."

Elizabeth murmured sleepily, then stirred and sighed. "You used to call me 'pom' all the time, but you don't any more."

"That's because you aren't any more. Good night, then."

Elizabeth thought drowsily about what Sheila had said, then smiled and nodded as she wriggled closer to Sheila.

They reached Wilcannia East seven days later, after having slowly driven the sheep across Penong Paddock and Wilcannia West. There were already some twelve thousand sheep in Wilcannia East, with a single stockman to keep them in a loose mass and move them about in the enclosure, check fences, and watch for dingoes. He was an old man and knew Sheila from childhood, and Elizabeth had seen him at the home paddock a few times. Sheila treated him with the easy familiarity that existed between her and the older men she knew well, but he had an unsure

317

attitude toward Elizabeth, the wary watchfulness of those
who spend much of their time by themselves. They spent a
night by his shelter, eating dinner with him and talking
over the fire before rolling up in their blankets on
opposite sides of the fire, and when they left the next
morning, they went to the north to check part of the
northern boundary fence and to familiarize Elizabeth
with the area as they worked their way back toward the
home paddock.

They covered the miles rapidly without the sheep, the
horses moving along at a swift trot and the dogs they had
brought with them running along behind them, and they
reached the northern boundary fence the next day and
turned to the west. The boundary fence was post and rail,
and posts had sagged and rails had fallen in a few places
since it had been checked. They repaired it, working their
way along the fence to the west, and crossed back into
Penong Paddock.

The sheep were moved about in the sections as the
graze was eaten down, loosely clustered by their herd
instinct and by the stockmen watching them and driving
back bands which strayed too far. An occasional stray
which had wandered off and had somehow escaped the
dingoes as they worked their way along the boundary
fence, but after they crossed into the northeastern
quadrant of Penong Paddock, there were a lot of them.
They rode along the fence for an hour, Sheila frowning
thoughtfully and looking around as strays kept bounding
out of the brush around them, then they turned south.

The dogs made wide sweeps to each side of their line of
travel and collected strays, and Elizabeth and Sheila
drove them along at a rapid trot, shouting at them and
cracking their stock whips. The cluster of sheep acted like
a magnet for strays along the way, and they were driving
several hundred sheep in front of them by the time they
began finding bunches of a half dozen on the edges of the
main body of the flock, which had spread out over a

distance of many miles. Sheila whistled at the dogs and called them in, and they coiled their whips and left the sheep, riding on to the south.

The stockman's shelter was a small structure of bark and poles on top of a knoll, and his dogs were sitting in front of it and his horse was hobbled and grazing in the valley below the shelter. A strong odor hung in the air around it, urine, feces, and a heavy stench of corruption, and the hot, dim interior of the shelter was almost overpowering. The man was lying on the pallet against the wall, and Sheila knelt by him and bent over him as Elizabeth stood in the doorway, choking back her retching.

"Bring me some water, Elizabeth."

She went back to the horses, drawing in deep breaths of the fresh air, and took the leather-covered water bottle from her saddle and carried it inside. Sheila took it from her, and Elizabeth scurried back to the entrance, holding her breath and gagging. The man stirred, groaned, and drank as Sheila lifted his head and poured the water between his lips.

"Off your feed, are you, Billy?"

"Aye, I've been better," the man sighed weakly.

"How long have you been this way?"

There was a long silence as the man pondered, then he sighed heavily and murmured. "Onto a week, I believe. See how my gut has puffed up?"

"Aye, I can see. We'd better take you back to the home paddock, then."

"Who'll bloody see to my sheep?"

"*She* will."

"Who in the bloody hell is she?"

"You know Elizabeth. She was married to Cummings, and now she's married to Colin."

"Aye, the mad one."

"No more than most, and a lot less than some," Sheila chuckled.

319

"She'll let my sheep stray to buggery."

"She can let them stray no worse than they are now, and you can't see to them in your state. I'll clean you up a bit, and then we'll bluie to the home paddock."

"You'll do no cleaning with her in here."

"She couldn't get herself a decent look at your cod piece anyway, the way your gut is puffed up," Sheila said, pushing the cork back into the water bottle, and her smile faded as she walked toward the entrance and motioned Elizabeth out.

Elizabeth drew in deep breaths again, trying to get the foul odor out of her nostrils and throat. "What's wrong with him?"

Sheila shook her head morosely and shrugged, handing the water bottle back to her. "I've no bloody idea, Elizabeth. But this is no good here. I'm going to have to take him back to the home paddock, and perhaps Colin or the cook can do something for him."

Elizabeth nodded, chewing her lower lip thoughtfully as she looked around. "If we had come through here on our way across, we would have found out sooner that he was sick."

"Aye, and we would have had a bloody pickle. The way this lot is spread out, our mob would have got all mixed up with it and we'd have to bring in help to build folds and runs to separate them again. But I'd rather have had that than have Billy in the state he is now." She turned away, sighing heavily. "Well, go catch his horse and saddle it."

Elizabeth nodded, picking up the bridle by the dead ashes of the fire, and she mounted her horse and tied the water bottle back to the saddle as she turned the horse down the slope.

Billy's horse had broken its hobbles, and was hard to catch. She drove it around until she cornered it in the decaying remains of an old sheep fold from years before, when the area had been unfenced, and she glimpsed Sheila walking back and forth between the shelter and a water hole down the hill from it, carrying buckets of water. Sheila was carrying the man's trousers back to the shelter after washing them in the water hole as Elizabeth led the horse back up the slope.

Elizabeth saddled it and tied it to a bush at the corner of the shelter, and Sheila backed out of the shelter, dragging the man on the pallet. His wet trousers were pulled up on him loosely, clinging to his legs damply and hanging open around his grotesquely distended stomach, and the fetid air from the interior of the shelter seemed to waft out of it with him. Elizabeth drew in a deep breath, and went to help Sheila drag the pallet along the ground. The horse began stamping nervously and tossing its head, and Sheila snapped at it as they pulled the pallet closer. She motioned for Elizabeth hold the horse's head, and she bent over Billy and put her arms around his chest, lifting him. His face was deathly white, and he winced and groaned with pain and effort as he tried to get his feet under him. Sheila pulled him up against the side of the horse, then bent over and took his legs and put her shoulder under his buttocks, lifting him. He clutched weakly at the saddle, and groaned louder as she lifted him and pressed his swollen stomach against the horse. She pushed his leg over and slid him into the saddle, and he slumped over the front of the saddle, holding onto the horse's withers and panting and gasping. A racking noise came from the seat of his trousers, and the foul stench intensified, eddying around Elizabeth as she held the reins.

"Oh, bloody hell. I've done it again, Sheila."

"Aye, well, you'll have to sit in it for a while, Billy. We'll reach Mullewa Creek by nightfall, and I'll have another swipe at you then."

"It's more than I'd do for another," he sighed, his face twisted with pain, then he suddenly began weeping. "You're a good sod, Sheila," he sobbed in a broken voice.

"Some would debate that and all," Sheila chuckled

wryly, patting his leg and turning away and walking toward her horse. "But I'll bloody well look after my own, Billy."

"Aye," the man murmured softly, sniffling and wiping his eyes with the back of his hand as he slumped over the saddle. "There's God's bloody truth." He gripped the horse's withers with both hands again, looking down at Elizabeth and nodding and sniffling. "Sheila looks after her own, by God."

Elizabeth smiled weakly and nodded, swallowing to keep from gagging. Her eyes kept moving toward his swollen stomach from some morbid impulse, and she cleared her throat and looked away.

There was a stiff moment of leavetaking. The horses moved their feet and relaxed, and the dogs they had brought with them and the man's dogs sat in a cluster, panting and looking at them. The breeze rustled the grass around the shelter and stirred the dead ashes in the circle of stones. Elizabeth looked around, then pushed her hands into her pockets and looked at Sheila. Sheila looked at Elizabeth, then sighed heavily and looked away.

"I wouldn't have put you to something like this so soon, Elizabeth, but there's bleeding little else I can do."

"I'll manage."

Sheila sighed again, taking off her hat, and she held it with both sets of reins in one hand and pushed at her hair with her other hand. "Your fence to the south and west are both brush fences, and if some have got through there we can sort that out later. They're still on Wayamba, and they'll join the flocks in the other sections if the dingoes don't get them. Make you a run around all four fences and get them back together, but don't mob them so tight that they can't graze. You saw how Fred had his in Wilcannia East, and that's about how they should be, or even a little tighter because the graze is better here. Don't worry about moving them once you have them mobbed, because this will do for a few days and I'll be back with someone by then."

322

"Very well."

She put her hat back on and started to mount her horse, then hesitated, moved closer to Elizabeth, and smiled down at her as she cupped Elizabeth's cheek in her palm and bent down to kiss her. "This place isn't bad for boars, but the flaming things can be about anywhere, so keep your musket at hand," she murmured, her eyes moving over Elizabeth's face. The tips of her fingers moved over Elizabeth's cheek, and she smiled fondly, her eyes warm. "Do what you can, and buggery take the rest. And look after yourself. I've bloody ample sheep, but I've only one of you."

Elizabeth smiled up at her and nodded. "I'll be all right."

Sheila's smile widened and she nodded as she kissed Elizabeth again, then her smile faded and she sighed heavily as she turned toward her horse. "Be careful, then."

"Aye, and you."

"Aye."

Sheila vaulted into her saddle, clucking to her horse, and it moved down the slope at a slow walk, the other horse following it and the man swaying heavily from side to side as he leaned over the front of the saddle. The dogs stirred and whined, looking from the horses to Elizabeth, and Elizabeth snapped her fingers and motioned them to her. They moved closer, sitting down around her. She put her hands in her pockets and stood watching the horses as they moved down to the bottom of the slope and up the next one. Sheila turned in her saddle and waved at the top of the next slope, and Elizabeth waved. Then the horses plodded on across the hill, disappearing from sight.

The man's dogs were starved, their ribs showing, their flanks sunken, and their eyes begging piteously. Elizabeth took her musket from her saddle and led her horse down the hill to the closest group of sheep, shot one of them in the head, tied a rope from its rear feet to the saddle and led the horse back up the hill to a tree near the shelter, pulling the sheep along through the grass. When she slit the sheep open and the entrails slithered out onto the ground, the man's dogs fell on them ravenously and began devouring them, vomiting, and eating the chewed bits again. It had seemed easy and simple when she had glimpsed men working in the slaughter yard at the home paddock, skins slipping away from knives and joints separating almost magically, but it was distasteful, difficult work, flies swarming around, bits of wool getting on the meat, and the greasy, bloody smell of the hot carcass blending with the stench coming from the shelter.

The responsibility for the sheep was a depressingly heavy burden in her mind, and it was difficult to restrain the impulse to mount her horse and immediately begin collecting them, but it was afternoon and Sheila had warned her repeatedly about being caught away from camp in unfamiliar terrain at nightfall. There were fences on four sides of her and she was in one of the smaller sections, but loss of orientation and the resulting panic could be dangerous. The section was still large enough for her to become lost and starve to death or die of thirst if her horse became injured and she was left wandering about on foot and looking for her camp. She moved the stones around the fireplace further away from the shelter to get away from the smell, built a fire, and made damper and put on a piece of the mutton to roast. The fire and having her belongings around her provided a sense of security against the lonely sound of the breeze moving through the grass, and she unsaddled her horse, hobbled it and turned it loose, and arranged her things around the fire.

Darkness fell. She ate, put the leftovers away, and lay by the fire in her blanket, shivering with cold and thinking about Sheila, already many miles away across the rolling hills and plains of brush and grass, camped somewhere with the deathly ill man. The stench from the shelter still lingered around her, and a burning in her stomach turned into nausea. She pushed the blanket away and got to her feet, walked a few yards away from the fire, and vomited.

The dogs lying by the fire stirred and looked at her, and two of them rose and trotted over to lap up the food she had vomited as she walked back to the fire. She lay down again, sighing heavily and pulling the blanket around her.

It was the first time she had ever been out of the immediate presence of others, and the loneliness was intense. She slept fitfully, every sound in the night awakening her, and she sat up at daybreak, built up the fire and put on a billy of water for tea, and walked down the slope to catch her horse. The water was boiling when she returned to the fire, and she poured tea into it and chewed a mouthful of cold mutton and damper as she dragged her saddle to her horse.

She started in the north, where the boundary met that of another station and strays could be lost to someone else's flocks, and she led the dogs to the fence and started them on a sweep back toward the camp. The seven dogs quickly stirred a large flock of strays out of the brush and began racing in wider circuits as they found out what she wanted, and other strays began running through the brush and joining the flock as she drove it slowly along, shouting and cracking her whip. The dogs began running much wider and chasing strays from behind nearby hills and out of gullies, and by the time she was halfway back to the camp there were hundreds of sheep in front of her. She called in the dogs and took them back to the fence, and started another sweep further to the west, driving the sheep collected as far as she had driven the others, then turning back to the fence again. By late afternoon, she had worked her way along a long stretch of the northern part of the section and had collected thousands of sheep, and she began driving them toward the camp. A large cloud of dust rose when they were all in motion, collecting more strays from the brush as they trotted along, and just before sunset they poured over the last hill in a flowing, rippling mass into the valley below the shelter.

The following day, she found the carcasses of eighteen

sheep which had been killed by dingoes. The hatred of dingoes she had heard expressed around her had been one of the many things she had noted in passing but had failed to fully understand, but understanding came as she sat on her horse and looked at the swollen, rotting carcasses. They had apparently been in a small group and had been attacked by several dingoes, because they were all within a few yards of each other. And only portions of a couple of them had been eaten. Fiery anger rose within her as she looked at the carcasses, and dingoes suddenly changed from small, yellowish, dog-like animals she had seen a few times to evil incarnate.

She glimpsed a pair of dingoes later in the morning, and rode stealthily toward them until they began running, then she whipped her horse into a gallop and raced after them, jerking at the leather thongs holding her musket on the saddle. The dingoes darted across an open space, and she jerked the horse around and fired both barrels of the musket at them. The recoil of the musket almost knocked her off the horse, and both dingoes yelped, rolled on the ground, then ran on. The distance had been too far for the pellets to kill. She whistled for the dogs until a couple of them came, and the dogs began following the blood trails through the brush and grass, the other dogs joining as they heard the excited barking. They caught the wounded dingoes in a ditch, and she sat on her horse on the edge of the ditch and watched the snarling, boiling mass of dogs fighting the dingoes and killing them.

Colin had given her a sense of belonging, in contrast to the way Cummings had continually harped on what a burden she was to him, and a feeling of participation had developed from the time she had started working with Sheila. But a sense of ownership over the sheep and land had been delayed, because her background and experience made her automatically view herself in the secondary role of a helper. A subtle but fundamental shift in attitude took place in the process of rising every morning to search through the brush for another flock of the strays. She was alone, and the sheep were her responsibility, and she was a member of the family which owned the sheep and the land. As her feeling of ownership developed, each of the sheep became an object of especial value, and she began scouring the brush even more thoroughly to make sure none would be left to the dingoes, and she began watching more closely for dingoes.

It took four days to work through the northern part of the section, then she started on the east side, working from the north to the south. There was a cluster of rocky hills in the southeastern corner of the section, and on the morning she started working the last stretch of the eastern fence, she found an area near the hills which was scattered with carcasses of sheep killed by dingoes. There were thirty or forty of them, and most of them had been partially eaten. She glimpsed a dingo as she rode around and looked at the carcasses, and she whipped her horse into a gallop and chased it as it darted away. The dingo disappeared between some boulders at the base of one of the barren hills, and she rode back and forth through the boulders with her musket cocked, looking for it. She noticed a hole in the ground under one of them, and reined her horse over to it and looked at it closely. The sides of the hole were worn smooth. It was a den. She reined her horse around and rode back out of the boulders, whistling for the dogs.

The dogs circled around the hole, whining and barking excitedly, and a couple of them ran up the hill above the pile of boulders and began digging at other holes. Elizabeth tied her horse, took her flint, steel, and tinderbox out of the saddlebags, and collected a pile of sticks and dry grass and kindled a fire in front of the hole. When it began burning hotly, she collected up a large armload of dry grass and green boughs from the brush and piled them on. The grass began burning fiercely and smoke boiled up as the green boughs hissed and popped, and she took a long stick and pushed the fire into the hole.

Smoke trickled from three holes a few yards up the hill, then began boiling from them in thick clouds. She could hear thrashing noises and yelping sounds in the hole over the crackling of the fire, and she picked up her musket and backed away, watching the holes up the hill as the dogs ran back and forth, yapping excitedly. A dingo shot out of one of the holes, panicked and blinded by smoke, and the seven dogs pounced on it, dragging it down and tearing at it. Another ran out of another hole, and she lifted the musket and fired. The pellets struck it in the rear quarters, and it yelped with agony as it spun around. The shot and yelping drew the attention of the dogs, and two of them ran toward the wounded dingo. Another dingo leaped out of a hole, and they swerved and attacked it. The other dogs left the dingo they had killed and ran toward the fight. Three more dingoes appeared, and the hill above the boulders was suddenly alive with dogs fighting and killing the dingoes. There was a stir in the hole under the boulder, then pain-crazed yelping as two dingoes tried to crawl past the fire and out of the hole. Elizabeth lifted the musket and fired the other barrel into the hole. Dust boiled up with the smoke coming out of the hole, and the yelping changed into hoarse howls which died into silence. She stepped closer to the hole and listened. There were still scurrying sounds coming from the hole, and the distant, muffled, high-pitched wailing of pups. She went back to the horse, took the powder flask and shot bag out of the saddlebags and recharged both barrels of the musket, then gathered more grass and brush to push into the hole.

An occasional dingo struggled to the mouth of one of the holes up the hill, blinded and almost suffocated by smoke, and the dogs jerked them out and killed them. When the fire burned down again, the sounds in the hole had stopped. She called the dogs to her and examined all of them. All of them had minor wounds from the fights, but one had several deep bites on a shoulder and was favoring a paw. She lifted the dog onto the saddle and carried it in front of her to her camp, driving the sheep before her and the rest of the dogs circling through the brush and stirring out more strays. When she got back to the camp, she endured the stench of the shelter and searched around in it, and found a pot of tar. She put it by the fire to melt, cut large pieces from the carcass of the sheep she had killed the day before and hung them over the fire to roast, and daubed tar on all the dogs' wounds and fed them all the mutton they would eat.

There had been scattered bands of sheep totaling a thousand or so in the valley when she had first seen it, and when she finished it was filled with a mass of thousands of sheep which overflowed the valley and spread onto the adjacent hills. She went all the way around the section again and found less than twenty sheep, killed several isolated dingoes and found two more dens and wiped them out, and settled down to a routine of camp chores and spending the days in making a circuit of the sheep and driving back bunches which were straying too far. She ran out of tea and found some in the shelter, but it tasted of the odor in the shelter and she threw it away and did without. Her loneliness had faded and changed into an expectant wish to see Sheila again. When she thought to count how many days it had been since Sheila left, she had already been by herself long enough for the days to begin to run together.

It was midmorning and she was working along the top of the hill east of the valley when she noticed the sheep stirring in on the opposite hill, and at first she thought it might be a dingo. Then Sheila and a man came into sight above the brow of the hill, their horses trotting along and bunches of sheep darting out of their path, and Sheila lifted her arm and waved. Elizabeth turned her horse back toward the shelter, signalling eagerly.

She reached the shelter first and reined up, waiting for

them. Sheila's smile was wide, her brilliantly white teeth gleaming against the darkness of her face in the shadow of her hat. Sheila reined her horse up, the man pulling his horse to a stop by hers, and she and Elizabeth smiled at each other in silence for a long moment. Then Sheila spoke in a quiet murmur.

"Are you all right, then?"

"Aye," Elizabeth replied. "Are you?"

"I am now. You know Clyde, don't you?"

He was a short, heavyset man with a thick mat of beard and mustaches and hard, prying eyes, and she remembered him from seeing him around the buildings at the home paddock. He always stared, though from a distance, and he looked as if he would be a lot like Cummings. Her smiled faded as she looked at him, they exchanged a silent nod. She looked back at Sheila and her smile returned.

"Did you steal this lot from the other paddocks, then?" Sheila chuckled, indicating the sheep with her chin. "There are thirteen thousand there if there's a one, a thousand or two more than we were supposed to have in here."

"I believe I found all of them."

"You bloody did and all. There's not a stray in this section now, and there's God's truth. And as good a bloody job as any stockman on this station could do, cod piece or no."

Elizabeth flushed with pleasure and looked away, tugging at her hat and pulling it down on her head more firmly. "How is the man?"

"Old Billy?" Sheila's smile faded, and she looked away and sighed. "He died on the way back. And a bloody chore it was and all, getting him back with him almost ready to fall apart by the time I got there and fighting that bleeding get of a horse to make it carry him. Then I had to wait for the vicar and constable to get up from Menindee, which is what took me so long."

"What was wrong with him?"

Sheila shrugged and shook her head. "His gut rotted out on him or something, Elizabeth—God knows. That flaming constable was determined to find that he'd been shot in the gut, miserable dag worm that he is and forever trying to cause trouble. He poked about in that mess until he was chundering so hard that he had to swallow to get his arsehole back where it belongs, and he knew no more when he finished than what I had told him before he started. But I had me a good laugh to his bleeding face and all, sod that he is." She chuckled, looking back at Elizabeth. "Well, get your swag together, and we'll bluie."

Elizabeth nodded, dismoutning from her horse. She tied it to a bush by the shelter and began gathering up her things from around the fire. The man dismounted and tied his horse, and untied the bags of rations and equipment from his saddle. He sniffed, turned and smelled at the shelter, then turned around and looked at Elizabeth.

"The bloody hut smells worse than he did. Don't you know how to build a hut?"

"If I'd bloody known it was himself coming, I would have built a bleeding palace for your worship. But in my flaming ignorance, I gave more thought to the bloody sheep than I did to your accomodations. So you'll be bloody well obliged to shift for yourself to keep your sodding arse warm!"

Sheila had started to reply to him irritably and had been cut off by the blistering tirade, looking at Elizabeth in surprise then with a wide grin of amusement as she raged at the man. Elizabeth ended with an angry snarl, glaring at the man with her fists clenched and her chin thrust out. Clyde looked at Elizabeth stolidly, looked at Sheila and started to turn back to his horse, then looked back at Sheila and suddenly laughed.

"It's no great chore to tell who's been bloody teaching her. Another month with you, and no one will speak to her for fear that she'll set the grass around them on fire with her bloody tongue."

Sheila laughed uproariously, slapping her thigh and gathering her reins tighter as her horse stamped and bobbed its head. Elizabeth relaxed, laughing and nodding, and knelt by the fire, collecting the rest of her things.

Elizabeth tied her things to her saddle and mounted, and Sheila turned her horse down the slope. The man waved, still chuckling, and they smiled and waved as they rode away. Sheila led the way down the slope and up the next hill through the sheep, and Elizabeth looked over her shoulder at the valley as she followed Sheila. It had become familiar during the past days, and leaving it stirred twinges of melancholy regret. She turned back around in the saddle, urging her horse forward to catch up with Sheila's, and they rode along at a swift trot.

"I would have been happy just to see that you're all right, Elizabeth, but you did a bloody good job and all."

"Aye, well, I'm happy that you're pleased. I had some bloody cold nights as well, you know."

"Did you, now? We'll see that right, then."

Elizabeth smiled, looked at Sheila's smiling face, and she nodded and looked away.

– 19 –

The most difficult part of the birth was immediately after it was over, the waiting while they murmured and shuffled around on the other side of the room, cleaning and examining the child. The monotonous sound of the digereedoos, rhythm sticks, and chanting came through the floor and filled the room, reverberating in her ears, and the feel of the house was hauntingly familiar, a blend of fragmentary memories of sorrows and joys. It was a clear, cold winter day, but in other ways it was much as it had been before. It had seemed dangerously close to tempting fate to come back to the head stockman's house to have the child, but the old man was ill and it had seemed preferable to the atmosphere of aged sickness that clung to the Garrity house.

The baby wailed, a sound of human protest against the situation into which the inexorable flow of time and immutable laws of nature had thrust it, and its voice sounded healthy and normal. Elizabeth's suspense was almost unbearable, apprehension and hopeful anticipation battling in her numb, weary mind. Water splashed in the pan, and one of the aborigine women commented to the other one in their language. Bessie's shoes scraped on the floor, and the old woman said something to her in a soft murmur of pidgin. Then they moved back toward the bed. Elizabeth turned her head slightly and looked at them. Bessie was carrying the baby in a blanket, and she beamed as she spoke.

"That's as pretty a baby boy as I've ever seen. Aye, what my man would give if any of mine had been as big and healthy!"

Her relief was almost overwhelming, but pride and the need to reflect a confident attitude had kept her from calling out to them and asking. The same impulses made her control her expression and allow only a slight, tired smile to show on her face. She could hardly restrain herself from rooting in the blanket and baring the baby to see for herself as Bessie put the bundle in the crook of her arm. The tiny face in the opening in the bundle was red, wrinkled, and twisted as the small mouth opened and closed, and its crying was almost painfully loud in her ears, drowning the sound of the digereedoos, rhythm sticks, and chanting. The old woman was smiling widely, her face a maze of wrinkles and lines as her teeth shone brightly and her eyes sparkled. She bent over her bed, touched her cheek to Elizabeth's and patted her head, then straightened up and turned away from the bed, glancing at the two aborigine women and indicating the doorway with a nod as she walked toward it. They slipped soundlessly through the doorway on their bare feet, and the old woman followed them, her stick thumping lightly on the floor.

334

Elizabeth looked back up at the ceiling, relaxing in a comfortable, satisfied exhaustion. Bessie moved about, dumping a bucket of water out of the window, clattering pans together on the table, and chattering.

"The old lady's more pleased than I've ever seen her. Did you mark the grin she had on her face? I've never seen her—" She broke off as the droning of the digereedooes, rhythm sticks, and chanting voices stopped, and she sighed heavily as she gathered up bunches of rags and put them in a pan. "That's finished, thank God. It would drive me bloody mad to have to listen to that while I was having a baby. Well, I'll go see who's out here so they can come in and have their look."

Elizabeth licked her lips and swallowed dryly. "Is Colin there?" she asked in a weak voice.

"No, he was like a wild boar this morning, and some of the men got him interested in that new bunch of cows so he'd go over to the stockyard and busy himself with something. He's all right with you, but it isn't as though he doesn't have a temper with others, you know. But I'll send for him if his mother hasn't. And I'll get Sheila—she's over across the road somewhere."

Elizabeth smiled and nodded at Bessie as she came back to the bed to tuck the edges of the blanket closer around the baby. Bessie's footsteps faded as she went through the doorway and crossed the front room toward the door. Elizabeth turned and opened the blanket around the baby. Her apprehension had built up over a period of months, strangely drawing sustenance from rather than being diminished by the confidence Sheila and Colin had radiated, and she had felt a dull resentment over the restrictions on her activities from the fear that the end result would again be shock and sorrow. But the tiny limbs, torso, and head were perfectly formed, and a lusty bellow came from the small, gaping mouth. She put the blanket back around the baby, pulled it closer to her breast, and put the nipple in the baby's mouth. The howling stopped, and he began sucking greedily, his small hands making pawing motions. She smiled happily, tucking the blanket tighter and holding him closer, and closed her eyes.

The feel of the baby's mouth on her breast was satisfying, a hearty, vital demand for nourishment and a confirmation at some deep level that she was all he needed. Sleep tugged at her, and light, quick footsteps racing across the veranda and through the front room penetrated her drowsy reverie. She opened her eyes as Sheila came through the doorway and crossed the room with long, rapid strides, beaming at her. Sheila bent over the bed and kissed her, pushing her hair back from her forehead, then lifted the edge of the blanket and looked at the baby, sighing and clicking her tongue in admiration.

"Would you look at that beggar? He's again the size my James was, and he knows where his tucker is, doesn't he? It's as well that you have two of them, because he's going to have that one off there. What are you going to call him?"

"Dennis," Elizabeth murmured, smiling tiredly.

"Dennis? Aye, that's a good name for him."

Elizabeth nodded weakly, and Sheila bent over the baby again, smiling and touching the fine, dark hair on his small head with the tips of her fingers. There was a sound of voices on the road in front of the house and a smell of smoke in the air, and Elizabeth lifted her head slightly and looked at the window. Sheila tucked the blanket back around the baby and smiled at Elizabeth, pushing at her hair again.

"Give no mind to that mob out there. My ma and the abos are building a bloody big fire out in the middle of the road, and most of the village is out there. It's their custom when a baby's born, but it's the first time it's happened for one of us. James came on the wrong side of the blanket, which means naught to them, of course, but they didn't want to get my dad's wind up. And Bessie's had two here, but they don't look on her as their own." She leaned over and kissed Elizabeth again, patting her hand. "I'll go see what's keeping Colin."

Elizabeth turned her hand under Sheila's and squeezed it, and Sheila patted her hand again and smiled down at her as she turned away from the bed. She left, and Elizabeth looked at the baby again. The nipple had slipped from his mouth, and he was asleep. She covered her breast and tucked the blanket closer around the baby, then closed her eyes wearily and dropped off to sleep.

Colin woke her, kissing her. His eyes were tinged with red from lack of sleep and there was rum on his breath, which was extremely unusual for this time of day. He looked at her anxiously as he sat down on the edge of the bed, his eyes moving over her face as he asked her how she felt, and he smiled widely when she patted his hand and reasured him sleepily. Sheila was behind him, and she looked over his shoulder at the baby as he lifted the edge of the blanket and smiled proudly at it.

There was a stir on the veranda, and heavy, hesitant footsteps crossed the room. Sheila turned and looked at the doorway, then moved away from the bed, plucking at Colin's sleeve. He looked over his shoulder, stood up, and moved away from the bed. The old man had got out of bed and come to make an appearance in recognition of the event. He had lost weight and he looked very ill, his face haggard, pale, and pouchy. His footsteps were slow and dragging as he followed the old woman, his hand on her shoulder. He was wearing a long, heavy sheepskin which looked too large for him, open in front, and she could see that his shirt wasn't tucked into his trousers properly. There was an expectant expression on his face, and he breathed loudly through his mouth. The old woman smiled at Elizabeth, one of her thin hands on the old man's hand resting on her shoulder and the other lifting and placing the heavy stick as she led him across the room.

The old woman stopped at the side of the bed, took the old man's hand from her shoulder, and guided it toward the baby. He leaned over, his blind eyes staring blankly ahead and his boots scraping the floor as he edged forward stiffly, his gnarled, blotched hand trembling slightly. The tips of his fingers touched the baby, and it began crying loudly. A wide smile spread across his face, the wrinkles and creases at the corners of his blind eyes deepening and his slack lips stretching over his toothless gums. He touched the baby with a light pressure, his calloused, knobby fingers feeling gingerly to transmit some sense of the baby's appearance to his mind, then he moved his hand away from the baby and felt for Elizabeth's shoulder, and he patted her with a rough gentleness.

They all congregated at the side of the bed, the old woman smiling down at the baby as it howled, Sheila and holding Elizabeth's hand, and the old man mumbling to Colin. He leaned heavily on the old woman's shoulder. Sheila and Colin hadn't seemed particularly worried about his illness, talking about similar stomach illnesses he'd had before, but it was the first time Elizabeth had seen him since he had become ill a few days before, and his condition appeared to her to warrant concern. His pleasure over his grandchild was very touching, his satisfaction with the conditional immortality of the transmission of his genes into another generation appearing as complete as physical immortality would have provided. Elizabeth pulled the baby closer, putting her nipple in his mouth, and he began sucking hungrily.

The old man talked to Colin, and the old woman murmured to Sheila in her language, pointing to the baby's hair and touching it. Their voices faded into a drone in Elizabeth's ear as she began dozing again. The stir they made leaving aroused her and she smiled sleepily at Colin as he kissed her, then she closed her eyes and went to sleep.

The baby stirred and began crying, awakening her. It was late afternoon, and Bessie was sitting quietly in a chair at the side of the room. She rose and came to the bed for the baby, took him across the room to wash him and put him in another blanket, and called to the two aborigine women in the front room as she brought the baby back to the bed. They came in, and the three of them helped Elizabeth out of bed and into the kitchen. There was a large bonfire with a sheep roasting over it on the road in front of the house and a crowd of aborigines were sitting around it singing. Yet another large fire burned near the cookhouse, surrounded by the employees at the home paddock, and Elizabeth glanced through the front windows at the activity as the three women helped her into the kitchen to drink some broth then helped her back to the bedroom. She dropped off to sleep again, and it was dark when she woke. A lamp filled the room with yellow light, Bessie sitting in the chair by the wall, and the two aborigine women were sitting on their heels by the doorway. The aborigines on the road in front of the house were singing louder, and the flickering light of their bonfire came through the windows and danced on the walls in the front room. Sounds of laughter and shouts from the fire by the cookhouse were boisterous, clearly audible over the singing in front of the house. The cause for the celebration, the heir to the lands, stirred and began crying, and Elizabeth turned toward him as she guided her nipple into his mouth.

Sheila brought a wet nurse from the aborigine village the next day, and the woman moved her belongings into the corner of the room and began caring for the baby under Bessie's watchful eye. Elizabeth was soon able to move around the house with more freedom, taking care of herself. The restrictions on her activities caused by her pregnancy had chafed, and she looked forward to resuming her work on the station. But there were things to keep her occupied. During the latter stages of her

339

pregnancy she had started working on the station accounts, an untidy and confused mass of papers which Colin and Sheila had gladly relinquished to her, and she continued working on them as she recovered her strength. There were also letters from James to answer. He continued to make exceptional progress, indicating that he would do better than average in college after boarding school. Sheila viewed his progress with motherly pride and a degree of wry amusement that a child of hers could do well scholastically, and she was agreeable to his going to college.

The correspondence with her relative who was a solicitor in England had continued, with a letter arriving every few months. Over a period of time, his letters had revealed more about himself and had become more personal, always conveying his wife's best wishes and once including a note from her. He was a man somewhat older than Elizabeth and had several children. There was another letter from him, in which he mentioned a client of his who was contemplating letting a son emigrate to Australia to find his place in the world. Elizabeth made her reply as candid as possible, describing Sydney as a city much like many in England in terms of opportunity and emphasizing the hardships of the Outback, and she wrote about the baby.

There were other letters to read and answer, one from George Cummings, the shipping factor in Sydney. Several months before, the factor with whom the Garritys had usually traded had quoted prices higher than usual on several kinds of goods being ordered. It had been at about the same time that Elizabeth was investigating more closely into the details of the operation of the station, and she had written to other factors and asked for price quotations, one of whom was her former brother-in-law. Cummings' prices were well below the others, and the goods on a trial order had returned promptly and in good condition on the supply wagons. Since that time, much of the trade from the station had been with him, despite letters from the former factor announcing reductions in prices.

It was one among several instances where Elizabeth had found reason for suspicion that the station had been taken advantage of by outsiders. There was little that the old man, Colin, and Sheila didn't know about sheep, but there was equally little they knew or cared about except sheep. Colin and Sheila were highly intelligent, could read and write well considering their limited education, and could both do impressive arithmetical calculations in their heads. But their tally sheets on wool shipments were grubby scraps of paper covered with symbols which represented knots in a rope and were impossible to deal with by conventional arithmetical procedures. Letters from the trading factor giving an amount of bank credit were the only documentation received as a result of shipments. Far too much trust had been placed in those who might not be deserving of it, and Elizabeth had been given what amounted to a free hand with the business affairs of the station when she had indicated a willingness to deal with them.

There was also a letter from the factor who handled the wool, a reply to a letter she had written a few weeks before in which she had asked him to make arrangements to return a tare bill and certified copies of bills of sale on future wool shipments. His letter was distant in tone, referring to the unusual nature of the request and the cost of the excise stamps for notarized bills, and requesting that a reply be made over the signature of one of the Garrity men. The letter was aggravating, and it increased her suspicions that the factor might have something to hide. It also started her again contemplating the possibilities of selling the wool directly through a dealer in London rather than through a factor in Sydney. For a smaller concern it would be unfeasible, but Wayamba Station generated a quantity of wool which made it practical. It would take longer to receive the proceeds of sale, but the profits would undoubtedly be far higher. She wrote a reply for Colin's signature, reiterating the request and stating that the notary costs would be paid by the station. Then she wrote a letter to Cummings and asked him to determine the cost per ton for shipment of freight to London, including the cost of his services to act as shipping agent at Sydney, and she added another page onto her letter to her relative in England, asking him to put her into contact with a commodities trader in London.

The business affairs of the station took up only a small part of her time, and she went for walks, cleaned out the flower beds and weeded the graves by the water tanks, and did other small chores to help get her weight back down. The baby did well with the wet nurse, the old woman began helping with him when Elizabeth moved back into the large house, and even the old man wanted to hold the baby at times after he recovered from his illness and began eating dinner with the family again. Elizabeth turned the baby over to them when he was three weeks old and her trousers began to fit again. She couldn't ride comfortably, but lambs had been separated and driven in for tailing and mulsing, and she went back to work in the pens.

When the baby was six weeks old, the situation had more or less returned to normal. On some nights she would be alone with the old man and old woman at dinner; Sheila, Colin, and occasionally, both of them were there on other nights, and on still others she was gone. A careless fossicker started a brush fire with his campfire in Wayamba Paddock, and there was a week of frantic activity in containing it, with most of the employees and the dozens of swagmen who flooded in fighting it. Elizabeth had recovered from childbirth, but she didn't have the physical strength and endurance that Sheila and the men possessed, and most of her time was spent in driving a wagon between Wayamba Paddock and the home paddock, transporting food, kegs of rum, and fire-fighting equipment to the paddock and taking injured or exhausted men back to the home paddock. When it was finally over, something over ten thousand acres were blackened and well over two thousand sheep burned to death.

It had been a bad fire in terms of injuries, and two of the employees and fourteen swagmen had suffered broken bones or severe burns. They were kept on pallets in two of the sheds, and Elizabeth and Sheila tended them, keeping them clean, feeding them, and smearing goose grease on burns. One of the swagmen died, the constable and minister were brought from Menindee and he was buried, and the others gradually healed to the point that they could look after each other and themselves. Eventually they recovered, the employees going back to work and the swagmen drawing their rations and leaving along the track.

Elizabeth drove a flock of two thousand to Windorah. They were young and freshly mulsed, and she drove them along the track at a moderate pace, stopping at every source of water to let them drink, driving them only a relatively short distance every day, and camping in the middle of the afternoon to give them ample time to graze and rest. Windorah Paddock was divided into four sections, and the flock was to go to Windorah Two Rocks, the northeastern quadrant. The track was a straight line north through the two western quadrants of the paddock, and when she estimated she was about halfway across the northwestern quadrant, she turned the flock to the east. It took another two days to get them into Windorah Two Rocks and to find the stockman's shelter, and she left the sheep and some supplies she had brought for him and went on to the north to check part of the northern boundary fence before she went back.

She traveled rapidly without the hindrance of the sheep, and she camped at the boundary fence and was back at the track the next afternoon. It was a straight line of trampled grass and brush, not as heavily traveled as the eastern track but still a distinct line, and it went south to the home paddock, became the road in front of the houses by the creek, then stretched on to the southern boundary to Wayamba Paddock, where it joined tracks across other stations to become the roadway to Menindee. One of the rails was down in the section of fence where the track crossed over onto the next station, and she dismounted, put the rail back into place, and mounted her horse and turned it to the south.

A man walking along the track to the south became visible in the distance as she topped a low rise and started down the other side. He was a swagman, tall and heavyset, with his blanket roll hanging from his shoulder and his billy and other possessions hanging from his belt. Small pieces of cork suspended on short lengths of string were spaced around he brim of his hat, dancing and swaying in constant motion as he walked and keeping flies and mosquitoes off his face, and he carried a staff in his right hand. Caution murmured in the back of her mind. Sheila had a habitual wariness toward men in general, keeping a wall of reserve between herself and all the employees except the older ones she had known for years, and she was especially wary about swagmen when she was alone and had repeatedly warned Elizabeth about them. Elizabeth momentarily considered turning off the track and riding around him, then dismissed the thought with a flash of contempt at herself for even considering it. She was on her lands.

The man looked over his shoulder when he heard the horse, still striding along and using the staff as a cane. She recognized him. It was Stapleton. The sheer terror she had felt for him as he had grappled with her in the storeroom returned, feeling like a frigid hand gripping her vitals, then it was swept aside and replaced by a more rational apprehension. She was no longer the frightened

344

woman who had been in the storeroom that day. Then he recognized her, and stopped in the middle of the track and looked at her, a sneering smile spreading across his face. She pulled her horse to a walk, then reined up a few yards from him.

"Well, I'll be swiped! It's the pommie what lost me my job! And on a bloody horse and carrying a whip and all!"

Her hands felt damp and her mouth dry as she looked at him, and she swallowed without moving her lips to control her voice and keep it from shaking as she considered what to say to him. Sheila would take the offensive. "You're on the wrong bloody track, Stapleton. Turn your arse back in the other direction."

His jeering smile faded slightly, then returned. "I walk where I bloody want to, pommie."

"Not on Wayamba you don't, sod. Get off this station."

"Aye, I heard you twisted your way around and married Colin and all," he sneered. "Sly bloody slut that you are. But it's naught to me, because neither Colin nor his pommie slut will put me off the track."

"Stapleton, there's no bloody room for you here, and no rations. I'm telling you to get your sodding arse off this station, and I'm telling you to do it bloody now."

He shrugged the blanket roll off his shoulder, tossing it aside with a quick movement, and took the staff in both hands, his face flushing and his features hard with rage. "I said once I'd find out how good you are, pommie," he grated, advancing toward her and swinging the staff. "And Sheila's not here to stand in my way, so I'll attend to that now."

She reined her horse back, moving away from him. The horse could easily outdistance him, and she could ride on into the night and escape. But he would spread the story along the tracks, and it would reflect upon Wayamba. She was a senior stockman on the station, and she had assumed the responsibilities of that position. A senior stockman was in a position of authority, but both the senior stockman and the station were regarded with derision if that authority wasn't enforced. A woman could assume such a position, but she couldn't use her womanhood as an excuse for failure to fulfill her responsibilities.

She let the coils of the whip spill to the ground. He hesitated, then he laughed jeeringly as he took a stance, spreading his feet apart and lifting the staff.

Handling the whip was an art, even though some men used brute strength and suffered a lack of accuracy as a result, and one in which a woman's precision and innate grace and judgement in movement offered an advantage. She wasn't as good as Sheila, but she was good because she had practiced for endless hours until the muscles in her forearm had knotted with fatigue, snapping the tops from blades of grass and flipping stones into the air. And the old storekeeper, an expert craftsman with leather, had made her whip, taking choice lengths of leather and carefully shaving them to reduce their bulk and weight, then braiding them over a slender piece of hickory to make a handle which fit her hand and into a thin, well-oiled twenty foot length which was light enough for her slender arm and supple for precise accuracy.

It was a dangerous situation. If he could catch the tip of the whip around the end of his stick, he could send all the force of the whip traveling back along it and jerk it out of her hand. Or he might snatch her off the horse with it. And his expression evidenced that he intended to do as he said. Even if she escaped from him, there would always be the danger that he would be lurking nearby when she camped, waiting for a chance to attack her. She had no option but to give him reason to fear her.

She flipped the long length of leather into the air, moving her wrist in a slight, rocking motion to make the whip glide back and forth in a flowing ripple, and she gathered her reins tightly in her left hand and nudged the horse with her heels to edge closer to him. His grin faded as he saw the expert movement of the whip, and his features tightened as he gripped the staff more firmly and lifted it higher. Elizabeth brought the handle back and pulled the length of the whip through a slow, casual curve to gather impetus, then swept it straight forward in an overhand to crack it high over his head, and he lifted the stick, thinking she was aiming for his face. The handle was coming back in another backstroke even as the tip snapped a foot above the staff with an explosive crack, and she pulled it through a quick underhand, cracking the tip an inch from his stomach while he still had the staff guarding his face and trying to catch the end of the whip. It unnerved him, and his face twisted with shock and fear as he jerked the staff down to guard his body. The whip became a blur as she leaned forward and put her entire arm and shoulder into it, and the tip of the whip cracked three times in rapid succession within an inch of his chin and nose. He reeled backwards in instinctive reaction to the deafening reports in front of his face, almost dropping the staff.

Stapleton recovered, uttered a roar of anger, and pulled his head down between his shoulders, holding the stick up for protection as he rushed toward her. She jerked her horse back, and the whip whistled as she swept it back and then into a forward overhand, aiming for his knee. The tip of the whip dug in, hundreds of pounds of force concentrated into the inch of leather, and it cut through the heavy fabric of his trousers and sliced into flesh. He screamed as his leg folded under him, and dropped the staff as he fell to the ground. She reined her horse around, snapping the whip back and forth again. He reached up, trying to catch the end of it with his hand. She pulled the whip through another quick stroke. He screamed again with agony as the back of his hand was slashed open. Her horse swung its head around, and she jerked it back. Stapleton was scrabbling on the ground for the staff. The tip of the whip cut into the back of his other hand. He howled with pain, trying to crawl to the shelter of a clump of brush. The whip snapped across his wrist, jerking his arm from under him, then worked down his back in a rapid tattoo of penetrating cracks, the tip biting into his flesh each time.

The memory of her helpless anger in the storeroom returned to Elizabeth, along with the memory of humiliation at other times and places, and of countless cruelties. Of hard fingers pinching the inside of her thighs as she wept and begged; of harsh, sadistic laughter. She stood in the stirrups, and she swept the whip back and forth in rapid strokes. The horse wheeled and danced, its eyes rolling and foam dripping from its lips, and she slammed her heels into its sides and jerked the reins as she ground her teeth together and continued slashing with the whip.

Then she stopped, her arm aching and her breath coming in quick gasps. He lay curled in the road, his arms wrapped around his head, his trousers and shirt covered with rents and blood showing on his skin through the rents. She loosened the reins and coiled the whip with trembling hands, breathing heavily and swallowing dryly.

"Now get off this station, dag worm."

He lifted himself to his elbow and looked at her, sobbing with pain and anger. "Aye, I'll leave, you bloody get!" he shouted in a quavering voice. "But I'll be back, no fear! And I'll turn this bloody place into a cinder, and there's God's truth! I'll fire every bloody inch of it!"

The memory of the fire on Wayamba Paddock was only weeks old, the terror still troubling her dreams at night, visions of smoke hanging in the air during the day and the yellow line of flames licking into the night sky still very recent. The smell of burned wool and flesh of roasted sheep and the sight of blacked carcasses scattered over thousands of acres lingered in her mind. The groans of injured men still rang in her ears.

And he meant it. It wasn't an idle threat. She turned in

the saddle, snatching at the thongs holding the musket across the back of the saddle. His mouth dropped open, and he scrambled to his feet. She swung the musket around, pulling one of the hammers back, and looked down the barrel at him as she brought it to her shoulder and pulled the trigger. The hammer snapped with a metallic sound, the barrel misfiring, and he leaped into the brush.

She slammed her heels against the horse's sides, pulling the other hammer back, and the horse sprang forward. Stapleton darted from one clump of brush to another, his legs pumping furiously as he looked over his shoulder in terror, and the horse pounded through the brush, wheeling after him as Elizabeth jerked the reins. Then he crossed a short open space with the horse almost on top of him, and she jerked the horse around, shouldered the musket, and pulled the trigger. Smoke belched from the barrel as it thundered, and Stapleton was knocked forward as though some invisible force had struck him. He collapsed and rolled on the ground. Elizabeth rested the butt of the musket on the saddle and rode over to him. Part of the pattern of pellets had struck him in the back of the head and neck, making shining spots of red.

Then she thought about what she had done. She had killed a man. Stories of murders were common, but murders were rare. A constable had to certify the cause of death of anyone before burial, and the constabulary was tenacious and painstaking in exploring the circumstances of any suspicious death or disappearance. There had been a number of times when a constable had come to the station looking for information on when a missing swagman had last been seen. Elizabeth rode back to the track and picked up the bedroll and other things he had dropped, took them to the body and tossed them down beside it, then returned to the track and turned south.

She rode on along the track at a rapid trot until dark, then camped. She vomited the food she ate, and lay rolled

349

in her blanket by the dying coals of the fire, looking up at the stars and thinking about the implications of what she had done. Sleep came, light and fitful, and she was up well before dawn, building up the fire to make tea. She caught her horse and saddled him at first light, and by dawn she was moving along the track at a swift trot.

Sheila was at the pens when Elizabeth arrived, and she turned her horse and galloped over to the stockyard, waving at Elizabeth. Her smile of greeting faded into a concerned frown when she saw Elizabeth's pale, drawn face. "What is it, then?"

Elizabeth dismounted, glancing around, and told her what had happened in a few quiet, terse sentences as she loosened the saddle girth on her horse.

"Sod him," Sheila said in a confident tone, shaking her head. "Who's to bloody know? He's off the track, you say?"

"Aye."

"Then forget it. The dingoes and crows will have him, and no bugger will be the wiser. And you did what I would have done and all. I might have picked a less messy way of doing it so he could be planted properly, but I would have done him, no fear. So don't let it plague, Elizabeth."

Elizabeth nodded doubtfully as she began untying her equipment from the saddle. Sheila patted her shoulder and smiled as she began helping her, and Elizabeth smiled weakly.

The incident gradually assumed a less prominent position in her mind in the press of day-to-day activities, and it returned to worry her at less frequent intervals as the weeks passed. There was a rash of fires, then a couple of heavy rains. A dry, early fall followed a hot summer, and shortly after shearing time there was a fire on the adjoining station to the north which threatened the northwestern quadrant of Windorah Paddock. Several of the employees and a large number of swagmen went to fight the fire and to contain it. During the cleanup of putting out small fires started by sparks, one of the swagmen found Stapleton's bones. Sheila was on the scene, working with Colin and other men driving the flocks into the eastern paddocks after shearing. Elizabeth was at the home paddock, pregnant again, when the swagman came to her and reported the discovery. She sent several men to look for bones and belongings, and one of the employees rode across the station south to Menindee to notify the constable.

The constable came and examined the remains. There was an identity disc among the belongings, pellet holes in the back of the skull and in two or three of the neck vertebra which had been found, and several gold pieces among the belongings. The constable began an exhaustive investigation which lasted for weeks, during which time he traveled back and forth between Menindee and Wayamba Station to interrogate employees on the station and further north to make inquiries on other stations. Elizabeth saw the full extent of Colin's temper for the first time when she and Sheila finally told him about it. He didn't have Sheila's casual attitude toward killing others, but he was enraged that he hadn't been told so he could have found and burned the bones before someone else found them, or at least taken the gold pieces so it would appear to be murder for gain. It was a bad week, during which Colin and Sheila were furious with each other, then they gradually made up with each other. The employees of the station closed ranks to protect one of their own. Everyone knew of the trouble Elizabeth had had with Stapleton, and everyone suspected that she had killed him.

The constable's investigation dragged on, with him showing up at unexpected times to question employees or passing through the station on his way north to other stations. Sheila kept reassuring Elizabeth that she was in no danger and Colin was also sanguine about it, and the immediacy of Elizabeth's concern began to fade.

The constable returned during the winter after an absence of a week or more. He arrived late in the day, after dinner, tied his horse in front of the house and came into the parlor where they sat after dinner. Colin was in the paddocks and the old man and old woman were smoking their pipes. Sheila sprawled in a chair and looked at the constable with a musing, sleepy expression as he talked with the old man on general subjects, and Elizabeth, swollen and heavy with pregnancy, sat and pretened to look at a sheaf of papers on the station accounts. The papers trembled in her hands as she kept her expression neutral, listening to the constable and the old man.

Their conversation faded into silence, then the constable took a folded stack of scraps of paper out of his coat pocket and cleared his throat as he unfolded them and turned them to the light of a lamp. "Ah...Mrs. Garrity, there is something I would like to ask you about."

Elizabeth steeled herself, lifting her eyes and looking at him, and she curved her lips into a polite smile as she lifted her eyebrows. "Yes, Constable?"

"In the course of my investigation into the death of the deceased man Stapleton, I was informed that you had...ah, some trouble with him."

"Who told you that?" Sheila snapped.

The constable looked at her and pursed his lips as he shook his head. "I'm not at liberty to divulge—"

"No one on this bloody station told you that."

"No," he said, shaking his head. "I can't say the man's name, but he's a stockman on Tibooburra Station, and—"

"Aye, and you've little to do if you've time to talk with that lot of scurvy gets," Sheila growled. "They must have ewes that have litters of lambs like bloody dogs the way they sprout sheep in their south paddock, and our sheep in Bulloo North disappear into the flaming ground. There's ample there to go to Tibooburra Station for, if you've time to muck about up there."

The constable cleared his throat uncomfortably. "Aye, well, if you wish to make a charge about—"

"We're not making any charge about sheep," the old man said quietly, turning his sightless eyes toward the constable. He slowly turned his head toward Elizabeth. "Answer him, Elizabeth."

Elizabeth composed herself. She smiled whimsically and nodded. "I *did* have a small difficulty with the Stapleton man, Constable. It was because..." She hesitated, letting her smile become embarrassed. "Well, actually, he wanted to kiss me."

There was an instant of frozen silence. The old man chuckled, puffing his pipe. Sheila looked at him, then sat back in her chair and guffawed, nodding. The old woman grinned, her pipe clenched between her teeth. The constable looked around, then sat back in his chair and laughed, nodding.

"Him and fifty more like him," Sheila chuckled. "But that wasn't what got him sent away, because I don't take a dog to task for barking. No, he started a bloody big fire in Windorah Paddock with his campfire one time, then he let a whole mob of sheep get killed by dingoes. He was no bloody good."

The constable looked at her, his smile fading, then looked at Elizabeth again. "Well, then, let's see." He looked down at his papers again, then looked back up at Elizabeth. "Mrs. Garrity, I understand that in October you took a flock of sheep to the northeast section of the paddock in which the bones of the deceased were found."

There was a sudden, frozen silence. "I took those bloody sheep there," Sheila blurted, breaking the silence.

The constable pursed his lips and shook his head, riffling through his scraps of paper. "No, Miss Garrity. You were at ... ah, in one of the southern paddocks when Mrs. Garrity left to—"

"Yes, I believe I was there in October, Constable," Elizabeth said. "I can't be sure, of course, because I'm about all the time when I'm able to ride."

353

He looked back at her, nodding. "I believe it's a practice to check the fences on such a trip, isn't it? That would normally involve coming back through the northwest section from the northeast section. Did you observe anything out of the ordinary that you would like to tell me about?"

Elizabeth mustered all her self control, and rested the papers she was holding on her swollen belly as she replied in her most pear-shaped tones, "Constable, are you suggesting that *I* might have had something to do with this man's death? *I?*"

There was another instant of silence. Then the old man began laughing, wheezing hollowly in his chest as he rocked back and forth in his chair. Sheila looked at him, then slapped her thigh and burst into peals of laughter. The old woman took her pipe from her mouth and bared her shining teeth as she rocked back and forth, laughing silently. The constable looked around, his face turning crimson, then he began chuckling weakly.

The old man coughed hoarsely, putting his pipe back in his mouth. "Pour him some rum, Sheila."

The constable looked at him with a shamefaced smile. "No, thank you, Mr. Garrity. I can't have a drink while—"

"Your chore is finished. Pour him some rum, Sheila."

The constable opened his mouth, then closed it again as he cleared his throat uncomfortably and sat back in his chair, putting the papers back in his pocket. The old man puffed on his pipe, still smiling. Sheila crossed the room to the sideboard, splashed rum and water into a pannikin, and handed it to him with a wide grin. He took it, nodding and smiling weakly, and she grinned as she returned to her chair and flopped into it again. Elizabeth examined the papers, trying to control the trembling of her hands. The constable ventured comments on the weather and the condition of the graze as he took gulps of the watered rum, and the old man replied in monosyllables, still chuckling occasionally. He finished the pannikin, put it on the edge of a table, then rose and took his leave. The old man grinned toothlessly, and the old woman smiled widely around her pipe. Sheila looked up at him with a broad grin, and Elizabeth smiled and nodded politely.

He left, and a moment later there was the patter of hoofbeats as he crossed the road toward the barrack building where he would spend the night. Sheila looked at Elizabeth and smiled widely, and Elizabeth nodded, breathing a gusty sigh of relief.

The old man stirred, lifting himself from his chair. The old woman stood, picked up her stick, then took the old man's hand and put it on her shoulder. They shuffled across the room with slow, short steps to the hallway, then turned into the hallway. They paused, and the old man turned his head back toward the room.

"The next time, fire the paddock. We can spare sheep and acres of grass, but we can't spare you."

"Very well, Mr. Garrity."

– 20 –

A second son was born to Elizabeth and Colin on a frigid
day in August, and she named him Earl. He was another
healthy, sturdy baby and it was an easy childbirth for her,
and by October she had turned him over to the wet nurse
and the old woman and had resumed her routine of work.
During her latest pregnancy and recovery she had worked
out details of the first shipment of the wool to be sold in
London, with Cummings acting as the shipping agent in
Sydney and a factor with whom her relative in England
had put her in contact awaiting the wool in London, and
she looked forward to the next shearing with both
excitement and a certain amount of trepidation. Summer
began with moderately cool temperatures, promising a
bountiful crop of wool, and the unusually good weather
continued.

The old man became ill again, spending much of his time in his room, with the old woman attending him. Occasionally he recovered enough to have dinner in the dining room for a night or two, then had a relapse. Sheila and Colin took it in stride and expressed no undue concern, but it worried Elizabeth. And what appeared to be an uncharacteristically despondent attitude on his part bothered her as much or more than his physical condition. On the nights when he had dinner in the dining room, he always played with Dennis and held Earl for a long time, and when Elizabeth was there he talked to her at length about rearing the children, the education she would have to provide for them and the necessity for having them fully clothed and wearing boots at an early age.

A herd of cattle had to be driven to the southern boundary to deliver to a drover who was taking them to market in Adelaide, and Elizabeth and Sheila took them. They were much more difficult than sheep to drive, more inclined to fight a dog than to obey as a sheep would, and more inclined to scatter at night. It was an aggravating, arduous drive, with one of them staying awake all night each night to keep the cattle together. They reached the southern boundary without losing any, turned them over to the drover and his men, and returned for a short distance along the track and camped two days to rest before starting back near the hill the aborigines called Wayamba, and Sheila took Elizabeth to show her a cairn of stones near which she and Colin had been born.

They traveled a long distance on the day they returned to make up for the time they had lost, and they arrived at the home paddock well after dark. The old man was ill again, and Sheila and Elizabeth made a meal on cold damper and salt beef in the kitchen, talking tiredly and holding the children. The aborigine women took the children away to put them to bed, and Sheila followed, stretching and yawning.

Elizabeth sat at the table for a while, absently

munching a piece of beef and feeling very tired and remotely depressed, then pushed her chair back from the table and rose. She went out onto the back porch, undressed in the darkness and dipped water out of the wash tub to bathe herself, then pulled her trousers and shirt back on, and went through the house to her room, carrying her boots and the rest of her clothes. She dropped the boots and clothes by the bed, pulled off her trousers and shirt, and slipped wearily onto bed, sighing heavily as she relaxed. The dull, unfocussed depression still hovered in the back of her mind, keeping sleep away for a few minutes, then exhaustion claimed her.

A shrill, agonized scream snatched her from sleep, snapping her to a sitting position in bed. Early daylight was coming through the window, and the scream still rang in her ears. It resounded through the house again, and she identified the voice as Sheila's, a long, wailing cry of sheer despair coming from the hall outside her door. She scrambled out of bed, throwing on her trousers and shirt, and running to her door. She threw it open, and darted into the hall, buttoning her trousers and fastening her belt. Sheila was kneeling by the wall near the door to her parents' room, barefoot, her shirt open, her hair down over her face, and holding her head between her hands. She screamed again, a penetrating, animal-like shriek. Elizabeth ran to her, and she motioned toward the door behind her, sliding lower toward the floor and making a choking, gagging sound. Elizabeth turned to the door. It was ajar. She pushed it open.

The old man's toothless mouth was gaping, frozen open, and flies were clustered on his blind eyes and crawling in and out of his mouth. He had apparently died during the night. The old woman was lying partly on top of him, her left arm around his neck and her head on his chest. The knife was still in her hand. A wide, gaping wound across her throat had released her blood in a sudden spurt which had drenched the bed. Flies were crawling around on it. The air was heavy with the stench of death. It was too much for Elizabeth to encompass at once. Then her stomach suddenly surged. She fought the impulse to retch, swallowing the bitter taste of bile, and she stepped back out of the room, closed the door, and leaned against it weakly, her knees trembling violently and her body soaked in a cold sweat. Sheila was vomiting on the floor and trying to scream again. The two aborigine woman who looked after the children ran into the hall from the parlor, carrying the children and looking around wildly.

Elizabeth pushed herself away from the door and stumbled toward them, waving them away. "Out! Out! Take baby other house! Out!" Their expressions reflected numb incomprehension as they looked from her to Sheila, and Elizabeth snatched one of them by the arm, wheeled her around, and kicked her solidly on the buttocks with the side of her foot. "Out of it, you bloody get! Go to the other flaming house! The other bleeding house, sod!"

They darted out and ran across the parlor toward the front door, and Elizabeth went back to Sheila and bent over her, putting her arms around her and lifting her. "Come on, then."

"My ma and dad, Elizabeth..."

"I know who they are!" Elizabeth shouted irritably, tugging at her and trying to lift her. "Come on in here!"

Sheila looked up at Elizabeth with a dazed expression, her hair hanging down over her face, and she put her hand against the wall and tried to stand. Elizabeth took a firmer grip on her and dragged her along the hall. Sheila leaned on Elizabeth heavily, and she began gagging again. They stumbled through the doorway and into the parlor, and Elizabeth eased her onto a settle. There were pounding footsteps on the veranda, and the front door burst open. Bessie ran in, her face pale and her eyes wide with shock.

"What is it? What is it?" I heard screams..."

"Sheila's ma and dad," Elizabeth replied, pushing her hair back and sighing heavily. "He passed away during the night, and she did herself in. Bessie, go find two . . . no, three men, and tell them—"

"She did *what*?"

"She cut her bloody throat!" Elizabeth stormed at her in sudden rage. "He died, and she went with him! Now close your bloody mouth and listen to me! Go find three men, and—"

"Dead?" Bessie wailed, bursting into tears. "Both of them . . ." She turned away, clutching her face in her hands and sobbing. "God . . . God . . ."

Elizabeth snarled with anger, seized her arm, spun her around, and slapped her solidly across the face. "Listen to me, you bloody get! You'll have your while to bawl, but I need you now!"

"You've no call to belt me, Elizabeth," Bessie sobbed, flinching from her. "You've no bloody call to do that. They're dead . . . both of them . . ."

Elizabeth ground her teeth together, taking Bessie's shoulders and shaking her viciously. "By God, I'll give you such a bloody swiping as you'll never bloody forget if you don't listen to me and do as I say," she grated. "We've things to do, and there's no bloody time for that now!"

"Aye," Bessie sniffled, wiping her eyes and nodding. "Aye, what is it, then? What do you want me to do?"

"Go over to the barrack or to the pens or wherever you can find them, and tell three men they're to come here at once. Then get some clean bedsheets, a set of clothing for both of them, some rags, and a half dozen buckets full of water, and put all that in the hall so I can get them cleaned up. You can find that pair with my boys and get one of them to help you carry the water, and tell the other one to keep the boys in the head stockman's house if you can get them to understand you."

Bessie nodded rapidly, sobbing heavily, and weaved out the door and across the veranda to the steps, pawing at her eyes. Sheila was slumped on the settle, weeping wildly. Elizabeth walked across the parlor to a window and looked out, pushing her hair back from her face. The heavy timbers of the floor were cool and rough under her bare feet, and the sun shone brightly down on the dusty ground and the buildings and pens. The rough, wooden chairs the old man and old woman had used when sitting on the veranda were in their accustomed place, together near the rail. Birds were calling brightly in the trees. The world seemed strangely normal. Sensory impression registered, but at the same time Elizabeth felt out of touch with reality.

She remembered her feeling of depression the night before. She was convinced that the old woman had been alive then, silent in her agony of grief in the room with her dead husband, waiting for the noises in the house to stop so she could go to the kitchen for the knife. A delay of only a few minutes before she had gone to bathe herself or some other slight alteration in what she had done the night before, and she might have seen the old woman and perceived what she was doing. And she might have been able to beg the old woman to spare herself, beg her to share her tears and her grief with others and wait until the sunlight came bringing courage to face the day. Her lips began trembling and her eyes filled with hot tears, and she pushed her hair back again, fighting her weakness.

"She didn't have to do that," Sheila choked thickly through her sobs. "She didn't have to cut her bloody throat."

Elizabeth wiped her eyes and drew in a deep breath, pressing her lips together in a firm line, and she watched Bessie running across the open space toward the buildings, her skirt flapping around her ankles and her large breasts bouncing.

"There's a flaming abo for you," Sheila whimpered. "No bugger can tell what the sods will do. Cut her flaming throat . . ." Her voice faded into sobs as she began weeping again. "And I loved her," she wailed brokenly. "God, I loved her. She was my ma, and I loved her! She didn't have to cut her flaming throat just because he had died. We would have bloody looked after her and took care of her. Didn't she know that? Didn't she know that we loved her?"

Elizabeth silently nodded, still watching Bessie. She was telling a couple of men, waving her arms and swaying on her feet as she wiped at her eyes, and they were looking at her and at each other in astonishment. Elizabeth sighed, nodding again. "Aye, she knew," she said quietly.

"Then why did she have to bloody do that? Why did she have to cut herself open with that great bloody knife?"

The men were running toward the house, waving and calling to another man, and Bessie was standing with her hands over her face. Elizabeth pushed herself away from the window and moved toward the door, buttoning her shirt. "Because she was through. He died, and she was through."

Sheila lifted her head and pawed at her hair, looking at Elizabeth through her tears as she shook with sobs. "You've turned a hard bloody slut."

"Aye," Elizabeth murmured quietly, pushing her shirt into her trousers. "I found myself in a hard bloody place."

She walked out onto the veranda, pushing her shirt into her trousers, and she walked to the edge of the veranda, buttoning the cuffs. The men ran toward the house, a third man running along behind them and racing to catch up. They crossed the road, then slowed to a walk as they approached the steps, looking up at her and panting. One of them took off his hat, then the other two took theirs off. They stopped and stood in a line, holding their hats and breathing heavily as they looked up at her. She straightened her shoulders and pursed her lips.

"The owner has died," she announced in a formal tone. "And his wife went with him. And we're going to see to them properly, the way the owner of Wayamba Station

362

and his wife should be seen to. Freedman, you're to ride to Menindee for the constable and the vicar. Change your horse for Marshall's at Wayamba Paddock, then get another horse at Newton Station. Go at a dead run every mile of the way, and if you kill your horse then run on foot. Tell Newton Station what has happened, and ask them to send riders to Powell Station and Mission Station. The funeral is to be day after tomorrow, and that'll give everyone ample time to get here. Fred, you're to ride to Bulloo Wilga for Colin, then go on through to Blair Station and tell them what happened and when the funeral will be. Take Aberly's horse from Bulloo Wilga if it's in any better shape than yours when you get there, but make sure Colin has a good horse to ride. At Blair Station, ask them to send riders to Tibooburra Station and Stanthorpe Station." She stopped talking, her eyes moving back and forth between the two men, then she nodded. "Go on, then."

The men wheeled and sprinted away, putting their hats back on. Bessie was walking toward her house, wiping her eyes and stumbling from side to side. Elizabeth looked down at the third man. "You're to see to things here. And it's to be done right, because this station won't be shamed before all the people who will be here. Tell the cook to kill a beef and a pig and to put the tables and benches over here in front of the house, and tell the storekeeper to see to the rum. They'll start getting here tonight, so we must be prepared. Get some men to build the boxes and to dig the holes, and find someone to cut some of those flowers. The head stockman's house will be used for station owners, the shearer's barrack will be used for women, and everyone else can bunk in what they find. You're to tell everyone—"

"Elizabeth?" Sheila called from the parlor.

"What is it, then?" Elizabeth replied, turning.

"Have someone tell the abos."

"What have they to bloody do with this?"

"They have to know."

"Aye, all right," Elizabeth said, turning back to the man. "Go down by the huts and tell the abos, then. And tell everyone they're to have on clean clothes and black their boots. And take care of the rest of it. If any sod argues with you about what he's to do or anything goes amiss, come over here and tell me."

The man silently nodded, turning and putting his hat back on as he ran away. Elizabeth turned and walked back into the house. Sheila was slumped on the settle, still sobbing dryly. Elizabeth crossed the parlor and went along the hall to her room, and pulled on her socks and boots, combed her hair and tied it back with a scrap of cloth, and went back into the parlor. There was a thunder of hoofbeats as the riders left, the sound quickly fading into the distance.

"Do you have a dress?"

Sheila looked up at her numbly, looked away and thought for a moment, shaking with dry, sobbing gasps, then nodded.

"That's good, then. You should see to it presently, because you'll want to have it on by tonight, when they start getting here."

Sheila silently nodded again. Footsteps thumped up the steps and across the veranda, and Bessie came in with an armload of linen and clothing, followed by one of the aborigine women carrying two buckets of water. Bessie's face was drawn and splotched and her eyes were red, and the aborigine woman looked terrified. They went into the hallway, slipping on the vomit on the floor, then came back out and silently crossed the parlor to the front door. Elizabeth turned and went through the kitchen to the back porch, and she washed her hands and face in the tub. Bessie and the aborigine woman were carrying four more buckets of water in as she went back into the parlor. She followed them into the hallway and waited until they left, then opened the door and began carrying the buckets of water, linen, and clothing into the room.

Elizabeth almost fainted after she closed the door behind her. The odor seemed to enter through her lungs, permeating her and becoming apart of her tissues and blood, mixing and blending with her living flesh. She pulled the bedclothes off the bed, dragging them from under the old woman's body and wadding them up, and stuffed them out the window. The old man's body was naked, and she took a wad of rags, dipped it in a bucket, and began washing him, turning his surprisingly heavy body over on the bed. Then she tore a piece of rag and tied it tightly from under his chin to the top of his head to pull his mouth closed, and she closed his eyes. The eyelids wouldn't stay completely closed, and a line of the glazed, sightless surface still showed below the edges.

The old woman's clothes were stuck to her body with dried, crusted blood, and Elizabeth tore them off and threw them out the window. Her body was much smaller, tiny compared to the old man's, but it was difficult to get the blood off, bucket after bucket of water becoming tinged with reddish-brown as she sponged the dark, withered body and rinsed the rag out. She closed the old woman's eyes and tied her jaw closed with a strip of rag, took a long piece of rag and wound it around the old woman's neck to hide the gash, then spread out a sheet on the floor by the bed to lay them out. The old man's body made a heavy, jarring thump when she pulled it off the bed, but the old woman's body was so light that she easily lifted it down to the sheet. Bessie had brought underwear for the old man, and Elizabeth threw it into a corner of the room and started putting the shirt and trousers on him. His feet were swollen, and she had to use the knife the old woman had used to cut her throat in order to slice the sides of his boots so she could get them on his feet. The old woman's clothes were the shirt and skirt-like garment she always wore. She finished and waved the flies off them and spread another sheet over them, then emptied the buckets out the window. Blood had soaked into the mattress, and she dragged it to the window and stuffed it through. The knife was on the floor where she had dropped it, and she picked it up and threw it out after the mattress.

When she was through and could leave, she remained for a moment, glancing around the bare, spartan room and looking at their few pitiful belongings. The old woman's stick was in the corner, where she had placed it after coming through the door for the last time, perhaps after getting the knife from the kitchen. A horn comb with some teeth missing lay on a rough, homemade table in the corner. A bark container of the type aborigine women used to carry water was on a shelf. It looked very old and desiccated, and was elaborately carved. Elizabeth took it down and looked at it. There was a crack in the bottom of it with slivers wedged into it to repair it. The slivers fell out of the shrunken bark as she held it, and she knelt, gathered them up, and dropped them into the vessel. There were other things in it, a small Bible, a few stones, bits of bone, a few decayed feathers, a handful of glass beads, and a tiny, stained mirror wrapped in shriveled shreds of wool. And four coins, three gold ten-guinea pieces and a Spanish doubloon. She took the coins out, put the bark container back on the shelf, then walked around to the other side of the bed and knelt, pulling the top sheet down. She closed their eyelids firmly and put a coin on each of them, then replaced the sheet and left the room.

Sheila looked up at her as she came back into the parlor. Her face was younger and softer in grief, the hard, proud planes and lines of her dark features blurred. Her eyes were red, and her lips still trembled as she breathed in shuddering gasps. Elizabeth walked to the settle and sat down, reaching for her. Sheila slid over to her, putting her head on Elizabeth's shoulder. Elizabeth put her arms around Sheila and stroked her cheek as she pressed her lips to the top of Sheila's head. The mournful, droning sound of digereedoos, clatter of rhythm sticks, and rise

366

and fall of chanting voices came from the aborigine shelters.

"I heard what you told the men," Sheila whispered in a trembling voice. "They're being seen to proper, aren't they?"

"Aye, we'll see them on their way proper, Sheila."

"And it was good of you to take care of them. I couldn't have done it."

Elizabeth chuckled dryly, patting Sheila's face again. "Aye, well, I'll do the same for you when the time comes."

Sheila lifted her head slightly, a resentful expression on her face, then she relaxed again and smiled weakly, her breath catching in her throat. "You're a rum bloody sod any more."

Elizabeth's smile faded. She looked out the window, her eyes unfocussed, and she slowly nodded, stroking Sheila's cheek with the tips of her fingers. "Aye, I'll do," she murmured quietly.

Part Three

The Outback

– 21 –

The shrill, penetrating sound of the steam whistle rose to a
scream in the hot, sultry air and lingered there, drowning
the sounds of the tightly-packed crowd on the siding and
becoming a battering pressure which went beyond noise
and absorbed other sound so that all the gaping mouths in
the red, bearded faces around the train were opening and
closing in meaninglessly. Then the screech of the whistle
slowly descended in scale to a trembling warble, rose
again in three short toots, and stopped. The ringing
vibration hung in the air for an instant, as though it had
filled the air with a volume which took an almost
measurable space of time to dissipate, then the noise of
the crowd became audible again, shouts, bellows, and
cheers in voices of deep and high timbre blending together

and drowning individual words in collective meaningless babble. They danced, waved their arms, hats, and bottles, and surged and shoved against each other, individual faces and movements becoming lost in the blur of the mass.

"There's a proper send-off and all!"

Williamson's deep voice rumbled in his ear over the uproar of the crowd, and James nodded slightly, turning the cheroot between the tips of his fingers and biting the end of it to let the strong, warm taste of the tobacco fill his mouth. The gate in the wrought-iron paling around the caboose vestibule rattled as another man started clambering up it, and Williamson pushed himself away from the door and moved toward the gate, shouting and making threatening gestures. He looked out of place in his baggy tweed suit, the shoulders of the coat too small for his brawny shoulders and the sleeves and legs too short for him, and he was still wearing his heavy, battered boots. And he was still the same Williamson. He gave one more warning, his deep voice booming as he shook his fist at the red, anxiously-grinning face above the top railing on the gate, then the ham-like fist shot through the air and blood burst from the nose as the face disappeared. Williamson turned and walked back toward the door, wiping his fist on his coat and shaking his head as he smiled wryly, the features above his beard ugly and honest, dart and heavy from the strong admixture of aborigine in his blood.

"The sods won't learn."

James smiled and nodded, taking another cheroot from the breast pocket of his coat. Williamson took it, nodding his thanks, and James took a match from the side pocket of his coat, struck it on the base of the coach lamp by the door, and cupped it in his hands as it flared to life. He held it out to Williamson, and Williamson bent over to light the cheroot, holding it carefully in both hands to demonstrate his gratitude for the cheroot and possibly his deeper appreciation for the thought behind the gift. Williamson stood erect again, nodding and puffing, and James lit his, clamped it between his front teeth, and shook out the match. The scream of the whistle rose in the air again.

"That driver likes his bloody whistle!" Williamson shouted over the sound.

James nodded, taking his cheroot from his mouth and exhaling, and looked up at Williamson. "When he kills his head of steam and has to recharge his boiler, he'll start playing with his cod piece instead."

Deep laughter rumbled in Williamson's chest, and his large, square teeth showed in the dark brush of his beard and mustaches. "Is it time to leave yet?"

James put the cheroot back in his mouth and took his watch out of his vest pocket. He nodded, replacing it. "If all the toffs are aboard."

Williamson grinned and nodded. James leaned back against the doorjamb and took short puffs on the cheroot, gazing at the crowd. He was rested, having slept well the night before and arisen at an unusually late hour to go about the day's activities at an unusually leisurely pace, but he was still weary with a deeply ingrained fatigue, the accumulation of months of exhaustive effort. A man started climbing the wrought-iron paling at the side of the vestibule, his hands slipping on the bars, then he fell. Another man started climbing the gate, gaining a better grip on it, and Williamson stepped forward and pointed a thick, stubby finger at him in warning. The man dropped back to the ground. A rumbling vibration ran through the train and the caboose jarred back and forth an inch as the drive wheels on the engine spun on the track, and James winced.

"Feels like we're leaving."

James nodded, frowning. "And like the driver is trying to spread the rails and take a wheel shaft off the engine and all. That bastard knows that the engine is on loan from South Railways."

The train shuddered again, then rocked heavily, a metallic clattering coming from the couplings between the cars as they slammed back and forth. A spluttering, staccato rattle of snorts came from the stack on the engine as the drive wheels spun again, then the engine began chugging heavily with a deep, sonorous sound which echoed between the flimsy, ramshackle buildings along the siding as the train began moving forward. The sounds of the crowd rose to a crescendo as they walked along the sides of the train and along the tracks behind it, filling in the space it vacated as it inched along. The rhythm of the engine slowly increased, and the people began running alongside, waving and shouting. A man leaped at the gate and gripped it, trying to drag himself up it. He clung to it, his red, wide-eyed, excited face visible through the openings in the iron work.

"Get his arse off there before we're going fast enough for the fall to kill the bloody fool!"

Williamson nodded, puffing on his cheroot and spreading his feet apart to brace himself against the rocking of the train as he crossed the vestibule, and he jabbed at the man's fingers with the toe of his heavy boot. The fingers disappeared, and the man was momentarily visible as he sprawled on his stomach between the rails, an astonished expression on his face. The crowd covered him, running along behind the train. The buildings at the outskirts of Cockburn came into view on the embankments above the rails. Children and a few women were scattered among them, waving at the train. Shouts of people leaning out of the passenger cars were dimly audible over the sound of the engine and the rumble of the wheels on the rails. The train began outdistancing the last of the crowd, but they continued running, waving and shouting. Williamson stood at the rear of the vestibule and leaned against the gate, waving. People in the crowd responded, waving both arms and screaming, their mouths reddish splotches as the train drew away from them. Then the train rounded a curve, seeming to reach it in a span of time which ridiculed the enormous distance of effort between the curve and the stationary siding, and the crowd was lost from sight. Williamson dropped his arm and started to turn away from the gate, and a man leading a yoke of oxen along the embankment above the rails came into sight. He was waving, and Williamson turned back and waved to him. The train rounded another curve, and the man disappeared. Williamson walked back across the vestibule, puffing his cheroot.

"Give them a wave to pay them for their wait, eh?"

James nodded, clamping his cheroot between his front teeth and turning to the door. He opened it, and Williamson followed him inside. The interior of the caboose was stifling hot, creaking and rocking from side to side and loud with the pounding of the wheels on the rails. Williamson slammed the door and began walking along the side of the caboose and opening windows, and James sat down on the bench built into the wall along one side, running his finger around his celluloid collar and wincing.

"Aye, this bugger is choking me to death as well," Williamson shouted over the noise, jerking at his collar as he opened a window with his other hand. "I believe I'll just have it off until we get there."

James smiled and nodded, taking his cheroot out of his mouth and knocking the ash off it as he sat back on the bench. Williamson took off his collar and tie and put them in his coat pocket, opened the rest of the windows, and walked back across the caboose and sat down on the bench by James.

"Will you be going up to the passenger cars?"

James shook his head firmly.

Williamson grinned, puffing his cheroot. "Would you have a little drop with me, then?"

James started to shake his head again, hesitated as he looked up at Williamson, then nodded.

Williamson's grin widened, and he pushed himself to his feet and walked to the other end of the caboose where he opened a locker built into the wall. He pulled a large, canvas bag out of it and rummaged around in the bag, taking out a bottle and a couple of pannikins, then closed the locker and came back to the bench. James took one of the pannikins from him and held it as Williamson carefully poured a trickle of amber fluid into it, then waited until Williamson had poured a drink into his. They lifted the pannikins and nodded to each other, and drank. The rum was unwatered, raw and burning in his throat. He swallowed, holding his breath, then took a puff on the cheroot and slowly exhaled. Williamson poured more into both pannikins, then pushed the cork back into the bottle and put it down on the bench by him, placing it carefully so the motion of the train wouldn't rock it off.

"Who's in the engine with the driver?"

"Franklin," Williamson replied. "I showed him that gauge to watch, and I showed him how to read it. And he'll rap the driver with a billet of wood if it goes over twenty five miles in the hour."

"Is he sober?"

Williamson looked at him, hesitated, then nodded. "Aye, he's sober."

The look, hesitation, and tone indicated mild affront, as though there had been a reflection on his judgement. They had grown close enough during the months that it was possible to inflict hurt upon Williamson, but not close enough to always be able to tell what would hurt him. And apologies were useless with him. "What are you going to do now?"

Williamson looked away, thinking, then shrugged and puffed on his cheroot as he looked back at James and smiled. "I'll go back up to Brisbane and see the family for a while, I believe, and then I might get me a boring engine and see if I can make my fortune with it. Or I might try fossicking for a while. I heard they were offering you another big job at Port Pirie. Is that right?"

James nodded. "There's one there, but I'm not interested. I believe I'll stop at Wayamba for a while."

Williamson nodded, taking a drink from his cup, and turned and picked up the bottle, pulling the cork out of it. James took a drink from his cup and held it out as Williamson poured more into it, then he relaxed on the bench and leaned his head back against the wall. The wall vibrated with a steady, jarring motion which was transmitted through his skull, making his ears and face tingle. It became uncomfortable, and he sat up straighter, sighing wearily.

The past months had been grueling. After the frustrations of Port Pirie, the opportunity to build the railroad line between Cockburn and Broken Hill had promised independence from interference, abundant capital to work with, and the challenge of a worthwhile undertaking. It had been gratifying to have a last meeting with the government functionaries at Port Pirie and dumbfound them by telling them to get someone else to build the breakwater within the criteria they had placed on it.

But the satisfaction had been short-lived. He'd heard and read bits of the background behind the railway project which had promised trouble, and after taking the position and learning the full details, that promise had been fulfilled. The genesis of the railway had been the massive silver strikes at Silverton and Broken Hill. The bullock wagons hauling the ore across the New South Wales border to the railhead at Peterborough in South Australia had been far too slow and inefficient to transport the ever-increasing produce of the mines, and the South Australian Railways had started building a line to haul the ore to the smelting works on the South Australia coast. The government of New South Wales had refused the government of South Australia permission to cross the border with the line. The line had stopped at Cockburn, on the border, and business interests in Broken Hill and Silverton had asked the New South Wales Government to build the remaining thirty-five miles. The request had been refused, a company had been formed and capitalized for fifty thousand guineas in stock issues, and permission had been requested from the New South Wales Government to build a private railway from Broken Hill to Cockburn. The request had been approved, contingent upon calling the undertaking a tramway inasmuch as the law of New South Wales specified that only government agencies could operate railways.

The squabbling between the governments involved had set the stage and established an atmosphere which had remained. The time schedule he'd had to work against had been unrealistic considering what had been involved, and despite what he'd been told before taking the position, there had been severe financial limitations. The initial limitation had been a thousand guineas for each mile of track, which was totally unreasonable, and he'd managed to get the directors to increase it to twelve hundred pounds. The gauge of the track was three and a half feet, which gave a less stable platform than the New South Wales standard gauge of four feet eight inches and far less than the southern South Australia Railways gauge of five feet three inches. The precipitant race in getting it completed had meant inadequate surveys, costly mistakes, and lives lost in accidents. And there had been constant petty arguments with one official or another.

So it had turned sour, as others had—the bridge at Melbourne, and the roadway between Adelaide and Mount Gambier, the stone pier at Newcastle, and the drydock at Hobart. All of them had turned sour because of the people involved. But always there was Wayamba as a refuge, the vast stretches where the pace was slow and the solitude nourishing to the spirit.

There were some satisfactions. The line had been completed, and it had been completed in spite of what had seemed at times to be insurmountable obstacles, all of them raised by other people involved. It was an undertaking which had been popularized far beyond its actual scope, and there had been offers of other projects, including one at Port Pirie. James had had a gratifying relationship with some of the people who had worked for him. Williamson had been a track foreman at the Peterborough yards and on the point of leaving, and he had found himself as foreman on the project. Working with him had been a pleasure, and there was even a family association of sorts, because he was the grandson of the man who had once owned the property which had been the nucleus of Wayamba Station. But there was even a sour note in that, because the vacancy for head foreman had been created when Charlie Howe, who had been with him on several projects, had been killed by a load of stone fill overturning on him.

The door on the other end of the caboose opened, and a portly man in a natty suit and tall hat came in, holding his hat on as he stepped across the coupling between the cars and into the caboose. "Ah, there you are, Mr. Garrity. We were wondering where you'd got to, man."

James smiled thinly as he stood and shook the man's proffered hand. "Just having a sit-down, Mr. Cockburn. I don't believe you've met my head foreman, Mr. Williamson. Williamson, this is Mr. Cockburn of the board of directors."

Cockburn's expansive smile faded fractionally as he turned to Williamson, and Williamson stood up and awkwardly shifted his pannikin to his other hand to shake hands. "My pleasure, Williamson. Please to meet you, yes indeed," Cockburn rattled as they shook hands, then he turned back to James. "Yes, we were looking around for you, Mr. Garrity. This is your day, isn't it?"

James shook his head. "No, my day was last Sunday, Mr. Cockburn. The day the last spike was driven."

Cockburn laughed heartily and nodded. "Yes indeed, yes indeed, Mr. Garrity. Without a doubt, without a doubt. Well, we're all very grateful for what you did, and you may be assured of whatever support we may render in your future undertakings. Splendid job, Mr. Garrity. Will you come up and have a sup with us?"

"No, I believe I'll stop here, thank you. But we should have another pannikin about if you'll have a drop with us."

"No, thank you," Cockburn said quickly, smiling widely and shaking his head rapidly as Williamson moved to step around him. "No, thank you, I've about had my limit. Thank you very much, but we've our speeches and all in Broken Hill, what? And ample toasts afterwards, I daresay. But thank you all the same. You'll be there for the celebration, Mr. Garrity?"

"No, I'm off to Wayamba Station directly we arrive."

"Ah, yes indeed, yes indeed. The family holdings, what? And how is your family?"

"It's been some time since I was there, but they're well, I understand. My mother passed away a few years ago, of course, and the only family I have now is my aunt and her children."

"Yes, a delightful woman, I understand. And very capable, I'm told. Yes indeed, yes indeed. Well, if you're not going to stop for the celebrations, perhaps you'll be able to return for the official opening in January. His Grace the Duke of Manchester will be here to officiate, you know, and I'd be more than pleased to present you to His Grace myself."

"That's very kind of you, Mr. Cockburn. Yes, I'll be here if it's at all possible."

"I'll be looking forward to seeing you, then," Cockburn said, smiling widely and putting his hand out again. "Yes indeed, yes indeed." He shook hands with James and nodded to Williamson as he turned away, then he hesitated. "Oh, by the way, there was a conversation between some of us in the car a few minutes ago . . . would you say we are traveling at forty miles in the hour or thereabouts?"

379

James laughed and shook his head. "I'd be bloody jumping off if we were. We're at about twenty-five, and I told the operation manager that anything over thirty would be a risk. This is a three and a half foot line, you know."

Cockburn's smile faded and he looked down at the floor with a disgruntled expression for a second, then he looked back up and his smile returned as he nodded. "Oh, yes indeed, yes indeed. Three and a half foot line, what? Yes, well, I'll see you gentlemen again."

They nodded, and he weaved to the door, bracing himself against the swaying of the car, and held his hat as he opened the door and stepped through the doorway. It slammed behind him, and James and Williamson sat back down. Williamson reached for the bottle, and James picked up his pannikin from the bench and held it out.

"Speaks like a pom," Williamson observed.

"He tries to."

Williamson poured several ounces into James' pannikin, refilled his own, lifted it toward James and nodded, and took a drink. "What would the Duke of Manchester be coming for?" he asked, smacking his lips and swallowing.

James took a drink, swallowed, and put the stub of his cheroot in his mouth and puffed on it. The fire in it had gone out. He tossed it down and put the pannikin on the bench beside him as he took two more cheroots out of his pocket. "Perhaps to piss on the tracks on Simpson Flats to keep the sand off them."

Williamson laughed heartily and nodded his thanks as he took a cheroot from James. He leaned over to light it as James struck a match and held it, and sat back up, puffing on it. "You're stopping at Wayamba, then? But you'll be going on again, won't you? An educated man like you wouldn't bide his time long on a station, I shouldn't think."

James took a sip of the rum and puffed on his cheroot,

shrugging. "The more educated a man is, the less he bloody knows, Williamson."

Williamson started to nod, hesitated, then looked at him with a puzzled frown. "The more...what do you mean?"

James glanced at him and looked away, taking a sip from his pannikin. James glanced at Williamson again and smiled whimsically and shrugged. "I don't know myself what I mean, Williamson. You're off to Brisbane, then?"

"Aye, but I'd be back soon enough if you take one of those projects you've been offered and you need me. This sort of work suits me."

"I'll think of you before I ask anyone else, if I do. It's been a rare pleasure working with you."

"And for me, Mr. Garrity. I'd welcome a chance to work with you again, and there's God's truth. And it's not only for the good wages you pay."

James smiled, taking another sip from his pannikin and puffing on his cheroot. The warm glow of the rum spread through him and relaxed him. The buffer it provided against irritations and frustrations was comforting, if dangerous in the possibility of making the bottle too much of a constant friend. The heat in the caboose was soporific, and the rattle of the wheels across the expansion cracks in the rails made a constant, drumming noise. The caboose swayed hard to the left and then to the right in an S-curve, and immediately afterward there was a slight dip, identifying the spot as Murray Creek. It had been difficult to bridge. And it had cost two lives.

The whistle began shrilling, and he put the pannikin down, stood up, and walked to a window on the other side of the caboose. Broken Hill was coming into sight, the clusters of sheet metal roofs, spidery lengths of conveyors, and cancerous masses of tailings. It had invaded a corner of Wayamba Station, to his aunt Elizabeth's utter rage, and when the shafts had been started she had sent a large group of men down to look for a cairn of stones which had some significance to her. But they hadn't been able to find it, undoubtedly because it had already been covered over or destroyed by the digging.

The amount of station property lost to the mining operations had been infintesimal, a matter of yards in hundreds of thousands of acres, but there had been a distinct danger that the old woman would arm her stockmen and protect her boundary with gunfire. A large contingent of constabulary had been rushed in to maintain peace, and an official from Sydney had made a binding settlement. As compensation, the companies which had edged onto the station paid a percentage of profits into the station's bank account, an amount which was many thousands of times what the property was worth, but the old woman had pulled in her boundary by a few yards, built a huge fence around the corner, and steadfastly refused to touch the money.

Elizabeth Garrity was a legend in the Outback, stories about her vying with those about Patrick Garrity, the founder of Wayamba Station. As a youth in college in Sydney, he'd overheard an old, grizzled swagman talking in a public house and spinning tales about her which the old man obviously believed and which the listeners wanted to believe. Most of the old man's stories had been about when she had first come to the Outback, about her and her first husband, and about how she had laid claim to the vast Wayamba Station. The old man had represented her and her first husband as Titans of the Outback, she a goddess in her beauty and virtue and he a demon in his wickedness, both of them larger than life and making the earth quake in their struggles. One of the stories had been of the baby she'd had by the handsome Colin while still married to her first husband, and how she had fled across the Outback to protect her baby from her husband's wrath, swimming swollen rivers and crossing the Gibbers Desert on foot. But her husband had resorted to subterfuge and arranged the baby's death through his evil cunning, provoking her into challenging her husband to a duel to the death with stock whips. The old man's story of the duel had been hair-raising, paddocks being torn up and whole flocks of sheep and herds of cattle in their path being killed as they battled back and forth across the northern part of Wayamba Station, and in the end she had been victorious and her husband had been so badly mutilated that the constabulary had made an official finding that he had been killed by a wild boar.

The stories, like others he'd heard, had been patently untrue and obvious fabrications. But the old swagmen and fossickers thrived on such stories, and anyone who challenged any point of them would find himself in a fight. There was a grave of an Infant Cummings at the home paddock on Wayamba Station. The official cause of death of her first husband was that he had been killed by a boar. And there were similar nuggets of fact which seemed to lend at least some basis to other wild stories he'd heard. But the old woman was tight-lipped about her early years on the station. And he'd never been able to summon the temerity to ask about any of the stories when looking into the sparkling blue eyes in the lined, hard face.

He looked out the window, smiling as he thought about her, and his smile became wry as he sighed and shook his head. The most unlikely story about her was that her father had been a minister. It was easy to be very fond of her, and respect for her was automatic because she was more of a legend than a person. But she could also be extremely exasperating, calmly demanding the impossible and then meting out a scathing, profane tirade when it wasn't forthcoming. And she could be loving. James' blurred, distant childhood memories of her were of a beautiful woman who kissed and caressed and demanded that the columns of figures be perfectly straight and the letters be formed precisely like the example.

The whistle began tooting rapidly, and the crowd came into sight as the train turned the last long, slow curve across the dry, scrubby flat and started along the straight stretch toward the sheet metal building which had been hastily erected to serve as a station. The crowd was even larger than the one at Cockburn had been, filling the road and overflowing onto the rubble-covered hill above the station, and bunched along both sides of the track. The train began slowing, jerking and rattling as the cars slammed back and forth against the couplings, and the whistle shrilled as the train crawled toward the station. The roar of the crowd swelled as they rushed toward the train.

James walked back from the window, picked up his pannikin and drank the last few drops, and handed it to Williamson. "Let's hope that fortified us to get through his lot, then."

Williamson laughed as he walked to the other end of the caboose with the pannikin and bottles, and he took the canvas bag out of the locker and dropped them into it. He moved and closed the windows, and James locked the door at the front of the caboose, picked up his portmanteau from the corner, and walked toward the back door. The train shuddered heavily, the wheels screeching on the tracks, and the whistle rose to a crescendo as the train came to a stop. The roar of the crowd outside was thunderous. James opened the door and held it for Williamson as he set the lock on it, and he slammed it behind them as he followed Williamson out. Most of the crowd was concentrated around the front of the train, with only a few stragglers to the rear. Williamson crossed the vestibule to the gate, opened it, and leaped down with his canvas bag over his shoulder, then turned and reached up for James' portmanteau. James handed it to him, leaped down to the gravel and cinders between the tracks. Williamson handed the portmanteau to him, reached up and closed the gate, and

384

they stepped across the rail and walked toward the siding.

"Where are you off to now, then?" James asked.

"I thought I'd spend a while with the boys we have on the train. How about you, Mr. Garrity?"

"I believe I'll see about getting a horse and go on..." His voice faded as he heard his name being called over the uproar of the crowd, and he turned and looked around. A tall, well-built youth was shoving his way through the edge of the crowd and calling to him.

"Colin!"

Colin pushed through the crowd toward him, smiling widely. He had his father's stature and his mother's features, a strapping youth of eighteen in a stockman's heavy shirt and trousers, boots, and wide, flat hat. "Are you all right, James?"

"Aye, I am and all," James said, smiling with pleasure as he shook hands with him. "Are you all right, Colin?"

"Aye, I am." His smile became a wide grin, and he chuckled. "Here I was looking for you up amongst the toffs, James," he said in a teasing tone.

"Then that shows just how much you bloody know about me, doesn't it?" James retorted, and he turned to Williamson. "Williamson, this is my cousin, Colin Garrity. Colin, this is Edward Williamson, the head foreman on this job."

"I'm glad to meet you," Colin said with his wide, friendly smile, shaking hands with Williamson.

"Aye, and I am as well," Williamson said. "Come down to see the train in, did you?"

"Not bloody likely!" Colin laughed explosively, shaking his head. "My ma would sew me in a raw sheepskin if I even mentioned aught to do with bloody Broken Hill. No, she sent me down for James here."

"Did she now?" James said. "Well, God bless her for thinking of me. That saves me from finding my own way to the home paddock."

"Save your blessings until you talk to her," Colin

chuckled. "She wants something of you, or I'll miss my guess."

"Not more bloody bores," James groaned, wincing.

"Aye, I believe that's what she has in mind," Colin said cheerfully.

"Oh, bloody hell," James sighed, shaking his head.

"A bore would give you no trouble would it, Mr. Garrity?" Williamson said. "Some lout like me might have his hands full with it, but I should think you would be able to sink one right neat and proper. Not that it's any of my affair, of course."

"You don't know my aunt," James said wryly. "She marks off a ten foot space in the corner of a paddock, and there's where she wants water found. And it can't be hot water, and it mustn't have too many minerals in it so the sheep and cattle can't drink it."

"Bloody hell," Williamson laughed, shaking his head. "You can't tell within a mile where you'll find water, or how deep you'll have to go. And you never know what the minerals will be like."

"Tell that to my aunt," James replied, chuckling and shaking his head. "When I went there after the job at Hobart, she already had the troughs built for a bore she wanted, and I didn't hardly have room to stand on the spot where she wanted it drilled. As luck would have it, I did hit water. But then she had her wind up because it was hot water."

All three of them laughed, and Colin looked at Williamson. "Will you come along with us, then?"

"No, I'm stopping here for a time."

Colin nodded pleasantly, looking from Williamson to James. It was time to go. The proximity of months and of common purpose was about to be severed. They had grown to know each other, and now their paths were to divide. James felt as though there must be some profound observation to be made or some expressive phrase which would make things less final. But he couldn't think of what it might be. He put out his hand.

"Thank you for everything, Williamson."

"It's me who's doing the thanking, Mr. Garrity. And if you need me again, just write to my name at Ipswich outside Brisbane. Everybody there knows me, and it'll reach me, regardless of where I might be at the time."

"I certainly will. Goodbye, then."

"Goodbye, Mr. Garrity."

Williamson and Colin exchanged a nod, and James followed Colin away from the track and up the low embankment of crushed rock and rubble, carrying the portmanteau.

"I left the horses down there away from all these ... here, I'll carry that, James."

"I can carry my own bloody swag," James snorted.

"Aye, I can see that and all," Colin said pleasantly, plucking it out of James' hand and lifting it lightly to his shoulder. "You got it here, didn't you?"

James grunted sourly, then smiled wryly in response to Colin's wide grin. They walked around the edge of the crowd along the embankment, and through the crowd James could see Cockburn and several more men on a makeshift platform by the station, apparently preparing to make speeches. They disappeared from sight behind the milling crowd. Colin hopped lightly down the outside of the embankment onto a dirt path which led past several dilapidated shacks used for dwellings, with ragged clothes hanging on makeshift lines and thin, drawn women and children looking through the doorways from the dark, hot, dingy interiors. There was a brushy opening on the other side of the shacks, then an odorous trickle of water with a cluster of withered, dying gum trees on the other side of it. Two horses were tethered to one of the trees, and Colin turned toward them.

"Someone could steal your horses, leaving them alone like this," James commented as Colin lifted the portmanteau to tie it behind the saddle on one of the horses.

"Aye, but then he'd want to be off to China, wouldn't he?"

The reply was soft, matter of fact, and with a total lack of youthful braggadocio. Colin looked suddenly ageless, neither youth nor adult, but something quite apart from and independent of age. As a person, and knowing him well, it was ridiculous to contemplate that he sprang from the stuff of legend. But there were moments when there seemed to be a charisma about the old woman and her children which made the legends almost believable. And the aura had nothing to do with them as people. It seemed to come from *what* they were rather than *who* they were. And Colin was suddenly a courteous youth again, showing friendly respect toward an older relative who was well-liked and regarded as one of the inner circle of the family as he mounted the horse with the portmanteau behind the saddle, swinging his leg lightly over the bulky bag.

"I should ride that one, shouldn't I? That horse will be loaded down with you and the portmanteau, great bullock that you are."

Colin laughed and shook his head. "He's a good horse. And it'll make him jog hard, and I can't bring you in with a sore arse now, can I?" He reined his horse around toward a road up the side of the hill. "You heard about Earl, didn't you?"

James nodded, nudging his horse with his heels and reining it around beside Colin's. Earl was the middle brother, older than Colin and younger than Dennis, and he had been killed in the gold fields near Melbourne a few months before. "Aye, and I was sorry to hear about that, Colin. As sorry as I could bloody be. How did your mother take it?"

"Bloody different than I'd look for. She threatened to sew me and Dennis in raw sheepskins if we so much as set foot toward Melbourne."

"And quite right she was and all. It would have been foolish to go to Melbourne looking for trouble. And after I thought about the matter, I decided it was the reaction she would have."

"Well, I don't think it's so bloody foolish. The sods did it, and a lot some pansy constabulary will do about it. And I don't see how you expect that of Ma, considering what a hellion she's been about this lot here at Broken Hill and plenty of others."

"Your mother didn't send Earl down there, I'll wager."

"You'd win. They had a fight about it."

"Then there you are. If he'd been in Melbourne on station business, there wouldn't two bricks left standing together down there."

Colin pursed his lips, thinking, then shrugged and dismissed it. He turned his horse onto the road, then looked at James with a sudden grin as he caught up. "We've something at the home paddock that'll interest you, I'll warrant."

"What's that?"

"A girl. A pommie girl and all. And a proper pommie too, not from Sydney or such. But ample sand in her, for all of that."

James laughed and shook his head. "And you're not interested? Or Dennis isn't?"

Colin snorted and shook his head. "We've no bloody time for interest in such things. And she's a bit old for us, but about right for you. A proper good-looking girl as well."

"Aye, well, I don't have much time for such myself."

"You might find time for her," Colin chuckled.

James smiled and shrugged. "What's she doing at the home paddock?"

"She's a relative of Ma's. She was in Sydney and needed some help or something, and Ma brought her to the station. Her name is Alice Willoughby."

James nodded disinterestedly, turning his horse to follow Colin as he turned off the road and across a barren stretch of rocks and sandy soil.

– 22 –

The thin voices chanted, the words melting together and becoming a string of sounds so that the last syllable of one word joined the first of another to form words which existed nowhere except in the lexicon of classroom recitation, where young minds were trained to travel along safe paths on the theory that embedding the appropriate symbols would lead to an adult life of conformity, hard work, respect for authority, and observance of God's law. The Psalms were always a safe way to fill the last few minutes of the day, and concentration on anything more involved would have been impossible because of Alice's horrified fascination with the mucus oozing from the nose of the boy who sat at the desk on her left. It was there on the edge of her vision regardless of where she turned her eyes, and some morbid impulse kept bringing her eyes back toward him in spellbound revulsion to see if the alternate movements of the greenish trickle and the pink tongue were going to intersect and fulfill her perverse urge to see the odious result. The mass crept down from his left nostril, following the shining trail it had made in previous trips, and approached the edge of his lip. Then a sniff would snatch it back into the nostril which was surrounded with a rim of crusty, pale brown matter, and the tip of his tongue would whip across his upper lip, as though parts of him were imbued with a life of their own, the mucus provided by the nose and sought by the tongue failing to reach its intended destination because of an unfortunate lag in coordination.

It happened over and over, with just a split second between the recovery of the mucus and the flicking of the tongue so that it seemed certain that they would eventually meet. Yet they didn't, and all the while his mouth opened and closed and he swayed slightly with the others in rhythm to the recitation. They were working-class children, indifferently clothed and inclined to dismaying secretions and odors. Moreover they were boys and she had little experience to fall back on in dealing with them. But they were obedient and respectful, stimulating impulses of affection in her that were also outside her experience in dealing with school children. For the young ladies in the day school where she had taught in Wexford a glance and a touch of her finger to her nostrils would have been a scathing reproof and would have immediately resolved any problem. But the young ladies had also been sufficient unto themselves, arriving and leaving in their carriages and needing nothing from her. She could glare at one of the boys in front of her and scour her nose with her hand until it was red, and the boy would conclude that her nose was itching. But a smile or a word of encouragement brought a beaming response from them which gave her a warm glow inside. It required a strong effort of will to control an impulse to affectionately embrace them all.

And then the small arm moved in a quick motion, and the mucus became one stain among many on the sleeve of his muslin shirt, and she felt a sense of relief and a touch of something approaching disappointment which was cause for bemused wonder at herself. The chant continued, the rhythm following the bobbing of the pointer in her hand, and there were small irregularities which signalled less than satisfactory familiarity with the syllables. But it was late in the day, she was weary, and there would still be thousands of repetitions for each of them which would eventually provide the necessary familiarity to satisfy the world that they were equipped to deal with those aspects of life requiring a detailed knowledge of the Psalms. The chant stopped.

"Very good. And now Psalm Twenty-Three. Would someone like to start us? The Lord is..." She glanced back and forth along the line of boys. They knew it well, but there was absolute silence. And she had found out that pointing to one of them to begin the chant would result in stuttering, blushing confusion on the part of the one designated and stares from the others incorporating relief that they had escaped and something resembling the sadistic enjoyment of watching a moth impaled on a pin flutter away its life. Again, far different from the young ladies, who displayed quiet, modest pride when they knew the proper response and who arose and serenely apologized when they didn't. "The Lord is my..." she said, hopefully providing another word, then nodded and started moving the pointer in the rhythm for the Twenty-Third Psalm. "Very well, then. All together. The Lord is my shepherd..."

They all started on the first syllable. She tried each time to get one of them to volunteer to start a well-known exercise in order to develop latent qualities of leadership in one or another of them, and each time she met a wall of silence. The only solution would be to get them all to volunteer at once, which in effect was what happened when she started them.

The sound of shuffling footsteps came from the adjacent room, but the rhythm continued in an unbroken pattern and the only indication that they even heard the rumble of the departure of the other class was the hopeful swivel of two pairs of eyes toward the door. Out of the corner of her eye she saw the door open silently and the bulky form of the headmistress standing in the doorway, and she kept her eyes on the boys and continued repeating the syllables with them as she moved her pointer. None of the eyes moved toward the door, but they all knew she was there. It was evident in their faces, in the subtle changes in the lines on the small, bright faces which reflected cowering fear. The atmosphere in the room changed. The chant stopped. They sat stiffly, looking straight ahead. Alice looked toward the doorway.

"You may dismiss."

"Very well, Miss Copely." She looked back at the boys, motioning with her pointer. "Let's line up."

They stood up, straightened their chairs, and formed a line. The doorway was empty again, the door standing open, but tension remained in the room and their faces were still haunted with apprehension. They knew the weight of cruelty which could be brought to bear on them by a fifty year old spinster. Alice walked along the line, and it was impossible to resist touching the rosy cheek of the cherubic eight year old who was such a lovely child. She stepped in front of the line and walked toward the doorway. They followed her trailing skirts, their quiet footsteps in an even rhythm. She walked through the doorway, across the entry hall, and through the front door, and stepped to one side outside the door. They grinned up at her as the line turned into a cluster moving across the porch, then the cluster dissolved into individual boys as they raced down the steps and out onto the street. She turned and went back inside.

It was an old dwelling, housing the day school provided by a government concerned that its citizens should be able to count their wages and read the Bible. The entry hall might once have been graced with mirror stands, a table holding a tray to receive calling cards, and other niceties, because the house was fairly large and well-appointed, but it had been turned into a bare space for the purpose of occasionally assembling all the students in neat lines to hear a lecture by the headmistress and for access to the classrooms. She crossed it and went back into the room, put the pointer away, stacked the small chalkboards neatly on the desk and straightened the stack of books on the desk, then picked up her reticule and turned toward the door.

Miss Copely was standing in the doorway again. There had been an instinctive defensiveness between the two women from the first day, when she had arrived with the Reverend Preston and the small, dark eyes in the pale, sagging face had moved over with a coldly hostile glare of jealousy. Alice's crinolines, bright dresses, and colorful ribbons had been adjudged frivolous, and she had been given a class selected on the basis of immunity from unsettling influence. And she had restrained herself and contained her temper, hoping that her unfortunate situation could soon be improved.

"Your pupils were doing very poorly on the Psalms, Miss Willoughby. Mrs. Cunningham had most of them before, and they were doing much better then."

"Then I shall speedily make amends and exercise them at greater length on the Psalms."

"You'd also do well to use your pointer for something besides waving about. A taste of it across their backs increases their interest in what they're doing." Her eyes moved up to Alice's hair, then back down to her eyes. "And you'll also have to do something about your hair."

"My hair, Miss Copely?"

"Yes, your hair. I've no doubt it catches all the young men's eyes in a ballroom, but it is far too frivolous for a classroom."

The crinolines had been put away, the bright broadcloths had been replaced by the heavy, plain muslins she had intended to use for housework, and the ribbons had been replaced with combs. She had maintained a humble silence in the face of cutting remarks and insinuations from one whose education and ability marginally qualified her for a post in one of the small day schools in Sydney. It had been a delaying tactic, and she had wondered when the confrontation would come, hoping it could be averted until her situation was resolved. But the problem was that those who derived pleasure from being cruel to others knew no limits. One small victory whetted their appetites, and they were never satisfied until they had devoured the spirit of their victims. Alice knew the process well, because she had seen it happen to her father, a kindly and weak-willed man who worked as a clerk, and she had seen him exploited by his employers and crushed by the casual malice of butchers, tailors, and virtually everyone else with whom he came into contact. Her mother, broken by poverty and ill health, had expected nothing else from life. But from the time Alice had reached the age of fifteen, many had found to their surprise that the spineless could beget a child with courage. By habit she maintained a polite and reserved manner until provoked, and in these strange and unfamiliar surroundings, her unfortunate circumstances, and her reliance upon the good will of others for the necessities of life, she had been even more compliant than before.

But the time had come. The one who derived a perverted nourishment from being cruel to others was going to be denied her feast. The mass of heavy, auburn ringlets would never feel the touch of scissors because of the jealous whim of a dowdy woman with a thin, stringy mop of grey-streaked hair.

"I shan't cut my hair, Miss Copely."

A touch of color came into the doughy cheeks and her wattles trembled as she stiffened and her nostrils flared. "*Shan't*, Miss Willoughby? I have told you that your hair is too frivolous!"

"In that event, I fear I must subject the Reverend Preston to the bother of undertaking to secure employment for me elsewhere."

"Aye, well, no doubt you can discover a means of repaying him for his vexation."

It was difficult for Alice to keep a smile of triumph from forming as satisfaction flowed through her. She had a weapon. Reverend Preston was a handsome, personable man under forty, safely married and with two children, an assistant pastor well liked by his superiors, including the bishop. His aggressiveness in helping her and his solicitude and sympathy over her situation had undoubtedly been increased by the same impulses which had generated the admiring gleam in his eyes, but he had been more than circumspect, always addressing her formally, making a point of placing her in contact with his wife, and always meeting with her in the presence of others. No touch of scandal was permitted. But Miss Copely's irritation had overcome her judgement, allowing her tongue to range too far. The school, and others like it in the city, were administered by the Church. Miss Copely was indirectly under Reverend Preston's authority. And she realized she had gone too far. It showed in her eyes as Alice looked into them. And she started stuttering something to cover the remark. Alice cut her off.

"I would be able to remain in any event, Miss Copely, if that is your assessment of my character. But aside from that, you have also impugned the Reverend Preston's motivations and intentions. He and his wife have been exceedingly kind to me, and beyond that he is a respected church official. If gossip is spread about him, I can do no less than communicate to him the sense of what I have—"

"What are you talking about, you silly girl?" Miss Copely snapped, her face flustered and a heavy brogue overtaking her cultivated accents. "I said nothing of the sort!"

"I beg to call that into question, Miss Copely. Indeed, I plainly heard what you said. Perhaps it was an unfortunate slip of the tongue, but even so it betrays an attitude which I cannot allow to pass unchallenged."

"You misunderstood me, that's what it was," Miss Copely said, trying to smile and regain her composure. "You've misunderstood me entirely, in fact. Who's saying anything about another position? You have a position here, don't you? And I've said naught which could be construed as a threat to it. All I did was venture a comment on your hair."

Those who were most cruel were also those who were most cowardly when confronted with courage. The splotches on her pasty face were darker, her lips were trembling, and she was panting breathlessly. She had been misled by Alice's retiring mien. She had not expected resistance, and Alice's retaliation was shattering.

"Miss Copely, am I or am I not to understand that my hair is unsuitable for my employment here?"

"Wear it as you wish," she replied sullenly. "I only passed a comment, and there's the end of it."

Alice pursed her lips and nodded slightly. She still had full control of the situation. And there were other things. Miss Copely routinely picked out a boy or two on some pretense or other to thrash with a pointer at assembly, instilling fear in all the pupils and satisfying some depraved urge within herself. Too often it had been Alice's boys. They suffered because they were hers. "There is a further matter I wish to discuss with you, Miss Copely," she said as the woman turned away. "As you know, my previous experience in instruction was in a young ladies' finishing school in Wexford."

"Yes?" Miss Copely said heavily, looking at her resentfully.

"The procedure to which I am accustomed is for the mistress to punish her own pupils and to be responsible to the headmistress for their conduct and obedience. I would like to have the same arrangement here."

Miss Copley's flush deepened, and she turned to face Alice. "What makes you think you can come here and change things? I'll leather any brat who has it coming, whether you like it or no."

"I have no wish to change things as such, Miss Copely. I was merely stating a condition of my continued employment here. If you find it unacceptable, and I will certainly accede that it is within your authority to do so, I shall simply seek employment elsewhere, with no more ado about it. The Reverened Preston did mention several alternate possibilities, you see. And I believe he will agree with me that there are other places where I might be employed with greater advantage to all concerned, if I find it necessary to go into the matter with him."

The headmistress glared at Alice, her lips in a thin line and hate and fear gleaming in her eyes, and she grudgingly nodded as she turned away. "Aye, all right," she grumbled.

"Thank you so very much, Miss Copely," Alice said cheerfully, sweeping briskly through the doorway and walking toward the front door. "Good afternoon."

Miss Copely muttered a reply, and Alice smiled to herself in satisfaction as she walked through the front door.

The school was near the center of the city, just off King's Cross and a short walk from her lodgings on the church grounds behind St. George's, and the street was busy. Carriages, wagons, and drays moved back and forth and the sides of the street were a bustle of pedestrians. It seemed rural to Alice despite the activity. The people's clothing was mostly rustic, a high percentage of the conveyances were loaded with produce, animals were occasionally seen being driven along the street, and the buildings were small, many of them only a single story high. But certain elements clashed with rural locations she had seen in England. In many respects it had an atmosphere all its own, far different from other places she had seen. It wasn't England. And she still felt severe pangs of homesickness, even though her situation was far better than had seemed possible at first.

Roger Warfield had been an exciting man, far different from others in his almost overpowering masculinity and engaging impatience with social conventions, and his accent was charmingly different. He commanded immediate attention everywhere he went. And he had chosen Alice. She had demurred, not wanting to associate herself with the giddy women fluttering about him, and he had pursued her with a dedicated, single-minded determination which had been the ultimate flattery and the topic of conversation on every tongue. To her utter horror, he even appeared at the school where she worked one day, but snatched success from the appearance of disaster in the way only he could, charming the headmistress and the other teachers so that they were fluttering and giggling around him with no more presence of mind than their charges. And all the while his eyes had been only for her.

There had been foreboding hints. Gossip had it that a couple of young men had been jealous enough to challenge him at fisticuffs, hardly an undertaking for a gentleman, and he had trounced them with a vicious thoroughness which revealed an alarming skill in such a rude enterprise. The uncle who had assumed a parental role in her life from an early age, Lawrence Willoughby, had been suspicious of him and had contradicted his stories of wealth in Australia, having information on it from another relative who was a barrister in London. Her uncle had also logically questioned why one from a land of such wealth would be traveling as a common seaman.

But for once she had gone against her uncle's judgement, because for the first time in her life she had felt truly alive.

And she had come to Australia to marry him. Wexford had appeared grey and dreary after he left, and the days had been long and dull.

Then his letter had come and her uncle had dipped into his resources for her again, and she had come to Australia, only to meet with bitter disappointment, disillusionment, and shame. He hadn't been there to meet her, and when she searched for him she found that he had gone to Tasmania. His family lived in a hovel on a small farm in Lithgow, an ironical testimony to the accuracy of her uncle's comments on his stories of wealth, and they were hostile and suspicious of her. An older sister of his had been more kindly, if still somewhat withdrawn, noncommittal, and cruelly amused, and it had been she who told Alice that he had gone to Tasmania. She also told her that he had raised the expectations of several other women in Newcastle and Melbourne, and it had been a similar situation closer to home in Sydney which had been the proximate cause of his departure for Tasmania, when the woman's father and brothers had become aware of the situation.

Alone, lonely, with shattered hopes and limited resources in a strange and unfriendly land, Alice had solicited the protection of the Church. Her initial reception by the vicar of St. George's had begun with a frigid attitude and marked lack of understanding on his part. Then in the process of relating her story, she gave him the name of a relative which had been given to her by her uncle. His attitude magically changed, and she was rushed to the bishop. It appeared that her distant cousin was a woman of distinction, substantial wealth, and great influence, as well as the daughter of a deceased member of the local clergy who was remembered with considerable reverence.

Alice had been given lodgings on the church grounds, and the bishop had appointed Reverend Preston to see to her immediate affairs, in the course of which he had secured her the post at the day school and had taken her to the offices of a shipping and trading factor in the city who conducted business for her cousin. It was an old and well-respected firm. The man who had interviewed her there simply asked her for details of her parentage and of her situation so he could pass them on. Her suggestion that she had sufficient money to take a post chaise to her cousin's establishment had resulted in hilarity, and she had found that her cousin Elizabeth lived a far distance away.

Since that day weeks had passed, and no response had been received. The postal system was subject to the vicissitudes of weather and apparently of the whims of the people involved, and Reverend Preston remained confident that a reply would eventually arrive. But part of Alice's worry lay in the fact that she wasn't sure of what she wanted. The uncertainties of her present situation were preferable to facing the derision which would be her fate if she returned to Wexford, unmarried and rejected after the going-away parties and the envy of others. She had no wish to subject her uncle to further expense on her account, so the bishop had acceded to her request to delay writing her father and uncle until some reply was received from her cousin. On the other hand, it was unreasonable to expect her cousin to advance her a loan to establish herself. The only other alternative seemed to be to ask for an invitation if her cousin's reply was cordial, but from what she had heard of the Outback, that might be the worst possible alternative.

Reverend Preston's wife and the wife of another member of the clergy were walking along the street in front of St. George's as she passed it, and they replied to her greeting with cool nods. She had been invited to take tea by each of the wives of the clergy as the discharge of an obligation which had probably been levied by the bishop, and there had been no further invitations or overtures of friendship. The barriers were various, ranging from jealousy towards her because of her education and accent, to the feeling that her coming to Australia without being married first was improper. But her situation wasn't unbearable, and to an extent she dreaded a reply from her cousin, because it would force her to commit herself in one way or another. Over the weeks she had become more or less adjusted, and the worst part was having no friends. It would be easy to get drawn into social circles in the city, because the several families who had invited her home with them after church had been congenial and some further invitations had been forthcoming. Men stared at her as she walked along the street, there had been advances toward acquaintance in church on Sundays, and it appeared that most of the invitations she received were for the purpose of meeting sons or other young male relatives. But she had no desire to satisfy wagging tongues with a full explanation of her situation, and her disappointment was too recent to contemplate even friendship with a man.

Alice turned onto the walk leading along the side of St. George's and into the church grounds, a pleasant expanse of grassy lawns, flower beds, and shade trees, and she turned off onto the path to her lodgings, a room in a small house which had once been the quarters for a curate. There were five other residents of the house, three aged invalids, a widow who cared for them and was in charge of the house, and a girl who was mentally deficient, and they were all relatives or widows of deceased clergymen. It was a pleasant enough place, because the widow was an amiable, motherly woman, the closest to a friend that Alice had, and the house was meticulously clean. The food was good and ample, and the charges were modest enough that she had a few shillings left over from her wages from the school. But Alice shared a room with the retarded girl, a seventeen year old, and some of her eccentricities were discomfiting. She occasionally locked herself in the privy for hours at a time, leading to the unseemly necessity for the widow to stand on the path and bellow for her to come out. She had a set of quoits someone had given her and she often played with them in the dark at night.

The widow was standing in the doorway, and she walked down the steps and came along the path toward Alice as Alice approached. Alice hesitated, seeing the piece of paper in her hand and her heart both sinking and leaping at the same time, and she forced a smile and began walking more repidly. "Good afternoon, Mrs. Hawkins."

"Aye, aye, love. A boy brought this for you not an hour gone. He said he was from the shipping factors Cummings."

Her face reflected curiosity, and Alice suspected that she couldn't read and write. Alice smiled and nodded, taking the paper and glancing over it. It was simply a request to call on Mr. Jeremiah Cummings at the offices of his firm. She had more or less expected a personal communication from her cousin. And while she had spoken with an officer of the firm before, she was to see one of the heads of the firm, judging from the name. "Yes, I'm to call around immediately," she said in a musing tone, glancing over the short note again. She looked up and smiled at the widow as she put the note in her reticule. "It appears that they've heard from my relative."

"Aye, no doubt. Well, I'll have your tea ready for you when you return, love. I have some good scones today, the kind you like."

"Lovely," Alice said, smiling brightly as she turned back along the path. "Thank you, Mrs. Hawkins."

"Aye. And I hope the news is the best, love."

Alice glanced over her shoulder and smiled and nodded again as she hurried along the path, but her smile faded as she turned her face away. In one way or another, the matter of her cousin must be settled. The curt, brief note from the factor's firm seemed somehow ominous. It wasn't beyond the realm of possibility that her cousin had replied to the effect that she felt no responsibility for a remote relative from England who was in dire straights. And that would undoubtedly make her something less than a welcome guest of the Church.

The streets were crowded and bustling with activity near the closing of the day, women shopping, tradesmen, porters, and workmen on their way home, and hawkers out to meet the crowd. She turned down Bridge Street toward the docks, following the route that Reverened Preston had brought her along, because she had heard that some of the streets were of an unsuitable character for her to frequent, and she weaved through the people. She crossed a last intersection and saw the sign ahead, and she slowed, catching her breath. She hesitated outside the door, glanced down at herself and tugged the waist of her dress straight, then pushed the latch and entered.

The outer office was small, dingy, and cluttered, a wooden fence enclosing a small space in front of the door and the elevated desk of the head clerk facing the door. He was an older man with thin, white hair and a drawn, wrinkled, unfriendly face whose pale blue eyes peered over the top of his spectacles. His celluloid collar stood out around his thin, withered neck, his tie was stained and greasy, and his woolen sleeve protectors made his forearms look burly, in strange contrast to his emaciated appearance and to the thin, white, veined hand holding the quill as he looked at her. Two younger men and a boy sitting at table desks against the wall glanced up and then looked quickly back down and began writing again. They were the same ones who had been there before. And the atmosphere was solemn and hushed as it had been before, so that the Reverend Preston's deep voice had sounded painfully loud. She quietly closed the door, walked softly across the wooden floor, and stood on tiptoe to speak to the head clerk.

"I am Alice Willoughby, and I have in hand a request to call upon Mr. Jeremiah Cummings."

He held his hand cupped behind an ear as she spoke, and belatedly she thought of giving him the note. But he had already put his quill down and was slowly and carefully climbing down from his tall stool. The two younger men and the boy looked at her from the corners of their eyes as the head clerk walked slowly toward one of the doors opening off the outer office, one of his shoes squeaking loudly in the stillness. Then he passed them, and one of the younger men looked directly at her and smiled. She averted her face. The squeaking shoe made a longer, dragging noise as he opened the door and slipped inside. Then a second later he came back out. His expression was stern, which could be interpreted as the expression appropriate to the gravity of speaking with one of the heads of the firm. Or it might be a reflection that her cousin had refused to assist her. He held the gate in the wooden fence open for her, and she nodded her head politely as she gathered her skirt and walked through it. Then he walked ahead of her to the door, his shoe squeaking more loudly at close range, and he opened the door for her. She nodded her head politely again, and he bowed slightly and closed the door behind her as she entered the office.

The office looked much the same as the one in which she had been interviewed with Reverend Preston, small, dirty, and untidy, with a large, littered desk, a couple of hard and uncomfortable chairs, shelves of papers around the walls, a small fireplace in the corner, and a musty, unaired odor. A man was standing with his back to her and putting on his suit coat, plainly a courtesy. He turned, tugging his coat straight, and bowed slightly. She kept her polite smile in place and pretended not to notice the large, dark brown birthmark which covered half of his face.

"Miss Willoughby? I am Jeremiah Cummings, and I am pleased to make your acquaintance."

She bobbed in a motion of a curtsy. "It is my pleasure, Mr. Cummings."

"Will you sit?"

"Thank you."

His tone and manner were extremely courteous, and he put his hand on the back of the chair in a token gesture of seating her. He shot his cuffs from his sleeves as he walked around the side of the desk, and sat down in the chair behind it, picking up a folded letter of several pages and clearing his throat. Her apprehension over what her cousin's response had been returned and intensified as he seemed to hesitate slightly in broaching the matter, turning one of the pages and clearing his throat again. She looked at the desk, keeping her eyes away from his face. There was a stack of gold coins on the desk among the papers, at least fifty guineas and perhaps more. He sat back in his chair, turning another page on the letter. She realized that she was nervously opening and closing her reticule, and she forced herself to hold her hands still.

"Miss Willoughby, Mrs. Garrity has requested that you come to Wayamba Station. Wagons transporting supplies there will leave four days hence, and I will personally speak with the man in charge to assure that you and your belongings will be transported safely and with all possible comfort. Mrs. Garrity had directed me to advance you the sum of sixty guineas against her accounts with this firm so you may discharge any obligations you may have incurred and to purchase any necessities you may require." He put the letter down, picked up the stack of gold coins and leaned over to put them on the edge of the desk, then put a piece of paper, a quill, and an inkpot by the coins. "Will you sign this bill as having received the money, please?"

It had all happened with stunning swiftness. There was no time to ponder and consider alternatives. Her cousin's generosity was overwhelming. Sixty guineas was a small fortune! But she had been given no latitude for decision. Alice hesitated. She cleared her throat and nodded then picked up the quill, dipped the tip in the inkwell, and signed the bill.

– 23 –

All of the man's hair seemed to have slipped down to the
sides of his head. The top of his head was a gleaming,
bright red, and his forehead, cheeks, and nose had the
same ruddy color. The hair came down in a wild, wiry
profusion that hid the lower part of his face and flowed
down onto his shoulders, knotted, uncombed, and
untrimmed. The sleeves on his sweaty, dusty shirt were
rolled up, and he sat with his elbows on the table, holding
a joint of mutton in both hands as he gnawed on it, then
holding it in one hand as he plied a large spoon rapidly
between his trencher and his mouth, shoveling in huge
bites of rice, peas, beans, and potatoes, and quaffing
deep drinks of small beer from an oversize pannikin. And
all the while he was talking to Russell, the head drayman,
who sat across the table from Alice.

But they were kindly, hospitable people. They were crude and inclined to bursts of profanity, but all along the rutted, bumpy road Russel called the track, people had made bed and board available as a matter of course when afternoon had found the wagons near a home paddock.

Not that poor table manners and lack of similar refinements was the rule, because some of the owners of the stations along the road lived and dined in a manner which would do credit to a lord, with good wines and the best of cuisine served by maids and manservants. But the style in which the people lived was apparently a matter of inclination or background rather than of income. A week or so before, they had been served a tasty dish of fowl with good wine from silver plate on a linen tablecloth, and the station and number of sheep had been much smaller than those owned by the man gnawing on the joint of mutton.

Sweat was running down Alice's face and she occasionally waved her hand in a vain attempt to drive the flies off her food. But one never ventured an observation that a host's house was overly warm, even if everyone's face was streaming and one's clothes soaked. And even if one made crunching sounds under foot with every step from the roaches and other vermin on the floor, and windmill one's arms to drive away the flies, it was extremely discourteous to remark on the possible presence of an insect or two. There was also great sensitivity about background, and the thousands of convicts who had been transported had apparently died childless or had been swallowed up by the earth and replaced by early immigrants of unimpeachable respectability. Her origin and accent drew attention from all and subjected her to a kind of analysis to see if she intended to criticize or complain. When she didn't, she was accepted.

Habits of a lifetime had been altered. Alice had been taught that one didn't arrive at another's house unannounced and uninvited, but along the road it was a matter of course to turn into the houses and buildings and stop.

Alice had accepted the practice happily, because nights in the wagon were extremely uncomfortable. The woman at the end of the table opposite the bearded man had been even more friendly and welcoming than most. She was in her forties, about the man's age, and massive in girth, with a round, red face lined from smiling. Her blue eyes constantly twinkled with good humor as she talked with Alice, telling about a distant relative in England in order to establish common ground. The table was large, with places set for several other people, and she talked about her sons who were out in the paddocks. Then she mentioned an unused bedroom which Alice could have for the night and shrugged off Alice's thanks. It was true to form. A bed was always made available for her, even if the owner or some of his children had to sleep in the parlor, and for Russell if there was room in the house. If not, he was always accomodated with his men in one of the barrack buildings for employees on the station.

"Stopping at Wayamba, are you?" the man asked through a mouthful of food, turning his attention to her. "Relative of Elizabeth Garrity's, are you?"

A direct and straightforward probing into one's affairs was also common, the undisguised curiosity a result of loneliness and isolation, and they were always very curious about her because few young unmarried women traveled along the road. "Yes, we are cousins."

The man started to speak again, probed a bit of gristle from between two teeth with a forefinger and threw it on the trencher, then began chewing again. "You've not met her, then?"

"No, we've never met."

"Aye, well, you'll bloody meet someone when you do. Covers more acres with more sheep than one bloody man in ten million can manage, woman or no. Rum old beggar she is and all. Did you hear what she did to Tom Stapleton?"

410

There had been a number of stories about her cousin along the way, and if any part of them were to be believed, her cousin was a mass of contradictions. Alice had heard stories of kindness and revenge, of helping some and killing others. Her cousin had advanced her the princely sum of sixty guineas for incidental expenses, indicating generosity, but when the men had been unloading a wagon stuck in the mud, Russell had stormed at them to be careful with the boxes and barrels because he would be held responsible for the loss or spoilage of a threepenneth of goods, indicating miserliness. And she was a minister's daughter, which seemed to belie many characteristics attributed to her.

"No, I don't believe I'm familiar with the name."

The man grinned widely, taking a drink of beer, and looked at Russell. "Have you?"

"Aye, I heard she shot him."

"Shot him?" the man snorted. "*Shot* him, you say? You've less than half the bloody story, mate. And I had it from Clyde Ayres, who was there when it happened. Shot you say? Not bloody likely, but Stapleton would have gone to his maker grinning if she had, I'll warrant. It's been over twenty years ago that it happened, but it still bears telling. By God, it still bears telling and all. And Clyde Ayres told me exactly what happened with his own mouth."

"Ayres?" Russell asked. "Is that the Ayres who was killed over at Silverton?"

"No, the one killed at Silverton was Charlie, Clyde's brother. And a man hung for that piece of dirt and all, or Clyde would have seen it right, no fear. No, Charlie was a fossicker, but Clyde never could settle for more than three days, even if he had made his campfire on the mother lode. Clyde's been a swagman from all the way back. And he was at Wayamba Station when Elizabeth done Tom Stapleton."

411

"What did she do to him?"

The man gnawed a large bite of mutton off the joint, looking from Russell to Alice, and chewed rapidly and pointed with the mutton for emphasis as he talked. "She made him eat a piece of damper that had a bait of dingo poison in it. Shoved it right down his throat, she did. Then she hung him in her shearing shed before the poison could kill him. Tied a rope around his neck and hung him from a rafter. Then while he was still kicking and choking to death and dying of the poison, she upped with her musket and shot him."

It was far from being the most improbable story she had heard about her cousin. And, happily, she had restrained her humor the first few times she heard such stories, because it had since become evident that the people who told them believed them implicitly. Then, after a time, she began worrying that the stories might be true. Russell listened intently, his mouth open, then he began chewing again. "Killed him proper, didn't she?"

"Killed him?" the man crowed, slapping the table with his hand. "She killed him *three times* before he had a chance to die from the first two! And then she sent to Menindee for the constable while Stapleton was still hanging there. Clyde told me that he stopped to see what was going to happen, because he didn't want to miss that. Well, the constable got there, and he started talking to Elizabeth about the way you'd expect. And she told him she still had some poisoned damper left, another rope, and a change in the other barrel of her musket. So the constable just took what was left of Stapleton and went back to Menindee. And that's nothing against the constable, either, because that was when Sheila and Old Pat Garrity were still alive. Sheila was every bit the brumby that Elizabeth was and is, and Old Pat Garrity was the one who taught them both. So it wasn't that the constable was a coward or didn't do his job. It was just that he wasn't a bloody fool." He took another large bite of the mutton and looked from Alice to Russell again. "So that's how it happened. And he's buried in the churchyard right there in Menindee. I've had fifty people tell me they've seen the grave."

"Aye, it's there," Russell said, nodding. "I've seen it myself."

"Then there you are, then," the man chuckled, nodding emphatically. "And now you know how he got there."

"Jeff, you do go on," the woman chuckled in a chiding tone. "Here this girl hasn't been in New South Wales long enough to get the shine off a new pair of boots on her way to Wayamba Station, and all you can talk about is killing. Elizabeth Garrity is a good woman, and there's God's truth. How about when the Claymores were burned out? Didn't she send them a whole flock for seed as soon as it started raining? And rations to tide them over? And how about when there was that epidemic up at Frome that was so bad that no doctor would come within fifty miles of it? Didn't she track right up there with a bunch of her people and with food and medicine?"

"Well, of course she did, Mae," the man grumbled, spooning food rapidly into his mouth.

"Then talk about things like that, Jeff. Anybody can kill, but there's bloody few who can do some of the good things she has. Or few that will, in any event."

"Aye, aye," the man mumbled, chewing rapidly, and he looked back at Alice. "How do you come to be going to Wayamba?"

The reply had been formulated while in Sydney as a response which revealed little, wasn't untruthful, and ended questions. "I came to Sydney to a position which I found was no longer available when I arrived. When I communicated with my cousin through her factor in Sydney, she invited me to come to her station. And Mr. Russell very kindly agreed to transport me there."

The man looked at Russell in surprise. "You wanted to?"

413

"That's her way of speaking," Russell chuckled. "But she's little enough pother for a doxie and a pommie. There's more sand in her than you can tell by looking at her. She can abide, and if she spends a few years in the Outback, you might be able to tell she's kin to Elizabeth Garrity without asking her."

Alice flushed at the compliment and looked down at her plate and took another bite as they looked at her. The hardships had been grueling, and it had come as a shock that Russell and his men endured such conditions as a matter of course. There were flies, mosquitoes, dust storms, heavy downpours of rain, places where the road turned into a sea of mud, dry, sandy stretches where no water was available, and the constant danger of being caught in a grass fire. But Russell had done his best to make her comfortable, and she had determined from the beginning to be as little of a burden as possible.

"I'll warrant you have a chore in keeping your bullockies in hand around her, as fair as she is," the woman chuckled.

"She's kin to Elizabeth Garrity, and she makes no display of herself," Russell replied, shaking his head.

"She has no need to display herself," the woman said, smiling warmly at Alice. "She is a comely bit and all. And a trek must be a sore trial for such a gentle girl. You could stop here if you had a mind to, love."

"And have Elizabeth Garrity collaring me at Wayamba?" Russell asked. "You leave her be!"

"Aye, and I'd never get my boys into the paddocks again," the man laughed.

"Some hopes," the woman snorted. "Slower sods never lived, unless it was the one who got them." She looked at Alice, her eyes twinkling. "It took my dad and three of my brothers to get him into church with me. There are a lot of men in the Outback that don't even think about getting married, you know. From the time they're born until the time they die, all they think of is bloody sheep."

"Aye, that's true," the man nodded, shoveling food into his mouth again, then he looked at Alice, chewing. "Does Elizabeth have you in mind as a wife for one of her boys?"

Alice started to shake her head firmly, then she hesitated and thought again. She had regarded her going to Wayamba Station as simply seeking the assistance of a relative, but her cousin might indeed have some ulterior motive. Others had mentioned that her cousin had three unmarried sons. And from comments of still others, there was no need for a school mistress at Wayamba Station. She cleared her throat and shrugged unsurely. "Well, it certainly isn't my intention to—"

"Oh, bloody hell, Jeff," the woman sighed. "See how you've plagued her? Just because you don't have a relative who'd give you the salt to put on a pickle doesn't mean that everyone else is the same. Didn't she just tell you that she didn't have work in Sydney? And do you think Elizabeth Garrity would let her own cousin starve and go without a roof over her head? Beyond that, Elizabeth Garrity doesn't have to hunt for wives for her sons, because every squatter within a hundred miles of Wayamba who has a daughter is doing it for her."

"All I did was ask," the man grumbled, gnawing on the joint again.

"And all the brains you have would rattle around in a parrot's head," the woman retorted. "Her youngest is too young to be married anyway. The next can't be more than twenty-one, and her oldest is no more than twenty-two or so. So even if they're not as slow as our mob and they were thinking of getting married, they're in no hurry at their age." She looked at Alice with a smile and glanced at her plate. "Here, take some more peas and rice, love."

Alice smiled and nodded her thanks, taking the bowls and putting another spoonful of each on her plate. She passed them across the table to Russell. The woman's remarks on the ages of the three unmarried sons had resolved her sudden concern about her cousin's motives.

415

She was twenty-three, and it was highly unusual for a woman to be the older of a married couple, even by as much as a year.

The food was delicious, the mutton tender and well seasoned with pepper and curry, and the side dishes were tasty and spicy. The flies unfortunately became embedded in the food, as usual, and she tried to keep from being too obvious about it as she scraped them from the food and into a neat pile on the edge of her plate with her fork. Her squeamishness had been more pronounced during the first days of the trek, and she had been reluctant to eat fly-infested food. But it had been overcome by hunger, and now she was content as long as she could keep from eating the flies.

The woman rose from the table and went into the kitchen for dessert. Alice helped her carry it back in. It was a heavy fruit pudding with mugs of strong tea, servings as abundant as the main course, and Alice was uncomfortably full. The beer had been homemade, powerful for small beer, and between the heat, the beer, and the heavy food, she became drowsy as she forced down her pudding and sipped her tea, listening to the conversation.

The sun set as they finished eating. The two men went into the parlor with their pipes and fresh mugs of tea, and Alice helped the woman clear off the table and wash the dishes. The sudden change from heat to an uncomfortably cool temperature began as soon as the sun went down. and the lingering warmth of the stove in the kitchen was welcome as a chilly night breeze blew through the window. The lamp drew flies and mosquitoes, but it cast a yellow, cheerful light and gave the room a comfortable, home-like atmosphere.

Alice collected her nightgown and other belongings, and the woman accompanied her to the back porch with a lamp, checking to make sure no snakes or opossums were lurking about, then took the lamp back in. Alice undressed on the porch in the darkness and dipped water out of the large tub and poured it over herself, shivering in the chilly air as the water ran through the cracks in the floor and splashed to the ground below. She hastily dried, put on her nightgown and gathered up her clothes, and went back inside. The woman was waiting in the kitchen for her, and she showed Alice to her bedroom, clucking over her with a fussy, motherly air as she got settled in bed.

The days began early. Alice heard a stir in the house and the yellow light of a lamp came through the crack around the door well before dawn. The men murmured drowsily to each other and scratched as they stood in the kitchen gulping hot tea and chewing leftovers from dinner the night before. The woman's smiling face was puffy with sleep, and the air was still chilly and alive with the constant din of insects and night birds outside. Alice burned her mouth with hot tea and choked down some cold potatoes and mutton, then hastily gathered up her things. The road in front of the house bustled in the darkness with the clank of harness, stamping of horses, und the men's sleepy, irritable cursing. Russell and the station owner disappeared into the darkness, and the woman walked along the line of wagons with Alice, holding her arm and exchanging a last few words with her as they dodged wheeling teams of horses and searched for the wagon in which Alice rode. When they found it, the woman pressed a greasy canvas bag of leftover pudding into her hands and hugged and kissed her with the sudden fierce affection of strangers met along the way, a poignant, wrenching stab of feeling which Alice had never experienced in Wexford and which brought stinging tears to her eyes. She hugged and kissed the woman and climbed the wheel over the side of the wagon bed to the seat. The woman stood near the wagon, a thicker shadow in the darkness. The activity along the road diminished then increased again with a different character, hoarse shouts ringing out, whips cracking and wheels squeaking and rumbling. The woman waved in the darkness and her voice was thick as she called out, and Alice waved and swallowed before she answered so her voice would not quaver. The driver leaped onto the other side of the seat, cracking his whip and shouting, and the wagon jerked and moved forward. The woman walked along the side of the wagon until she was lost in the darkness and her voice was drowned in the clanking and rattling of the wagon.

A glow of red touched the horizon in the east, and rosy light illuminated the fences as they passed the last of the buildings and rumbled along at the pace they would maintain during the day. Daylight came, and Alice stopped shivering, savoring the cool temperature before the heat of the day.

What had happened to her in Sydney would no doubt cause derisive laughter in Wexford, but her adventures since would undoubtedly stimulate fascination. Each day had its discomforts, but also its excitement. She was in a different world, endlessly vast, a moving vista of deep forests, arid deserts, and broad plains, all of the vegetation different from any she had seen before. The trees in the forests seethed with brilliantly-colored, raucously loud birds, kangaroos bounded and emus raced through the brush, and the deserts were lifeless in their burning heat. Choking dust storms filled the air with clouds which obscured the horses in front of the wagons, and the rains were deluges which soaked clothes through to the skin within seconds. She had adapted, reducing her underclothing to the minimum necessary for decency and tying her hair back out of the way so it would be less uncomfortable as it collected dust and became dirtier. She endured, waiting through the long, hot days for the cool of evening and scratching insect bites as she watched out for snakes. And she enjoyed it.

The stations became larger, taking many days to traverse, and the wide disparity in lifestyle continued.

More of the people were of mixed blood, and some of the stations were staffed by managers rather than owners. The women on the stations were widely disparate, at one time dressed in the latest English equestrienne fashions and riding splendid show horses to entertain themselves and the male members of their families while practicing for competitions held at some of the stations, and at other times working as stockmen and dressed in the same type of clothing as their brothers. Their interests were those of women in Wexford, and they frequently kept Alice up at night to discuss fashions, or to ask her about social life in England, and to talk about the parties and fairs that were periodically held at some stations and settlements. But their objectives were different than those of other women Alice had known, many of them having a lackadaisical or even a disparaging attitude toward marriage in general and motivated toward marriage only when they met a man they loved deeply. Their independence of attitude reduced their fathers' control over them to the point that the fathers sometimes went to unusual lengths to exert authority.

At one station where there were four daughters and a single son, the owner locked one of his daughters in a shed to persuade her to marry a man who had agreed to establish his household at the station and work there if she would marry him. There was a remarkable lack of rancor in the situation. The father bore his daughter no ill will, but simply wanted her to marry the man. The daughter felt no animosity toward her father for locking her up, but she had no intention of marrying the man. Alice sat with the mother and the other three daughters on a bench outside the shed, conversing between themselves and with the woman locked in the shed. The woman's voice from the shed sounded hollow and muffled as she participated in the conversation. Alice expressed a polite interest in how long the confinement might be expected to continue, and it was the consensus that the daughter would be

needed for shearing and her father would have to release
her at that time. The woman in the shed seemed confident
that she could endure the confinement that long.

The season slowly changed, the intensity of burning
heat fading into the softer warmth of autumn. Then it
rained for several days, and they arrived at the Darling
River. It was flooded, but an enterprising man had built a
large raft at the crossing to ferry animals and wagons.
Russell spent most of an afternoon and late into the night
haggling with the owner of the raft, and the next morning
they began crossing, the raft taking a load of horses then
coming across with a single wagon on each trip. It took
most of the day to get all the horses and wagons across,
and they moved along the muddy road for a short
distance and camped again.

Crossing the boundary of Wayamba Station was an
anticlimax. Whoops rang out along the line and whips
cracked. The wagons moved along at a smart pace
through a wide gate in a fence, then trudged along again.
The days followed each other as before. Some were cool,
and Alice sat with a blanket around her as the wagon
rumbled along. They went through another gate and into
another paddock, and the second day they were crossing
it Alice saw a flock of sheep several times as large as any of
the others she had seen, a sea of the wooly animals flowing
over irregularities in the ground and rippling around the
wagons as they went through the mass. Two men
following the sheep on horses waved at the drivers as they
passed. That night they camped at a bore, a well which
had been drilled into the ground to tap underground
reservoirs of water.

They went through other gates and though other
paddocks, and the conversation among the men began to
concentrate on when they would arrive. Some of the men
argued about it and others made wagers, then a concensus
began to develop among most of them when they were
about a week's travel away. The days seemed to pass more

slowly, and Alice felt something approaching regret that the trip was ending, a reluctance to discover what might disappoint her and an unwillingness to end the major adventure of her life. But the days passed, and little else but the station was discussed among the men. Then the last day arrived, and the wagons moved up a long, gradual swell in the land and started down the other side. The driver pointed, and she looked into the distance, seeing the fine, dark line of another fence and a blur of buildings beyond it.

The wagons went through the last gate, and even the horses seemed to sense that they had arrived at their destination. They began trotting heavily as the men cracked their whips and shouted. Three men rode out from the buildings, waving and shouting, and they galloped their horses around the wagons, passing the one in which Alice rode and looking at her curiously. Dust boiled up as the wagons went through a wide passageway through a maze of pens, and it billowed thicker as the wagons rumbled into the midst of the buildings. Dogs raced about and barked, adding to the uproar, and several aborigines ran along at the sides of the wagons, hooting and waving their arms. Men standing about waved and shouted. Alice gripped the edge of the seat as the wagon careened along, trying to see through the dust. Then the wagons began circling and slowing, and came to a stop by a long, low building.

The drivers leaped down from their wagons, laughing, shouting, and greeting the men gathering around, shaking hands and slapping shoulders. Alice climbed down, tentatively looking around. The sprawling maze of pens was massive compared to other stations, and more and larger buildings than at other stations, but size and number seemed to be the only difference. She saw bare, dusty ground, dark, unpainted wood, and rusty sheet metal. Then she turned and saw the thick greenery of tall trees over the top of the wagon. She walked around the wagon, dusting her dress and patting her hair, then stopped and gasped with delight. On the other side of a road at the edge of the bare, trampled area was a scene of stunning pastoral beauty.

Trees towered into the sky to a dizzying height, and below them there were clustered smaller trees. There was a large house with a wide veranda and three smaller ones, trees clustered around all of them and wide sweeps of greenery between them. The verandas had climbing vines hanging around them in thick mats, and vines almost completely hid the row of large metal water tanks beside the large house. The decayed remains of a row of smaller wooden water tanks were thick with vines, and between the large house and the adjacent one were beds of flowers and shrubbery around a small cemetery. It was beautiful, quiet and peaceful-looking, and the hint of wild, uncontrolled growth of foliage added a unique charm.

Then Alice saw her, coming along the path from the large house toward the road, an old woman, dressed in grey broadcloth of an old-fashioned cut, her grey hair pulled into a tight knot at the back, and leaning heavily on a cane as she walked. Her pace was dignified, she walked with her chin up, and her mouth was set in a hard, straight line. The men fell silent as Alice walked toward her. Her face was heavily lined and wrinkled, leathery from the sun and wind, and there was a haughty set to her features. The steely blue eyes fastened on Alice, and their gaze was like a physical force. Alice suddenly felt very much in awe of her. She was like a monarch among her subjects, and the role fit her well. She stopped on the road, leaning on her cane and waiting. Alice stopped a few feet from her and dropped a curtsy.

"Madame, I am Alice Willoughby, and I beg to express my grateful appreciation for your kind offer of hospitality for me in my need."

Elizabeth's eyes moved over Alice for a long second,

studying her, then she smiled slightly and her eyes warmed as she moved forward and put her hand on Alice's shoulder. "Aye, a pretty speech, from a pretty girl. And you are very lovely—very lovely indeed. Welcome to Wayamba Station, my dear. I'll call you Alice, and you may call me Elizabeth." She patted Alice's shoulder, her smile widening, then fading as she looked toward the wagons. "Dennis! Step over here and meet your cousin! Russell, did you steal me blind this time?"

Russell laughed heartily as he and another man walked toward them. "I'll not steal from you until Saint Geoffrey's Day, Mrs. Garrity. Are you all right?"

"I'm bloody here, and that's far more than many of my years can say. Are you?"

"Aye, I am now."

He and the other man approached, and Alice noted that the man her cousin had called Dennis was large and sturdy but looked younger than his years and somewhat younger than she. He also looked withdrawn and sullen, as though angry about something, and Alice received the distinct impression that he and the old woman were having an on-going argument about something. The old woman looked at him with undisguised irritation as he responded to the introduction with stiffly formal courtesy, then she took Alice's arm and turned toward the house.

"Come on, then, Alice. Russell, have her things brought in. You'll sup with us?"

"Aye, I will, Mrs. Garrity, and I thank you."

"If you'll clean yourself up before you come to my table, I'll thank you. Dennis, take his tally and I'll make out the draft on the bank. And see his men to a barrack and his stock to fodder and water."

The men nodded and turned back toward the wagons as Alice and her cousin crossed the road to the path to the house. "You have a very beautiful home here, Elizabeth."

"Aye, it'll do. Give no mind to that sod Dennis. He's

usually not so flaming dark, but he has his wind up just now."

"I'm sure he meant no discourtesy, and I'm not—"

"You'll find out directly, so I'll tell you now what it is. My boy Earl got killed down at Melbourne not a month gone. He never was much of a stockman, forever wandering around like a bloody swagman, then he got down there and fell in with some bloody bad mob and got his arse killed. And that Dennis there and his brother Colin were rolling their swag to go down there and see it right as soon as they heard about it, but for my part they were going for more of the same. So I told them they'd either stay or they'd die from my own hand. They stayed, but we've been at it tooth and nail since."

"Well, I'm sorry to hear that your son met with a—"

"Aye, well, it's bloody done, isn't it? And there's no mending that."

Her tone ended the conversation on the subject. They walked along the path in silence and started up the steps. She glanced at Elizabeth, slowing her pace to walk beside the old woman as she went up one step at a time, leaning heavily on her cane. Elizabeth's face was slightly averted, her attention on the steps but her mind far away. The lines and wrinkles on her face reflected grief. Fresh sorrow was added to the old represented by the stones in the small cemetery, and the mention of it had brought back upon a heart already overburdened the agony of a mother whose child is dead, the pain and conflict of battling with her other children to defend them. It was an excruciating weight borne alone and unshared. They reached the top of the steps, and Alice put her hand on the old woman's arm and stopped her as they started across the veranda.

"I wish there were something I could do to help. I truly wish there were."

Elizabeth's expression was inscrutable, the sparkling blue eyes like ice. Then there was a subtle alteration in the lines of her face, a softening, the hard blue eyes suddenly became misty, and her lips trembled slightly. She turned her face and looked away toward the buildings, sighing as she blinked her eyes rapidly, then she looked back at Alice. "A pretty face and a heart as well?" she murmured, smiling slightly. "There's a rare bloody combination. And if you've sand to go with it, it'll be even more rare. And then most rare of all, there might even be a brain behind those pretty eyes." She looked away and sighed again, then pursed her lips and slowly nodded. "Aye, I hurt for him. I've cut him out of my heart, and there's a great, bloody hole left in his stead. And if pain were tears, I'd have every ditch on Wayamba Station running a bloody banker, no fear."

"I know it must be agonizing for you. I've never been in anything approaching this situation, but perhaps it would be better to dwell on the happy times you had with him."

The old woman shook her head. "He was a bloody lout. I loved him because he was my son, but he was a worthless sod. And his dad would have killed him if he hadn't died before he found out what he was. But I got two good ones out of the three, so I did as well as most and better than some." She looked back at Alice and studied her face with a thoughtful expression, then smiled slightly as she lifted her hand and touched Alice's cheek with the tips of her fingers. "I was a pretty girl once, you know. And with a heart, so that I loved those around me. And the land. I have a brain too, and I grew me some sand. The heart, the brain, and the sand. It takes all three. Last year we had a bloody big fire in Windorah Paddock, and it got across Landers Creek on them. So I told Dennis to back fire all the way across Windorah." Her eyes misted again, and her lips trembled as she dropped her hand and looked away. "Aye, I told them to burn Windorah, and my sixteen thousand sheep I had there. Do you know what that cost me? No bloody bank can count that high. I bloody burned with them, that's what it cost me. But if the

425

wind had raised, Wayamba Station would have been one great, bloody cinder. So I lost my sixteen thousand sheep, but it could be that I saved Wayamba Station. It takes the brain to say what to do, the sand to go ahead and do it, and the heart to hurt over it when it's done." She looked solemnly at Alice, then smiled brightly. "Does an old woman's prattle mean anything to you? Well, we'll see if it does in time. As far as helping, you've helped already, Alice. Come, and I'll show you your home."

Alice worked on the station accounts, talking with
Elizabeth and poring over the yellowed pages covered
with neat, faded rows of figures from past years to
familiarize herself with how it was done, then she took
them over entirely. The accounts took only a portion of
her time, and she walked along the creek, explored the
buildings and learned their purposes, and pruned the
vines around the houses and the flower beds near the
cemetery so they would flourish when spring came. And
she studied the gravestones.

The names recorded there were a roll of the history of
the station, members of the Garrity family, aborigines,
employees, and swagmen who had died on the station.
Patrick and Mayrah Garrity were buried in adjacent

graves, their stones weathered and mossy. Sheila Garrity lay beside them, and there was a vacant space by Colin Garrity's grave. Earl Garrity's grave was fresh, and it was by that of Frank Garrity, an old one. Frank Cummings was buried in a corner of the cemetery. The grave of Infant Cummings was among the others. The aborigines were distinguished by a single name on the gravestones; Doolibah, Bahal, Narine, and others.

The old woman was about the place all the time, in and out of buildings, at the pens, talking to men, and examining stock. She and Alice were together much of the time and developed a warm friendship, and occasionally Alice contemplated some of the stories she had heard and thought about asking her about them. But Elizabeth could be irritable and had a fiery temper, and there was always an air of reserve about her which precluded unlimited intimacy. Alice decided that she didn't really want to know. She began to regard the station with an attitude of permanence, as her home, and she wrote to her father, mother, and uncle, relating the events which had led up to her coming to the station and describing it in glowing terms.

Three of the married stockmen lived with their wives in the three smaller houses, and one of the wives did the cooking and washing in the Garrity house. The three were amiable toward Alice and stopped to chat with her frequently when they passed, but they preferred the company of each other and regarded Alice with something of the same distant respect they had toward her cousin. The companionship at the station amounted to virtual isolation compared to the number of friends and acquaintances she'd had in Wexford, but she was contented.

The old woman had a watchful attitude toward Alice during her first weeks on the station, leaving her to her own devices but observing what she was doing with interest, and she was highly gratified when Alice

428

expressed a desire to learn to ride. "Aye, there's more sense in that than in mucking about out there around the graves so that a snake might run up your leg and bite you on your bandicoot."

"Elizabeth! Must you be so crude?"

"Crude is as crude bloody does. And a snakebite on the bandicoot would bring a tear to any eye. Not that we'd have any shortage of doctors who'd be willing to take care of you for something like that, or I'll miss my bloody guess."

Alice had intended riding sidesaddle, but there wasn't a sidesaddle on the station. The old woman rummaged around in one of the unused rooms in the rear of the house and found shirts and trousers of strong, heavy muslin which were years old and bleached and soft from many washings, a new hat with a crown large enough to hold Alice's hair pushed up under it, pairs of heavy socks in her size, and a pair of old-fashioned men's boots which were exceptionally small and dark with age and the thick coating of preservative tallow.

The old woman held the boots with a loving, almost reverential attitude as she cleaned them, telling Alice that they had belonged to Sheila Garrity when she had been a girl. Alice was surprised at the age of the boots, and at the way some things on the station were preserved with great care, things which might be thrown away elsewhere. She was also flattered that the old woman would let her wear boots which had once belonged to Sheila Garrity, because the old woman spoke of her extremely affectionately and at great length, even more often than she talked about her husband. And Elizabeth was highly pleased that the boots fit Alice well.

The weather had turned colder, and the old woman found a thick sheepskin coat for her to wear as she rode around the home paddock and explored further afield on horseback. Riding as an end in itself lost its novelty after she became accustomed to it. The work around the pens was at a relatively low level of activity, with a routine doseage for worms being administered to several thousand sheep, and some of the men let her help them move sheep between the pens and taught her how to control the dogs. She discovered something of a natural aptitude for it in herself, rapidly learning how to spot the surge of a break in a flock of sheep and sending a dog to block it, and she enjoyed it. Elizabeth frequently happened by and watched her, and Alice basked with pleasure in the old woman's warm regard.

A flock had to be driven to a near paddock to the east and another brought back for the worm medication, and Elizabeth sent Alice with Colin. The game-like atmosphere of working around the pens was gone and it was suddenly a serious undertaking with frigid wind whipping across the lonely stretches of grass and brush as she huddled in her sheepskin coat on the horse during the day and shivered in her blanket by the fire at night, but she enjoyed it even more. Colin was barely more than a boy, but he was in his element, and she learned from him. He began teaching her how to use a whip and let her take the flock ahead while he ranged to the sides for strays which had scattered from the main flocks, leaving her with the flock during the morning and returning in the afternoon to find a place to camp. The strained atmosphere between him, his brother and their mother remained, with both boys treating their mother with a formal courtesy. Alice subtly drew Colin out on the subject as they talked over the campfire at night. She found that Dennis was the instigator and Colin automatically followed his older brother's lead.

The time when her grooming had been a primary concern to her seemed in the far distant past, and when the home paddock came into sight again, she was sooty from campfire smoke, grimy with wind-blown dust, and sweaty and disheveled from sleeping in her clothes, her hat jammed down on her head and her hair an untidy mass inside it, her collar pulled up over her face and her shining eyes peering over the edge of it. She was supremely happy, with a deeply gratifying sense of accomplishment. The old woman was coming from one of the buildings to the house as Alice and Colin neared the pens, and she saw them and turned back to limp slowly along on her cane toward the pens, bundled in her long, heavy sheepskin coat. She stood by the side of the gate as Alice and Colin drove the flock in, and she and Alice beamed at each other.

Dennis was out in the paddocks, and Alice chatted happily with Elizabeth over dinner as the three of them ate. But her happiness was clouded by the pain in the old woman's eyes when Colin finished eating, rose from the table and left without saying anything. The following day, Alice and Colin separated another flock of sheep and drove them into a pen, and on the next day they left with them.

When they returned, Dennis was at the home paddock. Alice took her equipment and blanket roll to the house, put her saddle away and turned her horse into the stockyard, then went around to the other side of the pens, where Dennis was working with some other men. He looked up and smiled and nodded to her as she approached.

"Are you all right, Alice? You're coming along, aren't you?"

"I hope so. I'll talk to you for a moment, if you have time."

He nodded, turning away from the men, and followed her along the side of the pens. "That Colin hasn't been frisky, has he?"

She laughed and shook her head. "He wouldn't know how." She stopped and turned to face him, her smile fading. "It's about your mother, Dennis. This can't go on."

His smile abruptly disappeared, his youthful features

becoming hard and cold. "This is none of your flock, Alice. And not because I don't regard you as one of the family, because I do. But I'd say the same to Colin. Or to Earl, if he were alive so I could. Which he isn't, by God."

Alice sighed. She was tired, and she suddenly felt like an adult dealing with a small, stubborn child. "Dennis, this is a matter between human beings, and I'm a human being. Now you can't—"

"No, I won't listen to it," he said brusquely, turning away. "If that's all you have to talk about, then we've naught to say to each other."

"Stay!" she snapped, her temper suddenly flaring. "We've a lot to say—" She broke off, lifting her hand and shaking her head. "No, this won't do. If I start shouting, then you won't listen. And even though I want to shout, I want more for you to listen to me."

"There's nothing you can say or do to make me change my mind," he said, starting to move away. "There's naught no one could say or do."

"Then listen to this," she said, taking a quick step and catching his sleeve. She pointed toward the graveyard. "Soon enough, there'll be another stone there, right by your father's. And all I could do and every other person on this station could do will be nothing to what you'll be doing to yourself. Now you think about that. Dennis, you've a man's stature and you fill a man's job, but you've a long way to go before you have a man's mind. And if you ever do, you'll be thanking your mother for what she did. Then you can go over there and thank a gravestone. And you can see if it'll smile and answer you back. Now you just think on that, Dennis!"

She whirled away from him and stamped toward the house, fuming with anger. He made a movement to stop her, then began walking slowly back toward the men. When Alice got to the house, the old woman was working on the accounts, sitting at the desk in the parlor and blinking at the sheets of paper through the thick lenses of her glasses. She put her quill aside and went with Alice into the kitchen to make tea, chatting with her about her trip into the paddocks.

They sat and talked for a time, then Elizabeth returned to the parlor and Alice went out on the back porch, broke the thin film of ice on the tub of water and washed, and went to her room. She started to put on a dress, then changed her mind and put on clean trousers and a shirt and joined Elizabeth in the parlor. The old woman was working on the accounts again, and Alice went to the kitchen and brought in more tea and helped her until it was time for dinner.

They went in and sat down at the table. Dennis and Colin entered the dining room, and Alice looked up at them, trying to catch Dennis' eye, but he was looking at his mother as he came in. He walked around the table to Elizabeth, bent over her chair and kissed her.

"I'm sorry, Ma."

A radiant smile spread across her face as she looked up at him, and she pulled him back down and kissed his cheek. "If there's cause to be sorry, then I am too, Dennis."

Colin came around the other side of her chair, bending over and kissing her. "And I'm sorry too, Ma."

Her face was wreathed in a smile, and she pulled Colin down to kiss him. "And the same for you, Colin. Now you lads sit down and eat."

Alice looked from Dennis to Colin, smiling warmly. Colin grinned, and Dennis smiled sheepishly, dropping his eyes. They sat down, and the old woman suddenly put her hands over her face and burst into tears. Dennis looked at her, appalled, knocking his chair over as he sprang up. He went to her and bent over her, putting his arms around her. Colin ran around to the other side and leaned over and embraced her. She tried to control her tears, shaking her head rapidly and pushing at her sons as she attempted to speak, then began sobbing harder.

433

Colin's lips trembled, and tears ran down his cheeks, and Dennis was on the point of tears as well as he tried to calm his mother. As Alice looked at them, tears streamed down her cheeks.

It cleared the atmosphere far more than the apology had, and there was a warm, loving feeling in the room over dinner. The conversation around the table before had been stilted, consisting of instructions from the old woman and silent nods or terse questions from her sons, and now Alice saw them as a family for the first time. They laughed and joked, and they reminisced. They told anecdotes and laughed about events from years past. Then Dennis mentioned what a swagman had told him about a railroad being built from some other point to Broken Hill, and Alice started to cringe. In working with the station accounts, she had come upon references to a large bank account belonging to the station which came from mineral shares mining companies at Broken Hill, and her questions about it had brought only outbursts of rage and streams of profanity from the old woman. Eventually Alice had connected together enough out of what the old woman said to conclude that the government had given mining companies enormous tracts of land from the southern paddocks of the station. She had found out that the land given to the mining companies was measured in feet rather than acres.

But what Dennis said didn't provoke the old woman. He mentioned a James Garrity, the old woman's nephew who was building the railroad, and that the line would be finished some time during the summer. The old woman seemed greatly pleased by the news.

Elizabeth and Alice sat at the table and finished their tea after Dennis and Colin left the table to go to bed. They talked about the sheep for a few minutes, then they became silent, sipping their tea and musing. Presently the old woman looked at Alice again with a thoughtful smile. "You talked to Dennis, didn't you?"

Alice shrugged and nodded. "It was in his mind all the while. I only helped him find it."

The old woman chuckled and shook her head. "None of your sly talk with me, you little sod, because I'm not bloody Dennis. But it pleases me. In its own way, it pleases me as much as making up with my sons."

"What pleases you?"

The old woman reached for her cane, pushed her chair back and stood, and moved around the table to Alice's chair. She patted Alice's shoulder and leaned down stiffly to kiss her cheek. "To see that you're a sly little wench. And there's nothing wrong with that, because there are sufficient thick bloody men in the world that we need a few sly wenches to keep them from pulling it down about our ears." She turned away from Alice's chair and moved toward the door. "But always use it wisely, Alice." She hesitated in the doorway and smiled at her, then turned into the hall toward her room. "Always use it wisely," she repeated, her voice fading as she moved along the hall.

The weather began to moderate, warmer days alternating with periods of continued cold. Elizabeth gave Alice one of the heavy, single shot rifles from the storeroom and showed her how to use it, and Alice went out along the creek and practiced until she was familiar with it. Then she took a flock out by herself, driving it to the near quadrant of a paddock to the north, and brought another flock back. She caught a severe head cold and the old woman kept her at the home paddock for a few days, then she took out another flock by herself.

Alice received letters from home, expressions of surprise at what had happened and hopes that she was doing well from her parents, and an offer of money for her return passage from her uncle. The letters recalled a way of life which seemed very distant to her, and the phraseology and the meaning behind what was written brought back memories of a time which had been claustrophobically restricted. She answered the letters, writing about the station, what she had been doing, and about Elizabeth and her sons. The old woman had encouraged her several times to use the station accounts for anything she wanted to buy, telling her that she was earning far more than a stockman and spending nothing, and she cheerfully assented when Alice asked her for a draft to repay her uncle for the money he had spent for her passage to Australia.

Spring came, and Alice found the tailing distasteful and the mulsing revolting, but she became inured to it. Then the old woman became ill, having fainting and dizzy spells, and Alice remained at home with her. She changed back into her dresses, took care of the accounts, and spent a lot of time with her cousin, talking to her. The subject of Elizabeth's age came up, and Alice was surprised to learn that the old woman was hardly more than fifty, prematurely aged by hardship, toil, and worry. Elizabeth gradually improved as the weather became warmer, and most of the mulsed and tailed sheep had been driven out to the paddocks by the time she was well enough to remain alone again. Alice took a single flock out, then worked in the pens again when she returned.

Swagmen coming along the track from the south brought news of the railroad which was being built, and the old woman showed a continuing interest in it. There was some conflict in stories, and when the stockman from Wayamba Paddock was replaced by another man, Elizabeth summoned him to the house to talk with him about it. The stockman agreed with what some swagmen had told her, that the railroad would be completed in late November, and the old woman began to make preparations to send for her nephew, having the housekeeper prepare a bedroom for him and making sure that Colin was on hand to fetch him. Then all the swagmen coming along the track began relating the same story, that the first train would run from Cockburn to Broken Hill on November 28th.

Some of the stockmen to the north needed supplies and there had been an understanding that Alice would take them, but the supply wagons arrived during the third week of November, much later than had been expected, and Elizabeth told Alice that she wanted her there when her nephew arrived. It was something of a disappointment and a puzzle, but Alice agreed without arguing about it. Then the end of November approached, and Colin left with two good horses. The old woman's fondness for James Garrity had been abundantly clear when she talked about him, regarding him with an affection which matched her feeling for her own sons. She told Alice about teaching him as a child, and of his education as an engineer in Sydney, and she had talked about the things he had done on the station, designing the metal water tanks and a pump to fill them when the creek was flooded, and the bores he had drilled for water for the sheep and cattle, and she continued to rattle on to Alice as she limped about on her cane, excited by his imminent arrival and going in to check his room time after time.

Elizabeth woke Alice early on the day he was to arrive, and asked her to put on one of her brightly-colored dresses. The suspicion had dawned on Alice that the old woman was engaging in matchmaking, and she shrugged it off with a nonchalant expression when Alice asked her about it, telling Alice that it wouldn't displease her if she and James Garrity found each other congenial. Alice felt that the reply was understated, but she prepared herself to please the old woman, putting on a crinoline, a pale green broadcloth dress, and combing out her hair and tying it up with green ribbons.

Alice was in the parlor looking through the lists for the last delivery of supplies when she heard the horses come along the road and stop in front of the house. There was a murmur of men's voices, one of them Colin's and the other a deeper voice, and the horses moved away at a walk. She put the lists down on the desk and walked toward the kitchen to find Elizabeth. The old woman wasn't in the kitchen, and she walked back toward the hall to check in her room. The thump of footsteps crossed the veranda, and she hesitated and turned toward the door as it opened.

James was an extremely handsome man, not as tall as Dennis or Colin, and more slender. There were traces of aborigine blood in the shape of his forehead and eyes and in an olive tinge to his skin, and his eyes were large, deep blue, and with long lashes, almost beautiful eyes. He had a quiet, studious look about him, and was dressed in a neat wool suit, vest, and tie. There was an air of solid dependability about him, of seasoned judgement and a maturity which went beyond his years. He appeared to be in his thirties, though there was a touch of grey in his dark brown hair.

There was a wide smile of greeting on his face, which faded into an expression of stunned astonishment as he looked at her. Then it disappeared as he effortlessly brought his expression under control, and smiled politely as he put his portmanteau down and bowed slightly. "Miss Willoughby? I am your servant, James Garrity."

Admiration and interest gleamed open and unabashed in his eyes. She bobbed in a perfunctory curtsy. "I am pleased to make your acquaintance, Mr. Garrity. And I trust I didn't startle you."

"Not you, Miss Willoughby. It was that confounded Colin who startled me. He said you were attractive, which is to say the sun gives light. Colin is more capable in judging the points of sheep, it appears."

"La, la, Mr. Garrity, such a pretty speech. From what your aunt has told me and from what I hear myself, you are a man of unlimited parts."

His smile was wide and natural as he shook his head. "No, I'm not given to pretty speeching, Miss Willoughby. But you would inspire a post to poetry."

Her cheeks were starting to tingle and her smile was

about to slip from her control, and she breathed a sigh of relief as Elizabeth rushed into the room from the hallway. "James! James! Come here and kiss me, you young rogue! What have you been doing with yourself?"

He embraced her and kissed her fondly, then held her as he looked at her. "You haven't altered, Elizabeth. You look the same as when you were scolding me for not doing my sums properly."

"And you haven't altered," she chuckled. "You're still a bloody liar. Have you met Alice, then?"

"Aye, Miss Willoughby and I were just—"

"Miss Willoughby, you say? There'll be bloody none of that here. Her name is Alice and yours is James, and there's the end of it. Here, let's sit down, if you can see for that bloody big grin you have on your face. Come on and sit down with us, Alice."

"I'll see to tea, if you like, Elizabeth."

"Aye, do that, then. And hurry back in here, because I don't want him boring holes in my walls with his gimblets."

Alice turned and walked toward the kitchen, gathering her skirt to go through the doorway. She could feel his eyes on her, and she stepped out of sight into the kitchen and put her hands to her cheeks, drawing in a deep breath and trying to control her flush.

She had herself under firm control again as she came back in with the tray and put it on the table. His warm smile brought only a polite smile in response, and she poured the tea with a steady hand, passed their cups to them, then sat down with her cup, sipping it and listening to them. Colin came in, did an open-mouthed doubletake at her dress, then recovered and grinned at James as he crossed the room to sit down. Alice rose and got another cup for Colin, then one for Dennis as he came in, rushing across the room to James with his hand extended as he greeted him. She filled the cups with tea and handed them to Dennis and Colin, then sat down again. James brushed off the questions about the railroad and began asking her about Wexford.

He was a thoughtful, sensitive man rather than an aggressive one, but there was an unassuming determination toward her in his manner. He courted her, offering to take her to the adjacent stations to meet neighboring women, and to take her to a stage show scheduled to be presented in Menindee. She declined because she had no particular desire to go, but she didn't reject his suit. Nor did she encourage it. She found him attractive and there were stirrings of affection which could turn into deeper emotions, but the situation was complicated by the fact that she was already in love. She found that she had come to love Wayamba Station.

Elizabeth wanted several more bores drilled in some of the paddocks, and James left for a few days to see about obtaining boring equipment in Adelaide. Alice went into the paddocks to help move several thousand sheep between two of the paddocks, and when she returned he was at the home paddock. His smile was as warm when she was dusty, sweaty, and disheveled as it had been when she had been in her bright dress with her hair combed into ringlets.

There was a fire in a paddock to the east and a week's frantic activity by everyone on the station and a horde of swagmen to contain it, and even when he was stumbling with fatigue he could still smile at her, as she could at him.

The equipment arrived in bullock carts and he set it up on the home paddock to drill a bore for the pens. She was at the home paddock most of the time, taking care of the station accounts and working in the pens, and they saw each other frequently during the day and had dinner together at night. He talked about the projects he had completed, others he had been offered, and still others he wanted to do. Although he was an experienced stockman, he was like a visitor on the station, not a part of it.

Christmas approached, and preparations began for the

celebration. The drilling equipment on the other side of the pens stopped its puffing and snorting one day, and the massive beams mounted over the bore drill suddenly disappeared in a shower of water. Everyone ran to look, and the geyser died down into a belching stream of water pouring from the ground. The younger men capered in the water and splashed each other, then began dragging the long, heavy wooden troughs into place and cutting a ditch to channel the overflow to the creek. James dismantled the equipment and moved it to the side of the pens, and over dinner he and Dennis talked about going to Adelaide. There had been talk of exchanging gifts, and Alice asked him if he would fill a list for her. He quickly invited her to go along, then shrugged and smiled wryly when she demurred.

James and Dennis returned from Adelaide, and she wrapped her gifts and put them with the others under the small tree in the parlor. She participated in the preparations, but it was a strange Christmas for her, the fiery, summer days following one after the other. Swagmen began to collect at the station, filling all the barrack buildings and overflowing into empty sheds, then others came and slept on the ground between the buildings.

On Christmas day the cook and his helpers began roasting a beef and a hog and preparing large kettles of rice, peas, and potatoes. Other men put up trestle tables near the cookhouse, and the storekeeper rationed out tots of rum during the day. Alice felt in a festive, holiday mood despite the lack of snow and yule log, and she put on a colorful dress, put her hair up, and sat on the veranda with the others.

Near sunset the cook built up the fires and began putting out the food, and the storekeeper put out bottles of rum. Alice joined the old woman, James, Dennis, and Colin as they walked across to the feast, and stood with the other women at a table and ate and talked with them as the old woman sat in a chair, sipped a pannikin of watered rum, and talked to the employees and swagmen who gathered around her. Darkness fell, and the fires spread a yellow, wavering light between the buildings, silhouetting the men moving around and laughing and talking to each other. The old woman caught Alice's attention and motioned to her, and she went to her and walked back to the house with her.

James, Dennis, and Colin followed them, and they sat in the parlor and opened their presents. Alice had bought knives for Dennis and Colin, a shaving set for James, and a brooch for Elizabeth. She opened her presents. Dennis and Colin had bought her ribbons and combs, and James had bought her a beautiful gold locket and chain. Her present from Elizabeth was large and heavy, wrapped in plain, brown paper. She saved it until last, and she gasped with pleasure when she opened it. The whips she had used had all been thick and cumbersome, bulky for her to carry and heavy for her to use. This one was light but still long, hardly more than the width of one of her fingers below the handle, coated heavily with preservative tallow and almost black with age.

She became conscious of the silence in the room, and she looked up. Colin and Dennis were looking at the whip in surprise, and James was looking at Elizabeth with a thoughtful expression. Alice looked at her cousin. She was smiling at her.

"It was mine," she said quietly.

"The one you used?" Alice said. "But, Elizabeth, how could I . . . ?"

"It's of no advantage to anyone hanging on the bloody wall, and you can't use one of those huge, great things the men do. Soak that tallow off with oil before you use it, and keep it oiled so it won't split. It'll give you many good years of use, as it did me."

"Elizabeth, I don't know what to say!"

"Your face has said it," the old woman chuckled,

picking up her cane and gathering up her presents. "And I'm for my blanket. Late hours are for the young."

The others stirred, Dennis and Colin still looking somewhat bemused. Alice gathered up her presents, thanking everyone, and she followed Dennis and Colin along the hall as they went to their rooms. She put her things on the dressing table and looked at the whip again, then turned and went back out into the hallway. James was waiting for her at the end of the hallway.

"Would you join me in a glass of cheer?"

She smiled and nodded. "Just one, then."

He smiled down at her, offering his arm, and she put her arm through his as they walked toward the door. They went out the front door and across the veranda, and he held her arm more firmly as they went down the steps. As they walked along the path, he closed his hand on hers and stopped, looking down at her. "Will I have a Christmas kiss from you?"

She looked up at him in the dim light from the fires across the road, and she smiled and nodded. "Aye, but only one of those as well."

His arms closed around her and as his lips touched hers, a glow formed inside her. She felt herself melting against him, her lips turning up to his without conscious effort on her part. The scent of his hair and body were wholesome and fresh, and the feel of his arms around her gave a feeling of comfort and protection. She opened her lips, and the glow within her suddenly turned into a surging, fiery tingle racing through her. His arms tightened around her, and he kissed her passionately.

She pulled away from him abruptly, feeling the situation slipping out of her control, and swayed on her feet. His warm, strong hands were suddenly holding her arms and steadying her. She drew in a deep breath, putting her palms to her burning cheeks. He pulled her closer, and she leaned against him. His breathing was more rapid, and she could feel his heart pounding.

"Alice, I love you. Will you marry me?"

Conflicting desires raged within her. She wanted to. She wanted the feel of his arms around her, and she wanted his lips on hers. But she also wanted to remain where she stood. Her breath caught in her throat as she sighed. "James, this has come to be my home more than any other place I've ever been. When I'm here, I can . . . do things . . . it's hard to explain, James, but I can't leave Wayamba . . ."

"Then I'll stop here as well."

Her heart leaped, then she thought again. She slowly shook her head. "James, I'm not sure that would be fair to you. Your work, and—"

"I am. Wayamba will suffice if you go with it."

She drew in a deep breath and sighed again, looking away, then looked back up at him. "May I think about it?"

"Of course," he murmured, smiling down at her. "You may take as long as you wish, as long as you don't take it amiss if I keep talking to you about it."

She smiled and nodded. "And may I forego the drink of cheer? My spirits have been lifted amply."

"Aye," he chuckled, patting her shoulder as he bent down and kissed her cheek. "And mine have, but I'll join the lads for a while."

She smiled and nodded again as she turned away and walked toward the steps, lifting the front of her skirt. "Good night, James."

"Good night, Alice."

She went into the house, crossed the parlor, and walked along the hallway toward her room, chewing her lower lip and looking down at the floor, then stopped in front of the door to the old woman's room. There was a glow of yellow light showing under the door. She knocked on the door lightly.

"Who is it?"

"It is I."

"Come in, Alice."

Elizabeth was sitting up in bed, the lamp on the table by the bed casting deep shadows in the lines and hollows of her face. She was holding an aborigine water vessel made of bark on her lap. Alice closed the door behind her and leaned back against it.

"James has asked me to marry him, Elizabeth."

"That was bloody foregone. What did you tell him?"

"That I'd think about it."

The old woman nodded firmly, pointing toward a chair in the corner of the room. "Then do so, and I'll help you if I can. Pull that over here and have a sit-down."

Alice looked at the bark vessel as she sat by the bed. "The aborigines use those, don't they? I don't think I've seen one quite like it."

"It's an old one. Put it on the shelf there, will you?"

Alice nodded, taking it. There were some things in it, stones, bits of bone, a dessicated piece of a feather, a small Bible, a piece of a mirror, a few glass beads, and four gold coins. "Is it a keepsake?"

"Aye, you might call it that. It and that stick over there."

Alice nodded, putting it on the shelf and glancing at the stick in the corner, then went back to the chair and sat down, adjusting her skirt as she smiled at the old woman.

"Do you love him?"

"I believe I . . . no, I do. Yes, I love him."

"Then where's your worry?"

"I find that . . . well, I don't want to leave here, Elizabeth."

The old woman's face paled, and she suddenly looked faint. She closed here eyes, pressing her lips together, and Alice leaned toward her in sudden concern, taking her hand.

"Elizabeth, are you well?"

A smile spread across the old woman's face, and she nodded slightly, her eyes still closed. "Aye, I am," she murmured. "Better than I've been for a time." She opened

445

her eyes and looked at Alice again. "He can stop here, if he wants to marry you."

Alice shook her head. "He said he would, but I'm not sure that would be fair, Elizabeth. And after a year or two..." Her voice faded, and she shrugged.

"Bugger him," the old woman growled. "He'll have what he wants, you'll have what you want, and I'll bloody have what *I* want."

"What do you mean? What do you want?"

The old woman looked away, pursing her lips and thinking, then she looked back at Alice and took Alice's hand betwen hers. "Alice, what's to become of this station has been a burden to me. Old Pat Garrity put his heart and soul into building it, and I've put my heart and soul into keeping it together. And I've been afraid it'll go to nothing when I die. Now you know Dennis, and you know Colin. Good stockmen, both of them. But any ram I have out there in the pen would make as good a station owner. They're mine and I love them, but neither of them have it in them to be station owners."

"But this property will be theirs, Elizabeth, and that's—"

"No, it'll belong to them and *James*. Now listen to me. It doesn't have to be a man, you know. I'm living proof of that. But I know every woman on every station around here who's of an age to marry Dennis, and God never put a more ninny lot of sluts on earth. Powell Station, Newton Station, Ivanhoe, Stanthorpe, Blair, Tibooburra—I know all of them, and not a one of them can do anything but burn a piece of mutton and have a baby." She smiled and patted Alice's hand. "And then you came."

"But, Elizabeth, I can't—"

"No, now listen to me. James has said he'll stop, you say, so let him stop. Dennis and Colin will look to him, because he's the oldest. Now you have a lot to learn and you have a way to go, but when you're there they'll look to

446

you as well or I'll miss my guess. But I'm not dead yet, and I'll be here to help you. I'm not sure James would do any better than Dennis or Colin as a station owner. But I think *you* can." She squeezed Alice's hand tightly between hers, leaning toward her. "Did you think that I gave you only an old whip for Christmas? Your arse, I did! I gave you bloody Wayamba. And I think you have the heart, the sand, and the brain to do it. But it starts right here and now. You tell him you'll marry him, and let him stop with you or come back here between his trips on his foolishness. It's all the same as long as he'll give you whelps to take this place after you. I'll help you get it in hand, and I'll help you with it as long as I'm here, but I can't do a bloody thing if you don't have it in you. Now do you?"

Elizabeth's eyes bored into hers as she gripped her hand tightly. Alice looked away, staring absently at the dark wall on the other side of the room as she pursed her lips in thought, and she looked back at the old woman and nodded. "Aye, I can do it."

THE Capricorn People

In this sprawling
sequel to *OUTBACK*,
Earl Garrity, son of the
domineering Elizabeth, defies
his powerful family to pursue
a life at sea, and to win the
love of a woman who belongs to
another man.

AARON FLETCHER

Historical Romance

Price: $3.95 US, $4.50 Canada

0-8439-2012-2